Forever Mine

Hayden Falls

Book One

By:

Debbie Hyde

This book is a work of fiction. Names, characters, places, and incidents are the product of the author's imagination. Any resemblance to a real person, living or dead, events, or locals is entirely coincidental.

Debbie Hyde Books.

Cover Design by: Debbie Hyde
Couple Image by: fotostorm @ Istock
Background Photo: Carrie Pichler Photography (Facebook).
Photographer Website: https://carriepicherphotography.weebly.com
ISBN: 9798448179440

This book is dedicated to all the wonderful people who are a part of the Facebook group For All Who Love Montana. Thank you for the wonderful stories and pictures you all shared with me. You are all amazing! If you liked or commented on my post for Montana stories, you will find your name on the Acknowledgment page. A special shout-out to the group Admin, Christine Migneault, for letting me make the post.

And a BIG shout out and thank you to our wonderful photographer, Carrie Pichler! Thank you for the beautiful photos of Montana! These covers wouldn't be the same without you, girl! I love working with you!

Chapter One

Aiden

Going home causes so many mixed emotions for me. I don't know which one to focus on. I'm not sure if I'm anxious, nervous, or just plain scared. I'm probably all three and so many more, which means I'm seriously messed up in the head.

Not all of my emotions about going home are bad, though. A part of me is happy. In a way, this is a dream. The only problem with my dreams of a happy life in Hayden Falls is the dream, once again, stirs up all of the bad feelings, too. It only proves the messed-up part.

All of my wonderful dreams for my future were destroyed six years ago. The decision I made before graduating high school destroyed everything. There's so much I need to fix, but I'm not sure if the people in this town will let me fix any of it. Once you get on the bad side of the good citizens of Hayden Falls, Montana, you seem to stay there forever.

The only two things I wanted to leave my hometown for were college and to be a pitcher in the MLB. I had a sports scholarship for college already secured, and a Major League Baseball career seemed to be a sure thing. I was good, and I knew it. The truth was, and I'd never admit it to anyone, but college and the MLB career were just to pass my time. I had a forever goal in mind, and it was in Hayden Falls.

My forever goal had long, wavy brown hair and deep blue eyes that captivated me every time I looked into them and a smile that warmed every part of me. The timing never worked out for me to make her mine, though. Our age difference was an issue. There are only three years between us. Those three years were enough to cause legal problems. I wasn't willing to put us through that type of heartache. People frowned at an eighteen-year-old being with a girl who was only fifteen. Well, she turned fifteen just before I left town that summer. It was the first time since meeting her I didn't get to see her on her birthday. My original plan was to remain her friend until her eighteenth birthday, but I messed things up royally.

Six years ago, I lost it all—my reasons for going and my reason for staying. A split-second decision when I was eighteen would probably haunt me for the rest of my life. I'm not sorry for why I made that life-altering decision, and if given a chance, I'd more than likely do it all over again. I'm just sorry for what it cost me in the end. I'll never admit that. The only people who knew my regrets were the friends I left behind four days ago in Tennessee. They don't even know the whole story. The only person who knows the entire story is sitting next to me, driving my truck.

Today, I'm going home. In a matter of minutes, my little brother, Brady, will drive us across the wooden bridge and into Hayden Falls. Even though I insisted I was okay to drive, my brother wasn't so sure. He's done all of the driving for the past four days. Whenever I protested, Brady called in reinforcement. Mom quickly settled me down every time.

My mom didn't care that this was my truck. Her reasoning was the same every day of this trip. I was injured, and I had no business driving. As always, our mom was right. Even if she weren't right, I'd never argue with my mom. I think she knew this fact because she has always been able to talk me into doing just about anything. I built the back deck on my parent's house during high school just because my mom saw a design she liked in a magazine.

"How's the arm?" Brady's question brings me out of my thoughts.

I looked down at my left arm propped up on the console between us. The cast that went from my hand to halfway up my upper arm is a constant reminder of the accident I was in a few weeks ago. That accident is the reason I'm going home now.

"It's a dull throb right now." I could have lied, but what's the point? My brother wasn't going to let me drive.

"You might want to take your pain meds."

"Does mom have you monitoring my medication now?" I lightly laughed. It sounds like something our mom would do.

"Naw, man." Brady chuckled. "Just thought you might want to numb what pain you can before we drive into town."

Brady's eyes flicked to me for a moment before going back to the road. That one small glance was enough to quieten us both down. My brother wasn't talking about the pain in my broken arm. Well, he's probably concerned about my arm, but he also means the pain in my heart.

Brady's the only person who knows everything about what I did six years ago and why I did it. It's the only thing he and I argue about. Yeah, six years later, he and I still have words on this subject. The only part of my pain Brady doesn't know about is *her*. I never told anyone from my hometown, not even my family, that I was in love with someone. Shoot. I've never told *her*.

"Yeah. You're probably right," I say after a long pause.

We'll be entering Hayden Falls in about thirty minutes. I grab the bottle of pain medicine from the console. I should have taken it about an hour ago, anyway. It will take care of the pain in my arm, but it won't fix anything else. I doubt there's a medicine strong enough to take away the pain in my heart. It's an ache I'm destined to feel forever.

Hopefully, my brother will drive us straight to our parents' house. If this fool stops in town, I'll break one of his arms. On the few and far between visits I've made home over the past six years, I've avoided going into town as much as possible. It's safer for me to stay on our family's ranch. No one would physically try to hurt me. At least, I don't think so, anyway. Still, the people of this town knew how to rip you apart with their hateful words. Gossip and rumors run strong in our little town.

I sigh deeply as my brother drives over the old wooden bridge. Technically, it's not that old. The wooden boards and support system are checked often. The town council refuses to let go of the style and update to newer material. I fully support their decision. The wooden bridge is a landmark for this little town. None of us want it to change.

It's impossible, but I swear the air felt different once we crossed the bridge. When I was younger, I felt freer here. Now, I have a lot of burdens on my shoulders.

I cut my eyes at my brother when I realized this fool was taking me straight to town. I'm tired and want to go to our parents' house. The town square is the last place I want to go right now. My luck, our mom has planned something grand to welcome me home. Surely, it's not in the town square.

"Where are we going?"

"Home."

"You're driving us straight to the town square." I look at my brother like he's crazy.

"Chill out, man." Brady flashes me a grin before turning back to the road. "We're not stopping."

"Then why are we heading to the square?" My annoyance with my brother could be heard in my voice. Sadly for me, the jerk didn't care.

"Just thought you'd like a glimpse." He still has that stupid grin on his face.

"Brady." I sigh deeply. I don't know how much more of my brother's nonsense I can take today. "I was here for Mother's Day. I highly doubt Hayden Falls has changed in three months."

"Oh. You never know." Brady's still grinning. He makes no sense whatsoever.

Ignoring my protest, he takes us down South Main Street, right into the heart of town. This side of the square runs from the hardware store to the diner on the driver's side, which puts the gazebo in the center of the square on my side. The moment the square came into view, I knew immediately that nothing, absolutely nothing, had changed in our little town.

I groan loudly. I want my brother to know he's pushing my buttons today. Still, I look out my window at the town square. There's nothing I could do anyway except take in the view. A view I already knew like the back of my hand.

"Perhaps you'd like to get a coffee or catch up with Crawford." Brady points towards the coffee shop on the side street across from the gazebo.

"The *last* person I want to catch up with is Roman Crawford." I roll my eyes and shake my head. My brother's a complete idiot. He knows Roman and I don't get along.

I look toward the coffee shop as if on cue from my brother's suggestion. My eyes widened, and my mouth dropped open. What in the world? I sat up straight in my seat and turned my body as best I could for a better view as we passed the square.

Right in front of the coffee shop, on the sidewalk, is indeed Roman Crawford. My eyes dart between Crawford and the woman standing in front of him. I'm not even in town for two minutes, and Roman Crawford has, once again, managed to get to the top of my bad list. My eyes narrow, and a growl comes from deep in my chest.

The man I despise the most is talking to *her*. I have no right to feel the way I do but darn it. I want to hurt Crawford right this very minute. Never mind my broken arm. The pain would be worth it. As they fade out of sight, I turn back around. *She has a fiancé*. I have to keep reminding myself of this. *She's not mine*. But she should be.

I snap my head toward my brother. The jerk is sitting there whistling like nothing's wrong. Well, for him, nothing's wrong. Did he do this to me on purpose? Of course not. My brother couldn't have timed our arrival at that exact moment. It was a coincidence. It was a friendly chat among fellow townspeople. Nothing more. *Absolutely* nothing more.

"Did you see something interesting?" Brady's grin widens.

"No," I say sharply as I glare at my brother.

"I think you did." Brady pushes the issue.

There's nothing I can say here. I can't admit what I saw because if I did, I'd have to admit to a whole lot more. So, I stay quiet and ignore my brother.

"Come on," Brady coaxes. It doesn't look like my brother is going to stay quiet. "Admit it. You saw her."

"I saw a lot of people," I grumble.

Brady blows out a breath and shakes his head.

"How much longer are you going to deny it?"

"Deny what?" I play dumb.

"You care about her." Brady gets right to the point.

Those were words I never expected to hear him say. I stare at him, unsure of how to respond.

"I've known for a long time," Brady informs me. "You don't hide it as well as you think you do."

I don't know how my brother figured it out, but this was one conversation I didn't want to have. Brady and I have always been close. We aren't just brothers. Brady's one of my best friends. He and I share a lot of secrets. We share one of the biggest secrets in our family. It's probably one of the biggest in our town. But, my feelings for her were something I'd never told him. It's hard to talk about it now. Too much bad has happened, so nothing can ever become of my feelings for her.

"It doesn't matter anyway," I mumble.

"Just don't hurt her," Brady says sternly.

Did my brother just threaten me somehow? That makes no sense. He knows my situation. There's no way I can get close enough to her to hurt her. She's engaged. I waited too long. Not only that, but I destroyed my chances with her six years ago. Nothing will ever happen between us.

"That's not a problem," I tell my brother.

I swallow the lump in my throat. We need to let this conversation end right here. We can't show up at our parents' house arguing. Our mother will have both of our hides for fighting with each other.

"How's Colton?' I change the subject, not that this is a better one.

"As grumpy as always." Brady laughs. Thankfully, he let the subject change with ease.

There are three of us. I'm the middle son. Brady's the baby of the family. He's three years younger than me. Colton? Well, he's our older brother. Colton's destined to run our family's ranch just like our father and grandfathers.

"How did you know they'd be in the square?" I guess I'm not letting the subject drop. It has me baffled. Did my brother set it up?

"Well," Brady drags the word out. "It's Saturday. I knew *she* would probably be walking around town this afternoon. I wasn't expecting her to be talking to Crawford."

That's a relief. I'd hate to think my little brother set that horrible sighting up. I'm still fuming over it. Maybe he should be warning Roman about hurting her instead of me. No. I shake my thoughts away. She's engaged to a douchebag from college. There's no way she'd be interested in Roman Crawford. At least, I sure hope not. If I had to watch *that* relationship happen, there's no way I could ever stay in Hayden Falls.

Chapter Two

Aiden

Walking into my parents' house finally made moving back here feel real. I've denied a lot of things over the past three weeks, but I can't deny this anymore. One of the biggest things I'll have to admit and accept is that I'm, once again, living in Hayden Falls. Until now, it didn't feel real.

Not only will I be living here, but I'll be working here too. This isn't just an extended vacation or time off to heal. I still own the house in Tennessee, and I've been telling myself I can always leave if things don't work out here in Montana. I was wrong, and I knew it. I can feel it just by stepping into this house.

Today's different from my visits over the past six years. Today, I'm coming home for good. Home to what? I don't know. There's a lot of bad stuff here, and I'll have to face it all soon enough. Whether or not I can fix the bad things, this will be my home until the day I die.

"Aiden!" My mother shouts as she rushes from the kitchen.

"Hey, Mom." I wrap my good arm around her.

"How are you feeling?' Mom asks as she looks at my left arm. I have it in a sling now to keep from jarring it too much.

"Tired, but I'm okay." I give her a tight squeeze.

I could have left the tired part out, but my mom would have been able to see it in my expression anyway. My mom has a way of reading people's emotions. She would see through me in a heartbeat. She's the main reason I came home. It broke me when she showed up in my hospital room in Tennessee after the accident a few weeks ago. She was an emotional mess. I gave in to her pleas to come home. I can't handle seeing my mom cry.

"Why don't you go up to your room and get some rest?" Mom suggested.

My room? I groan within. I couldn't let Mom hear it. Sadly, I will be staying in my old room for a few weeks. I have a house to remodel and a new job to start once my mom realizes I'm going to survive this broken arm. Yes, I'm being dramatic here.

My mom wasn't too concerned about a broken arm. It was the tour bus accident that made her a nervous wreck. I won't lie. The accident scared me, too. I'd never been unconscious before, and I didn't like it. I saw my life flash before my eyes just before everything went dark. I used to think that was a cliché, but it sure happened to me. I had things I wanted, no needed, to do before I left this earth.

"I don't want to rest right now, but I am hungry." I smile, hoping it doesn't show how tired I am.

Since we were so close to home, my brother and I decided not to stop too often so we could get home faster. It was probably a mistake on our part and the reason I feel so tired. Then again, it could be the pain medicine I took about thirty minutes ago. I should have eaten something first.

"If you boys feel like riding back into town, we could go to the diner," Dad suggested as he walked into the room.

"Hey, Dad." I give Dad a one-arm hug like I did Mom.

"Glad you're home," Dad said. I swear his voice cracked a bit.

It wasn't often you caught Rafe Maxwell choked up over anything. Well, my mom has a special way of bringing him to his knees. Any other time, my dad was as tough as they came. He didn't take crap off of anyone, and most people would go out of their way to avoid an argument with him. The accident I was in broke something in my usually strong father. My dad was as scared as I was that day. I saw it in his eyes. I never doubted my father's love, but after the accident, I saw it as raw and real as it truly was. Family is everything to him.

"Rafe, I'm sure the boys want to sit down for a while. I can fix something for them." Mom started back toward the kitchen.

"Don't do that, Mom," I call out. "I don't mind going to the diner."

"I'm good with the diner." Brady grins at me.

Yeah, he knows why I want to go back to town. My brother and I will have to talk more about this later. He's going to have to tell me how he figured things out. Was he the only one to figure it out? I hope so. It wouldn't look good for me if the rest of the town knew I had feelings for an engaged woman.

"Well, if you boys are sure." Mom turns and points at me. "But you're not driving."

"Okay, Mom. You win." I couldn't help but laugh. I haven't driven since the accident.

We all went out and climbed into my dad's extended cab pickup. Mom tried to get me to sit in the front with Dad, but I refused. My dad always said Mom's place was by his side. That included in a car. He never let her sit in the backseat unless he sat back there with her. I wasn't about to change that. I have a broken arm. I'm not dying. Sooner or later, Mom will relax and realize she doesn't have to baby me all the time.

"Is Colton meeting us?" I ask Dad as he pulls into the parking lot behind the diner.

"Naw." Dad hurries around and opens Mom's door. "He and Drew are mending fences in the lower pastures today. We won't see them until dinner time."

Drew Larson has worked on my family's ranch since he and my brother Colton were in high school. The two have been best friends since the first grade. Mom serves dinner every day for our family and the farmhands around six. It would be another four hours or more before I saw my overly grumpy brother.

My parents led us into the diner. They go straight to a table in the middle of the room. Great. I sigh deeply. This puts me on full display to everyone. I requested we sit at a table, not a booth, so I wouldn't have to worry about bumping my arm against whoever sat beside me. I should have requested a table in the back dining room. After we're seated, Dad walks over to speak with Mr. Hamilton. His son Miles is one of my best friends. Hopefully, I'll see Miles soon.

Since it was the middle of the afternoon, there weren't a lot of people in the diner yet, but a few already noticed me. Most of them give me a small smile. A couple of people look away. Yeah, not everybody here will forgive me. Still, I'll have to make the best of it. I'm sure a few people aren't happy I got the deputy job. It's going to be interesting around here for a while.

"Hey, Mrs. Maxwell," a woman behind me greets my mom.

Every muscle in my body stiffened at the sound of her voice. I close my eyes and take a deep breath. I hoped to see her, but now that she's here, I'm at a loss for words. What do I say to her? Sensing the change in my mood, Brady taps my foot with his to snap me back to the present.

"Hey, sweet girl." Mom stands and gives her a hug.

I turn in my chair and look up at the woman my mom's hugging. I have a picture saved on my phone of these two women hugging. Brady sent it to me from last year's fall festival. Is it possible to be jealous of your own mother? Honestly, I think I am.

She's beautiful, always has been. Her long, wavy brown hair falls loosely over her shoulders. I want to reach out and run my fingers through those soft strands. Her deep blue eyes practically dance with happiness. Her smile. Oh, her smile has always felt like sunshine to me. If only she weren't engaged.

"Aiden Maxwell, it's good to see you." When she spoke to me, I felt like she had stolen my breath.

My eyes drop to her left hand for a moment. Nothing. No ring? My heart beat faster in my chest. Is she not engaged anymore? No one in my family has mentioned this. Manners. Oh my gosh, where are my manners? I quickly stand to greet her as a gentleman should.

"E Hayes, I assure you, the pleasure is all mine." And it is. I extend my hand and almost melt on the floor when she places her tiny hand in mine.

"How are you feeling?" E's gaze moves to my broken arm.

Words. I need words. I'm an idiot right now. I don't know how to talk to her. Not seeing an engagement ring on her finger has me dumbfounded. I glance over at my brother. Brady grins at me. He knew. He knew she wasn't engaged anymore, and he didn't tell me. Yeah, I'm seriously going to hurt my little brother later.

"Would you like to join us?" Mom asked E.

I look between the two women. *Please say yes*. I would love for her to join us. I should say something. Why are words so hard to form right now?

"We can pull another chair over," I offer. Yeah, it wasn't the best line, but it was all I had at the moment. I reach for a chair at a nearby table.

"Oh, don't trouble yourself." E held her hand out to stop me. "I'm meeting my aunt and the ladies from church." She points toward the group of ladies gathering in the back corner of the diner.

"Oh. I need to speak with your aunt," Mom said and hurried over to the group of ladies from church.

E laughs and turns back to face me. There's so much I want to say to her. The teenage boy in me wants to shout out how much I love her. The man I am today won't let me do that to her.

"E, please tell me you are not part of the *'old ladies'* club," I tease.

"They're not *old ladies*," E protests.

She glances over her shoulder at the women across the dining room. She rolls her eyes and shakes her head when she turns back to me.

"You're the only one under the age of forty in that group," I point out.

"The Hayden Sisters are a respectful group of women." E lifts her chin. Her grin turns into a light laugh. It's adorable.

"You know I'm right." I nod my head. She does know it. We used to call them the old ladies' club when we were kids.

E leans towards me and whispers, "But you can't call them that."

I lean close to her ear and whisper back, "You started it." And she had.

Being this close to her is driving me mad. I don't know what shampoo she uses, but her hair smells like coconut. I need to get a grip on myself. Hopefully, no one noticed I smelled her hair. I couldn't help it. Being around her is intoxicating. I want to wrap my arms around her right here in front of everyone. I groan, hopefully not too loudly. She has me so messed up. I'm not going to survive this.

"Shh." E holds her hand at the corner of her mouth, trying to silence me.

"E!" Her aunt calls out. She waves E over to their group.

"I have to go." E smiles up at me again. Her voice sounds a little sad. Does she not want to go? "But I'll see you tomorrow."

Tomorrow? I have no idea what that's about. I glance at Brady. Am I missing something here?

"Mom planned a Welcome Home Party for you at the ranch tomorrow," Brady answers my unspoken question.

I groan *very* loud this time. Of course, Mom would plan a welcome home dinner. I'm not fond of big dinners anymore. But then again, if E's going to be there, I'll gladly welcome this one.

"I look forward to it." And oh, how I do.

With a huge smile on her face, E gave my brother and me a little wave before joining the Hayden Sisters. I stand there and watch as the elderly women of our little town lovingly welcome E with a hug. I understand how they all can love her. What I don't understand is why a woman so young is a part of the Hayden Sisters.

I didn't realize I was still standing by our table until my parents rejoined my brother and me. I'm a bit embarrassed because people are staring at me. Brady snickers at my awkwardness—the jerk. As I take my seat, I glare at my little brother. However, I'm grateful because, from our table, I can watch E the entire time we're here. Tomorrow can't come soon enough for me. Maybe tonight, Brady will tell me why E's no longer engaged. That one fact gives me more hope than I thought possible.

Chapter Three

Etrulia

This meeting with the Hayden Sisters turned into the longest in history. Everything for the town's upcoming Fall Festival next month is on schedule. I don't understand why nearly every woman in this group had to ask questions today. By the end of the meeting, I was practically pulling my hair out. These ladies would know everything if they read the flyers in the folders I gave them earlier.

"Are you okay?" My aunt reached over and placed her hand over mine. She can sense my frustration.

"Our dear girl is distracted today," Laura Murphy, the President of the Hayden Sisters, said.

I snap my head toward my best friend Beth's mother. She's sitting at the head of our table on my right. Thankfully, she said that low enough to where none of the other ladies heard her. With a huge smile on her face, Mrs. Murphy's eyes dart across the dining room and back to me. I sit up straight and stare at her. What can I say? She's right, after all.

Mrs. Murphy and my aunt lightly laugh before turning their attention back to their plates. Thankfully, our food arrived, giving the rest of these women something to do besides bombarding me with useless questions. Honestly, I believe half of these women only want to prolong our meeting so they don't have to hurry back home to their husbands. Knowing the demeanor of some of their husbands, I can't blame half of them.

I glance across the dining room when I'm sure no one is paying me any attention. My *distraction* is looking at me. Every time, over the past hour, whenever I looked his way, I found Aiden Maxwell looking back at me. From where we both are sitting, we're facing each other.

I can't believe he's back in Hayden Falls. Of course, he visited a few times, but those visits were few and far between. I hardly ever saw him when he came home. When I did see him, it was only for a few minutes. He always disappeared without speaking to me. I don't understand why he did that. It deeply hurt me, but I never let it show. Well, not publicly, anyway. When I was alone, I allowed myself to break down. Aiden used to be my friend. My best friend, actually, and somehow, I lost him.

Aiden was the first friend I made when I moved to Montana. I was eight years old and starting the third grade when I moved here. Aiden was eleven. His mom and my aunt were best friends, so we were together often. He's the only friend I made that summer. Being shy and afraid of your own shadow didn't help much in the friend-making department. Thankfully, I met Beth when school started. It took me a few weeks to open up to her, and we've been inseparable ever since.

During my middle and high school years, Aiden was something more to me. He never knew it, but I had a crush on him—a *big* one. Nothing ever happened between us, though. Why would it? We were friends because of our families. He probably thought of me as a little sister. I thought of him as so much more. By the time he got to high school, I was only in the sixth grade. I was too young for him. I hated watching him date girls, but there was nothing I could do about it. So, I loved him from afar.

We're older now, and today feels different somehow. I might get my hopes up if I was brave enough to venture back into the dating world. I'm not brave, though, and I don't date anymore. The relationship with my last boyfriend, who used to be my fiancé for a little over a year, didn't go well. Dating is not in the cards for me right now. I'm not sure if it ever will be.

Still, those soft brown eyes across the dining room call to me. They always have. Since he took the job at the Sheriff's Office, hopefully, it means Aiden will stay in Hayden Falls for a long time. He spent years working for a country band. I fear our little town will be too small and slow for him now. People who went on to bigger and better things hardly ever returned to live here. I don't see myself living anywhere else. Not now, anyway.

"E!" My best friend, Beth Murphy, shouts as she hurries over to our table.

"Hey, Bethie." I stand and give her a hug. "Are you on a break?"

"Nope. I'm done for the day. So, I'm all yours."

"Lucky me," I tease.

"You sure are," Beth proudly boasts. She holds out a to-go cup of coffee. "And I brought your favorite. Caramel Macchiato with all the extras."

Beth is the best. She knows I love lots of whipped cream with extra caramel drizzle, and she never disappoints me.

"Thank you." I happily take the coffee.

"Now, let's get out of here," Beth loudly whispered. She's not usually quiet about things.

"Aunt Sara, do you need anything before I go?"

"No, Dear. Laura and I will finish up here. You two go on." My aunt stands and gives me a hug.

Beth hugs her mom while I grab my purse. Thankfully, my aunt and Mrs. Murphy are taking over the meeting now. My friend grabs my arm and pulls me toward the door before one of these women finds a reason to keep me here longer. Beth knows how hard it is to get away from the Hayden Sisters.

The Maxwell family starts to leave as we get near their table. Aiden's eyes lock with mine as he gets to his feet. Something's wrong. He looks tired, but this feels like something more. I'm sure the long drive he and Brady made from Tennessee wore them out.

Aiden's eyes close as he weirdly drops his head. This isn't normal. Something's very wrong with him. Aiden's good hand lands flat on the table to brace himself, causing Mr. Maxwell and Brady to grab him. Brady's careful not to jostle Aiden's broken arm.

"Aiden." Concern fills my voice as I step closer to help.

"He's okay, E." Mrs. Maxwell lovingly puts her arm around me. "It's the medicine they have him on. Brady said it's been affecting him like this for the entire trip."

"Are you sure he'll be alright?" I watch helplessly as Aiden's father and brother carry him to their truck.

"I'm sure." Mrs. Maxwell walks out the door with Beth and me. "He just needs to get some rest. We shouldn't have come out today."

From the concern on Mrs. Maxwell's face, she blames herself for Aiden's condition at the moment. Still, I wished there was something I could do to help.

"If your family needs anything this evening, give us a call," Beth offered. "E and I can make store runs for you and help prepare dinner for your family."

I look at Beth from the corner of my eye. She's acting weird. I could see us making store runs, but Beth doesn't cook often. She bakes some and makes sandwiches for her coffee shop. But dinner? I'm not sure that would be edible.

"You girls are so sweet." Mrs. Maxwell pats my arm. "But I can send one of the boys out if we need anything."

"Well, the offer still stands," Beth insisted. It's getting weirder by the minute. Beth's beginning to sound like one of the Hayden Sisters. That's laughable.

"Thank you both. I promise I'll call if we need you," Mrs. Maxwell said politely.

Mr. Maxwell holds the passenger door of the truck open. Lovingly, he reaches for his wife's hand and helps her inside. After twenty-seven years of marriage, Aiden's parents are still very much in love. The Maxwells are a perfect example of relationship goals.

"We'll see you, ladies, tomorrow." Mr. Maxwell waves to us as he gets into the driver's seat.

"Yes, Sir," Beth and I say in unison.

Aiden sits in the seat behind his mom. He releases a breath and rubs his face with his hand. He looks so drained. Hopefully, he won't have to take those meds too much longer. When he looks at me, I smile and wave. He groggily does the same. My heart breaks seeing him like this.

"You still like him," Beth said after Mr. Maxwell drove away.

Of course, I still like Aiden. I probably always will. Nothing will ever come of it, though. I'm not good at relationships. The last one left me broken in so many ways. The happy girl everyone thinks I am is totally fake. I only smile when I'm in public so people won't ask me questions.

"Is that why you offered to cook?" I tease. This is a safer subject than my feelings for Aiden.

"It's the only reason." Beth laughed.

I knew it. She's always meddling. I narrow my eyes at her and shake my head. My friend is going to play matchmaker. I'm sure of it. It's pointless, though. I don't date, and all of the single women in Hayden Falls will be flocking to Aiden's doorstep soon enough. Karlee Davis will more than likely be the first one there. She and Aiden dated in high school. I really don't like Karlee.

"He likes you too." Beth's words shocked me.

"Yeah, like a sister," I mumble.

"Oh, girl. A man does *not* look at his sister the way Aiden Maxwell looks at you." Beth grabs my arm and pulls me towards the beauty salon. It looks like she got the last-minute appointment she wanted. I agreed to go with her if she did.

"He doesn't look at me like that. Besides, he's on some strong medications right now." I refuse to believe anything else.

"I wasn't just talking about today." Beth paused outside the salon. "But if it took medication to get that man to act on his feelings for you, somebody should have broken his arm a *long* time ago."

"Beth," I scold my friend. "You can't mean that."

"I do." Beth nods and opens the door. "I couldn't do it, but I bet I could talk Spence into it."

"That would never happen."

She knows it wouldn't. Her brother Spencer and Aiden were best friends way before they were in high school, along with Miles Hamilton. When Aiden's well enough to start work, he and Spencer will be working beside each other as deputies.

"You should ask him out," Beth suggests.

"What?" I almost spew the sip of coffee I just took into my hand. "I don't date. I'm not asking anyone out."

"Come on, E," Beth whines. "You can't stay single forever."

"I can," I insist.

"I know you're afraid of getting hurt, but that's Aiden," Beth continued to push the matter. "He won't hurt you."

"Beth, you know I can't." I struggle to hold back tears.

Beth puts her arm around me. "I'm sorry. Maybe someday you'll get past what happened to you. If not, I promise not to push you anymore."

I plaster on a fake smile and nod my head. Thankfully, I'm able to sniffle and blink back the tears before they escape my eyes. Falling apart in public is so embarrassing. Every time it happens, I hide away at my aunt and uncle's bed and breakfast for weeks. So far, I've been able to keep what happened to me out of the local gossip circles. Thank goodness it hasn't shown up in Hayden's Happenings. I personally believe our town's local gossip blog is pure evil.

I often wonder if I will ever fully mend. Probably one day. Would I mend enough to where I could try to have another relationship? I highly doubt it. So, I don't see any sense in dreaming about anything with Aiden. Sadly, I'll have to watch as he falls in love with someone else. Just please don't let it be Karlee.

Chapter Four

Aiden

Yesterday was horrible! Well, not all of it. I did see E, and I even spoke to her. Usually, I avoid talking to her during my visits home. It hurt too much, and I couldn't handle it. To be honest, I wasn't handling *not* talking to her too well either. After every visit, I'd go back to Tennessee in a sullen mood. Several times, I lashed out at one of my friends and needed someone to talk me down. I didn't mean to be a jerk to them, but that's exactly what I had been.

The horrible part about yesterday was that I almost passed out in front of everyone. Well, mainly in front of E. I knew half the town already thought poorly of me. I don't want that from E. I know it was because of the medication and the long ride, but it made me look weak. Weak was not a way to start out in this town, especially for me. By a few of the stares I got yesterday at the diner, I knew I was going to have a hard time proving myself to this town. I'll have to find a way to do it because I'm not leaving.

E Hayes is single, and I'm *not* missing another chance with her. It looks like Bryan Dawson and Harrison Shaw will get their wish. One day soon, I'm going to tell E how I feel about her.

I was the sound guy for the country band Dawson for four years. The job started as a side gig. It was a rebellious act on my part. I didn't want to train as a cop and a detective, but I did it anyway. I didn't have a choice in the matter.

I took the job with the band as a temporary way to make some extra money. Those five guys became my family. It's why I stayed on with them as long as I did.

I wouldn't be here now if it weren't for the tour bus accident in Chattanooga about three weeks ago. Sheriff Barnes probably thought I was never coming back to Hayden Falls or that I'd ever use the law enforcement training he sent me away for. Fate had other plans for me, though. It took a serious accident, but here I am, right where the good sheriff said I'd end up someday.

Today, I'm going to use my detective skills and try to uncover why E isn't engaged anymore. That's the technical way of putting it. Some might say I'm being nosy by hounding my brother for information. Others would even go as far as calling it gossip. I, on the other hand, preferred the term investigating.

My mom planned a welcome home party this afternoon. It was only one o'clock, but a few people showed up after church to help set things up. My brother Colton wasn't happy about having to set up tables around the backyard. Truth be told, Colton wasn't happy about doing anything. The only thing he seemed to enjoy was riding. Most days, he would saddle his horse way before noon, and we wouldn't see him until dinnertime. I have no idea what he does out on the ranch all day. It's fine because it keeps him out of my hair.

After yesterday's mishap at the diner, I collapsed in bed and slept until almost ten this morning. A time or two, I woke up and took a glass of water from my mom. Doing so kept mom from calling 911. I was in such a medicated stupor. I don't remember talking to my mom at all last night. I'm not about to tell her that, though. She would drag me to the doctor's office in town to have these meds checked if she knew how out of it I was last night. After yesterday, it might not be a bad idea. Maybe my meds are too strong.

I find Brady in the backyard getting the grill ready. Grilling is one of my favorite things. I'm a master at it. My father and grandfather taught me everything they knew. I've also tested out other techniques. I put all my grilling skills to use during the summers in Tennessee at Ms. Shaw's outdoor dinner parties.

Here in Hayden Falls, Pit claimed the title of Pitmaster. He rightly earned the title, too. Pit won the BBQ cook-off at every Fourth of July celebration. Most people thought that's why he's called Pit. It's not why the nickname started, but people around here have called him Pit for so long that most of them don't even know his real name. Next summer, I'm going to enter the town cook-off and try to take Pit down.

"Need some help?" I hand my brother a beer from one of the nearby coolers.

"Thanks, man." Brady takes a break and pulls up a couple of chairs. "I don't need any help, but the company would be nice."

Brady eyes the glass in my hand. He gives me a sympathetic look when he realizes I have a glass of tea. I can't drink alcohol with the medication I'm taking for my arm.

"So," I begin. "What happened to E?"

Brady freezes for a moment. He briefly looks me in the eye before dropping his gaze to the ground. He wants to tell me something, but I'm pretty sure he won't do it. Brady and I don't keep secrets from each other, so this is an awkward situation.

"What do you mean?" Brady won't look at me now. Something serious is going on here.

"She's not engaged anymore. You knew and didn't tell me." If my brother knows how much I care for E, why wouldn't he tell me?

Brady sighs and nods. It looks like he's going to make me work for information today.

"When did it happen?" I might as well start here since I have to treat him like he's five.

"January."

January? That's all he's going to tell me? Really? Just one word. That was seven months ago. Why hasn't anyone said anything before now? I was here for a few hours on Mother's Day. Brady is the only one who knows I care about E. He could have told me before now. He's been with me every day for the past three weeks.

"Why didn't you tell me?" I throw out baby question number two here.

"It's not my story to tell." Brady rubs his eyes with his thumb and index finger.

No, little brother, there's more to this than that. This really is turning into an investigation. Glad I have the training for this. Brady knows more about this than what he's saying.

"That's lame." We both know it is. I don't understand him. "You know I care about her, but you didn't tell me."

"You weren't here, Aiden." Brady shakes his head. "You were halfway across the country, living a different life."

"That's beside the point," I snap. "You should have told me."

"And what were you going to do? Were you going to leave your new life to come home for her?" Brady's temper is rising. Why does he protect E like this?

"Yes." I lean back in my chair and release a long breath. "I would have come home for her."

"You love her that much?" Brady's voice softens. He, once again, looks at the ground.

Does my brother love E, too? That would not end well for any of us.

"Yes," There's no point in me denying it now. "And you should have told me."

"I couldn't." Brady's voice cracks.

Now, I fear coming home is a problem. If my brother loves E, and she loves him, I'd have no choice but to leave again. I couldn't watch that relationship happen. And there's no way I'd ever hurt either of them. It's a good thing I still have my house in Tennessee.

"You love her too." I swallow hard. I'm sure of it. It appears I'm destined to lose E Hayes no matter what I do.

Brady finally looks me in the eye. At least he's going to be a man about this.

"I do," he admits. "But not like you do. E is family to me."

I blow out another breath and let my head fall back. That was a huge relief.

"Then why can't you tell me what happened to her?"

"For one, I promised her I wouldn't talk about it. And two, I don't know everything." Brady slumps down in his chair.

"Brady, you have to give me something here. You have to tell me what you do know." I have a bad feeling, and all of this sidestepping my brother's doing is grating on my last nerve.

"It hurts to talk about it." Brady downed his beer before leaning forward and dropping his head into his hands.

"Why?" I continue to ask simple questions. Usually, people talk more when I do this. With Brady, it's like pulling teeth.

"I don't know everything that happened, but I feel like it was my fault." Brady rests his forearms on his knees and shakes his head. Whatever happened, it's hard for him to talk about it.

Every nerve in my body goes off. This is serious. Brady doesn't act like this. My chest tightens. He's going to have to tell me more.

"I get that you can't tell me everything." It's okay. I'll figure it all out in the end. "But explain *that* to me. Why do you think it's your fault E's not engaged anymore?"

Brady leans back in his chair and crosses his arms over his chest. He can't sit still. Something is seriously agitating him. He's trying to figure out what to say without breaking E's trust. I admire that, but this is about her, and I need to know. I don't push my brother. I'm a patient man. I wait quietly while he works it all out in his head.

"We went back to college after Christmas. We were only two weeks into the new semester. E and I didn't have classes right after lunch on Mondays. I found her outside the library, by herself, building a snowman." Brady chuckled, but there was no humor in it.

E had always loved the snow. When we were kids, she was the first one to hurry outside on snow days to build snowmen. Well, she loved them so much that she created snow families. The thought made me smile. Still, I don't push. This is serious, and I need answers. Brady's reliving that day in his mind. I can see how much this hurts him.

"I went and got us a couple of hot chocolates and went back to help her build snowmen. We built three that day." Brady briefly smiled. See? Snow families. "It was then that Garrett found us."

Garrett? That must be the ex-fiancé. I never asked who E was engaged to, and thankfully, nobody bothered to tell me. It would have given my hate a name. From the way my brother talks, I'm about to *really* hate this guy.

"He never said anything to me. He only glared at me." Brady takes a deep breath. "But he grabbed E's wrist and pulled her away. I should have stopped him." Brady shook his head again. "Anyway, they paused at the edge of the parking lot. I couldn't hear what they were saying, but it was clear he was angry with her. He looked at me a couple of times and fussed at her some more. E tried to pull away, but he jerked her arm. When she screamed, I started running toward them. He shoved her in the car and drove away before I could get to her."

Brady leans forward and places his forearms on his knees again. I swear, the way his voice cracked, I thought he was about to cry. He blames himself for whatever happened to E that day. As bad as this was, I don't believe he's finished telling this story.

"I didn't see her again after that. A couple of days later, I heard that her uncle and a couple of the guys from town came and cleaned out her dorm room. She's been taking her classes online ever since. Mom said it was over a month before anyone saw E in town. Whatever happened that day, they're keeping it quiet."

Quiet in Hayden Falls? That's not possible. If these people weren't gossiping, they were spreading rumors. I have a feeling somebody in this town knows exactly what happened that day. I just have to figure out who I need to talk to.

"Who helped move her stuff?" Maybe this would help me out.

"Spencer and Alan."

Cops? That's alarming. Spencer Murphy is my best friend. Soon, he and I will be working together. Alan Whitlock is the deputy I'm replacing. He's already moved to Texas with his son. I'll have to find Spencer and get him to tell me what he knows. I have a pretty good idea of what happened, but I need to know for sure.

"Aiden." Brady looks up at me. His eyes are filled with pain. "Please don't tell her I told you anything. I promised her I wouldn't."

"Don't worry, little brother. I won't." I reach over and pat him on the back. "Whatever happened, it's not your fault."

"But it is," Brady insists. He blinks back tears. He's probably already guessed what happened. "He was fussing at her about me. I'm sure of it. If he hurt her…" Brady runs his hand through his hair.

"I know. Trust me, I know." I nod my head at my brother. He doesn't have to say anything more. I completely understood how he felt.

From what little Brady knew, I'm almost positive the jerk physically hurt E. I vow to get to the bottom of this. Being a deputy, I should be able to get some inside information soon. I should have listened to Bryan and Harrison. I should've come home a long time ago and told E how I felt about her.

Chapter Five

Etrulia

By the time we got to the Maxwells' house, Aiden's welcome home party was in full swing. I wanted to arrive early to help set up, but I was too nervous. So, I waited until my aunt and uncle went to the party.

Some of the things Beth said to me yesterday had my mind running wild. She doesn't believe Aiden looks at me like I'm his little sister. Could that be true? Did I want it to be? Yes. I do want that, but I can never be more than a friend to him or any man. Who knows, I may never be ready to try again.

Seven months ago, I vowed to myself that I would never get involved with another man. My relationship with Garrett wasn't great. It was darn right horrible. In the beginning, everything was fine. We were both in college, taking hotel management classes. Garrett's family owns a hotel and casino in Las Vegas. My aunt and uncle own The Magnolia Inn, a bed and breakfast in Hayden Falls. It's the only place to stay within the city limits of our town.

Garrett and I are destined to take over our family businesses someday. It made talking to Garrett easy when we first met. I thought having something in common would help us to have a good relationship. It turns out that's not a key factor. Nope. Not at all.

I was surprised when Garrett proposed to me at Christmas almost two years ago. We were close in the beginning, but our relationship didn't seem to be growing. I thought we were on the verge of breaking up. We should have done so that year. I liked Garrett, but I wasn't in love with him.

Garrett proposed to me at a party with all our college friends the night before everyone went home for Christmas. I was floored when he got down on his knee. Being put on the spot like that had always been a huge embarrassment for me. I never knew how to respond in those situations. I don't know why I said yes. Actually, I didn't say yes. I was stunned and couldn't speak. I nodded my head, and a cold ring slipped onto my finger.

A part of me thought getting engaged might help our relationship grow, and the true feelings of love would finally blossom between us. Well, for me, anyway. I thought Garrett loved me since he proposed. I was an idiot. Since I wasn't in love with him, I should have never agreed to marry him. Sadly, I was too afraid to end things with him. My childhood planted fear in me, and I never broke free from it.

My college friends thought my being the future Mrs. Garrett Preston would be the greatest thing ever. The only greatest thing my relationship with Garrett turned out to be was my greatest nightmare. Some nights, I jolt awake from actual nightmares. I'm an emotional mess most of the time. I've learned how to hide most of my emotions from the people in my life. I'm not sure I'll get past this enough to heal properly.

The only thing I can do about my feelings for Aiden is to love him from afar as I have for years. He's the one good thing from my childhood. I never want to destroy that. It doesn't matter how I feel about him. Karlee will run into Aiden soon enough. She'll drown out any slight hope I have with him. Karlee's far more outgoing than I could ever be.

"Hey, E." Mrs. Maxwell hands me two glasses of tea when we walk into the kitchen. I love her sweet tea. "Will you take one of these out to Aiden?"

Well, there goes my hopes of hiding on the sidelines today. I was going to find a quiet corner and watch everything going on around me today. I could refuse to take this to Aiden, but my aunt and uncle didn't raise me to be rude. I smile and nod before heading out the back door. My aunt stays in the kitchen to help Mrs. Maxwell.

I love the H. H. Maxwell Ranch. It's named after one of the founding fathers of Hayden Falls. This ranch has one of the biggest backyards in town. The outdoor grilling area is more like its own kitchen, and that's exactly where I find Aiden. He and his brother, Brady, are manning the grill. Or rather, I should say grills. We only have one grill. The Maxwells have at least six out here. Well, I think some might be smokers or something. I don't know a lot about the equipment, but grilling out is one of my favorite things to do.

Aiden's eyes land on me when I step out the back door. A slow smile crosses his face as I get closer to him. I don't miss the moment he looks me over from head to toe. Oh my gosh. Could Beth be right? My heart beats faster. No. She can't be right. In my mind, I willed Beth's words to be false. I don't like how the rest of my body says differently. Well, that's a lie. I *do* like it, but I can't let anything happen between us. Aiden deserves someone who isn't as broken as I am.

"Well, hello, Sunshine." Aiden leans back in his chair and smiles up at me.

He's called me Sunshine since the day we first met. I don't know why. It never made any sense to me. I was a terrified little girl when I came to live with my dad's brother. I honestly believe my Uncle Silas is the only decent man in our family. He's a million times better than both of his brothers. I don't know why he and Aunt Sara agreed to take me in. Without them, I would have been placed in state custody. I thank God for my aunt and uncle every day.

"Hey." My lips betray me, and I smile back. "I brought you a glass of tea."

"Thank you." Our fingers touch as Aiden takes the glass from me. His eyes snap back up to mine.

I sigh as our eyes lock. Yeah, this man is going to be trouble for me. It's just me that's messed up here. Aiden doesn't feel anything for me other than friendship. Could I betray my private vow if he did feel more? No. I can't let anything happen between us.

"You'll have to thank your mom." I quickly pull my hand away.

"Recruited, huh?" Brady teases as he turns back to flip the steaks and burgers on the grill.

"Still, I'm glad you're here." Aiden points to the chair next to him. "Join us?"

I look at him questionably. I would love to sit and talk with him, but it's not safe for me to be around him. Declining his offer would be best.

"Come on, E." Brady points to the chair with his spatula. "Don't leave me here to talk to this grumpy jerk by myself."

"Grumpy? Jerk?" Aiden playfully threw an empty beer can at Brady. Naturally, he misses him on purpose. "If you'd let me grill, I wouldn't be grumpy or a jerk."

"That, dear brother, is not true." Brady laughs at Aiden. "And mom says you aren't supposed to do anything today."

Brady motions toward the chair between his and Aiden's. Great. They're putting me in the middle. I take a deep breath before sitting down. Truthfully, I don't mind sitting here. All the Maxwell men are handsome. Even at his age, Rafe Maxwell is just as handsome as his sons. Any woman would consider herself blessed to be in their company. Of course, my heart is pulled towards one of these Maxwell men.

"How's your arm?" I ask—anything to keep my mind off the feelings my body has right now.

"Good. Considering," Aiden replied. "Thanks for asking."

Unsure of what to say, I smile and nod my head. Being this close to Aiden makes me extremely nervous. I take a sip of my tea to have something to do. I look around the yard for Beth. Hopefully, she'll get here soon and rescue me. It's only a matter of time before I do something to embarrass myself. Knowing me, I'll embarrass myself several times.

"E, do you want a steak or a bacon cheeseburger?" Brady asked over his shoulder.

"Ah." I gasp in shock, causing Aiden to laugh wholeheartedly.

"What?" Brady turns around. He looks confused at first, but then he smiles and winks at me. Aiden growls, causing Brady to laugh harder.

"You know you have to give her both," Aiden said.

It's true. I love both and could never choose, but taking both at a party would make me look like a pig. I want both, but people will think my aunt and uncle never fed me.

"I can't eat both." I kindly refuse the offer.

"You can take half home with you, but you're getting both," Aiden informed me.

Bossy man. Aiden points at his brother. Brady nods, saying he understands and I will indeed be getting both. There's no winning against the two of them.

"There you are!" Beth shouts.

She flops down in the chair on my other side. Brady glares at her for taking his seat. I hoped she would pull me away when she got here, not join us.

"So." Beth leans towards me and grins. "I'm calling Friday Night as girls' night."

"Dinner and a movie in Missoula." I nod. It's been our go-to for girls' night.

"No." Beth jabs her finger in the air. "If we keep doing that, the crazy folk in this town will swear we're dating."

Aiden spews tea. Brady glares even harder at Beth with his mouth hanging open. I giggle. My best friend has a special way of shocking people. I love her.

"We need something much more exciting." Beth wiggles in her chair. She's being mischievous. I'm in trouble here. "We're going to Cowboys for drinking and dancing."

"I think not!" Aiden roars.

"Oh, calm down, big guy." Beth waves Aiden off with her hand. She turns back to me. "You need to let loose and have some fun."

"Beth, I don't know." I was never a partying person.

"I do, and it's happening." Beth doesn't back down.

"Beth," Aiden warns.

"That's not a good idea," Brady agrees with Aiden.

I look between the two brothers. Do people really think I'm not capable of making my own decisions? Everyone knows drinking and dancing aren't something I do. Still, it should be my decision. Everyone expects me to always do the good and sweet girl things. Maybe I am becoming a true member of the *old ladies'* club after all. That has to change. I may not be as outgoing as Beth is, but I don't want to be a twenty-one-year-old grandma.

"You know what?" I grin at Beth, totally ignoring the guys. "Let's do it."

"Yay!" Beth claps her hands.

Aiden and Brady weren't expecting me to agree with Beth. They're staring at me with their mouths hanging open. Good. It's past time I shocked a few people in this town. Honestly, I have no idea where this bravery is coming from. I'm not the spontaneous type. I don't drink often. I don't dance in public either, but I'm doing this.

Before the guys regain their senses, I grab Beth's hand and pull her away. Gotta go. Can't sit here and get a lecture from the Maxwell men on how wrong a wild night out would be.

"E!" Aiden calls out. Guess he regained his senses. *Too late, Cowboy.*

Nope. I'm not letting him talk me out of my stupid decision. And it's a *very* stupid decision. I'll have to avoid Aiden for the rest of the party and probably the rest of the week. He'll find a way to talk me out of our girls' night out.

Beth, on the other hand, is super excited. She's practically bouncing on her toes. I have a gut feeling I'm going to regret this. Friday Night is going to be very interesting.

Chapter Six

Aiden

What. Just. Happened? I think the world may have ended. It has to be the medication messing with me. There's no way I just heard E Hayes agree to a wild girls' night out.

"What just happened?" Sorry, but I had to ask.

"Lightning struck." Brady looks as dumbfounded as I am.

"Please tell me that was a joke. They're messing with us. Right? There's no way that was real." I can't believe it.

"Oh, that's Beth Murphy. Of course, it's real." Brady grabs another beer from the cooler. "I'd give you one, and you probably need it right now, but with your meds, you can't have alcohol."

He's right. I sure need alcohol right now, and a lot of it. Beth is E's best friend and my best friend Spencer's little sister. She usually looks out for E and protects her as the rest of us do. She should know better than to suggest a wild night out. I'll have to make a point to visit the coffee shop this week and talk to her about this crazy plan. Dinner and a movie would be a much safer girls' night out for them.

"I guess I know where we will be Friday Night." Brady pulls me out of my thoughts.

"We?" I ask.

"Yeah. We," he insists. "Even without a broken arm, you'll need help Friday night." He sure has a point there.

"We have five days to talk them out of it," I point out.

"Oh, we'll be at Cowboys Friday Night." Brady nods. He's right. We will be. "Just be glad it's Cowboys and not O'Brien's Tavern or a bar in Missoula."

I'm beyond glad it isn't a bar in Missoula or O'Brien's. Missoula is a bigger city, which means bigger trouble. Cowboys is a country bar here in Hayden Falls. It's where most of us hung out. For a long time, it was the only bar here. About twenty years ago, the O'Brien's moved here and opened an Irish Pub on the other side of town. The Crawford family hangs out there. The O'Brien's are great, but the Crawfords are another story. Since our families don't get along, I avoid the tavern whenever possible. Still, if Beth and E were going there, I would chance a fight with Roman Crawford to ensure E was okay.

My mind is going crazy with all the wild scenarios that could happen on this girl's night out. There has to be a way to stop it. I didn't figure out a plan because Sheriff Barnes joined us.

"Aiden, how's it going?" Sheriff Barnes shakes my hand before sitting in the chair E just vacated.

"Good," I lie. Things are far from good right now.

My eyes dart around the yard. I don't see E anywhere. I also can't avoid my boss. Hopefully, he won't notice how preoccupied I am. I owe Sheriff Barnes a lot. He also reminds me of my past. Somehow, I'm going to have to make peace with that.

"You should come in toward the end of the week and let me show you around the station," Sheriff Barnes suggests.

A tour of the station isn't necessary. I've lived here my whole life. Well, except for the past six years. While I was away, I trained for a job that would lead me back here. However, getting out of the house would help me feel like my life wasn't at a standstill.

"Yeah. That would be great." Even though I'm talking to the sheriff, I'm still scanning the yard for E. Where did they go?

"I'm assigning you Deputy Murphy's section of town," Sheriff Barnes said.

Section? That's odd. Less than five thousand people are in our little corner of the world. How do you section off something that small?

"Is Spencer quitting or getting promoted?" Surely my friend isn't moving away without telling me. Spence and I talk all the time on the phone. He hasn't mentioned moving.

"Neither," Sheriff Barnes replied. "He's moving to patrol Alan's old section of town."

"What section am I getting?"

"You'll patrol the west side of town." Sheriff Barnes is off duty today. He takes the beer Brady offers him.

I'm the new guy on the force, and he's giving me the side of town the schools are on? Interesting. I still don't understand why we have our own sections.

"Is Hayden Falls so big now that we have our own beats?" I laugh at the thought. We're far from a major city.

"Of course not. I give you guys an area of town for you to connect more with the businesses and people on a daily basis. It helps some of them feel more comfortable having the same officers all the time. Or, so our dear citizens claimed when they asked for this at a town meeting last year." Sheriff Barnes doesn't sound so sure.

"Where's Spencer going?" It made no sense to me why he would move Spencer. It would be easier to give me Alan's section to patrol.

"The north side." Sheriff Barnes drops his eyes.

Ah. The north side. The Magnolia Inn is on the north side of town. I would have gladly taken the north side. It would have given me more reasons to investigate what happened to E. It makes absolutely no sense. Then it hit me. Alan and Spencer were the ones who helped Mr. Hayes pack up E's dorm room. They don't want to risk anyone else finding out what happened to her. When did Hayden Falls become so secretive? This made me want to seriously investigate what happened to E now.

"I don't mind taking Alan's section." I'm testing my theory here.

"Well." Sheriff Barnes rubs the back of his neck with his hand. Yeah, he's hiding something. "I've talked with a few of the businesses on the north side of town. Several of them requested Murphy."

Sure, they did. I disagree with him, but I nod anyway. My wonderful boss is indeed hiding something from me. It makes no difference. I have ways around this. First, I'll need to know precisely what my daily job entails. From there, I'll figure out what lines I can technically cross. This is about E. I'll uncover all these secrets soon enough.

"So, I'm not allowed anywhere but the west side of town?" I watch the sheriff real close. Body language can reveal a lot.

"No. That's not the goal I have for this *little* program." Sheriff Barnes smiles and nods to a few people as they walk by.

"I'm totally confused." It's best to play dumb for a while.

"I'll explain more when you get to the station." Sheriff Barnes rubs his forehead with his fingers. "Most of the businesses on the west side are friends of your family anyway. You'll be better received there."

Now he's going to pull my past into this. My past will cause me enough problems, but it isn't the issue in this. I already hate this little program the townspeople requested. In large cities, this type of thing is necessary. In smaller communities, I think it causes more harm than good. The way the sheriff is talking, he hates this program, too.

At least on the west side of town, I won't have to deal with the bank and Roman Crawford every day. A smile crosses my face. The west side puts the coffee shop in my section. I'll be making regular rounds by there for sure.

Maybe I can get Beth to slip up and share some information with me. She's bound to know what happened to E. Even if Beth doesn't tell me anything useful, E will visit Beth several times each week. I'm all for anything that lets me be around her more.

"So, we're allowed to go anywhere in Hayden Falls, but we just communicate more with the businesses in our sections?" I want to be clear on this. It's a stupid program, but the last thing I need is someone giving me grief because I'm in the wrong place.

"Yes." Sheriff Barnes glances at me and rolls his eyes. He already knows this program is stupid.

I laugh and shake my head. Even with all the ridicule and judgment I've received over the past six years, I still love this crazy little town. These people have never made much sense to me, but you can't help but love them.

Fitting in here won't be easy for me. The sheriff is right. Most of the people on the west side of town are friends of my family. Our ranch is even on this side of town. I guess it's best to put me there. Little by little, I'll find a way to make things work out.

"When do you see the doctor again?" Sheriff Barnes points to my arm.

"I start physical therapy Wednesday morning in Missoula, and I have a doctor's appointment with the office here that afternoon." I'm ready to start physical therapy. The doctor's visit has me feeling uneasy. I don't want to hear any more bad news.

"If those visits go well, why don't you come to the station Thursday morning? We can talk more there, and your uniforms should be ready by then." Sheriff Barnes laughed.

"What?" I don't understand why he's laughing.

"I never thought this day would really come." Sheriff Barnes shakes his head. "Aiden Maxwell in a Hayden Falls deputy uniform."

That has me laughing too. "Well, this law enforcement career was *your* idea," I remind him.

"I had my reasons for that." Sheriff Barnes became all serious. His eyes flick to my brother and then back to me. "From what I hear, your training went very well. My friend in Nashville says you're a natural."

Detective Walter Young in Nashville was a great mentor. He went to college with Sheriff Barnes. When I made the decision two months before graduating high school to destroy my already laid-out future, Sheriff Barnes sent me to his friend. Why the good sheriff thought I'd make a fine officer of the law is beyond me. I'm sure the real reason he looked out for me back then was because of his friendship with my parents.

"Well, I'm here now. Let's hope this career choice wasn't a mistake."

"It's not," Sheriff Barnes assured me. "Some of us need you here."

The Sheriff's eyes move across the yard. I follow his gaze. E is standing with a group of women, laughing about something. She's so beautiful. Her smile is warmer than the sun. I snap my head back toward the Sheriff when I hear him laugh.

"Maxwell, I'll see you on Thursday. Don't worry. That doctor's appointment will go just fine." Sheriff Barnes stands and holds out his hand. "Welcome home, lad."

I stand and take his hand. "Thank you, Sir." I dip my head once. "For everything."

"I don't think you hide your feelings for E all that well." Brady nudged my shoulder with his after the sheriff walked away.

By the Sheriff's reaction just now, I'll have to say my brother is right. Could the sheriff be right, too? Did E need me here? I sure need her. When the time comes, I *am* going to tell her how I feel about her. I also have two more missions where she's concerned. One, I'm going to find out what happened to her. And two, I have to do something about this wild girls' night out.

Chapter Seven

Etrulia

It's only Tuesday, and I'm already regretting my decision for this week's girls' night out. Beth is over-excited about it. She has already turned our best friend's girls' night out into a full-blown party. I've probably received a hundred text messages since Sunday night. Our friends Ally, Sammie, and Katie will now be joining us this Friday night at Cowboys. The other girls know I don't party, so they're not missing this night. It's going to be a disaster. I have to find a way out of it.

Sure. I'm tired of being the quiet little pushover everyone thinks I am. A wild girls' night out doesn't sound like the way to change anyone's mind, though. The last thing I need is to be the headline of Hayden's Happenings. Megan Sanders is constantly reporting on people's lives in her famous gossip blog—the good and the bad. Well, she mainly shares rumors and gossip. It's a gossip blog, after all. Still, most of her predictions about relationships have happened. I swear the girl has hidden cameras all over town. Thank goodness her blog is only famous to the people in our odd little corner of the world. So far, I haven't been mentioned in any of her articles.

Today, I decided to ignore my phone and all of these crazy messages from my friends. They're having way too much fun with this. So, I made our bed and breakfast my main focus. The Magnolia Inn isn't a large bed and breakfast. We only have eight rooms for guests. We also have a small restaurant. We serve breakfast and a light lunch through the winter. During the summer, when it's busier, we include dinner. The restaurant is open to the public as well as our guests. Most people in town go to the diner, though. It's bigger and has a larger menu.

Since my aunt's flower garden behind the inn is one of the prettiest in the area, I convinced her to allow the inn to cater to small weddings. The restaurant is big enough to hold approximately sixty guests for the reception. Of course, the bride and groom have the option of renting a tent for larger weddings.

Today is not going well at all. I have another meeting with Isabell Richardson. This is our third in-person meeting in the past two months. I have heard plenty of bridezilla stories from my online wedding planner friends. Isabell is my first unhappy bride-to-be.

I'm looking forward to next Saturday when I can happily pass Miss Richardson off to her extremely wealthy fiancé, Julian Whitlow III. Come on. Even the man's name screams money, lots of money.

"I have some new decoration ideas for you to incorporate into the ceremony," Isabell stated.

Of course, she does. It's not a request. She's telling me to do it. I roll my eyes as she digs the photos from her expensive shoulder bag. I groan inwardly as I flip through the pictures she hands me. Yes, they're beautiful, but this woman doesn't think things through at all.

"Miss Richardson, these are lovely. However, most of them are for indoor weddings. You requested an outdoor ceremony in the garden." I motion toward the area where her wedding will take place. She insisted on seeing it again.

"So?" Isabell's tone is from what I call an overindulged spoiled brat. "This is what I want."

I turn my attention back to the photos. There's no way I can look this woman in the eye and keep a straight face right now. There's also no way I can give her what she wants here, and I already know she's not going to like it. Que rich girl temper tantrum.

"We can do something similar to these, but it won't have the same effect since you will be outdoors. We can change some of your other design choices so the style in these photos will incorporate in without throwing the theme off." I look up and give her my best professional smile. Fake. It's totally fake.

"I don't want to change anything." Isabell jabs the pictures on my clipboard with her perfectly manicured fingernail. "I want to add these to what I already have."

By the expression on her face, Isabell is frustrated with me. I knew she would be. When she called last week and asked for this appointment, I started preparing the moment we hung up the phone for the temper tantrum she would throw.

"Miss Richardson, I think you have already chosen a wonderful theme with the perfect flowers and decorations for your garden ceremony. Why don't we incorporate these new ideas into the reception tent?" I offer her the only solution I believe will work.

"I don't pay you to think. I pay you to do your job." Isabell taps the pictures on my clipboard again for good measure. "Now, do your job, and give me what I asked for." Her voice rose on the last part.

It would be so nice to remind her she doesn't pay me. Her parents are paying for this wedding. Isabell's parents have almost as much money as the Whitlows. Two powerful families will be joining together through their spoiled children. Lucky me. Unfortunately, I can only smile and try to find a way to work through this.

"I will see what's left in the budget your parents set. If these ideas can be added, I will happily include them. Just know, they will not have the same effect in an outdoor setting." There. That's the polite way of reminding her who's paying for her wedding. I also have no choice but to do what she's asking. Never mind that it's not going to look right.

"You're an idiot." Isabell huffs and throws her hands in the air. I brace myself for more of her tantrum. "Do you not know who we are? Money is no obstacle here. You and your decorating skills obviously are." She puts her hands on her hips and glares at me.

"I'm sorry, Miss Richardson, but your mother set a budget. I will have to get the additions approved by her first." Once again, all I can do is smile and hope for the best.

"If it wasn't so close to my wedding, I would cancel this and fire you right now." Isabell's eyes bore into me. She folds her arms across her chest. "I want to speak to your manager." She looks at my name tag. "Miss… E? What kind of name is that?"

See? Like I said, spoiled little brat. Isabell has known my name since she and her mother booked The Magnolia Inn six months ago. Little does she know I *am* the manager here.

"I think she has a beautiful name," a deep male voice says from behind us.

I look over my shoulder and smile. The handsome man walking toward us has always looked out for me. He's been a constant staple in my life for the past seven months. I don't know what I'd do without him.

"Well, hello, Officer Murphy," I greet my best friend's brother as he gives me a hug.

"Everything okay here, ladies?" Spencer looks from me to Isabell.

Isabell's eyes widen, and she bites her bottom lip. Her eyes roam over Spencer from head to toe. Yeah, if I didn't think of him as a brother, I might have that reaction, too. The lanky kid in high school is now clearly a full-grown man. A lot of single women, and a few of the married ones, give Spencer this look all the time. As far as I know, he doesn't give any woman in town the time of day. I'm sure that will change when he meets the right girl.

"This is Miss Richardson. She's getting married here next Saturday," I introduce Spencer to Isabell. She glares at me like I shouldn't have added the getting married part.

"Well, Miss Richardson, it's a pleasure to meet you. Congratulations on your marriage." Spencer shakes her hand. "I'm sure you're in great hands with E." He leans towards her and loudly whispers," It's short for Etrulia. Beautiful name." He says the last part louder as he winks at me. He gives my bridezilla a sly smile.

I hate my name. My parents gave me an old lady's name. My middle name is the same as my grandmother's. When I first moved here, I didn't want to be called by my first name anymore because that's what my parents called me. Uncle Silas told me everyone used to call his mother E, short for Etrulia. So, I adopted the initial, just like my grandmother.

"Beautiful," Isabell softly repeats. She's not referring to my name here at all. Her eyes continue to hungrily take in Spencer. Disgusting.

Spencer turns to me. "I need to speak with your uncle. Is he around?"

"Yes. He and Aunt Sara are having lunch." I point toward the path that leads to our house behind the flower garden.

"Thanks, E." Spencer leans down and places a kiss on the top of my head.

I know I will always be another little sister to him, but my body tenses up from his touch. Spencer places his hands on my forearms. His eyebrows raise in question. Releasing a breath, I nod my head to let him know I'm okay.

"Have a good day, ladies. I can't wait to see the amazing job E will do for your wedding." Spencer nods once at Isabell before hurrying down the path to see Uncle Silas.

"Will he be at my wedding?" Isabell is fanning herself as she watches Spencer walk away.

"If you're still having your wedding here, he probably will stop by. Officer Murphy makes regular rounds on this side of town," I reply.

"Wow." Isabell's voice was a breathy whisper.

I roll my eyes again and wait. Spencer's out of sight now. She'll regain her senses soon enough.

"Well." Isabell's eyes lock with mine. "Why don't we go ahead and add the new designs to the reception tent?"

"Excellent choice." I smile and motion toward the inn.

After finalizing everything with Isabell, I slouch down in my office chair and let my head fall back. That woman gives me a headache every time we talk. Phone calls with her are just as frustrating.

"You okay?" Spencer asks from the doorway.

I sit up straight and nod. “Thank you.” He has no idea how much he helped me out today.

“No problem, little one.” Spencer walks over and kisses the top of my head again. This time, I don’t tense up.

I know all of his affection toward me is done in a brotherly way. His sister Beth and I have been best friends since the third grade. Thankfully, Spencer doesn’t do this in public. I’d hate to hear the rumors that would circulate from it.

“Have you talked to Aiden yet?”

“I did for a few minutes at his welcome home party.”

“Does he know?” Nervously, I bite my fingernail.

“Not that I’m aware of.” Spencer’s expression looks torn. Aiden is his best friend. I’m sure this isn’t easy for him.

“Please don’t tell him,” I softly plead.

Spencer releases a breath and runs his fingers through his hair. He’s battling on who to be loyal to here. He’s a good man. I shouldn’t put him in this position, but Aiden is the last person I want to know what happened back in January.

“If you’re not in any danger, I won’t.” Spencer walks to the door and pauses. “But, E, if your safety is in jeopardy in any way, I’ll have no choice.” That’s really all I can ask.

“Thank you.” I drop my head. Asking this of him is wrong, and I know it.

“E?” Spencer waits until I look up at him. “Aiden is a good man. You should consider telling him yourself before he finds out.”

This subject is an emotional one for me. I can only nod my head to say I’ll think about it. I don’t want to think about it. I don’t want anyone to know what happened to me. Too many people know already. They all pity me. I can see it in their eyes when they look at me. I *never* want Aiden to look at me that way.

Chapter Eight

Aiden

Thankfully, my physical therapy and doctor's visit went well yesterday. They weren't as great as I had hoped, but they were enough to get my mom to ease up on me some. I've been here less than a week, and I'm already going stir-crazy just hanging around the house. My mom is relentless in her watch over me.

Today, I'm touring the station with the sheriff and picking up my uniforms. It's almost laughable. I never thought I'd actually come back to Hayden Falls to be a deputy.

"Well." Sheriff Barnes grins as he looks up from the letters I gave him from my physical therapist and doctor. He asked for a written update on my condition. "According to these, I can put you on light duty next week."

I groan, and not inwardly. "You mean a desk job?"

Sheriff Barnes nods his head and wholeheartedly laughs. I hate my boss. Not really, but he's laughing at me.

"It's either that or you can continue to hang around the ranch for a couple more weeks." Sheriff Barnes is still grinning at me.

The Ranch? That means being under the thumb of my wonderful mother. Oh, she's wonderful, alright. However, she's become a drill sergeant with her constant watching out for me. I know how badly the tour bus accident scared my mom. I do my best to take in all her overbearing care with a graceful stride. The truth is, it's seriously wearing on my nerves, but I'll never tell my mom that.

"I'll gladly take the light-duty desk job." I quickly accept the offer, causing the sheriff to laugh again.

"Murphy!" Sheriff Barnes calls out as Spencer walks by the door.

"Morning, Sheriff. Aiden." Spencer walks over and gives me a fist bump.

"Good to see you two are still buddies," Sheriff Barnes says.

Of course, Spencer and I are still buddies. He's one of my best friends. We've been friends since we were toddlers. We talked on the phone almost every week while I was in Tennessee. It kind of hurts knowing Spencer knows what happened to E, but he's never said anything about it.

"That's never going to change," Spencer assures Sheriff Barnes. I nod my head in agreement.

"Good." Sheriff Barnes points to the uniforms hanging by the door. "You can carry Aiden's uniforms out to the truck, and if he feels up to it, walk him around to the businesses on the west side of town. Let them all know he's taking your section soon."

Spencer and I look at each other and shake our heads. It's pointless to remind the sheriff that everybody in town already knows who I am. From the look on Spencer's face, he hates this little section program as much as I do.

I don't even protest the sheriff's suggestion and follow Spencer out to my truck. No. I still can't drive, according to my mom. Brady drove me to town. I look around but don't see him anywhere. Oh well, he'll turn up sooner or later. Besides, I want a few minutes alone with Spencer. I didn't really get a chance to talk with him at my welcome home party, and this is a subject I don't want to talk about on the phone.

I glance over at Spencer as we walk toward the town square. He's fidgeting, which means he's nervous. The way he's acting confirms to me he does know the whole story about E. I don't understand why everybody is keeping this from me.

"Are you going to tell me what happened to E?"

There's no point in beating around the bush with Spencer. He and I have always been upfront and honest with each other. Well, except for this.

Spencer pauses at the side of the ice cream shop. He looks up and down the street to confirm there's no one within hearing distance. His action has me on high alert. I'm scared my worst fears on this are probably true.

"I wanna tell you." Spencer looks me in the eye and shakes his head. "But I can't."

"Can't, or won't?" I snap. Spencer's eyes widen. "I'm sorry, man," I hurry to apologize.

Taking a deep breath, I step away for a moment to calm myself down. None of this is Spencer's fault. Getting mad at him won't get me the answers I need. Not knowing what happened to E has me on edge.

"You still love her. Don't you?" Spencer's words cause me to jerk my head toward him. He chuckles. "Come on, man. Give me some credit here. I ain't blind. You never said so, but I knew."

My brother was right. I didn't do as well of a job as I thought about hiding my feelings for E. The whole darn town probably knows it. I don't answer his question. He knows I love her.

"Can you tell me anything?" I won't push if he can't. I'll secretly investigate harder to get the answers.

"She asked me not to." I narrow my eyes and point my finger at him. He holds up a hand to stop me from speaking. "I promised her I wouldn't unless she was in danger."

Danger? That told me more than he realized. Then again, Spencer may have been giving me a hint here. He knows all about my training as a detective. He knows I'll read more into his words. I will, without a doubt, be digging deeper into this.

"He hurt her." It wasn't really a question. I already knew he had. Spencer looks away and swallows hard.

Anger burns inside of me. If I ever find this scumbag, I'm going to rip him apart. I run my fingers through my hair and tug on the ends. I seriously want to hurt this guy. I don't even have his last name yet, but I'll get it soon enough.

"How am I supposed to do my job and keep her safe if nobody will tell me what happened to her?'

"Are you asking as just a deputy?"

Just a deputy? I could never be just a deputy where E's concerned. Even if I tried to be just a deputy, my heart would get in the way. I know it will. Spencer knows it, too.

"No," I reply honestly as I look my friend in the eye. "I love her," I admit. "I always will."

It's the truest statement I've ever spoken in my life. No matter what happens, I will always love E.

"Come on, man." Spencer nods towards the square. "Let's go talk to the wonderful business owners." He could see my disappointment with not getting the answers I wanted today. "Don't worry, my friend. It'll all come out sooner or later."

I sigh and nod. He's right. It'll all come out one day. I hope it's sooner rather than later. I'll keep searching until I have all the details. The detective in me won't let the matter drop. I'll find a way to do it without causing the people who cared about E to break her trust in them.

Before we step into the town square, someone barrels around the corner of the ice cream parlor and almost slams into us. Spencer and I grab the old man to keep him upright. I stare in amazement at his bushy beard, wild eyes, and dusty overalls. Spencer leans down and picks up the tattered hat that fell to the sidewalk in the old man's haste. I can't believe this guy is still alive.

"Hey, Mags." Spencer hands him his hat. "Where you off to in such a hurry?"

"Hardware store," Mags looks around, trying to find the store. "Gotta buy a new axe."

"What happened to your axe?" I immediately regret asking the question.

"Bigfoot took it," Mags grumbles.

"Bigfoot?" I look to Spencer for answers. He just rolls his eyes. "Well, Mags, you're headed in the wrong direction," I tell him.

"The hardware store is right over there." Spencer turns Mags around and points toward the east side of the square.

How anybody could miss the huge store on the corner is beyond me. It's not like Mags has never been there. I want to ask why Bigfoot would want his axe, but I don't have an hour to listen to the ramblings that will come out of his mouth. You can't piece half of what he says together anyway. It looks like he's back on the Bigfoot trip. Last I heard, he was hunting aliens in the woods around his cabin.

"There it is!" Mags shouts. You'd think he'd found some hidden treasure. "Bye, boys." The old man throws his hands up as he walks away, mumbling about something.

I cut my eyes to Spencer for an explanation. Honestly, I don't think anyone can explain that old man.

"Don't ask," Spencer said. "He gets weirder every year. He stays up at his shack with nobody to talk to but those dogs most of the time. Every now and then, he wanders into town."

"Dogs? What kind did he get?" This was new. I guess Mags got tired of being alone.

"Who knows." Spencer shakes his head. "I'm not going up there to find out."

"Now, Deputy Murphy, what if Mags calls for help?" I ask.

"What's he going to call with?" Spencer looks at me like I've lost my mind.

"Well, I'm sure Bigfoot or the aliens can call 911," I tease.

Unable to hold it in, both of us burst out laughing. Every town has a weird one, I guess. Hayden Falls has several people whose sanity is questionable. Mags is at the top of our list.

"Come on, man." Spencer is still laughing. "Let's get this over with."

We visit Frozen Scoops Ice Cream parlor and Sweet Treats Bakery. So far, so good. There are no issues with any of the people on this side of town. Brady comes running up as we're about to go into the coffee shop.

"Where have you been?"

"Hardware store." Brady holds up the bag. "Dad asked me to pick up a couple of things.

"We're going to grab a coffee and say hi to Beth. After this, we can head home." I motioned to the coffee shop.

The medicine I'm on still makes me groggy at times. I don't want to overdo things today and cause a setback. I need to get out of the house more, or I will go insane. If I show any sign of weakness, Mom will have the doctor pull my light-duty work status in a heartbeat. Spencer and I can visit the grocery store and the diner on Monday. I'll be sharing these two places with him and another deputy.

Brady grins and grabs the door, holding it open for Spencer and me. My little brother enjoys giving Beth a hard time. I should probably warn him. It's not a good idea to aggravate her in front of her big brother. Spencer will wrestle Brady to the floor in a matter of seconds if he upsets Beth too much. I'd be the same way if I had a little sister. Thankfully, I don't. It was just us three boys. Mom said we were enough to keep her busy. Deep down, I'm almost sure my mom wouldn't have minded if she'd been surprised with a daughter.

I smelled the coffee before we stepped inside the shop. Now, the wonderful aroma hits me full force. With the bakery next door, the sweetness from there lingers in the air. Beth does a little baking here, but she also gets a few of the items in her case from Sweet Treats. Her decision to put her coffee shop next to the bakery was a great idea.

"Hey, guys," Beth greets us. She's working behind the counter today. "What can I get you?"

We give her our orders and move to the side to wait while she prepares our drinks. Brady leans on the counter. His smirk lets me know he could care less that Spencer is standing here.

Beth hands Spencer and me our drinks and goes to prepare Brady's. I would love to talk to her about this girls' night out, but this is probably not the time. She hands Brady his coffee. I'm sure her smile is fake. My brother wraps his hand around the cup and Beth's hand. Without letting go, he leans closer to her.

"How come you named your shop Beth's Morning Brew when you're open all day?" Brady asks. He's an idiot. "It makes no sense."

Beth looks at me and then back to Brady. "I did it just so morons would ask me that question."

She pulls her hand from his and raises an eyebrow. Spencer and I laugh and shake our heads. These two have been going at each other for years. Most times, it's comical to watch. Beth can hold her own for sure. Spencer will only step in if he has to. Hopefully, Brady won't push things to that point.

"Still, you should have come up with something more original and catchier." Brady sips his coffee. He's enjoying this too much.

"If I *ever* need your help, Farm Boy, naming anything, I'll let you know." Beth lifts her chin before walking away to take another order. Spencer and I laugh again.

"Farm Boy?" Brady calls out. Beth is pretending to ignore him. "I have you to know that I'm a baseball player."

My brother really is an idiot. We grew up on one of the largest ranches in the area. Technically, it does make him a farm boy. I will give him credit, though. Brady is a great baseball player. He'll probably end up with the MLB career I was once destined for.

Beth prepares the drink and hands it to Mrs. Ramsey. "Thank you." She turns to Brady. "I know. I look for you every Saturday at the Pee Wee games."

Brady's mouth drops open. Beth is winning the battle today. He takes a step forward only to have Spencer's large hand clamp down on his shoulder. Without saying a word, Spencer pushes my brother toward the door. I'm not sure if he's saving my brother or protecting his sister here. It's probably both.

"So." Spencer turns to Beth. "What's this I hear about a girls' night out at Cowboys tomorrow night?"

Of course, he heard about this. Nothing stays quiet in this town for too long. I want to shout '*thank you*' to my friend. This is one of the things I wanted to talk to Beth about.

"The girls and I are getting together for a few drinks and dancing." Beth shrugs like it's no big deal.

"Little sister, I don't think this is a good idea," Spencer tells her, and I totally agree.

I should speak up, but since this is his sister, I'll let Spencer handle things for now. He's the only person in town who can reign Beth in when she gets out of hand. E tries, but sometimes, she's not enough.

"It's a great idea. We do it all the time." Beth goes over to take another order.

"Yeah, but you don't usually take E with you on those types of girls' nights." Spencer's expression turns hard.

I watch and listen closely. I'm sure both of them know what happened to E. Maybe one of them will slip some much-needed information out here.

"It's about time she did more than just dinners and movies. She's never going to break out of her shell if she keeps hiding away with the Hayden Sisters all the time," Beth says sharply.

I do agree with her. E doesn't belong in the *old ladies'* club. Still, E doesn't drink often. A night out partying is bound to end badly.

"Bethie, I don't think this is a good idea," Spencer says again, shaking his head.

I admire my friend's determination to keep E safe. I won't lie. It's a struggle not to feel jealous here. Spencer isn't in love with E. Well, he loves her, but not like I do. Somehow, it hurt just the same. Being Beth's best friend, E's like a little sister to Spencer. Now, because of a traumatic event, there's a deeper kind of bond between them. I want a deeper bond with E, too. I have to find out what happened to her. I'm a patient man. I'll let things play out for now, but eventually, I'll know everything.

"Neither do I," I add.

Beth looks between us for a moment. "Well, I guess if you two don't like it, then you should be there to protect her." Beth shakes her head. "I'm not changing it."

Stubborn woman. If Spencer weren't standing here, I'd probably snap off something smart-mouthed at her. Instead, I look at my friend and shake my head. There's no point arguing with her. Beth isn't going to back down. One thing's for sure. Brady and I will be at Cowboys tomorrow night. With any luck, Spencer will be there too.

Chapter Nine

Etrulia

Friday night! Yay! I close my eyes and take a deep breath. Nope. It didn't relax me or settle my nerves at all. This night is going to be a total disaster.

Should I give myself a little pep talk? Can I enjoy a night of drinking and dancing with my friends? While staring in the bathroom mirror, I tell myself this night will be just fine. Maybe if I said it enough, I could convince myself there's nothing to fear. I blow out a long breath. I don't think this is working. Bravery is not my strongest trait. Bravery was knocked out of me when I was a little girl.

Perhaps I should just lock the door and hide away in my comfy chair with a good book. A movie sounds nice. I can order a pizza or something from the diner. Both places will deliver since I'm so close to them. Well, the diner doesn't offer delivery, but they delivered the few times I asked them to.

"Hey, Bestie!" Beth shouts as she barges into my room. I grab the counter to brace myself. I wasn't expecting her.

See? Right there is why I should have locked my door. There's no getting out of this night now. Lifting my head, I put on a happy face and walked into the bedroom to see my best friend. She already looks too happy. Why can't I be as outgoing as she is?

"What are you doing here?" Yeah, it's a dumb question. I know why she's here. "I told you I would meet you at Cowboys."

"No. No. No." Beth waves a finger at me. "If I left you alone, you would find a way out of this night."

She's right. I sure would have. It would probably be best for me if I just refused these types of girls' nights out in the future. Why did I even agree to this in the first place? I groan. I already know the answer to that question. I want to prove to Aiden that I'm a true member of the *old ladies'* club. I shouldn't let anyone's opinion of me matter, but for some reason, Aiden's did. I can't let my mind go there right now. If I think about him, my true feelings for him will show. I'm ready to feel those feelings. I probably never will be, and it wouldn't be fair to Aiden if he did have feelings for me.

"Well, I must say, at least you've been giving this some effort here." Beth walks around my bed, looking at all the outfits I'd tossed there.

My bed is completely covered in clothes. I rarely go to bars and clubs. I have no idea what to wear tonight. It's probably another reason why Beth is here now.

At college, I only went out like this when I was with Garrett, and I don't want to think about those nights again. The only times I've been to Cowboys or O'Brien's Tavern are for special occasions like a friend's birthday. I could walk to Cowboys from here, but I've always driven. I wanted to make sure all of my friends got home safely. I have a feeling Beth won't let me be the designated driver tonight.

"There's no need to overthink this." Beth pauses and grins at me. "Unless you're hoping to turn this into a date."

Is she insane? Scratch that question. Beth is totally insane. I love her, but she knows I don't date. I shake my head and look away.

"Here." Beth tosses my favorite pair of jeans at me. "Those boots will do." She points at my black leather boots by the dresser. They aren't cowboy boots like she's wearing, but I love them. "Now, all you need is a cute top, and that's it."

Cute top? That's it? Beth can throw an outfit together in a matter of seconds. She just proved how much I was overthinking this night. Now, the only problem is, which top? I decide to follow Beth's lead and just grab one of my favorite tops. It's a navy blue summer sweater with a low neckline. It's not low enough to show off too much cleavage. I always felt pretty when I wore it. The only thing I didn't like about it was the length. It barely fell below the waistline of my jeans, so I always wore a long tank top under it.

"You don't need that." Beth snatches the tank top out of my hand. She pushes me into the bathroom. "Now, hurry up."

While I get dressed, Beth puts my discarded clothes back into the closet. She knows me well. I would have insisted on doing it before we left. I have a feeling she's ready to get this girls' night out started. The thought made me laugh. Beth's the fun one in our relationship. I'm the one who keeps us grounded.

Once I was dressed, Beth practically pushed me out the front door. She barely gave me enough time to lock up my apartment. I have no idea why she's so eager to get to Cowboys tonight. Normally, I would have walked or driven myself, but Beth's car was in the driveway. My friend loves to party. There's no way she can be our designated driver tonight.

I give one final glance at my front door. I live in the one-bedroom apartment above my aunt and uncle's garage. It might sound sad to most people, but I feel safe here.

I was eight years old when I moved in with my aunt and uncle. We lived in the huge Victorian house that is now The Magnolia Inn. Aunt Sara's mother lived in the two-bedroom house behind the flower garden. Uncle Silas and Aunt Sara are legally my parents now, but they never insisted on me calling them mom and dad. Those two words are hard for me to say.

When I was ten, we went on a family vacation to Washington State and stayed in a bed and breakfast inn. Even at such a young age, I immediately fell in love with the place. From that moment on, I knew I wanted to own a bed and breakfast someday. When Aunt

Sara's mother passed away two years later, my aunt and uncle moved us to the smaller house and turned the main house into The Magnolia Inn. After coming home from college earlier this year, I moved into the small apartment above the garage. My aunt thought this would give me a sense of peace and freedom at the same time. She was right. My little home is perfect for me. It gave me a safe place to hide and heal.

"Come on. Let's go." Beth's already in the driver's seat.

The drive to Cowboys takes less than five minutes. Still, Beth talks the entire way. There wasn't a lot of time to talk about much. That's a good thing because Beth talks all the time. I mean, All. The. Time. Beth wasn't the only eager friend I had tonight. Ally, Sammie, and Katie were already inside, waiting for us.

"You're not getting out of this now," Beth said. She notices me staring at the front door of the bar.

"I don't know why I'm so nervous." Well, that's not exactly true. There are lots of reasons why I'm nervous tonight. One, in particular, I don't want to admit to.

"Oh, he's going to be here tonight." Beth grins slyly. Her words shocked me.

"What?" My stomach is in bigger knots now.

"Aiden will be here." Beth jumps out of the car.

"Aiden is hurt and on some strong medications. He can't drink," I protest as I hurry to catch up with her.

Beth whirls around and holds both of her hands out. "The man has a broken arm. He's not dying. Geez." She rolls her eyes. "Trust me. He will be here, but not for beer." Beth winks and turns to open the door before I can say anything more.

The once muffled sounds from inside the bar fully hit me as Beth quickly pulled the door open. She's beyond ready to get this party started. Fearing I might bolt and run home, Beth grabs my hand and pulls me inside. Our friends already have a table on the far side of the dance floor. I don't even have time to take everything in because Beth is pulling me to our table. We hug our friends before taking our seats.

"I can't believe you're doing this," Ally squeals.

"What can I get you, lovely ladies?" Noah Welborn comes over to take our drink orders.

Noah's father owns the bar. He's been working here since he was twenty-one. Of course, he's been in and out of Cowboys his whole life. He's also one of the biggest flirts in town. I mean, he flirts with every woman he sees. Even the Hayden Sisters love Noah. He has all of the single women in Hayden Falls chasing him. Rumor has it that a few married ones have tried as well. Still, no one has been able to rope the charming bartender.

"A round of shots," Beth shouts. I glare at her. Shots? Not a good idea.

"And a bucket of beer," Ally adds. Noah nods and turns to go.

"Wait!" Sammie calls out before Noah can walk away. "And one pina colada." She points at me. "E's not fond of beer."

Well, that's embarrassing. My friend has no problem throwing my little quirk out there for everyone to hear.

"I gotcha, pretty lady." Noah winks at me before walking away.

Of course, I blush at his words while my friends make *ooh and awe* sounds at me. They know how flirtatious Noah is. I don't understand why they're making such a big deal out of this.

"I told you," Beth leans over and whispers in my ear.

"What?" I'm confused.

Beth slightly motions with her head toward the opposite side of the bar. I look across the dance floor to the upper section of the bar, where more tables and booths are. Cowboys serves food as well as drinks. They even serve lunch. Naturally, it's all bar food, but it's really good. My eyes lock with Aiden's. How did Beth know he would be here? He's not alone, either. Brady and Spencer are sitting at the table with him.

I watch several guys stop at their table to shake hands with Aiden. No doubt they're welcoming him back to Hayden Falls. Aiden only looks away long enough to say hello to them. His eyes automatically come back to me every time. I can't say anything because I'm having a hard time keeping my eyes off him.

Noah soon returns to our table. He sets a cold beer in front of each of my friends. A bucket filled with beers and ice is placed in the middle of our table. Next, a round of shots is placed in front of each of us. I'm not so sure about this.

"And one pina colada." Noah slowly sets my drink in front of me. Of course, he winks at me again. "Enjoy, pretty lady."

Again, the oohs and awes come from my friends as Noah walks away. My friends are acting like five-year-olds tonight. Nothing, absolutely nothing, will ever happen between Noah Welborn and me.

"Time to drink up, E," Katie said as she grabbed her shot.

"I don't know about this." I pick my shot up and eye it as if it might explode. "I've never done shots before."

"Uh oh," Beth said.

"What?"

Beth's not looking at any of us. I follow her gaze across the dance floor to Aiden's table. Uh oh, is right. Karlee Davis. I knew it was only a matter of time before she found Aiden. She's already making her move. She has one hand on his shoulder while leaning against his side. Aiden's looking up at her. He shakes his head at whatever Karlee's saying. Aiden's eyes quickly come back to me. I watch as Karlee continues to rub herself up against him. The sight makes me sick.

Embarrassed, I drop my eyes to the shot glass in my hand. I hate Karlee. I never understood why Aiden was so interested in her. Karlee is rude and selfish. She's beautiful, but there's not a nice bone in her body. Before I could talk myself out of it, I downed the shot and set the glass on the table, causing my friends to shout.

"I think I'm going to need more than one of those," I say without looking up.

"Yes!" Ally shouts. She stops Shelly, one of the waitresses here, and orders another round.

"Are you okay?" Sammie asked. She and Beth are sitting next to me. Both of them are rubbing my back.

"Oh, I'm great," I reply without looking up. I grab my pina colada and take a sip. I'm far from great right now.

"Would you like me to go throw her out?" Ally literally growls.

I snap my head up. My friends are all staring at Karlee and Aiden. They don't even try to cover up what they're doing. I look around the table and gawk at them.

"Come on, E," Katie says. "We all know that you like Aiden.

"I have no problem with getting her away from him." Ally's eyes shoot daggers into Karlee.

Ally has a deep hate for the woman. Karlee interfered in one of Ally's relationships back in high school. My friend is not letting go of that grudge. Ally vowed to make Karlee pay for what she did.

"No," I whisper. "If he wants her, let him have her."

The band starts up again after a fifteen-minute break. It's a slow song, and couples make their way to the dance floor. A throat clears next to me. I look up into a set of deep emerald green eyes.

"E, would you like to dance?" Jesse Calhoun holds his hand out to me.

Jesse and his friends are sitting at the table next to us. I wasn't expecting to dance with anyone tonight. I glance over at Aiden again. He's not looking at me. Karlee is still rubbing up against him. I close my eyes and take a deep breath. Forcing a smile on my face, I look up at Jesse.

"I'd love to," I reply.

Placing my hand in his, I hop off my stool. I don't miss the shocked gasps from my friends. Yes, this is totally out of my normal. Stepping onto the dance floor, I let Jesse pull me into his arms.

"Pit! Four! Get down!" Noah shouts across the bar.

I look over Jesse's shoulder to see Pit and Four dancing on top of one of the pool tables. From the looks of things, class clowns never grow up.

"I think your brother is about to get thrown out," I tell Jesse.

He looks over his shoulder at Four and shakes his head before turning back to me. He doesn't seem too concerned.

"If Mick gets in trouble tonight, he's on his own." Jesse grins at me. "My attention is right here tonight."

Oh, darn. I wasn't expecting anything like that from Jesse. I have no idea how to handle this situation. A glance at my friends tells me they won't be any help tonight. Those four crazy ladies are giving me thumbs-up signals. All I can do is look up and smile at Jesse. Jesse is cute and really sweet. He's just not the guy my heart wants.

I shouldn't be dancing with anyone, but seeing Aiden with Karlee is more than I can take. I knew this night was a bad idea.

Chapter Ten

Aiden

My eyes were on her from the moment E stepped into the bar. Beth practically dragged her across the edge of the dance floor to the table where several of their friends were waiting. I arrived early so I could get this very table. It's in the middle of the row overlooking the dance floor. From this spot, I have a clear view of every area in the bar.

E looks adorable tonight. Of course, she looks good to me, no matter what she's wearing. Her long, wavy, light brown hair falls loosely over her shoulders. I've often dreamed about running my fingers through those wavy curls. The dark blue sweater suits her. Blue is her favorite color. I can't tell from here, but I'm sure it makes her eyes a deeper shade of blue.

My only problem with her outfit is the length of her sweater. When E hugged each of her friends, the sweater lifted slightly to expose a sliver of her skin. Skin I desperately want to touch.

Her jeans hugged her, revealing the curve of her hips. A quick look around the bar and knowing the reputations of half of the guys in here is enough to know I'll have to keep my eyes on E all night. Wolves have a habit of circling a woman like her.

The first wolf I'll have to handle tonight is Noah Welborn. If that bartender doesn't stop winking at my girl, I'll poke both his eyes out. You can't wink if you can't see. And my girl? Why yes, yes she is! E doesn't know it yet, but I'll fix that little detail in time.

"Easy, big guy." Spencer puts his hand on my arm, drawing my attention to him.

"What?" I snap.

"We all know Noah means nothing by it." Spencer raises an eyebrow.

"Bro, if you're that jealous, you need to get over there and claim that." Brady chuckles.

"She is not a *that*," I inform my brother.

"You're right." Brady puts his hand on my other shoulder. He's careful not to jostle my broken arm. "I shouldn't have said it like that. But whatever you do here, do *not* hurt her or jerk her around. I won't have it."

Whoa! It looks like my little brother is more protective over E than I thought. I can understand where he's coming from, though. He feels responsible for what happened to her. I respected that. He has nothing to worry about here. I have no intention of hurting E or jerking her around.

"I'm with him," Spencer throws in.

I nod to both men to let them know I understand. I could argue with them, but there's no point. I could explain myself to them, but they already know how I feel about her. We all were close growing up. It's strange how easily we understood each other without words. It freaked our parents out every time.

I sit up straight when Noah returns to the girl's table with their drinks. That's a lot of alcohol. I want to rush across the room and tackle Noah to the floor. He just set a shot in front of E and a pina colada. The man has no brains in his head.

Before I can stand up or even speak, something rubs up against my right arm. I look up to see the one face I never wanted to see again. Karlee Davis. My on-and-off girlfriend from high school found me. I don't know why I ever dated her or took her back as many times as I did. Well, yes, I do. Sadly, and I'm not proud to say this, I was drunk every time it happened.

We would be at a party. Karlee would beg and cry until the fool I was would agree to take her back. She then spent the next few months destroying my life. Karlee knew I wasn't in love with her. When we were alone, she reminded me of the fact. In public, she was hanging all over me. It made no sense, then or now. Sadly, I wasn't always a gentleman in my teenage years. I'm not about to repeat any of that nonsense with her.

"Hey, Aiden." Karlee puts her arm around my shoulders. "I heard that you were back. You should have come to see me."

"Goodbye, Karlee." I roll my eyes. "I don't wish to see you."

Rude? Why, yes, I am. This woman tormented me for months at a time. Usually, I am a gentleman. This is just one time I can't do it. My grandfather's probably rolling over in his grave right now. I was raised to be a better man than this.

I look across the dance floor and suck in a breath. E just downed a shot and set the glass on the table. Brady and Spencer look over and now have the same expression on their faces as I do. Brady was right at my welcome home party. Lighting had indeed struck in Hayden Falls.

"I should have known," Karlee mumbles as she leans closer to my side.

"What?" I nudge her away with my good arm. Still, Karlee comes back against my side.

"You've had it bad for Miss Prim and Proper over there for years." Karlee huffed.

Does Karlee know I've always cared for E? That's surprising. I really didn't do a good job hiding my feelings for E. It doesn't matter what she knows. I don't want Karlee touching me. I nudge her away once more. Before Karlee can settle against me again, a body wedges between us.

"You need to go away." Miles Hamilton shoos Karlee away with both his hands. It's about time my other best friend showed up.

Karlee huffs again and shakes her head. Thankfully, she's backing away from our table now. There's no love lost between Miles and Karlee. Miles cussed me out every time I took Karlee back during high school. He's the one who caught Karlee cheating on me with Phillip Crawford when she and I dated the first time. Miles took a girl he was interested in up to the falls to make out. They found the spot already occupied by Phillip and Karlee.

"Bye, Aiden." Karlee gives me a little finger wave. "I'll see you around."

"No, you won't." Miles jabs his finger toward Karlee. He vowed years ago he would never let me be foolish enough to take Karlee back again.

"Thanks, man." I smile and shake my friend's hand. "It's good to see you."

"I would apologize for being late, but it looks like I got here right on time." Miles grins. He's seriously proud of himself right now.

"You sure did." Spencer laughs and hands Miles a beer from the bucket on our table.

"There was a house fire in Willows Bend today. It took a while to put it out." Miles sits down next to Spencer.

Willows Bend is another small town about twenty minutes away. Our school teams have always been rivals.

"Everybody okay?" Brady asked.

We all understood why my brother asked that question. It's a hard subject for most of us here. When we were kids, there was a fire here. Even though they got the family out, the parents didn't make it. I think it's one of the reasons Miles became a fireman.

"Yeah. They lost everything, but the family is okay." Miles takes a drink of his beer. He's one of the best firefighters we have in Hayden Falls.

"Bro." Brady wildly taps my shoulder, ending the awkward silence we fell into. "If you don't do something about that, I sure will."

What in the world is my brother talking about? I look across the bar to E's table. She's not there. How could I have taken my eyes off her? I'm here to watch over her. I franticly scan the area from the restrooms to the bar. I don't see her anywhere. Every muscle in my body tightens. Every nerve is on high alert. I have to find her.

Spencer reaches over and grabs my chin. He jerks my head toward the front of the dance floor next to the stage. Any other time, I would have punched my friend. However, what my eyes land on makes me jump to my feet, almost tipping my chair over.

Jesse Calhoun has my girl, *my girl*, on the dance floor, dancing to a slow song. Not that a faster one would be any better. I'm sure the lyrics to this song are something sappy and romantic. I don't care. I can't hear them anyway. All I can hear is my blood boiling.

Right here is where a man would cuss. I've already rolled my grandfather over in his grave enough tonight by not being a gentleman. I can't be a hypocrite here and start throwing cuss words around. I hounded my friends in Tennessee rigorously about their bad language. It took a few months, but I worked them out of it.

I won't cuss, but I will stop this for sure. I glance over and see wolf number one working behind the bar. The guys are right. Noah isn't a problem. He charms all the women in town, even the elderly ones. I lock my eyes on Jesse Calhoun. Wolf number two, however, *is* a problem.

As my temper builds, I growl deep in my throat. There's a set of hands I need to get off my girl.

"I got this." My voice is deeper than normal and laced with something primal.

I storm around the tables and down the steps to the dance floor. My eyes never leave Jesse. I have no idea what I'll do with one arm in a sling, but I can't handle seeing him touch my girl.

I hear Noah shout at someone. None of it registers, though. Hopefully, he isn't yelling at me. It doesn't matter if he is. I have one focus here. Get Jesse Calhoun away from my girl. E might hate me tomorrow, but tonight, I'm rescuing her.

Chapter Eleven

Etrulia

Dancing with Jesse isn't bad at all. He's a good dancer. I feel the effects of the pina colada and the shot I downed a few minutes ago as we slowly moved around the dance floor. I think Jesse senses it, too. I stumble a little, and his hand on my waist tightens. I'm overly aware of his touch, but it doesn't feel too intimate. I mean, slow dancing is a bit intimate. Thankfully, Jesse isn't being a jerk and pushing for more.

"You look good tonight." Jesse moves us closer to the stage.

"Thank you." I look up and give him a shy smile.

"I didn't think you'd dance with me." Jesse spins us around slowly. He really is a good dancer.

"Why wouldn't I dance with you?" I keep my eyes locked on his. I can't handle watching Karlee touching Aiden.

Jesse chuckles. "I think we both know why."

"Because I'm shy, and this isn't something I do?" I ask.

"Well." Jesse pauses for a moment. "Both of those are true, but it's not the reason."

"And what would my reason be?" I'm playing dumb, and we both know it.

Jesse chuckles again. "Don't worry. Remain calm. He's on his way."

"What?" I narrow my eyes. "Who?"

"And you're welcome," Jesse whispers.

"I don't understand." I shake my head. It's like we're having two different conversations here.

"Come on, E." Jesse keeps the grin on his face. "Maxwell wasn't going to make a move unless something prompted him to."

Oh my gosh. I can't believe this is happening. He did this on purpose.

"You didn't really want to dance with me. Did you?"

"Oh, I wouldn't say that, and don't you ever believe it." Jesse's tone is serious, and I do believe him. "If Maxwell had never come back to town, this dance would be something totally different."

A glance over Jesse's shoulder confirmed Aiden was indeed heading our way. He looks mad. Now, I fear for Jesse. Dancing with me could lead to an argument with Aiden tonight. I'm not sure why Aiden thinks he has a right to be mad. I mean, Karlee was all over him just minutes ago.

"Jesse, I'm so sorry." I shake my head. "I don't want you to get hurt."

"Nothing is going to happen." Jesse sounds sure. I'm not. "Trust me. Okay?"

I nod and bite my bottom lip. I don't have Jesse's confidence about this. Jesse grins and winks at me when Aiden taps him hard on the shoulder. Hopefully, Jesse's right about this. It would have been better if I had never accepted this dance.

"Hey, man." Jesse looks over his shoulder at Aiden.

"I'm cutting in," Aiden informs Jesse.

Jesse looks back at me and winks again. How can he be so calm? Aiden is practically fuming.

Jesse looks back at Aiden again. "Only if this pretty lady in my arms says so."

Aiden growls loud enough for me to hear him. I now have a new kind of respect for Jesse Calhoun. The sweet man with emerald green eyes, whom half of the women in this town swoon over, can hold his own.

Jesse turns back to me. “E, would you like to dance with Aiden?”

For a minute, I want to laugh at how comical this situation is. Or perhaps it’s the alcohol that’s making this seem so funny.

“It’s fine, Jesse.” It’s not a yes or no. I want to dance with Aiden, but I’m scared to admit it. “Thank you.”

“No problem, pretty lady.” Jesse winks at me again, earning him another growl from Aiden before he walks away.

The band moves into another slow song as Aiden and I stare at each other. I could walk away, or I could use the opportunity Jesse has given me. This might be my only chance to dance with him. I guess the alcohol is making me brave tonight.

“How are we going to do this?” I hold my hands out.

“What?” Aiden looks confused. At least he’s calming down now.

“Dance,” I reply. “You cut in. Remember?”

“Right. Dance.” Aiden looks down at his arm in the sling.

Thankfully, I hold it together and don’t burst out laughing. I’m a little tipsy, and I want to laugh. Aiden didn’t come down here to dance. He wanted to get Jesse away from me. That’s sweet, and it proves Beth just might be right. Aiden has feelings for me, too.

Since he’s still confused, I bravely close the distance between us. We can’t dance the same way Jesse and I did. Aiden can only use one arm. So, I have to decide if I want him to hold my hand or my waist. That’s easy. I reach up and place both of my hands around Aiden’s neck. He seems to be frozen in place for a minute. Taking his right hand, I place it on my waist. With my hands back around his neck, I look up into his soft brown eyes.

“I think we’re supposed to move,” I tease.

“Right.” Aiden snaps out of his trance. It’s probably more like shock. “We need to dance.”

Slowly, we start to sway to the music. It only takes a moment for Aiden’s mind to catch up with what’s happening. He takes over leading and moves us to the edge of the dance floor. I'm careful not to bump the injured arm between us.

Somehow, with his broken arm as a barrier and only one of his hands touching me, this feels more intimate than dancing with Jesse. Aiden's touch pulls at my feelings for him. Feelings I can't act on.

"Are you enjoying your girls' night out?"

"I am." It's true. I'm enjoying this.

I never thought I would ever dance with this man. Sure, I've dreamed about it, but it's not something I believed would happen in real life.

"Do you do this often?" Aiden's eyes hold mine. I can't look away, nor do I want to. This is crossing lines I swore I'd never cross again.

"Girls' night? Yes. Bars? No. Dancing? Not really." Hopefully, I answered all the hidden questions he was asking.

Aiden relaxes even more. His fingers on my waist move slightly. Feeling his fingertips on my skin causes me to gasp. I forgot how short my sweater is. With both arms around his neck, my top exposes a small part of the skin at my waist.

"E." My name is a whisper on his lips.

The way he says my name pulls at every part of my body. I swear I can feel it in my toes. How can that be real? His eyes drop to my lips. Oh, dear. Is he about to kiss me? I'm not sure I'm ready for that. Oh, I want it, but I'm not ready to take that step. If we cross this line, there'll be no coming back from it. Our friendship will be a thing of the past.

Thankfully, the song ends, and the band moves into a faster-paced song. Dropping my arms to my sides, I take a step back, breaking contact with Aiden. I glance toward the stage. Jake Campbell gives me a little nod before turning his attention back to his audience. Did our local musician just purposely give me an out here? Do I want this out? I do, and I don't. I want more with Aiden, but I'm too broken to do anything about it.

"Thanks for the dance, Aiden." With that, I turn and hurry back to my friends.

When I get to the table, another round of shots is waiting. I grab the glass and quickly down this one, just like the first.

"Girl, that was hot." Katie dramatically fans herself.

"You should have kissed him," Ally adds.

"Kiss him? She should be going home with him," Sammie said.

Hot? Yes, it was. Kiss him? I want to *so badly*. Home with him? Not happening. Aiden lives with his parents. There's no way I'd ever go home from a bar with him or any other man. I grab a beer from the bucket in the center of the table. After a few swallows, Beth wraps her hand around my wrist.

"Are you okay?" she asks.

"I don't know," I admit. "I want all of that, but I'm not ready."

"It's okay." Sammie takes my other hand in hers.

"What you did tonight was brave and a huge step." Katie smiles at me. It's a caring smile and not the one of pity I'm used to seeing from everyone else.

Beth is the only one out of the four who knows what happened with Garrett. The others have never pushed me to talk about it. Still, they know it's bad. I have some great friends, and I'm so thankful for their support. I would still be hiding at home if it wasn't for these four ladies.

I look up to find Aiden back at his table. Once again, his eyes are on me. His expression is unreadable, but I swear I can feel the heat from his eyes from here. Tonight, whether I'm ready or not, I'm going to have to come to terms with some things. My feelings for Aiden are at the top of the list.

Noah magically appears with another round of shots for us. This is not good. I really should refuse this one. My nerves and emotions are all over the place tonight. When my friends grab their shots, I grab mine. I'll pay dearly for this night in the morning. It's a good thing I'm not the one driving tonight. Right now, I'm not even sure I can walk to the door.

Chapter Twelve

Aiden

Well, I just royally embarrassed myself. Oh, not the part about dancing with E. That was beyond great. It would have been better if I could have used both arms. Hopefully, tonight won't be my only chance to dance with her.

I froze for a moment. I didn't think things through before walking onto the dance floor. The only plan I had was to get Jesse away from E. I wasn't expecting Jesse to walk away so easily. I wouldn't walk away if someone tried to cut in while I danced with her. I also didn't think E would dance with me anyway. When she agreed, I became a wordless idiot for a moment. It was like my tongue wrapped around my teeth, and my brain forgot how to function.

I was a goner when she placed my hand on her waist and looked up at me. She already had me, but that moment changed everything. I can't hide my feelings for her anymore. I don't know how I've managed to hide them all these years. She's my forever, and I'll do whatever it takes to officially make her mine. Hopefully, I'll be able to get past her fear and brokenness.

I wanted to kiss her right there on the dance floor. It would have been a jerk move. I can practically hear my grandfather scolding me for forgetting how to be a gentleman. A man should never kiss a woman for the first time on a dance floor.

When she stepped away from me, I saw the emotional damage her traumatic experience had caused. It's why I didn't try to stop her when she fled to the safety of her friends. Those beautiful blue eyes should never have to hold that much pain. Soon, I'll discover exactly what happened that horrible day. Tonight, I made a silent vow to love her through it all, no matter how long it took.

All I can do right now is sit here and watch over her. I don't want to risk pushing her too far tonight. The amount of alcohol E and her friends are drinking has me concerned. My eyes widen as she downs another shot. I have to admire her bravery tonight. Sadly, she's going to crash hard before the night is over.

"Every guy in here is watching them," Brady grumbles.

He takes a drink of his beer and sets the bottle on the table with a little too much force. Something has my brother riled up tonight.

"None of them are dumb enough to try anything." Spencer leans back in his chair and scans the bar.

Spencer's little sister is at E's table. He isn't about to let anything happen to those five women.

"A few might be drunk enough." Miles' words are not comforting.

"Pit! Four! I'm not telling you two again!" Noah shouts from the bar.

Everyone looks over to the pool tables. The town clowns have their shirts off. Their attempt to dance with the group of girls at the table next to them isn't going well. Both men are beyond drunk. Four's trying to dance with a girl with short blonde hair. He's failing miserably. The girl sidesteps to get out of the way, causing Four to faceplant on the pool table. People laugh and go back to what they were doing.

The concerts I've worked with Dawson had some crazy situations at times. Pit and Four could probably give the Zoo Crew a run for their money. Noah looks over to our table and holds his hands up. Spencer nods to Noah's silent, frustrated plea for help.

"Come on, man." Spencer stands. "Looks like it's time for you to learn what most Friday and Saturday nights around here look like."

Reluctantly, I get up and follow Spencer to the pool tables. There's not much I can do to help here, but I'll follow his lead.

"Hey, guys." Spencer pats his hand on the pool table next to Four's head. He's still lying there from his faceplant.

"Oh, man." Pit gives Four a shove. "Somebody called the cops on us."

"We didn't do nothing." Four abruptly stands and rubs his hands over his face. The way he staggers, I doubt he can see straight. These two have had enough alcohol for tonight. Maybe for a few nights.

"Come on, guys. Put your shirts back on, and we'll get you home." Spencer tosses them the shirts they threw on the pool table.

"You ladies okay?" I ask the group of girls.

"We are now." One of the girls fans herself as she looks between Spencer and me. They've had more than enough to drink, too.

"I don't wanna go home," Four mumbles.

At least his shirt is back on. Never mind that it's on backward. Pit isn't in much better shape. His shirt is on inside out. These two are a few years older than us, but it looks like they'll never grow up. They never do anything bad. They're just crazy. How these two function normally during the day is beyond me. Both men are talented. I have no idea why they act like idiots on the weekend.

"You get Pit." Spencer nods toward Pit. "I got this one." He grabs Four before he falls again.

"Whoa!" Pit steps back and points at me. "One arm here is not a cop."

One arm? Seriously man? This is getting crazier by the minute.

"Aiden is a cop. He starts on Monday," Spencer informs him in a sharp tone. "Now, come on."

"I ain't being taken home by no cop!" Four shouts, but he lets Spencer lead him away from the pool tables.

"Your brother is right over here. He can take you home," Spencer said.

That sounds like a good plan to me. The only problem with this plan is the fact it takes us right by E's table. Jesse Calhoun is still sitting at the table next to hers. For different reasons, the Calhoun brothers are a problem tonight.

"Jesse!" Four shouts when he sees his little brother. He acts like this is the first time he's seen his brother all night.

"Jesse, you wanna take your brother home?" Spencer asked.

"It doesn't look like I have a choice." Jesse narrows his eyes at his brother. He's probably tired of having to do this.

"I can take him to the station," Spencer tosses the option out there. He knows it won't happen, though.

"Naw. Mama would never forgive me," Jesse mumbles.

"I ain't going to no station." Four jerks his arm away from Spencer.

He's so drunk he stumbles again. This time, he stumbles into E. She's standing next to her table and not sitting on the stool. She's not sober either, but E manages to catch Four before he hits the floor.

"E!" Four grins at her as E helps him to stand up straight. Well, as straight as the two of them can manage anyway.

"Easy, Four." E pats his arm.

"You danced." Four nods his head. The movement causes him to sway.

"I did." E catches him again.

I don't like this situation at all.

"I saw you." Four lays his head on her shoulder like he's a two-year-old.

"Really?" E asks. I don't think she's fully comprehending the conversation.

"Are we dancing?" Four's eyes are now closed.

Somebody needs to get this fool off of my girl. If I let go of Pit, he's bound to hit the floor or flee out the front door. I'm not sure which scenario would be worse, probably fleeing. He could get hit by a car in the parking lot.

"I don't think so." E giggles.

"I'm a better dancer than one arm." Four leans further into E. She can't hold his weight, and they stumble to the floor.

"Jesse! Get your brother!" I roar.

"Easy there, Maxwell." Jesse grins at me. He's as crazy as his brother is. This is not funny. "I got him."

Jesse's friends help him lift Four off of E. I want to shove Pit aside and help my girl off the floor. Thankfully, a couple of Jesse's friends take Pit and start pulling him toward the door.

"I told you, one arm, you weren't taking me in." Pit jabs his finger toward me.

Really? When did he say that? They seriously need to drop this one arm crap. These two think they're being hilarious tonight. Their actions have me wanting to punch both of them. The sheriff wouldn't like it, but right now, it would feel good.

"Let it go." Spencer puts his hand on my shoulder.

I nod but glare at Pit and the Calhoun brothers as they walk out. There's nothing else I can do anyway. Well, I should help E up. I look down to find Beth now sitting on the floor with E.

"Okay, ladies." Spencer pulls Beth and E up at the same time. "It's time to call it a night."

"But, we're having fun," Beth protests.

"It's not our fault Four and Pit got drunk," Katie adds. Her words are a little slurred.

The two men aren't the only ones who are drunk. All five of these ladies can barely stand. I quickly move to E's side and put my arm around her. The alcohol is having a greater effect on her now. She easily falls against my side.

"I don't need your help." Beth jerks away from Spencer. Brady's there to catch her before she stumbles to the floor.

Spencer shakes his head and looks at me. "You and Brady get these two home. Miles and I will carry those three."

Miles is struggling to keep the others from falling off their stools. Brady and I nod while Spencer hurries over to give Miles a hand.

"Home!" E gasps and covers her mouth with both hands. "I can't go home like this."

"You're going home with me. Remember?" Beth leans into E's other side. E nods, but I don't think she remembers their plans.

Brady and I take E and Beth out to my truck. Now I'm really glad I insisted on him driving my truck tonight rather than his. Like our father's, mine has an extended cab with full backseats. My brother got Beth into the passenger seat before helping me get E into the back. Man, I'll be so glad when this arm heals, so I don't need all this help.

Thankfully, the other three girls are staying the night at Sammie's apartment above the jewelry store. Five women. Two locations. That makes it easier for us to get them all home safely.

Well, it was easier until E fell over with her head in my lap. With my good hand, I gently rub my fingers up and down her arm. I hate having a broken arm, but I'm grateful for it, too. If that accident hadn't happened, I wouldn't be here now. Sadly, this arm isn't letting me hold her like I should be doing. Soon. I'll hold her soon.

Chapter Thirteen

Aiden

There are only two apartment complexes in Hayden Falls. Thankfully, Beth's apartment is in the one just outside of town. These apartments are all single-story—no steps to climb.

E woke up as Brady was helping me get her out of the truck. Even though she was drunk, her smile still warmed me like the sun. Brady had to unlock the door because Beth kept dropping the keys. He finally managed to get her to the kitchen table and is now making a pot of coffee. Of course, Beth loudly protested everything Brady did for her.

I'm sitting behind E on the bathroom floor, holding her hair back while she empties her stomach. It's not how I want to touch her hair, and this is far from romantic. I darn sure wasn't going to let anyone else do this for her.

Sadly, this happens most of the time when people mix alcoholic drinks. The girls had three rounds of shots, which I know were whiskey. E had two pina colada drinks and a couple of beers. For a girl who only had a glass of wine every now and then, it was way too much alcohol. It was inevitable we'd end up where we are right now. She's going to really hate herself in the morning.

When I'm sure she's through being sick, I get a washcloth from the linen closet and wash her face. She's so out of it she can barely keep her eyes open. When she smiles, I drop the washcloth and let my fingertips gently roam over her cheek. She won't remember this, and I shouldn't do it. However, I'm powerless to stop myself. It feels like heaven when she leans into my touch. Her eyes flutter open, and she smiles again. Yep. This is heaven.

"You're here," she says.

"I am." As much as I don't want to break this moment, I need to get some water in her. "Here. Drink this."

I hold the glass Brady brought in earlier to her lips. She pushes it away.

"I can't. No more," E mumbles.

"Sunshine, it's just water. It'll help you feel better." I manage to coax her into taking a couple of sips. It's better than nothing.

"I'm sorry." She sniffles.

"It's okay." I doubt she's ever been in this situation before. She needs to get off this floor and into bed. Again, here's another reason I hate my broken arm. "Put your arms around my neck."

E does as I ask. There's not an ounce of fight in her. At least I'm having better luck than Brady is. Every now and then, I still hear him and Beth arguing.

Cautiously, I slip my arm out of the sling. I know it's not a good idea, but I can't leave my girl on the floor like this. As gently as I can, I place my arm against her back. I lift E off the floor with my good arm under her knees. It's a little painful, but the cast protects my arm from most of the pressure. I carry E to the guest bedroom and lay her on the bed. Brady must have pulled the covers back earlier. All I had to do was slip E's boots off so she could slide under the covers.

Even though she lives alone, Beth's apartment has two bedrooms. The other side of this room appears to serve as a home office. According to Spencer, Beth is saving to buy a house. I guess her coffee shop is doing better than everyone thought it would.

I turn on the small lamp by the bed. The soft glow is much gentler than the overhead light. Somehow, I managed to get E to take a few more sips of water. I'll leave the glass and a bottle of ibuprofen on the nightstand for her.

It's wrong of me to stand here and watch her like this, but I can't help myself. Kneeling by the bed, I softly run my fingers across her cheek again. She's so beautiful. E's eyes flutter open. I didn't mean to wake her.

"Hey, Cowboy," she said softly.

"Hey, Sunshine." I can't help but smile.

"Where's your hat?"

"It's at home." I have a hard time wearing my Stetson. It reminds me of her nickname for me.

"Aiden." Her voice is softer now. Sleep will come for her soon.

"Yeah, Sunshine?" I push a few strands of hair from her face as her eyes close again.

"I like you," she whispers.

My heart just exploded inside my chest. I close my eyes and swallow hard. I've waited years to hear those words. My heart also broke. She's not going to remember any of this tomorrow.

"I more than like you," I whisper back.

She's quiet for a few minutes. For a moment, I thought she had fallen asleep.

"Don't leave me again," she all but pleads. Who knows. Maybe she had. Her words broke something inside me.

"I won't." My voice cracked a little.

"Promise?" E's eyes flutter open and quickly close again.

"I swear." I could barely get the words out.

With a sigh, E settles deeper into the pillow. Her breathing evens out, and I know she's fallen asleep. She won't remember my promise, but I'll keep it just the same. Staying here any longer would be wrong. Standing, I drop my head and squeeze my eyes shut to hold back the tears. Who am I kidding here? Those simple little words were the rawest conversation I've ever had in my life. I wipe the corner of my eye. Yeah, that tear betrayed me, but it was for a good reason. It was for her.

Unable to help myself, I lean down and kiss her cheek. It's another thing she won't remember tomorrow. In sleep, her lips slightly turn up in a smile. Hopefully, it meant she subconsciously felt the kiss. It's the first kiss I've ever given her. She should have been awake for it. Kissing her now probably made me a jerk. Since she'll never know about it, I guess it doesn't matter. From here on out, I'll make sure she's sober when I kiss her.

If I don't get out of this room now, I'll climb into the other side of this bed and pull her to me. Now, that would be a jerk move. I don't want to leave her, but I need to go. Looking up, I find Brady, Spencer, and Beth standing in the doorway. Well, it looks like I had an audience. I'm not sure how much they heard. With one final glance at E, I quietly leave the room.

"She loves you. You know?" Beth said when we got to the living room.

"And I love her." I look Beth in the eye. It's the first time I've openly admitted my feelings for her to anyone other than Spencer and Brady.

"Don't hurt her," Beth warns. She's drunk, but she's still protecting her best friend.

"That's not my intention." I shake my head. "But somebody needs to tell me what happened to her."

"I won't without her permission." Beth holds her ground. E deserves that type of loyalty.

"You know." It's not a question, but Beth nods anyway.

Something tells me Beth knows more than anyone does about what happened. There's no point in asking any more questions tonight. Beth isn't going to betray E. Good. Still, I'll get those answers soon enough.

"Did you get the others home okay?" I ask Spencer. It's best just to change the subject.

"That depends on how you define okay." Spencer rubs the back of his neck with his hand. "They tripped a few times. At one point, Katie punched Miles. It did nothing to him, and I made sure her hand wasn't broken."

Wow. I don't remember Friday nights being so rough in my hometown. Guess I'll have to get used to this. After the promise I made to E just now, there's no way I'll leave. It doesn't matter if the people of this town forgive me or not. I'm staying for her.

"Little sister, I'm going to need a pillow and a blanket," Spencer said.

"Why?" Beth cuts her eyes sharply at him.

"Because I'm sleeping on your couch tonight," Spencer informs her.

"Why? I'm fine," Beth insists.

"You're nowhere near fine." Brady huffs.

"Farm Boy, you stay quiet." Beth folds her arms across her chest and glares at my brother.

"Bethie." Spencer draws her attention away from my brother. "You're in better shape than E is tonight, but neither of you are sober. I'm not leaving."

"Brady and I can camp out on the floor," I suggest.

"No!" Beth holds up both hands. "Spence can stay, but I'm not waking up with all three of you here."

"Why? Do you sleep naked?" My brother needs to shut up.

"That's none of your business!" Beth snaps. She moves toward Brady. Thankfully, Spencer steps in front of her.

"Aiden, I promise you I have this under control." Spencer wraps his arms around his sister's waist to hold her in place while he talks to me. "But, you might want to get your brother out of here."

Yeah. That's probably a good idea. From the looks of things, Beth might hurt herself trying to get to my brother. Somebody sure needs to teach this idiot how to treat a woman. I motion toward the front door for Brady to head that way. I pause and look toward the guest room door.

"I promise she's safe," Spencer assures me. "If I need you for any reason, I'll call."

"Thanks, man," I say.

Reluctantly, I push my brother out the door and leave. This girls' night out was just as I predicted it would be. Still, it had some wonderful memories too. It's too bad I'm the only one who will remember what happened between us tonight. I know, without a doubt, E's safe tonight. She's probably the safest person in Hayden Falls right now. Spencer won't let anything happen to her or Beth. I only wished I was the one who was watching over her.

Chapter Fourteen

Etrulia

My mouth feels so dry, making swallowing impossible. My eyes aren't even open yet, and I already feel miserable. Someone shifts next to me on the bed, causing me to bolt upright. The pain in my head is so sharp I grab it with both hands. Note to self: move slower.

"Morning, sleepyhead." Beth sounds way too cheerful this morning.

I wipe my mouth with my hand and move my lips, but no words come out. Too dry. Beth shoves a glass of water and a couple of much-needed ibuprofen tablets into my hands.

"Thanks," I manage to say after a few sips.

"Hurry up and get dressed." Beth bounces off the bed. The sudden movement did not help me at all.

"Why?" Again, I hold my head to try and ease the pain.

"We're going to the diner for breakfast." Beth waves her fingers before leaving the room.

The diner? I really do not want to go out in public today. Hibernating sounds like such a good idea right now. Beth won't have it, though. With a groan, I pull myself out of bed. How my friend is so cheery and functional right now is beyond me.

The first thing I notice on the way to the bathroom is the fact I'm still wearing the same clothes I wore last night. Sleeping like this wasn't ideal, but at least my friend put me to bed. It's a wonder she didn't just drop me onto the couch with a blanket when we got home. Come to think of it. I don't remember getting to Beth's apartment last night.

Beth set clean clothes on the bathroom counter for me. I smile at her thoughtfulness. She had more to drink than I did. Yet here she is, taking care of me. Maybe it's eagerness because she's yelling for me to hurry up. Shaking my head, I jump into the shower. The warm water feels great, but I can't linger too long. Beth will barge through the door and pull me out of here if I don't hurry up. So, hurry is exactly what I do.

My outfit today is just jeans and an old t-shirt. Beth and I have had so many sleepovers we keep simple outfits like this at each other's apartments. We don't need to dress up to go to Davis's Diner anyway. I still don't think going out is a good idea, but Beth doesn't cook often. She probably doesn't have anything here to make for breakfast. She might have some cereal, but she has a weird taste when it comes to cereal. You never know what kind she's binging on from one week to the next. The diner is a safer bet for a decent meal.

The moment I walk into the living room, Beth hands me my purse and a pair of sunglasses. I look at the sunglasses questionably.

"Trust me. You're going to need those." Beth puts her sunglasses on and opens the door.

Stepping outside, I squint my eyes and drop my head. She's right. Sunglasses are necessary this morning. Sunlight is a killer when you have a hangover, and I most definitely have a hangover. Beth laughs as I quickly shove the sunglasses on. It's her way of saying, *I told you so.* It makes me wonder how often my friend has a hangover. She seems to be a pro at this.

"Come on, slowpoke." Beth opens her car door. "I'm starving."

"Did you drive home last night?" I point to her car.

"No," Beth replies. "Miles took Spencer to get it about an hour ago."

That's good. Beth had more to drink than I did last night. There's no way she could have driven us home safely. They should have let me be our designated driver last night, and I wouldn't feel so bad now.

"Are you sure this is a good idea?" I ask as I buckle my seatbelt.

"Coffee and a good meal are crucial right now." Beth flips her wrist like it's no big deal and drives the short distance to town.

It's hilarious she said that. She owns the only coffee shop in town. It's a fact I do not point out right now. Beth gets very defensive over her baby. Yes, she treats Beth's Morning Brew like it's her child. I'm proud of her for making her dream of being a business owner come true. It's just surprising that her dream would have anything to do with food. Beth seriously cannot cook. I guess making coffee isn't exactly cooking. Still, she has a few baked goods and sandwiches. Of course, sandwiches aren't hard to make either.

The moment we walk into the diner, I second-guess everything. Everyone here seems to be watching us walk to an empty booth next to the front windows. Hopefully, it's just my imagination playing tricks on me. Could a hangover do that to you? No idea. To be on the safe side, I slide into the booth and grab a menu.

"Morning, ladies," Miss Cora greets us. "What can I get you?" Her eyes flick back and forth between Beth and me a few times. "Coffee, for sure." She writes something on her order pad and raises an eyebrow at Beth. Can she tell we're hungover? Well, I am. Beth seems fine.

"We'll both have the Sunrise Platter." Beth places our order without asking me what I want.

"Figures," Miss Cora mumbles as she writes the order down. She turns and heads for the kitchen.

Taking off my sunglasses, I lay them to the side and rubbed my eyes. I desperately need the coffee, but the Sunrise Platter is huge. There's no way I can eat all of that. With the queasiness in my tummy right now, dry toast might be a better choice.

Miss Cora hurries back with our coffee and a little silver pot of creamer. Miss Cora's husband's family opened this diner in the 1960s. The Davis family isn't one of the founding families of Hayden Falls, but they've been here for around a hundred years. Miss Cora's family is well-loved in our little community. Well, I have no love for her granddaughter, Karlee, but that's not Miss Cora's fault.

I still feel like everyone is watching Beth and me. At times, I catch a few people whispering. Okay. Hangovers make you paranoid.

"Hey, E," Four says as he slides into my side of the booth.

"Hey, Four," I return the greeting.

Okay. Something is definitely wrong. As drunk as Four was last night, he should have a hangover, too. Yet, somehow, he looks like this is a normal day to him.

"We danced last night." Four lays his head on my shoulder.

"Four, we didn't dance." I laugh and pat the top of his head.

Since I can't remember everything about last night, I narrow my eyes at Beth. She gives me a little shake of her head. Whew. For a minute there, I thought I danced with him.

"It's more like you fell with Four," Beth said.

I groan and drop my head back. The memory of sitting drunk on the floor at Cowboys with Four comes rushing to my mind. Is this why everyone was staring at us when we came in?

"I remember dancing with Jesse." I raise a finger while I go over my foggy memories from last night. "And with…" I snap my head toward Beth. "Aiden."

Beth laughs. "Yeah. You sure did."

"I'm a better dancer than one arm." Four smiles up at me. His head is still on my shoulder.

I cover my mouth with my hand to hide my smile. One arm? Four's little name for Aiden is funny. It shouldn't be. Aiden was in a horrible accident. From what I've heard, his left arm was broken in at least two places.

Four sits up and puts his arm on the back of the booth behind me. Mick Calhoun really is a sweet guy. He got the nickname Four back in middle school. I don't know the story behind it, but he adopted it as his gamer and tag name.

It's hard to believe someone as crazy as Four could be a talented artist. Oh, he can paint on canvas, but some of his best work is with spray cans. He even went to Detroit to compete in a few contests. Rumor has it he even taught a few teenagers while he was there. To this day, he denies it. I don't think he wants people to know he has a sweet and caring side.

The town even set up billboards, one on each of the four major roads into Hayden Falls, so that Four could paint. I honestly believe it's so he would stop tagging the buildings in town. Just about every weekend, you could find him having to clean up what he painted. The billboards sure make the business owners here happy. Since Four uses them to decorate for holidays and town events, those billboards have brought in hundreds of tourists.

Miss Cora sets our plates on the table. Beth wastes no time digging in. She doesn't look hungover, but I swear she's starving.

"You know." Four grins at me. "Mama always loved Jesse more."

"Four, that's not true." I totally disagree with this. His mother is one of the Hayden Sisters. She would never treat one of her children better than the other.

"It is." Four nods. He looks so serious. "You can tell by who gets more hashbrowns."

His eyes drop to my plate. I follow his gaze and laugh. My friend's silly antics are one of the reasons I love him.

"Four, do you want my hashbrowns?" I ask.

He nods, and I push my plate in front of him. There's no way I can eat all of this food anyway. Once he finishes off the hashbrowns, I'll finish my breakfast.

"So, you danced with Aiden." Beth grins at me.

"Yeah, I did." I'm pretty sure I'm blushing by this point.

I was a little tipsy when I danced with Aiden. Thankfully, the memory's there. It's one memory I never want to lose. A huge part of me wants to dance with him again when I'm sober. I'm not sure if I can, though. Our dance last night only happened because Jesse set it up. Was Aiden really jealous last night? The thought has me smiling even more.

"I'm going to call Megan and have her get her information correct." Four doesn't look up from eating my hashbrowns.

"What?" I ask quickly.

"You danced with me." Four looks up and nods his head once. "She can't leave that out."

Oh no! With eyes wide and my hand over my mouth, I turn to Beth. I'm in full panic mode now. Beth's already pulling Megan's gossip blog up on her phone. After reading it, she laughs and slides her phone across the table to me.

Oh. My. Goodness. There it is in black and white. Well, it's actually in color. It's an online blog, after all. I'm going to seriously hurt Megan Sanders.

Romance on the Dance Floor

Well, Good Morning, Hayden Falls. It looks like our little shy town mouse is not so shy after all. After a couple of drinks at Cowboys, she dances with not one but two of our town bachelors.

It looks like our newest deputy won the little lady's affection in the end. Who could blame her there? Right? I guess you could say that our handsome deputy one-handedly roped our little mouse in.

Stay tuned, Hayden Falls. Only time will tell if those sparks become full-blown flames.

After pushing Beth's phone back to her, I drop my head to the table and groan loudly. This is why everyone was staring at us and whispering. How could Megan do this to me? She's never written about me before. It looks like the safety net I used to enjoy has fallen. For the first time, I'm front-page gossip in Hayden Falls.

Chapter Fifteen

Aiden

Groaning, I shove back the covers and get out of bed. Sleep was not my friend last night. I tossed and turned for most of it. When I did sleep, I dreamed of dancing with E. At the part where I left her, I jolted awake. Even the pain meds I took couldn't keep me in a peaceful sleep.

A man should never leave the woman he loves as I left E. She was passed out, unaware of the world around her. If something happened to her, I'd never forgive myself. Yeah, I know she was safe with Spencer there. Still, leaving her like that did not sit right with me.

The need to know she's okay this morning is overpowering. So, I dress as quickly as I can and hurry downstairs. After a cup of coffee, I'll head to Beth's apartment. My mind knows everything's fine. Spencer sent a text earlier this morning letting me know E was still asleep when he left for his shift. Beth's awake and keeping an eye on her. Still, every nerve in my body is on edge. Seeing her for myself is the way I'll settle down.

Mom sets a cup of coffee on the table as I walk into the kitchen. Guess she heard me coming down the stairs. She starts fixing me a plate, but I shake my head. I usually need at least one cup of coffee before I can eat in the mornings.

Brady walks in and tosses the mail on the table. It's a good thing he hasn't taken off yet this morning. Mom's still cautious about letting me drive. Another reason I hate this broken arm. The doctor lowered the dose of my medications this week because of how they were affecting me, but it doesn't mean much to my mom.

"You ready to head into town?" Brady seems as eager as I am to leave.

"Yeah," I reply. "Just let me finish this."

As I take a sip of coffee, one of the letters on the table catches my attention. Reaching for it, I already know what it is. The size of the envelope tells me this is a card and not a letter. I pull it from the stack of mail. As I expected, it's addressed to me.

"I thought these stopped." I hold up the unopened card.

Mom looks over her shoulder. She knows what I'm holding.

"They started again around the end of February." Mom wipes her hands with a towel. "I forgot about them. I'll go grab the others."

This is another mystery I need to solve. Not long after everything happened six years ago, cards started showing up for me. It's one of the craziest things I've ever seen. There weren't just one or two cards, mind you. These came once a week. Well, they stopped for a while at the beginning of the year.

Mom sets the box of cards on the table in front of me. I flip the one in my hand over. As always, there's no handwriting on the envelope. My name and address were always on a sticker or printed out. There's never a return address, either. For six years, someone sent me a card with an encouraging message printed inside, a prayer, or a scripture from the Bible. The cards are never signed. For all I know, it could be more than one person.

"Somebody sure believes in you." Brady lifts a couple of the cards from the box and drops them back inside.

Our eyes lock. It was never confirmed, but we all know these are connected to what happened. There's no point in saying anything, though. Every time this subject comes up, Brady and I end up arguing. He wants to do something about that night. I refuse to let him. It's the perfect formula for a fight between us. We've gotten good at avoiding this subject for that very reason. I don't want to fight with him. I hate it every time it happens.

I put the box of cards in my room and hurry out to meet Brady at my truck. I'll read them later. Being home now might let me figure out who's sending these little messages to me. Even when the worst ridicule from the town came, I could always depend on getting a card that lifted me up. I owe someone a great thanks. Hopefully, I'll find them to do just that.

"Where are we going?" My brother is heading to the town square. I don't want to go to town. I want to go to Beth's apartment.

"To the diner."

"Brady," I warn, but before I can say anything more, he holds up a hand.

"It's Saturday morning. Beth always goes to the diner for breakfast after a night of drinking."

Really? A slow grin crosses my face. How does my little brother know that about Beth? I look out the window to keep from laughing. I don't know how I missed it before. The hard times Brady gives Beth might be for a deeper reason. Thinking back on it, I'm almost sure of it. It's that, or my brother really is a jerk. I glance over at him. Is he even aware of what he's doing? It's something he'll have to figure out for himself, though.

"See." Brady points to Beth's car after parking a few spaces down from her.

If they're here, they're okay, but I won't relax until I see E. That's what I thought, anyway. One look through the front windows of Davis's Diner has my blood boiling. Four is sitting in the booth next to E. It's bad enough I had to deal with this fool last night. The last thing I need this morning is to see him with E. I know nothing's going on between them. Still, I don't like him sitting with *my* girl.

I storm through the front door and straight to their table without saying a word. I pull the chair out at the table next to E's. With my good arm, I grab the back of Four's shirt and move him over to the chair.

"Hey, man! I was eating that." Four holds his hands out toward the plate on E's table.

"Here," I say roughly and set the plate in front of him before sitting down beside E.

One look at E and I fear I just messed up. Her eyes are wide, her mouth falls open, and she's pointing at Four. Beth breaks out into a fit of laughter. Brady takes a seat next to her. He looks proud of me.

"That's…" E seems genuinely shocked.

"What?" I'm totally confused.

"Never mind." E turns and takes a sip of her coffee.

She looks okay, and I have no idea what just happened. Before I can figure things out, Miss Cora walks up to our table. Even though I'm not dating her granddaughter anymore, Miss Cora has always been nice to me.

"What can I get for you, boys?" Miss Cora asked.

"Coffee." Brady holds up a finger and nods.

Miss Cora comes back with two cups and a fresh pot of coffee. She sets a couple of plates of food on the table in front of Four. I guess the man's hungry this morning.

"Here you go, E." Four holds the plate I set on his table towards us.

"Wait." I hold my hand up. Turning to E, I point at Four. "Is that your plate?"

E nods. I growl and shake my head. This fool was sitting here eating her food.

"Keep it, Four." I motion for him to set the plate back down.

"I can't eat all of this," Four protests.

"He was just eating the hashbrowns," E says.

This is insane. There are no other words for it. Our little town gets crazier by the minute.

"Take some of it home with you," I tell Four.

"But…" Four shakes his head.

"It's okay, man," I assure him. I look up at Miss Cora. She seems as baffled as I am. "I'll take care of the tickets for both tables. Will you get E another plate, please?"

"No, Aiden." E's hand falls to my thigh. I don't think she's aware of what she's doing. Trust me here—my body is *very* aware. "That's too much food."

"What would you like then?" There's no way I'm letting her leave here without eating.

"Pancakes and bacon." She grins shyly.

That's what I thought. This was usually her go-to breakfast.

"Any toppings?" Miss Cora asked.

"Just butter and maple syrup, please," E replied.

"Make that two," I say. "And whatever my brother wants."

Brady orders the Sunrise Platter. He'll have to share his with Beth because he's eating from her plate. What is it with the men in this town? At least Beth isn't fully aware of what's happening. She hasn't broken my brother's wrist yet. A baseball player should know better than to take chances like this. If he ticks this woman off badly enough, Beth will start breaking bones.

Miss Cora soon returned with our food. She even puts one of Four's plates into a to-go container for him.

"It's good to see you, Aiden." Miss Cora pats my shoulder before she walks away.

Our meal goes well with light conversation. That was until Four stood up to leave. I was doing my best to forget he was sitting at the table next to us.

"Don't worry, E." Four grins at my girl. "I'll call Megan and get those facts straight."

Megan? Facts? What's this fool talking about?

"It's okay, Four. Leave it be." E tries to reason with him.

"No, ma'am." Four sounds irritated. "She forgot to mention that we danced. I can't have that."

"You didn't dance with E," I firmly tell him. I need strength right now because I'm about to kill this idiot.

"I was on the floor with her." Four nods once for good measure. "Close enough."

"Four!" I roar as I stand up.

"Gotta go. Thanks for breakfast, one arm. Bye, E." Four waves and rushes out the door.

I'm going to go to jail having to deal with this fool. Spencer will probably be the one who has to arrest me. At least he's gone now. Sadly, I now have to sit down and find out how bad the situation is. If Megan is involved, something about last night is on her gossip blog. We haven't even talked about last night yet. I can handle the gossip, but I hate this happened to E.

"How bad is it?" I asked Beth. Asking E might embarrass her.

Beth pulls up the website and hands me her phone. After reading the little part about E and me, I want to hug Megan and yell at her at the same time. One-handed? These people seriously need to lay off my broken arm. She didn't have to reference E's dance with Jesse, either. No names are mentioned, but the descriptions are clear enough that the entire town will figure out it's us. My only real concern is, what E thinks about this? She's never been the center of town gossip before. For me, it happened nearly every time I came to visit.

"Are you mad?"

"Not at all," I assure her. "I only have a problem with this if it upsets you."

E looks over at Beth and back at me. She's struggling with something. I'm not sure what it is. Hopefully, she's not about to rip my heart in two here. She reaches up with one finger and slightly pushes my Stetson hat up. Yeah, I wore this just for her.

"I'm good, Cowboy," she says softly.

Her words, her smile, and the blush on her cheeks have me wanting to pull her into my arms. I need to get this cast off soon so I can wrap my arms around her.

"So am I, Sunshine." I wink at her, causing her blush to deepen even more.

Realizing that I'm staring at her lips, I turn around to find Beth, my brother, and half of the diner watching us. Good. Let them watch. I want them all to know something is building between us. I have to push back my emotions. Being next to her like this makes me want to pull her out of here. I glance over at her again. My eyes automatically fall to her lips. If I don't get to kiss this woman soon, I'm going to lose my mind.

Chapter Sixteen

Etrulia

Rumors and gossip in this town were horrible. Everywhere I went last Saturday, someone stopped me to ask about my dance with Aiden. Most people seemed happy about Megan's little article. Several asked if romance was really blooming between our handsome new deputy and me. The only answer I could give them was, '*It was just a dance.*'

It was just a dance? That's laughable. It's one of the biggest lies I've ever told in my life. Dancing with Aiden will never be just a dance. Still, it's the reply I gave to everyone. For a week now, I've tried to convince myself I'm not falling for Aiden. Staying busy with the upcoming Richardson and Whitlow wedding let me lie to myself during the day. My mind and heart betray my fake beliefs when I'm alone at night.

Not everyone in town was happy over the gossip. Roman Crawford let me know point-blank it was a huge mistake. I know he and Aiden have never gotten along. He wasn't the only one with negative comments. A few of the older gentlemen in town took it upon themselves to let me know that Aiden Maxwell was nothing but trouble.

If a wedding or a party weren't booked at The Magnolia Inn on Saturday afternoons, I often walked around the town square visiting the businesses just to say hello. My walks around the square always had me running into most of the people living in or around Hayden Falls. Usually, I finish my walks at the park on the edge of town.

Last week, I cut my walk short. The gossip I might have been able to handle. The hateful words and warnings about Aiden had seriously gotten to me. The person who practically drove a knife into my heart was Ms. Betty Taylor. The little elderly lady is known for bluntly speaking her peace.

"Shame on you for throwing away a fiancé for that Maxwell boy. You sure didn't live up to your raising." Ms. Taylor's bitter words and tsk sounds were more than I could take. She probably would have spit at my feet if it wouldn't have people saying she wasn't a lady. She had me rushing home to my apartment in tears.

Once again, facing the people of Hayden Falls became too much for me. I didn't leave the safety of the inn all week. My nerves and emotions were a complete mess. I hate the coward I've become. Will I ever be free of this?

Very few people know what happened with Garrett. So far, those people remain loyal to my family. They're keeping my secret. The people who don't know the truth make up their own versions of what happened. None of it has anything to do with Aiden. How can anybody compare Aiden to Garrett? If I let the secret I hold get out, the people of this town will quickly change their minds.

My secret isn't the only town secret I hold. The people of this town harbored many secrets. Not everything makes it into Hayden Happenings or the local gossip circles. There's one secret, in particular, I want to shout from the rooftops. It's not my story to tell. Doing so will cost me the friendship of two people I deeply care about. I've often prayed that the secret will come out on its own.

Today will be another Saturday that I won't be walking around town. Today's the Richardson and Whitlow wedding. Finally! It's almost over. Naturally, my bridezilla is in her true form today.

Isabell and her bridesmaids started being hateful to the youngest bridesmaid. Mindy is eighteen and the groom's cousin. Isabell only asked the girl to participate in the wedding because her mother said it would be a kind gesture towards the groom's family.

Isabell's screams and the rudeness from the other bridesmaids finally became more than Mindy could take. The young girl threw her bouquet on the floor and ran out of the inn with her parents right behind her. Isabell is not making a good impression on the groom's family. I wanted to applaud Mindy for not taking any more of Isabell's crap, but I had to remain quiet. The Richardson's are paying customers, after all.

Now came my next problem, or rather Isabell's. I'm the lucky one who has to find a way to fix it. Being minus a bridesmaid sent Isabell into another tantrum. I've gotten used to her fits by this point. I didn't let it bother me. Instead, I simply stand to the side with my clipboard held to my chest and wait for the new storm to die down.

"Now we have to remove a groomsman!" Isabell shouted.

"Dear, I don't think Julian will appreciate that." Isabell's mother tried to soothe her daughter. "Those men are close friends of his. It would be wrong to ask one of them to stand down now."

"Then what do you suggest, Mother?" Isabell shouted. Even her mother isn't safe from her tantrum.

"Can't someone else take Mindy's place?" Ms. Richardson suggested.

"No, Mother." Isabell rolled her eyes. "We don't have another bridesmaid's dress. Mindy has on the only matching dress."

If I ever have a daughter, she will never speak to me as Isabell does to her mother. From the look on Mrs. Richardson's face, she's more than ready to marry her bratty daughter off.

"What do you suggest?" Mrs. Richardson asked me. For a moment, I thought they had forgotten about me.

"Unless she can produce another bridesmaid with a matching dress, there's nothing *she* can do." Isabell huffed and folded her arms.

Ms. Richardson sighs and shakes her head ever so slightly. She's at her wit's end with her daughter. The only people in the room catering to Isabell's distress are her maid-of-honor and the three remaining bridesmaids.

The issue for Isabell is the fact she's short a bridesmaid. Which means one of the groomsmen won't be able to escort someone out. To her, this throws the entire ceremony out of order, and she has to have order. See? Spoiled. I wanted to let her squirm a bit longer but thought better of it. So, I offer the only solution I can think of.

"I would have the best man escort the maid-of-honor out because you'd want them to follow behind the bride and groom. Since you now have more men than women in your party, starting with the groomsmen, let them leave single file, boy-girl, boy-girl." I smile politely and wait for their decision.

"Well, that's just stupid!" Isabell shouts.

"Hush!" Mrs. Richardson points at her daughter. It looks like the mother-of-the-bride has had enough today. She turns back to me. "Can you make sure the groomsmen know what to do?"

"Yes, ma'am," I reply and quickly leave the room. I'm more than happy to leave Isabell to her mother.

In the hallway, I run into Spencer and Aiden. Both men look good in their deputy uniforms. My eyes may have roamed over Aiden a little. Okay. I admit it. I checked him out.

"Hey, E." Spencer's holding a piece of paper. "Do you have a minute?"

"Not really, but if it's important, I'll see what I can do right quick." I would rather talk to Spencer, but I have a job to do here.

"We're just passing out these flyers around town." Spencer hands me the paper he's holding. It's a missing person's flyer of a teenage boy from Missoula. This is an important matter, so I pause for a moment.

"I haven't seen him, but I'll keep my eyes open." I give the two men a nervous smile.

Aiden's eyes stay locked on me, but he doesn't return the smile. I drop my shoulders and groan when Isabell's shouts ring out.

"Is that your bridezilla from last week?" Spencer asked. I press my lips together and nod. "Let me see what I can do."

I go to stop him but think better of it. Isabell was making eyes at Spencer last week. Perhaps the good deputy can settle my spoiled brat bride down a bit. I watch him walk down the hall and knock on the bride's dressing room door.

Now, I'm alone with Aiden. My heart begins to beat faster, and my muscles tense up. The sight of this man alone has a way of affecting me, but it's not the reason I tense up today. I know he's upset with me. I look up at him, unsure of what to say.

"You've been avoiding me," Aiden says.

I nod again. It's true. I've been avoiding everybody.

"I'm sorry."

"I thought you were okay with that article." Aiden takes a step toward me. Until now, he's kept his distance.

"It was okay." Megan's article wasn't what upset me so badly.

"The people in this town," Aiden mumbled. He shakes his head and looks away. He knows.

"It's okay. Don't worry about it." I'll get past it eventually.

"I'm sorry, E." Aiden takes another step closer to me.

"It's not your fault," I assure him.

"But it is." He shakes his head again. His expression shows a lot of pain. "My failures are now hurting you. I never wanted that to happen."

"You didn't fail, Aiden." I place my hand on his arm, and our eyes meet. "This town failed you. One day, they'll see it."

Spencer's walking back towards us. Mrs. Richardson stands in the doorway. She gives me a little wave. I hold up a finger indicating for her to give me a minute. I hate leaving Aiden, but I need to get to the groom's dressing room.

"I can't promise, but I think she may settle down a level or two." Spencer lightly laughs. I'm sure he laid his country charm on thick for the bride.

"Thank you." His help is greatly appreciated. I look between the two men. "We're short a bridesmaid, and there's a new walkout order. I need to explain this to the groomsmen before we start."

"It's okay. Call if you see the kid." Spencer points to the flyer he gave me.

Aiden reaches out and gently grabs my arm. "Can I call you?"

I take a step back. I wasn't expecting that. It's a simple question, and it deserves an answer. This shouldn't have hit me so hard, but after what happened with Garrett, I'm not sure if I should do this. Where would phone calls lead? Taking a deep breath, I push most of my fear aside. Beth's right. This is Aiden. He won't hurt me.

My therapist has been telling me for months not to shut myself off from the possibility of another relationship. But am I ready? If I'm going to try again, I want it to be with Aiden. I trust him more than I do anyone. Still, I feel it's too soon for anything more than friendship with him.

"Here." Aiden must have sensed the battle in my mind. He writes something on the back of a business card. "You call me when you're ready."

"Thank you." I take the card and hold it like it's a lifeline.

I'm thanking him for more than giving me his number. His patience and understanding mean a lot to me. No. This man won't hurt me. Sadly, I don't have time to process all of this right now. I need to get this wedding started. Once Isabell says *I do*, she's no longer my problem. Hopefully, her husband will have better luck with her.

With a wave to Aiden and Spencer, I hurry down the hall. I glance over my shoulder before going into the groom's dressing room. Aiden is still watching me. He adjusts his hat and winks at me before following Spencer out the front doors. I have a lot to think about where he's concerned.

I smile down at the card with his phone number on it. It's his business card from the Sheriff's Office with his personal cell phone number written on the back. I'll call him soon. Right now, I need to focus on this wedding.

Chapter Seventeen

Aiden

This town makes me want to punch half of them in the face. I already knew why E was avoiding me. Having her confirm the reason made me angrier than I already was. I'm mad, but not at her. Several people told me about E's run-ins with the Crawford and Martin families and a few people who are loyal to them. Ms. Taylor was the rudest of the bunch.

My ancestors, along with the Crawfords and Martins, were the founding families of Hayden Falls. The Maxwells and Crawfords have fought over one thing or another for decades. Every once in a while, the Martins joined in. Usually, they were on our side. After my little mishap six years ago, the Martins were no longer an ally. Well, they didn't like me anymore, but I hadn't heard anything about them being rude to my parents.

On Saturday, I gave E my phone number. She hasn't called or texted like I was hoping. Mom said she missed the past two Sundays at church, which wasn't like her. I know she's in a fragile place mentally and emotionally. The last thing I want to do is to push her too hard.

After being around her for a few days and dancing with her, I'm finding it hard to stay away from her. I need some form of contact with her other than random meetings. Usually, I'm patient and have control of my character. Both are slipping where E's concerned. I want a future with her, so I have to fight my own emotions to stay calm and wait.

Mondays aren't one of my favorite things, especially after a frustrating weekend. At least I'm working on light duty status at the station. I hate desk work. Thankfully, the sheriff lets me ride with Spencer for a few hours each day. Whenever Spencer had to go to The Magnolia Inn, he made sure I tagged along. He can't tell me everything I want to know. Still, my friend is silently rooting for E and me to become more than friends.

After a shower, I head down to the kitchen for breakfast. Spencer will be here soon to pick me up for our shift today. This week, I'm going to insist the doctor tell my mom I can drive. A grown man shouldn't have to resort to such things, but my mom is still ruthless with her watch over me.

Mom is always up early. She makes sure my oldest brother eats breakfast before heading out on the ranch. I still don't know what he does out there all day. Colton is grumpy this morning. Of course, he's always grumpy, so it really isn't surprising. Still, the way he keeps glancing over at me is ticking me off. I don't have a good relationship with my older brother. We hardly ever talk. His judgmental looks this morning aren't helping my already irritated state.

I'm about to call him out on it when my phone dings with a text. I figure it's Spencer or one of my law enforcement contacts in Tennessee. I can't use the people I know in Montana to help me find out what happened to E. Last night, I called in a few favors from my southern friends.

I open the message and freeze. It's not from someone in my contacts, but I know instantly who it is. This one simple message changed my entire day.

E: *Good Morning, Cowboy.*

She's the only one who calls me Cowboy. I refuse to let anyone else call me that. She's called me Cowboy from the day she arrived in Montana. Even when I was eleven years old, I wore cowboy hats.

Me: *Good Morning, Sunshine.*

I quickly saved her number in my contacts. There's no way I'll lose this connection to her. Her little message gives me hope and has me smiling.

"Good news?" Mom asked as she set a plate in front of me.

"You could say that." I'm still smiling down at my phone when another text comes in.

Sunshine: *Have a great day at work.*

Oh, this feels domestic, and what I would give for more of this.

Mom sees the text and pats my shoulder before going back to the stove. These are simple little messages, but after what E's been through, this is a huge step for her. I hear Spencer pull up outside—no time for breakfast.

Me: *Thanks, Sunshine. Duty calls. Talk to you later.*

I grab the bacon and toast off my plate and head for the door. Once I get the paperwork I'm sure Sheriff Barnes has waiting for me out of the way, I'll make a few rounds around the town square on foot. The Hayden Sisters usually meet on Mondays at the church. Perhaps I'll stroll by there today. Okay. I was, without a doubt, going to see if E was at the church today. Setting up random little meetings isn't ideal, but I'll do anything to see her.

Spencer talks nonstop on our ride to the station. He's excited about the upcoming weekend. It's Labor Day weekend. Most of our townsfolk either grill out at home or head to the lake for camping. It's more like a big party at the lake with bonfires, fishing, and hiking. The town doesn't hold a big event for Labor Day since a lot of families go out of town. We wait until the following weekend to have our Fall Festival. The festival usually brings in people from the surrounding towns, plus a few tourists.

The paperwork I had to deal with wasn't too bad today. There isn't an update on the missing teen. Spencer and I passed out flyers about him to every business in town over the weekend. I managed to stretch the paperwork out for a few hours. It's now eleven o'clock.

The Hayden Sisters will end their meeting soon and head to the diner for lunch. It's time to arrange another random meeting. With a wave to Ms. Ruth at the front desk, I leave the station. I quickly work my way around the square and to the church. Thankfully, only a couple of people stopped me for a quick hello.

As I round the corner and the church comes into view, I see what I hoped to find. E's car is in the parking lot. A couple of the ladies are heading to their cars. *Right on time.* Is this sneaky of me? Yes, it is. The prize, however, is worth it.

"Hello, Aiden." Mrs. Murphy, Spencer and Beth's mother, hugs me when I walk into the fellowship hall.

"It's good to see you, Aiden. Is everything okay?" Mrs. Barnes, the Sheriff's wife, asked.

"Everything is fine," I assure her. E's pulling the strap of her purse over her shoulder. I couldn't have timed my arrival more perfectly. "I just stopped by to see if I could borrow your assistant over there."

E dips her head, but I see the blush on her cheeks. My smile widens, and my confidence grows.

"Borrow?" Mrs. Barnes laughed. "Young man, you came to steal."

E narrows her eyes and shakes her head at Mrs. Barnes. Her silent plea only causes the Sheriff's wife to laugh harder. The next thing I knew, E had me by the arm, pulling me out to the parking lot. She doesn't stop until we get to her car. Did my showing up here unannounced upset her?

"I'm sorry." E blows out a breath. "Those women can be so ruthless sometimes. I swear, they're only modest around their husbands."

Well, that's a relief. At least she's not upset with me. This gives me a little more confidence today.

"Would you like to go for a walk and have lunch with me?" This isn't technically me asking for a date. It's just lunch. Hopefully, she'll see it that way too.

"Aren't you working?"

She seems a bit nervous when she looks up at me. Yeah, I guess the uniform says I'm working. Is she looking for a reason to say no?

"I am," I reply. "It's my lunch hour. We could grab a couple of sandwiches and coffee at Beth's and walk to the park."

Her silence concerns me. I want more with her, but if phone calls and text messages are all I'll get for now, I'll take it. When she looks up at me again and smiles, I have to stop myself from putting my hand over my heart. Her smile alone can bring me to my knees.

"I'd love to." She just made me the happiest man on the planet.

I want to take her hand in mine, but it might be too intimate for her. So, with a huge smile on my face, I motion toward the square. We can walk since everything is only a few blocks away.

Beth was happy to see us when we placed our orders. A few people smiled and whispered to each other. More gossip about us is sure to follow. Of course, there were also a few glares as we made our way to the park. What the townspeople think doesn't bother me either way, but it could affect E. She's been through enough lately. I don't want to add more grief to her life. I'm just at a point where I can't stay away from her anymore.

If the reactions from the people in town bothered her, E didn't let it show. We sit at one of the picnic tables by the river and enjoy our lunch. Her stories about her bridezilla last weekend are hilarious. Her laughter is as warm to me as her smiles are.

"Do you have plans for this weekend?"

"We've been invited to a few cookouts this weekend." E drops her eyes, and her laughter dies. I noticed how she tensed up at my question.

"There's a party at the lake, too." I nod.

"Bonfires and smores." She lightly laughs.

"You go out to the lake?" I playfully slap my hand to my chest and fend shock.

"I haven't gone in a while. I like seeing everybody and the smores, but I don't go camping." She nervously gathers up our empty food wrappers.

I want to ask her out, but her actions have me doubting my decision. If I push her too soon, I'll lose her. She tosses our wrappers in the trash can. When she turns around, I'm pressing and rubbing on my cast. I don't know why I do this. It doesn't help the itching at all.

"Here." E sits beside me on the bench and pulls a pen from her purse. She eases it under the cast. I sigh at the contact. "Does that help?"

"Tremendously." I don't know why I didn't think to do this.

E giggles at the noises of relief I make. With her head bent over my arm, I can smell the coconut scent in her hair.

"Oh, I can't thank you enough for this," I tell her.

"I remember how horrible the itching can be." E continues to move the pen slowly under my cast. I watch her closely. "This was the only thing that helped."

E suddenly pauses. I wondered how long it would take her to realize what she was saying. Slowly, she raises her head until our eyes meet. It takes everything I have in me to keep the anger in my body from showing.

"It does help. Thank you." I place my fingers over hers and move the pen again. "Don't stop yet."

"My friend at college said this worked." E concentrates on my arm again.

A friend may have taught her this little trick, but I know she's referring to her own experience. That douchebag broke her arm. I'm going to find him, and he will pay dearly for hurting her. For his sake, he best pray he's still in jail.

"If you'd like, we could ride out to the lake this weekend." I quickly changed the subject back to the weekend. "We don't have to camp."

"You want to go to the party?" Her eyes lift to mine again.

"Yes." It's best to keep my words short and simple here.

"With me?" She seems surprised.

"Definitely with you." I push a lock of her hair behind her ear.

"No camping?" She shakes her head.

"No camping," I promise. I would love to have her alone in a tent, but it won't happen this weekend. Or ever. E hates camping.

My heart explodes when she replies, "I'd love to."

Chapter Eighteen

Etrulia

What's wrong with me? Do I have a magnet on me that attracts problems? Somehow, I managed to make my life hectic without even trying. I never had to look for trouble. It always finds me. Disaster, heartache, and pain seem to have my name, address, and phone number on speed dial. At this point, I'm beginning to believe all three are permanently connected to me in an unseen way.

The gossip in this town hasn't stopped. Because I had lunch with Aiden on Monday, everyone now has more to talk about. Their staring, whispering, and pointing have me avoiding town altogether. Beth was kind enough to bring me my favorite coffee a few times this week.

The uneasiness I felt had me calling my therapist again this week. It's sad to say I talk to a therapist. After everything that happened to me, I needed someone to talk to who wasn't a family member or a close friend. My therapist convinced me not to shut myself off from the world this weekend. Technically, going to the party at the lake with Aiden isn't a date. At least, that's what I'm telling myself. I'm not sure how he views it.

Beth quickly agreed with everything my therapist said. She was already planning on going to the lake. Naturally, she appointed herself as my guardian. She used that term because it sounded cooler. My friend has seen way too many fantasy movies.

"Guardians are a major part of those worlds, and you need a Guardian," Beth informed me when I told her she was taking this a little too seriously. She's crazy. What would I do without her?

Early Saturday afternoon, there was a lady's luncheon at the inn, which didn't allow time for us to go to the lake. We decided to go on Sunday evening. Sunday morning was church as usual for me, with a cookout after. Aiden has a shift at the station Monday morning, so I wouldn't have to worry about staying out too late tonight. Honestly, I was just looking for an excuse to end the evening if I felt a panic attack coming on. Sadly, I have to prepare ahead of time for the possibility of those.

Invites to family cookouts came from several families around town. Thankfully, my family chose to go to the Maxwells after church today for their cookout. Aiden and I can drive out to the lake from here. I'm glad we decided to go to the party at the lake today. I haven't been out there in years, but rumors of those parties lasted for weeks afterward. Saturday nights were the wildest, and Monday afternoons had often gotten out of hand with a few fights breaking out, and not just between the men.

Since I'm struggling with my nerves and anxiety today, I stay close to Beth for most of the cookout. When she left early for the party at the lake, I went inside and helped Mrs. Maxwell in the kitchen. I'm not trying to avoid Aiden. I needed to do this to keep from overthinking things. Let's face it. There's a lot here I can overthink about.

"Mrs. Maxwell, where does this go?"

We're doing the dishes. The odd-shaped bowl in my hands doesn't seem to fit with the other bowls I put into the cabinets. Aiden's mom and my aunt are talking at the sink. For some reason, women love to talk while doing the dishes. I heard a lot about Aiden's family during these times. Today is no different. Of course, my aunt is sharing our family stories too.

"Oh, that one goes in the cabinet above the fridge," Mrs. Maxwell replied. She goes back to talking with my aunt.

One look at the cabinet above the fridge, and I know I need a step stool to reach it. I'm five foot six. Why people think I can reach the top shelf is beyond me.

"I got it," Aiden said behind me. I didn't hear him come inside. Once the bowl is put away, he turns to me and holds his hand out. "Are you ready to go?"

The quietness from the other side of the room catches my attention. My aunt and his mom are never this quiet when they're together. My eyes dart to them and back to Aiden. Yes, they're watching us.

"We're heading out to the lake for a little while," Aiden answered their question before they could ask.

"Be careful. That party gets crazier by the year." My aunt can't hide her concern. I see it in her eyes. Her fear is one of the reasons I don't go to the party at the lake.

"Is Brady going with you?" Mrs. Maxwell asked Aiden.

"He already left," Aiden replied.

Before more questions can be asked, Aiden takes my hand and leads me to his truck. He helps me into the passenger seat before jogging around to the driver's side.

"What's the rush?"

"If we stick around long enough, Mom will have Colton driving us. The last thing I want is to show up at the lake with a pretty girl and my brother driving." Aiden looks over and winks at me as he pulls out of the driveway.

We aren't teenagers sneaking out of the house. Still, this nondate is starting to feel like a real one. Me dating Aiden Maxwell? Is that even possible? Sure, I have dreamed of it since middle school. Am I ready for this? I look over at him and smile. I think I could be. Until he officially asks me for a date, I can't consider us dating, though.

We ride the rest of the way to the lake in silence. The radio is on, and I think the CD playing is of the band Aiden used to work with. Seeing the tour bus accident on the news sent me into a full-blown panic attack. I called Brady the moment I could think clearly. He tried calling and texting me during my panic attack. He left no details, just a text to call him back. They were at the airport, already on their way to Tennessee. His updates on Aiden were all that kept me from losing it completely.

"Wow. Everyone is here." I don't remember seeing this many people at the lake before.

"Are you okay with this?" Aiden sounds worried as he helps me out of the truck.

Come to think of it, a lot of people use this tone when they talk to me. I didn't notice it until now. It's irritating. My therapist told me I would start noticing little things like this one day. It would be a sign that I was moving forward and making progress. I have a lot of things to let go of for sure. I don't want to feel like a victim for the rest of my life. I release a long breath and push past a few of my fears.

"It's great." I smile at Aiden. Is it fake? I'm not sure yet, but here's to finding out.

I'm not sure if I take his hand or if he takes mine, but this simple touch feels intimate. It feels like something more than holding hands. Maybe it's because of the look in Aiden's eyes when it happened. I don't know, but I'm not going to over-analyze it. I'm simply going to enjoy it.

"Do you want a smores?" Aiden motioned toward the bonfire.

"I don't trust that." I shake my head.

The sight before us is unreal. I've never seen a bonfire at the lake this huge before. The moment I realized Pit and Four made this fire, it explained everything.

"Is that safe?" I can't take my eyes off the huge flames.

"Miles is here, and he looks prepared." Aiden puts his arm around me as we walk over to Miles.

Seeing the fire truck across the field assures me that Miles is indeed prepared tonight. Miles and a few other firefighters are sitting on the tailgate of Luke Barnes' pickup truck.

"Aiden. E." Miles shakes Aiden's hand and gives me a hug.

"E!" Luke hops off the tailgate and hugs me. "You're looking good tonight."

I don't know why he would say that. Jeans, a t-shirt, and no makeup aren't considered '*looking good*' by any means. Aiden growls, and the next thing I know, I'm out of Luke's arms with Aiden between us. I'm having trouble comprehending how fast it happened.

"Gotta problem, Maxwell?" Luke grins slyly.

Having Aiden in his face doesn't seem to bother Luke at all. Honestly, I don't think much has ever bothered Luke before.

"Not at all." Aiden's voice is deep and holds a level of authority to it. Of course, Luke's father is the sheriff, so he's used to hearing this tone. I guess cops sound that way without much effort. Without taking his eyes off of Luke, Aiden says to me, "Let's get you that smores."

"Are you mad?" I ask as we walk toward the bonfire.

"Yep," Aiden admits. Well, at least he's honest. "But not at you."

"Luke is not a problem," I assure him.

"Oh, I know." He sounds confident on the matter.

"Then, what's the problem?" I'm a little confused here.

"It's what he said, how he said it, and he said it to you." The possessiveness in Aiden's tone is not missed.

Coming to this party might not have been a good idea. It seems as though half of the guys in this town are pushing Aiden's buttons lately. Is it because of his past? Could it be because of me? I glance up at Aiden. His eyes are focused straight ahead, his jaw is set, and his arm around me tightens slightly. If this is about me, I don't like the guys using me to hurt Aiden.

Aiden gets us a couple of smores from Maddie Gibson. She seems to be the only one brave enough to approach the huge fire. The firepit the city built here is huge, and for the most part, it keeps the fires at the lake contained. Yet, when Pit and Four are involved, anything could happen. It's probably why Miles has one of the fire trucks here tonight.

We walk back over to Aiden's truck. At first, I thought we were leaving until he let the tailgate down and spread a blanket over it. The only help he allowed me to give was to hold our smores. Doing things with one arm has to be frustrating, but he managed it well enough.

We got here late and had to park more to the side, away from where most of the party-goers were. This little bit of privacy is nice. Not everyone in town has accepted Aiden back with open arms. I've heard some hateful gossip floating around town already.

Just the two of us sitting here takes away my fear of having everyone watching me. Having people watching me makes me extremely nervous. The people of this town stared at me from the moment I arrived in Montana. I guess it was kind of hard not to stare at a broken and battered little girl. It wasn't their fault. It was my parents, the biological ones, anyway. Eventually, their stares softened, and I was accepted as one of their own. If we could pick our parents, I would have chosen my aunt and uncle. I'm theirs now, and that's what matters the most.

Sitting here alone with Aiden also gives me reasons to feel nervous. It's just us, and every part of me is fully aware of the man sitting beside me. I'm battling with several issues about relationships. They scare me now, and with good reason. Still, I can't help myself. I *want* to be here alone with him.

"It's beautiful," I say softly.

Montana sunsets are amazing. The sunrises here are spectacular, too. I love watching the colors as they dance across the sky. With the lake and mountains in the background, it's majestic. No matter how many times I watch the sunset, it always calms me and leaves me in awe.

"Very beautiful," Aiden agreed.

Turning, I find his soft brown eyes looking at me, not the sunset. Gone are the hardened lines on his face. His anger with Luke is now replaced with such tenderness. I can't say for sure, but I swear, I see my feelings for him mirrored back at me. I've never been good at reading guys, and that landed me in trouble.

Aiden's hand comes up. His fingers lightly move across my cheek. His palm settles on my neck as his thumb softly moves back and forth under my bottom lip. Those soft brown eyes drop to my lips and back to my eyes. After all these years, is he about to kiss me? Oh, please. I sure hope so.

"E." Aiden's head lowers slightly. His voice is so soft.

"Aiden," I whisper back.

"Go out with me?"

"Out? A date?" I can't seem to form a complete sentence.

"A real date." Aiden nods. His eyes never leave mine.

What would this town think? How would they treat us on a real date? Dancing and lunch in the park caused several rumors to circulate about us. I'm overthinking again, and I know it. My therapist urged me not to waste valuable time on things I can't control. The citizens of Hayden Falls and their wagging tongues are definitely something no one can control.

"We can go to Missoula," Aiden suggests. "We don't have to go anywhere in Hayden Falls."

Can this man read my mind? I know it's impossible, but I swear he can. It was like this when we were kids. Back then, he swore I could read his mind, too. We were close when we were kids. How did we drift so far apart?

"Go out with me, E?" he asks again.

His thumb gently moves across my bottom lip. Those brown eyes beg me to say yes. I'm not sure if my heart beats or stops. I'm lost in his gaze. Caution. I should proceed with caution. Play it safe. No. That's not what I want with him. Still, I'm scared, and at the same time, I want more.

"Yes," my reply was a whisper.

"Yes?" Aiden smiles.

I nod, confirming he heard me correctly. "I'd love to go out with you."

His smile widens as he lowers his head even closer to mine. Why is he drawing this kiss out? He needs to kiss me. I want to feel his lips on mine. My eyes close as I anticipate our first kiss.

"Umph." I can barely breathe as Aiden and I fall back into the bed of his truck.

"Hey, guys." Beth smiles down at us.

"Come on, Beth." Katie's there, pulling her off of us.

Did she really just ruin my first kiss with Aiden? Did my best friend just tackle us? Yes. Yes, she did. What's wrong with her? Why would she do that? I'm going to hurt my best friend. Not really, but I can imagine it.

One look at Beth and I understood why she did it. Katie's having a hard time keeping our friend up straight. Beth has been here for hours. From the looks of things, she's had too much fun this afternoon. I hop off the tailgate. I slide under one of Beth's arms to help Katie hold her up.

"We got you," I tell Beth. She's in tears, but I don't know why.

"Let's get her home before Spencer sees her." Aiden opens the door to the backseat of his truck. He helps us get Beth inside before turning to Katie. "I think she rode here with Brady. Will you tell him we have her?"

Katie doesn't want to leave our friend. I know she's worried. I am, too. Finally, Katie nodded and went back to the party. She'll be checking on Beth later.

"He went that way." Beth points to the woods across the field. "With Tabetha Sailors."

I wrap my crying friend in my arms. Aiden didn't protest when I chose to sit in the back with Beth. He quickly drives us to Beth's apartment.

It looks like my dear friend has some feelings for a certain baseball player she's going to have to come to terms with soon. I would have never thought it was possible. The arguing between them has been foreplay to hide her true feelings. Will Beth admit it? Probably not.

What did Brady do today to cause Beth to act this way? Maybe when she's feeling better tomorrow, she'll tell me. Tonight, I'll stay by her side. Will Beth be okay tomorrow? Well, that remains to be seen.

Chapter Nineteen

Aiden

Dreams and fantasies have a way of either coming true or blowing up in your face. Mine are the explosive kind. That's why I spent the past week tiptoeing around everything. I've never been this kind of man, and I pray this ends soon. Sure, I could be the normal me. Stand firm, stand tall, and don't give or waver for any reason. That's the man I was raised to be, and I am that man. Well, except for the past seven days.

If anyone noticed the change in me, they didn't comment on it. It's best they didn't. I probably would have popped off something smart. Then I'd be apologizing for months. There was no need for them to point out my irrational behavior. I could feel it. I'm not sorry. If I had to do it all over again, I would. My dream, my fantasy, my everything was too valuable to screw things up now. I finally got E to agree to go out with me, and I wasn't letting anything stop it from happening.

The only problem with this date was that I didn't secure a day and time. It wouldn't be happening this week, though. Today is the Hayden Falls Fall Festival. It's all hands on deck for the station today. Unless we had third-shift duties, every deputy was scheduled for four to six-hour shifts at the festival.

The festival officially begins around 9 am when the stores around the square open for business, and it ends around eight in the evening. The streets around the square are blocked off during festival hours. A few people complain every year because they can't drive straight down North and South Main Streets, but thankfully, the city council never gave in on this one. The Fall Festival is a huge event in our area. Business owners who don't have a store on the square and several local at-home businesses, including crafters, set up booths along the sidewalks.

A temporary stage was built in the center of the square next to the gazebo for this special event. Jake Campbell and his band will take the stage around four this afternoon and play until the festival ends. Until that time, there's a children's talent show. The adult talent show got too crazy years ago, causing it to be canceled completely. The church's adult and children's choirs will sing, contests will take place, and announcements will be made. It's a day filled with fun activities for everyone.

Spencer and I are on dayshift. We're scheduled to be at the festival from 8 am until two in the afternoon. The Magnolia Inn will set up a booth near Beth's coffee shop. Beth gave me that little bit of information on one of my visits to her shop during my regular rounds this week. We have to keep those business owners in our assigned sections happy. I roll my eyes at the thought. It's a dumb program, but it got me some inside info for today.

Beth also thanked me with a couple of free cups of coffee for rescuing her from the party at the lake last weekend. I still don't understand everything that happened that day. I sensed right away that whatever happened to Beth was strictly a girl's conversation, so I didn't push for any details. The best I could piece together from Beth's ramblings, it had something to do with my brother. Brady, however, was clueless on the matter.

Since my visit with Doctor Larson a week and a half ago, I no longer have to depend on Spencer or Brady for a ride. I knew before the visit he was going to release me to do more. So I carried my mom with me. Yes, she drilled the good doctor with every question imaginable. Thankfully, Matt was able to win Mom over in the end.

The new modern-style cast he put on is a thousand times better than the first one. It's more of a sturdy brace. I can take this one off to wash my arm. Trust me. It seriously needed it. My arm was broken in two places, and I had a hairline fracture in another. The first cast was needed to keep me from bumping my arm too much. The doctor in Tennessee said the slightest movement could shift the bones, which would cause me to need more surgery.

I park my truck in the parking lot at the station and sign in before heading to the town square. Everyone will be setting up their booths and displays for the next hour. Maybe I'll get to help E set up the booth for the inn. I've seen her a few times around town this past week. We even talked and texted on the phone every day. Her schedule was easy to figure out, so those random little meetings happened often.

As I rounded the corner of the ice cream parlor, The Magnolia Inn's booth came into view. My smile fades, and my heart sinks. Mrs. Hayes is decorating their booth. E's aunt is a kind woman. She was kind to me when the rest of the town wasn't. Most of the people here love her. Since she's loyal to my family and not the Crawfords, a few people turn their noses up at her. Small-town rivalries are a real thing here.

"Mrs. Hayes, let me help you with that." I grab the garland-type decoration she's trying to attach to the top of the booth.

"Oh, thank you, Aiden." Mrs. Hayes steps back so I can attach the end to the hook.

"You should have asked one of the guys running around here to help you." I'm concerned about her safety. She isn't very tall, and I don't see a step stool nearby.

"I should have, but everyone seems so busy." Mrs. Hayes motions around the square with her hand.

Everyone does look busy, but I'm sure someone would have stopped what they were doing long enough to have helped her. The Magnolia Inn's booth looks completely set up now, so I won't have to worry about this little woman getting hurt. Mrs. Hayes lightly laughs as I glance around the square again.

"Don't worry." Mrs. Hayes puts her hand on my arm. "She's here."

That brought a smile to my face. Of course, E would be here today. I didn't ask her what time, though. I should have realized E wouldn't let her aunt set everything up by herself. I'm still scanning the square for her when the bell above the door of Beth's coffee shop chimes behind me.

"Here you go." E hands her aunt a cup of coffee from the tray she's carrying. Of course, she would be in the coffee shop. "And this is for you."

My eyes drop from her face to the cup she's holding towards me.

"You got me coffee?" I wasn't expecting that.

"House blend. Cream. Lots of sugar." She smiles, causing her entire face to light up.

Interesting. That's exactly how I like my coffee. My large hand wraps around hers and the to-go cup. The smile on my face matches the one on hers. The deep shade of her blue eyes tells me, without having to look, that she's wearing blue today. I swear her eyes always changed like this, depending on what she wore. I've never seen it happen with anyone else. Maybe she's the only woman I've cared enough about to notice.

A glance down confirms my theory. She's wearing a navy blue sweater, jeans, and a pair of ankle boots. She's also the only woman I've paid attention to her shoes before. Man, I'm going soft here. How could I not? She's cute, and I'll do anything to keep that smile on her face. And yes, I let my hand linger on hers longer than necessary. Hey. She's in no hurry to pull hers away, either.

"Let me pay you back for that." I go to reach for my wallet.

"It's my treat." She puts her hand over mine, stopping me.

Wow. Her slight touch lights up every nerve in my body. I really like these hand-holding moments with her. Okay. This isn't holding hands, but she's touching me. Sadly, she removed her hand way too soon for my liking. Let me see what else I can come up with to get her hand back in mine.

"A gentleman never allows such a thing," I tell her. My grandfather would insist on this fact.

"You can pay for dinner," E suggests shyly.

"Dinner?" I'm a little shocked she brought it up.

Her smile is tight, and her eyes blink a few times. I notice when her foot wiggles a time or two. This is a bold move for her, and it gives my confidence a major boost. She wants this date almost as much as I do.

"You did ask me out," she reminds me.

She fidgets a little more. I can't leave her squirming like this. I like that she's been thinking about our date, but I don't like seeing her nervous.

"Of course, I'll pay for everything on our date." There's no time like the present to lock this date down. "When would you like to go on our date?"

She sighs with relief. Surely, she didn't think I would back out of this date. If I had my way about it, we would have already had our first date and maybe one or two more by now. Yeah, two or three dates in a week may sound like a lot, but I want even more than that with her.

"How about this Thursday evening?"

Her eyes do that blinking thing again. Gracious, can she get any cuter? There's no way I'll ever turn her down.

"Now, just how did you know my day off?" I'm pretty sure I know the answer already.

"Spencer."

That's what I thought. The Magnolia Inn is in Spencer's assigned section. It's still a dumb program. I'm kind of jealous, though. My friend gets to see her almost every day. Oh, I'll get that, too, one day. Except, I won't be doing it as part of a community program for the Sheriff's Office. Cocky? Not at all. Sure of myself? Absolutely.

"Thursday is perfect," I assure her. That's actually a lie. Thursday is too far away if you ask me, but I'll take it.

Someone clears their throat behind me. It's a gruff sound that's bordering on disgust. Alarmed that something could be wrong, I turn toward the sound. My beautiful, perfect day just got an unexpected thunderstorm.

Mr. Wentworth looks me over a couple of times before settling on glaring at me. The elderly man was a friend of my grandfather's. My life-altering decision six years ago revolves around this man. I'm almost positive he still hates me. I knew I was going to run into him sooner or later. I hate this confrontation is going to happen in front of E and her aunt.

"I see the sheriff is still trying to make a decent man out of you." Mr. Wentworth looks at my badge.

"Yes, Sir." There's no point in telling him I *am* a decent man. He won't see it.

"It's been a long time. Doubt it'll ever happen." Mr. Wentworth sighs and shakes his head.

"I'm doing my best, Sir." I don't want him to think I'm a lost cause.

Mr. Wentworth shakes his head again and adjusts his hat. He hasn't forgotten that night, and neither have I. No one in this town has forgotten it.

"Are you, though?" he asked.

I'm not sure if he's seriously asking or if he's trying to goad me into an argument here. His expression is unreadable. It makes me uncomfortable.

"I am." I nod once.

"Bad blood it is." The old man nods his head once, too. He would see it that way. "It ain't right." Now, he's shaking his head. "You shouldn't be a deputy, boy."

Half the people in this town weren't happy when Sheriff Barnes didn't arrest me. They all believed I got the easy way out. Nothing that happened to me over the past six years has been easy. Well, except for the friends I made in Tennessee, but that's it. I lost everything that night. Nothing I say to this man will make amends, so I stay quiet. Once again, I'm throwing my gentleman's character out the window. I could say more, but he won't listen to me, so remaining quiet is the best choice here. There's no point in wasting my energy when he won't believe me.

"You need to remember who you are, boy." Mr. Wentworth looks me dead in the eye. His jaw is set tight, and his eyes are hard. He's not happy.

Nothing I say or do will fix things with this man. I nod. It's best to let this drop before his blood pressure rises. He doesn't care that I spent the entire summer that year working to make amends for what happened. He knows. He was there every day to make sure I suffered. I paid for that night for six years.

Brady comes around the corner with his friend Dalton Edwards. Dalton is a good kid. They go to college together in Billings. Both have baseball scholarships. Mr. Wentworth narrows his eyes at Brady. He looks at me and shakes his head again.

"At least two of the Maxwell boys are worth their raising. One of you, there's no hope for," Mr. Wentworth grumbles. His face softens when he looks at E and Mrs. Hayes. The glare is back when he looks at me again. "Don't go disgracing decent women." With that, Mr. Wentworth turns and stomps down the street.

Elijah Wentworth, Mr. Wentworth's grandson, is leaning against the wall of the bakery. He listened to the entire conversation. He's as protective of his grandfather as I was of mine.

"Eli, I'm sorry for what happened. If he feels I owe your family anything more, I'll gladly pay it." I just want to live in this town peacefully.

"It's not what happened or the debt owned for it that he's hung up on." Eli pushes off the wall and steps closer to me. His eyes flick between my brother and me. "It's how it was handled."

"I can't change that." I had no idea back then that Sheriff Barnes would go easy on me.

"Maybe. Maybe not." Eli shrugs.

"Just tell me what your family wants from me," I reduce myself to pleading. "I'll do it to put this behind us."

"You're a grown man, Aiden, and a cop." Eli shakes his head. "Nobody needs to tell you how to fix things. You already know, but you won't do it."

I blow out a breath and run my fingers through my hair. There's absolutely nothing I can do to fix things. This town and the

Wentworths are never going to forgive me. Maybe being here really is a mistake.

"I'm sorry," I apologize again. I'll probably be apologizing to this family for the rest of my life.

"Without action, that means nothing." Eli looks Brady over with disgust. Like his grandfather, his eyes soften when he looks at E and her aunt. "Ladies." Eli nods and tips his hat. He turns to look me in the eye. "You shouldn't be a cop." With that, Eli walks away.

No, I shouldn't be a cop. I should have gone to college. I should have been a pitcher in the MLB. When she was old enough, I should have come back here and married Etrulia Hayes. None of that happened.

One look at her now, and I'm not so sure I can put her through the bashing this town will give her for being with me. Everything in me shatters to pieces. There's no way I can date her. This town will destroy her. She deserves a better life than I can give her. What kind of man would I be if I let them hurt her?

Chapter Twenty

Etrulia

This town is famous for holding grudges. I don't understand why the Wentworths won't forgive Aiden. The look in his eyes breaks my heart. He's trying. He really is.

"E," he says my name, but his eyes are on the ground. "I can't. You deserve…" Aiden pauses and shakes his head.

I close my eyes and shake my head. I know what he's about to say, and it already hurts.

"Aiden, please don't," I plead softly.

"I'm sorry, E, but I have to cancel our date." His voice cracks.

He swallows hard, and without looking at me, Aiden turns and walks away. When I take a couple of steps to chase after him, Brady grabs my arm, stopping me. A silent tear escapes the corner of my eye. Last week, it was Beth. Today, it's my turn to cry.

"Give him a little time. He'll come around," Brady said.

From the look in Brady's eyes, I'm not so sure he believes that. I know I don't believe it.

"It's not right what this town does to him." I wipe the tear away with my fingertips.

"It's not," Brady agrees and drops his eyes to the sidewalk.

"Why don't you go inside and wash your face before the crowd starts coming?" Aunt Sara suggests.

I turn to go into the coffee shop, but Brady's still holding onto my arm. He looks as torn as Aiden.

"Don't worry. I'll talk to him," Brady said.

"No." I shake my head. "If somebody has to talk him into going out with me, then I'd rather not."

Brady releases my arm, and I hurry to the restroom inside Beth's Morning Brew. Of course, my friend noticed I was upset and followed me into the restroom. Unable to hold it back, I tell her everything that happened outside.

"You shouldn't let him call off your date." Beth hands me a few paper towels to dry my face.

"I can't force him to go out with me," I tell her. "I'm not going to beg."

My life is already pathetic enough. As much as I want to go out with Aiden, I refuse to resort to begging. It looks like I'll be calling my therapist on Monday to talk this one out. I finally get brave enough to try dating again, and thanks to Eli Wentworth and his grandfather, it's no longer going to happen.

"You're not begging," Beth insists. "You're standing up for what you want. You've wanted Aiden for a long time. Don't let this crazy town come between you two. Trust me. He wants this date as much as you do."

"What do I do if I stand up and it still doesn't work? I'll look like a fool."

"You *will* be a fool if you let him go without a fight." Beth takes my hand and gives it a little squeeze for encouragement.

"I don't know." I sigh and shake my head. "Even if I can convince him to go on this date, what happens next time? This town is never going to stop."

It's true. They won't, and we all know it. The Wentworths, or someone else in this crazy little town, will keep bashing Aiden for what happened all those years ago. If we do go out, and I'm not sure I can convince him to still go out with me, will I have to plead with him every time someone brings up the past?

"You know." Beth taps her bottom lip with her finger. "Something about that night doesn't add up."

On that, I have to agree. Sadly, no one seems to think so. Well, no one with the power to make a difference in this town agrees. The wonderful citizens of Hayden Falls prefer listening to dirty gossip over digging into the true matters of things.

No one would believe me if I told them what I knew about that night. I tried speaking up six years ago, but the sheriff politely dismissed me and sent me on my way. Being fifteen at the time and the shy girl in town didn't give me a lot of credit among the people here. I know it wasn't my story to tell. It still isn't. But these people have it all wrong.

"Look." Beth holds her hands up. "I can't tell you what to do here, but if I were you, I'd fight for Aiden."

My mouth drops open, and my eyes widen. I know the look on her face. It's fine if she thinks that about the other guys in town. I don't like her saying that about Aiden.

"Oh, come on, E." Beth laughs at me. "Every woman in this town, and I'm sure in a few other towns, knows Aiden Maxwell is hot."

Nope. I do not like her thoughts. She can have her fill with every guy in this town, just not this one guy. Of course, Beth wouldn't act on it. This is Aiden. She knows how I feel about him. I just don't want my friend crushing on him like this. Sure, I know women do, but I still don't like it. Can we say jealous? Why, yes, we can. Besides, I'm pretty sure Beth has feelings for someone in town.

"Okay." I hold my hands up in surrender. "I'll think about it."

I wasn't going to think about it. I don't have a plan yet, but I will do something. Hopefully, in the end, I don't look like a fool.

"Well, that's better than a straight-out no." Beth gives me a hug. "Now, I have to get back to work."

After she leaves, I take a long look at myself in the restroom mirror. For most of my life, I've been cautious and safe. I've always been the quiet one who never took a stand. For the most part, I'm scared of just about everything. It's no way to live, and it can't continue.

If I don't stand up for myself and what I want, no one else will. Relationships terrify me. Still, my heart has always wanted Aiden. I didn't think he would ever come back to Hayden Falls, but he's here. I have to take a chance.

Rejection is a hard pill to swallow. What will I do if Aiden doesn't want me? I'll be the talk of this town for sure. Well, I'd be more like the laughing joke for years. In the past, that was enough to stop me from speaking up. I don't want to be the quiet little mouse anymore. It's time to be brave.

I want Aiden Maxwell. In the end, I may lose, but I have to try. If I fail, I could pull one out of Aiden's playbook and leave town. I'd have to leave because I won't be able to show my face in Hayden Falls again.

I also can't stay in this restroom all day. My aunt and I are handing out flyers for The Magnolia Inn and promoting our wedding and party services. Plus, we made goodie bags for the kids and gift bags for the women.

When I got back outside, the mayor was giving his speech to start the fall festival. We have a clear view of the stage next to the gazebo from our booth. This festival is one of my favorite events in our town. The event at the top of my favorite things here is the tree lighting at Christmas. That event is probably bigger than this one.

Last year, at this time, I was engaged. Not happily, I might add. Garrett and I were already having problems. Well, we had problems long before we were engaged. Garrett's temper grew every month when I didn't set a wedding date. During Christmas Holidays last year, he demanded I set a date, or he was taking me to Vegas to elope. I still never set a date. My entire world changed two weeks after the new semester started at college.

"You shouldn't let this town stop you from pursuing a relationship with Aiden," Aunt Sara whispered.

"You don't have a problem with me dating Aiden?"

We've never had this conversation. My aunt hates the gossip around this town as much as I do. I assumed she wanted to avoid any gossip involving our family. I thought what happened years ago changed my aunt's opinion of Aiden.

When Aiden got in trouble, people openly voiced their opinions about him. None of it was good. I overheard my aunt and uncle talking one night. It broke my heart to hear my uncle say the best thing Aiden could do was to leave and never come back.

"No," Aunt Sara replies. "You two should have been together a long time ago."

We should have. Still, it surprised me to hear my aunt say this. Looking up, I notice Aiden walking around the town square with Spencer. It's not lost on me how he avoids getting close to our booth. It's okay. Soon, I'll find a way to get close to him. If I have anything to say about it, our date on Thursday night will happen.

Chapter Twenty-One

Etrulia

The fall festival went well. Everyone laughed and had a great time. Many of the businesses in town held little contests for the festival-goers with cute prizes. Several ladies even booked The Magnolia Inn for birthday parties and luncheons.

Pit joined in with the guys from the fire station and grilled out in the park. A portion of the profits from their hamburger and hotdog plates went to the church's food bank. The rest went to the fire station.

Brady was kind enough to bring Aunt Sara and me a plate. He even carried one to Beth, but she refused to take it. Those two need to figure some things out and soon.

In the middle of the afternoon, Aiden disappeared from the festival. He probably finished the rest of his shift at the Sheriff's Office. That was hours ago, but he never returned to the square. He didn't come back to our booth to talk to me either. Guess we're playing the avoiding game.

At 8 pm, Jake Campbell and his band left the stage. Nearly everyone had already packed up and gone home by this point. My aunt and I had to hang around until Uncle Silas arrived with his pickup and trailer to carry our booth back to the inn.

Four and Pit came over to help my uncle load everything up. These two guys don't get enough credit around here. Sure, they're crazy, but they have big hearts.

"How about another dance?" Four puts his arm around my shoulders.

It's funny how he thinks we danced at Cowboys a few weeks ago. Beth assures me we did not dance. Still, Four always knew how to make me smile.

"Jake is gone. There's no music." I motioned to the empty stage. Tomorrow, some volunteers will start taking it down.

"We have *YouTube*." Four pulls out his phone from his back pocket and waves it at me.

He's so cute and, to my surprise, serious about this. He opens up the *YouTube* app and starts playing a song. I yelp when he grabs my hand and pulls me into his arms.

"Four, we can't do this." I push against his chest.

Protesting anything to Four is a lost cause, anyway. He doesn't release me. Instead, he twirls me around. This is unreal but funny.

"Four, stop goofing off and get over here," Uncle Silas shouts.

Reluctantly, as if it's the worst thing he's ever done, Four releases me to go and help secure the booth onto the trailer. Aunt Sara laughs and gives me a one-arm hug. We're used to Four's silliness.

"Are you riding home with us?" Aunt Sara asked as she opened the truck door.

"No," I decline the offer.

It's a lovely night. I'm not ready to go home just yet. The festival is over, but I have a lot to think about. I could do that at home, but a walk through the park sounds like what I need tonight. The park isn't too far from the inn. Hayden Falls is a safe place. I can walk home later.

After saying goodnight to everyone, I walked to the park. Four wasn't happy, but Pit convinced him to let me go. Of course, Pit had to agree to buy the first couple of rounds of drinks at Cowboys.

It is a lovely night. I haven't taken a walk after dark in a long time. Usually, Beth is with me. Tonight, she's at Cowboys with everyone else. It's okay. I need this time alone to clear my head. I also need to come up with a plan on how to convince Aiden to keep our date on Thursday night. I shouldn't have to come up with a plan, but this town doesn't play fair.

I walk through the park to the river. No one is here but me. The town council installed street lights throughout the park a few years ago. They're spread out enough to where the light isn't overpowering. Lazily, I follow the river to the wooden bridge at the edge of town. Three other main roads lead into Hayden Falls, but this one is my favorite.

The first time I crossed this bridge, I was eight years old. It quickly became an emblem of safety for me. A broken and battered little girl finally found a home with people who loved her on this side of that bridge. It isn't covered as I've seen bridges in pictures of other small towns. It's fine. The openness gives the bridge a feeling of safety and freedom, too. Strange how that is.

Placing my forearms on the railing, I slightly lean forward and watch the water flow under the bridge. Simple things like this help to clear my mind. I need that right now. This day sure didn't go the way I hoped it would.

The sound of footfalls when someone steps onto the bridge alarms me. Immediately, I stand up straight and turn to face them. Aiden. I thought he went home. He must have because he's no longer wearing his uniform. As much as I want to see him, I'm still hurt because he avoided me all day.

"Are you all right?" He stops a few feet from me.

I lightly laugh. There's no humor to it. Did he seriously just ask me that?

"Great. I'm just great," I lie and turn back to face the river.

I want to talk to him, but I haven't figured out what to say that would help. I'm not ready for this conversation. I like thinking things through first. It looks like I'm going to have to wing it tonight, though.

"E, I'm sorry." He steps closer and leans on the railing beside me.

"You're apologizing a lot today."

"I have a lot to apologize for." Defeated, he drops his head.

"But you don't." I shake my head and look away.

Aiden sighs and turns around. He leans back against the railing and crosses his ankles. Watching him from the corner of my eye, I can tell he has a lot on his mind, too. We need to talk, but neither of us knows where to start.

"So, where are we going on our date?" I decide to take a chance.

"E, we can't go on that date." He releases another long breath and folds his arms across his chest.

"Why not?" I bravely step in front of him.

"This town will never give you a moment of peace if we go out. I can't destroy you like that."

Beth is right. He wants this date as much as I do. I can see it in his eyes. It's time to be very brave. I take a step closer to him. Both of his feet are now between mine. Something flashes in his eyes, but he quickly shakes it away. I saw it, and I'm not letting it disappear.

"Aiden Maxwell, are you saying that you do not want to date me?"

Our eyes lock. He's struggling to stay strong. Realizing I may have a little more say in how this goes gives me more confidence. I have no intention of letting him stay strong tonight.

"I would never say that." At least he's being honest here. "Dating me would hurt you. These people will descend on you like wildfire."

Ah. The noble Aiden Maxwell. Some people in this town may think he didn't live up to how his parents and grandparents raised him, but that's far from the truth. This town is wrong about him on so many things.

"But we're already hurting." I lift my chin, daring him to tell me I'm wrong. He can't, and he knows it. "This town is going to talk whether we go out or not. They talked before we were born, and they'll still be gossiping hundreds of years after we're gone."

"E." He sighs again.

He doesn't want things to be this way between us, and neither do I. I have loved this man for a long time. Tonight, I'm going to push my advantage with him. Beth said I should fight for him, and that's exactly what I'm going to do.

I place my hand on his arm. They're still folded across his chest. I take a tiny step closer to him. His sharp intake of breath causes me to smile.

"I want to go out with you. I have for a long time." I place the palm of my hand against his cheek. "If there's nothing between us, nothing at all, then I will release you of this date, and I will walk away forever."

"Forever?" He can barely speak.

"Forever," I repeat and slowly nod my head. "But, if there's anything, anything at all, between us." I pause and cup his face with both of my hands. "Then, I don't care what the people of Hayden Falls have to say."

He unfolds his arms and gently places his hands on my waist. Even though his broken arm is still in a cast, this new one gives him a lot more freedom. His hands feel good on me. His eyes search mine. He's still fighting this in his mind. It's time to be braver than I ever have before. It's time to fight for what I want. Rejection is a possibility, but I don't care right now.

I take the final step that puts my body against his. My hands slide down to his shoulders and around his neck. Words cannot describe how right this feels.

"Sunshine, what are you doing?" He's no fool.

"Cowboy, I don't think you need instructions." I want to laugh, but I'm too wrapped up at the moment. He is, too.

Aiden opens his mouth to speak, but I stop him as I press my lips to his. Finally! The stars in the universe have aligned. Aiden doesn't need any more prompting. His arms tighten around my waist, pulling me closer to him. Better. This feels even better.

At first, his lips slowly move with mine. Heaven. This is so heavenly. With a moan, I fully give myself over to this kiss. I feel the growl in his chest just before Aiden's right hand fists in the hair behind my head. He takes over and deepens the kiss. No one has ever kissed me like this. This kiss could go on forever, and I wouldn't mind one bit, but eventually, we come up for air. Gotta breathe, after all.

Aiden rests his forehead against mine, but he doesn't loosen his arms around me. It's fine. I don't want to remove my arms from around him, either.

"I'll pick you up around six on Thursday." He hasn't fully caught his breath yet.

"I'll see you before then, right?" I lean back enough to look at him.

"Oh, Sunshine. You'll see me every day," Aiden assures me.

His hand moves behind my head again, pulling me back to him. His lips eagerly claim mine again. If I thought our first kiss was passionate, this one proved to be something more.

Chapter Twenty-Two

Aiden

Saturday Night will go down in history as one of the best nights of my life. There aren't enough words to fully describe what that night did to me mentally, emotionally, and physically. I am very aware that I sound like a teenage girl right now. I don't care if I do. Something wonderful happened to me. I'll never be ashamed of how E makes me feel.

After running into Mr. Wentworth and his grandson, I had every intention of staying away from E to spare her the cruelty of this town. It was a struggle, but I managed to avoid her for the rest of the festival. Still, I glanced her way every chance I got.

Truth be told, I failed miserably at staying away from her. When she was talking with someone, I would stop and stare at her. I couldn't help it. My eyes automatically sought her out.

After my shift, I went home, showered, and hurried back to town. I intended on staying at the ranch. The thought of her being at the festival with all those single guys roaming around town had me in my truck and on my way back to her. Of course, I stayed in the shadows and watched her from afar.

Jake and his band were on stage, and people were dancing all around the square, even on the sidewalk. The last thing I needed to see was Jesse Calhoun dancing with E again. That's not what happened. No, what I got to see was something far worse. Jesse's older brother, Four, tried to dance with her. There wasn't any music playing at that point. Okay. I admit it. It made my blood boil. Of all people, it had to be Mick Calhoun. Idiot.

I was a little surprised when E didn't get into the truck with her aunt and uncle to go home. So, I followed her at a distance through the park and to the wooden bridge. She had a lot on her mind. That would be my fault. I could see the weight of the hurt I caused without getting close to her. I was a jerk.

I hurt her. I hurt myself. Seeing her broken like that only drove the knife I plunged into my heart even deeper. A part of me whispered to walk away. Only I couldn't. I love her. And I couldn't leave her standing on the town bridge, almost in tears.

I was just going to apologize and make sure she got home okay. Well, that was the lie I told myself. My plan didn't work at all, and I'm beyond glad it didn't.

When she stepped in front of me, placing her tiny feet on the outside of mine, every muscle in my body took notice. When she moved forward, practically straddling my legs, I couldn't move. The moment her hands cupped my face, oxygen left my lungs, and my brain forgot how to work. I was putty in her hands, and I always will be.

It's been five days, and I'm still in shock. I have a hard time processing the fact she used a kiss to convince me not to cancel our date, and I let her do it. It was a bold move on her part. E isn't that kind of girl. I expected her to tell me I was wrong, but a kiss? A slow smile crosses my face. This beautiful woman already owns me. If there's such a thing as a man card, that kiss lit mine on fire, and the ashes were long gone by now.

Like the gentleman I am, I kept my promise to her. I saw her every day, even if it was just random meetings at Beth's Morning Brew or a quick stop by the inn on my way home. The one thing I didn't do over the past few days was kiss her again. It took all my strength not to do it. She initiated our first kiss. The memory of it will be etched into my mind and heart forever. Our next kiss is going to be all me.

Tonight is date night. Around six, I pull into the private drive behind The Magnolia Inn. Using the main entrance to the inn would give this town more to talk about. They have enough to talk about already.

As special as our first kiss was, it wasn't a private moment for us, thanks to Megan and her gossip blog. I swear that woman has hidden cameras hidden around town. That's illegal. Maybe I should talk to her about it. Her little article about us was short, but everybody in town knew who she was talking about.

Steamy Night on the Bridge

The hot nights of Summer have lingered over into Fall. That hot kiss on the town bridge last night has me still fanning myself. Looks like our handsome new deputy won the final prize of the night.

I thought Sunday's article would send E into hiding. She hated being the center of things. Surprisingly, she laughed. Seeing my girl with her head held high and walking proudly around town was amazing. I swear she even made extra trips to town the past few days.

This date still has me a little nervous. The people of this town can cut you to pieces with their hateful words. One of the reasons I agreed to take the sheriff's offer to go to Tennessee was because of the way my family was treated back then. I don't want people harassing E and her family now because of me. Seeing the strength she's displayed since Saturday night makes me believe she can handle the town gossip after all.

At six on the dot, I walk up to E's apartment and knock on the door. I haven't seen her yet today, so I'm a bit antsy at this point. Watching the clock every half hour or so made this one day feel like a month. My smile widens when the door starts to open.

"Hey, Aiden," Beth said.

My smile fades. She's not who I was expecting to see. Of course, I should have known Beth would be here today.

"Beth," I greet her with a smile back on my face.

"Come on in." Beth steps aside, opening the door wider. "She'll be out in a minute."

Stepping inside, I give E's apartment a quick scan. It has an open kitchen and living area. The total space is only large enough to have one bedroom and one bathroom. The decorations are different shades of blue. I figured that. Blue is her favorite color, but she could never decide which shade she liked the most, so she liked them all.

"I'm so sorry." E rushes out of the bedroom. "Avery at the front desk got another call from Mrs. Gibson about the birthday party she has scheduled on Saturday. I had to call the woman to assure her everything was in order."

"It's not a problem," I assure her, holding out my hand. "Are you ready to go?"

"More than ready." Her smile is infectious.

She hugs Beth and thanks her for everything. I'm guessing Beth helped her get ready for our date tonight. Since I don't have a sister, I have no idea what women do to get ready to go out. My friends have told me plenty of stories on the matter. A few guys complained while others didn't mind. One look at E, and I'm definitely in the *do not mind* category.

E's gorgeous tonight. The only detail I gave her about our date was that I would be taking her to dinner, and she could dress up if she wanted to. To me, she looks good in anything, but I'm going to find more reasons in the future for her to dress up.

The dark blue dress she's wearing clings to every curve of her body. It ends just above her knees. There's still a lot of bare leg showing. Her matching shoes have low heels, nothing crazy, as I've seen on the girls who chased after the band members of Dawson. Her outfit is simple but elegant. It's enough for me to know I'll have to keep my eyes upward all night. Looking down will create some serious problems for me.

When we get to my truck, the first obstacle of my troubles for the night presents itself. She will have to climb into my truck in that dress and those shoes. The running board isn't going to help this situation at all.

With an inward groan, I open the passenger door and offer E my hand to help her climb inside. *Eyes up. Eyes up. Eyes up.* I have to mentally prepare myself for this. The feel of her hand in mine intensifies everything I'm feeling. My eyes stay locked on her face as she steps onto the running board. If only they stayed on her face. Yes, my downward glance got me a glimpse of her thigh. Somehow, she manages to sit on the seat and swing her legs inside gracefully. A moment of jealousy shoots through me. She's done this before. I don't like the thought of anyone else seeing her legs like this.

After closing the door, I blow out a breath. I have to get myself together before I climb into the driver's seat. Beth laughs from the doorway of E's apartment. I glance up and narrow my eyes at her as I walk around the truck. My eyes dart from E to Beth a couple of times. I know. Without a doubt, I know they did this to me on purpose. Beth's laugh is a sure sign.

I climb in and glance over at the little temptress sitting next to me. She has her sweater lying on her lap, covering her beautiful legs. It's still a problem. Her shoulders are now bare. Well, the dress has straps, but they aren't very wide. There's a lot of skin showing. Now, looking up is going to be a problem. I can't be mad at her for messing with me like this, even if I wanted to. Maybe it's just me. Maybe she didn't mean to do this.

"Are you okay, Cowboy?"

The gleam in her eyes has me shifting in my seat. Nope. I was right the first time. She meant to do this to me. This is going to be an interesting night. There's no way I'm going to let her have all the fun.

"Oh, I'm good, Sunshine." I lean over the console and gently tug on her seatbelt. "Are you secure enough?"

I lean a little closer. I know she's secure, but it's not the point. My eyes roam over her face while my finger gently moves up and down her jawline. My eyes linger on her lips as I rub my thumb across the bottom one. Soft, pink, and all mine. Her lips part slightly, and I feel the warmth of her breath run up my arm. I want to kiss her. I really do, but I won't just yet. If she wants to tease and have foreplay, then that's exactly what she's going to get.

"I'm good," she whispers.

"Yes, you sure are," I whisper back.

I wink and give her a devilish grin. It takes every ounce of strength I have to pull away and start the truck. I catch her sharp intake of breath when I move away. This is already the best date of my life, let alone the best first date. We're both playing with fire here. I, for one, don't mind getting burned. I'm going to enjoy seeing just how hot the flames between us could burn.

Chapter Twenty-Three

Etrulia

Beth's bright idea for me to act sexy tonight is backfiring on me fast. I have no idea what I'm doing. It's obvious Aiden does, though. Of course, he would know how to act sexy. Sexy seems to roll off of him in waves. I can't fight it. Those huge waves are pulling me under.

I've only dated two guys, seriously. So, I don't have a lot of practice in being sexy. Beth tried to give me a crash course this afternoon. There's no way I can remember everything she told me. She goes out every weekend. I'm usually at home, curled up with a book or binge-watching something on TV.

My nerves are all over the place. Finally, I peel my eyes from the passenger window and glance at Aiden. He looks good dressed in slacks and a button-up shirt. I can't tell if he's wearing boots or dress shoes, but the all-black outfit seems to fit him. He's not the same guy who left Montana six years ago. As sexy as this looks on him, I think I prefer him in jeans and wearing his cowboy hat. The Stetson is in the backseat behind him.

This sexy attitude isn't me. There's no way I can pull it off all night. I should have never let Beth talk me into this. Is this the type of woman Aiden wants? I wish I hadn't thought of that. Now, I wonder if I'm enough for him. He's dated a lot of women. He had several girlfriends in high school. Karlee was the only repeated one. It was hard enough for me to watch that.

Hearing that Aiden was working with Dawson only made things worse. I've kept up with the band in hopes of seeing him in the pictures and videos. Nothing ever showed up on social media about him. There were no pictures, no videos—nothing. I guess being the sound guy let him go unnoticed. Still, I saw all those women shamelessly throwing themselves at the band members. I assumed the same was happening to Aiden. Now, I really hate those women. Thinking of them clinging to him makes me physically shudder.

"You okay?"

"I'm good." I'm not. I should have never thought of those women.

He slightly tilts his head and narrows his eyes before turning back to the road. He doesn't believe me. I'll have to be more careful at hiding my actions. A cop is trained to sense a lie.

"We're going to Missoula?" We didn't take the road that leads through the town square.

"I have no desire to share you with Hayden Falls tonight." He glances over at me like I've lost my mind.

Wanting to go on a date in Hayden Falls would classify me as crazy. I don't want to hide from anyone. I don't want all those busybodies in town gawking at us all night, either. What Aiden and I have isn't a relationship yet. The last thing we need is someone interfering. If we go to Davis's Diner, someone will meddle.

"There are more people in Missoula," I point out.

As Beth suggested, I lean on the console and tilt my knees toward him. Aiden notices from the corner of his eye and quickly returns his attention back to the road.

"I'm not sharing you with them either," he states firmly. "They can look, but that's it." Aiden pauses and quickly looks me over. "No. They can't look."

Someone is possessive tonight. I lean my head back and laugh. It's not a sexy move, but I can't help it. Seeing him like this is cute.

"If my house was remodeled, I would grill out for you tonight."

Well, that's one way to get me to himself. It would have been fine with me. I don't need fancy dates. I'd feel more comfortable grilling out than acting sexy. Wait.

"Your house? You bought a house?" I stare at him. I had no idea he was even looking for a house.

"I did."

"In Hayden Falls?" I can't believe this.

"In Hayden Falls," he confirms with a smile.

Oh my gosh. Is this real? He's staying? He's really staying. I was scared he would only be here for a few months, a year at the most. If he bought a house, he's making Hayden Falls his home again. I would have gone to Tennessee for him if he asked me to. I don't want to leave Montana, but I would for him. As crazy as our little town is, I love it here. Can I finally have the future I've always dreamed of with him?

"When? Where?" I'm happy, but I'm confused.

"I bought Ms. Rowland's place a few months ago. She moved to Oregon with her daughter."

Months ago? How long has he been planning on coming back? That house and land connect to his family's land. I thought his parents bought it for either Brady or Colton. I had no idea it was Aiden.

"Well, when you remodel, if you need help, I don't mind."

"You want to demo, replace, and paint?" He sounds surprised.

"I do. And when it's finished, you can grill out for me."

"Sunshine, I'll grill out for you while we're remodeling." Aiden's grin widens. "And when we finish, we'll throw a big party. Mom would love that."

We spend the rest of the ride talking about the house. He has some great ideas on how to fix up the place. I'm impressed and proud of him. He deserves something good in his life.

Aiden pulls into Rainer Steakhouse in Missoula. I haven't been here since high school. I stare at him when he opens my door and offers me his hand.

"What's wrong?"

I look toward the restaurant. "I haven't been here since…"

"Your fourteenth birthday?" he finishes my sentence.

He remembers. I slowly nod. His family and mine came here on my birthday that year. Memorial Day was the day before. My aunt didn't want me to feel like my special day was lost because of the town's cookout in the park.

On Memorial Day and the Fourth of July, our town has a huge cookout and a baseball game. The high school teams play against the men of Hayden Falls in a charity game. I was on the girls' softball team in high school, and few of us got to play in the game. That year, we had a private birthday dinner for me here. The following year, things changed, and not for the better. Aiden left that summer, and I couldn't bring myself to come back here.

"Neither have I," he admits. "I remember how much you loved it, and the online reviews are still great."

He's trying to put some humor in this. I take a deep breath. I didn't think men remembered things like this. Aiden was only seventeen when we ate here, and he remembered it. Oh, my goodness. He's going to make me cry. Somehow, I manage not to do so. Garrett never remembered anything I liked.

"I didn't mean to upset you. If you want to go somewhere else, we can."

"No." I quickly put my hands on his shoulders. "It's perfect."

He nods and helps me out of the truck. First dates are supposed to be special. I wasn't expecting this one to tie in with my last good memory with Aiden.

The hostess takes us to a table for two near the windows. This place looks almost exactly how I remember it. To my right, I notice the larger table where we all sat on my birthday and smile. My emotions are all over the place right now. I hope all of this is a good sign. Does Aiden want a relationship with me? I don't think I can handle it if this is just another date for him.

"Do you want the sirloin or the T-bone?" His question pulls me from my thoughts and back to the menu.

"Oh," I gasp. "They have bacon cheeseburgers."

Aiden's face loses all expression. For a moment, I hold a straight face. Only for a moment, though. When I laugh, so does he.

He leans forward and whispers, "This isn't a bacon cheeseburger kind of night."

"What kind of night is it?" I *really* need to know.

"You wear that dress, those shoes, and look at me the way you do, and you think this night involves cheeseburgers?" His voice is deep, and his eyes never leave mine.

What have I gotten myself into? Does acting sexy automatically lead to having sex? Oh, dear. I mean, I want that someday. I lean back in my chair, a little shocked. I should have never trusted Beth on this. Is this night nothing more to him? He's used to women doing this and disappearing forever. I've never done anything like that before.

"Hey." Aiden reaches across the table and takes my hand. I slowly look up until our eyes meet. "I don't know what just went through your mind, but if it's what I think, you have nothing to worry about here."

I don't know what to say. I didn't mean to throw us into such an awkward moment, either.

"I don't do one-night stands, E." His expression is serious, and apparently, he can read my mind. "You look amazing tonight. Not that you don't every day. I'll never push my advantage with you. If I've said or done anything to make you believe otherwise, then I'm so sorry. You mean too much to me, E. I would never hurt you. *Never*," he said.

"Thank you," I whisper. Thankfully, no one is sitting close enough to us to hear our conversation. "It's just…" How do I even tell him?

"Hey." He draws my attention back to him. "You don't have to talk about that right now."

What? Does he know? Has someone told him? My breathing quickens. I'm not ready for him to know.

"Take a deep breath, Sunshine." His voice is soft and soothing, so I do as he asks. "I don't know what happened, but I'm no fool. When you're ready, you can tell me, but not tonight."

He's shaking his head, so I shake mine.

"Not tonight," I repeat.

The waitress comes over to take our order. I'm grateful for the distraction. We need to change the subject anyway. I feel better knowing Brady and Spencer haven't told him what happened to me. Both are in a position to do so. By not telling him, it shows their loyalty, but it puts them in a hard position with Aiden. He deserves the loyalty of his brother and best friend. It's wrong of me to ask them to keep something from him. One day, I'll have to tell him. Well, that is, if we continue dating.

"Sunshine?" Aiden raises an eyebrow and taps the menu.

"T-bone," I reply, bringing a smile to his face.

"Baked potato and salad?" He knows me well. I nod and return his smile. "That's my girl."

Aiden orders us the same meal. It's a typical steak dinner, but it's my favorite. After the waitress leaves, he takes my hand and brings it to his lips. The feel of his lips on my skin makes every part of my body feel warm. This man is my favorite thing of all.

Chapter Twenty-Four

Aiden

Dinner was great. Well, we had that one little glitch when we first got to the restaurant. I'm not sure exactly what caused E to throw her walls up, but I feel it has something to do with her ex-fiancé. That's one situation I need to do more investigating on. Maybe I could help her overcome her fears if I knew what happened to her.

After dinner, we went to a miniature golf course. It's not the same one we went to on her fourteenth birthday. That one closed down a few years ago. This new one was a lot more fun and even had an arcade room. It might be childish, but my girl loves arcade games.

We played a couple of rounds of golf. No, I did not let her bend over in that dress to pick up the balls. It's bad enough several guys got to see her knees. No way was I letting them see her thighs. Yes, I glared at every guy who looked her way, causing them to quickly turn their heads. I'm the only man that dress will rise for. Possessive? Absolutely.

After playing a few arcade games, we left Missoula and headed home. We're having so much fun tonight. I don't want to go home yet. I haven't seen her laugh like this since I've come home. Unfortunately, I'm running out of ideas on what we can do.

I have to work tomorrow and need to sleep, but I need her more. We could go to the lake or the waterfall, but going there would give her the wrong idea. Both spots are famous around here for make-out sessions. Oh, I want her, but I don't want her to think that's all our date is.

If I give in here and date her, even knowing what this town could do to her, then there's no way I'll take her to make-out spots tonight. Why am I even saying *'if'*? After spending time with her tonight, there's no way I can walk away from E. Dating is definitely happening for us.

"I had fun." E twists in the seat to face me. The glow of the radio illuminates her face.

"So did I." My eyes fall to her hands folded over her knees. Those are pointed toward me again. Silently, I cuss my broken arm. Yeah, I sometimes use cuss words in my mind. Rarely do they cross my lips. "I'd love to hold your hand right now, but I'm not supposed to drive one-handed with my left one just yet."

"It's okay. You need to let your arm heal." She understands, but for some reason, she drops her eyes. "I'm not ready for this date to end."

We're on the same page there. It took a lot for her to admit that. She's usually shy. I admire her honesty and boldness tonight. She's stronger than she believes. It may take some time, but I'll help her get past what her ex did to her.

"I don't want it to end either. I've been trying to think of something to do that wouldn't put us in the middle of town with all eyes on us."

Even if nobody were in town, Megan would somehow know we were together tonight. Being in one of her little blog articles would give people more reasons to harass E.

"You don't have to hide me." Her eyes drop to her lap again.

"Sunshine, I'm not hiding you. These people are ruthless. This is our first date. I don't want our wonderful townspeople to be a part of it."

"First date? So, there will be more?" Her voice is full of hope and happiness. I love that sound.

"Only if you want more, pretty lady." I glance over and return her smile. If I weren't driving, I would kiss her.

"I want more," she whispers.

Her soft words have my heart beating faster. I chance another glance at her. She means more than just dates. Wow. It's supposed to be me making those suggestions. It *is* me, but I wasn't expecting *her* to be the one to say so first.

"So do I, Sunshine. So do I." I can't let her think she's alone in this.

"You could show me your house."

That might not be a bad idea. Why didn't I think of it? My house is at the edge of my parent's property. There's not another house around for miles. The house isn't ready to move into yet, but it does have electricity and water. No one from town would see us there. It sounds perfect. I nod in agreement and drive us out to the ranch. Well, technically, my house is part of the ranch.

It only takes a few minutes to drive out to the house. You can get almost anywhere in Hayden Falls within fifteen to twenty minutes. From here, I can take E home without driving through the middle of town. I'm serious about not wanting to share this night with our nosy townsfolk.

Walking into my house has me second-guessing this decision. There's no furniture in this house. It's been sitting empty for months, waiting for the remodel. There's dust everywhere. E can't get dust on her dress. It's too pretty to mess up.

Before I can stop her, E walks further into the room. I brought her through the front door. It's not ready, but I want her to have the homey feeling I get when walking across the huge front porch and into the living room. You can't see it in the dark, but the mountain view from the front porch makes this really feel like home to me. I know I belong here. One look at E in my empty, dusty living room, and I know she belongs here, too.

"This is amazing." She takes everything in as she walks toward the kitchen.

Her beautiful blue eyes are filled with wonder. Is she seeing this house as home? Wow. The feeling that just ran through me has me putting my hand on my chest. Flashes of a future with her leave me speechless.

"I love this kitchen." She runs her finger through the light coat of dust on the counter. She picks up one of the hardware store flyers my dad left here. "Are these the cabinets you're getting?"

I can't fully explain what I feel right now, but the need to touch her is more than I can stand. Walking over to her, I stand behind her and put my hands on her waist. Looking over her shoulder, I see the picture she's referring to. I am considering those cabinets.

"My dad got that at the hardware store. I haven't made a final decision yet." I want her opinion. "Those are pretty. Do you like them?"

"Well." She flips through a couple of the pages and turns to face me. "The first set is white."

"You don't like white cabinets?"

That's kind of shocking. Most of the homes I've been in have white cabinets. My parent's house doesn't, though. I think back to my quick scan around E's apartment. Her cabinets are wood. Maybe white cabinets are a modern thing.

"Why not white?" I'm curious. "Is there a code or rule I don't know about?"

"It's your kitchen. You can install whatever you like. For me, I think the wood look gives a kitchen more character. Besides, if you get married and have kids, you'll be cleaning sticky fingerprints off those white bottom cabinets every day."

Her words have me in a trance. Married? Kids? My eyes drop to her lips. How did kitchen cabinets turn into something so serious?

"Kids?" I whisper. E slowly nods. I can barely speak. The thought of her carrying our child almost drops me to my knees. "Oh, Sunshine, there's going to be kids."

My arm goes around her waist, pulling her to me as my lips claim hers. I know I said no make-out session tonight, but I can't help it. The thought of a family with her causes me to snap. I love this woman. I've waited so long to have her. Moments like this make it hard for me to control myself. I wish I could say this was the sweet, soft kiss she deserves, but it's not. My mouth moves hungrily over hers, laying claim to what's mine, what should have been mine years ago.

Fearing I'm too rough or giving her the wrong idea, I slow the kiss. E's hands slide up my chest and around my neck. Her arms tighten as she pushes up onto her toes. She presses her lips firmly against mine, seeking the passion we were sharing seconds ago. I smile against her lips as I take over the kiss again. She wants more than soft and sweet, so I happily give it to her.

If my arm wasn't broken, and this counter wasn't dirty, I'd pick her up and set her on it. That might not be a good idea, though. Putting her on the counter would cause her short dress to rise and show off her bare thighs. We'd need a bed after that. We can't go there just yet.

Okay. This is getting too hot and steamy. We have to slow this down. The feel of her against me and the hunger of her lips is enough for me to know she won't be the cautious one here. Gentleman. I'm a gentleman. It's going to have to be me. Using all my strength, I slowly pull my lips from hers. The sound of her protest makes me want to give in and claim her lips again.

I have to remind myself again to be the gentleman she deserves. Still needing to touch her, I keep my arm around her and drop my forehead to hers. We're going to need a few minutes to catch our breath.

"E, I'm…" She cuts me off with a finger to my lips.

"Please don't say you're sorry," she whispers.

"I'm not." I shake my head with our foreheads still touching. "But I broke my word to you."

"How?" she asks softly.

"I told you that's not what this night was about."

"It was a kiss, not sex." She shakes her head.

"You're not disappointed in me?" I couldn't bear it if she were.

"Only that the kiss ended."

I lightly laugh. She likes being kissed. Good to know.

"Sunshine, I'll happily kiss you any time you want."

"Promise?"

"Promise." I have no problem making this promise.

"Aiden?"

"Yeah, Sunshine?"

"Kiss me."

A promise is a promise, after all. This one, I'll never break. I press my lips to hers again. This time, I give her the slow, sweet kiss she deserves.

Chapter Twenty-Five

Aiden

Thankfully, my date with E didn't end up in Hayden's Happenings. If anyone in town knew about it, other than Beth and our families, no one said anything. Mission accomplished.

Most of my contact with E since Thursday night has been through phone calls and text messages. Those on-purpose random little meetings around town still happen every day, though.

I'm beyond the point where I can stay away from her, so I don't try anymore. I want to ask her if she'll officially be my girlfriend. I kind of feel like she already is. Is there a timeframe from your first date until you're officially a couple? Naw. There can't be. That sounds dumb.

Last night, E and I stayed up late talking on the phone. After her fourth yawn, even though she swore she wasn't sleepy, I insisted we get some sleep. Hopefully, she isn't dragging as much as I am today.

It's almost lunchtime when I get up from my desk to get another cup of coffee. It's probably my fifth one this morning, but who's counting? If anyone asks, I'll blame my grumpiness on the fact that it's Monday. Lack of sleep has nothing to do with this.

"Here you go." Ms. Ruth hands me another file.

"More paperwork. Lucky me," I grumble as I take the file.

"You won't be on light duty forever." Ms. Ruth pats my arm before going back to the front desk.

Back at my desk, I open the new file. It's more about the missing teenage boy from Missoula. There are a few interviews with some of his classmates we didn't have before. Some of these statements kick my brain into overdrive. It's not one person's interview in particular that sets me on alert. If you take a few sentences from each one, it paints a different story. Am I reaching here? Not sure, but it's enough to make me doubt the original information from the missing person's report.

My attention is pulled away from the file when Spencer runs past my office. What on earth happened? I rush to the door to see Spencer getting into his cruiser. He doesn't turn his lights and siren on, but he's in a hurry. Something serious is going on.

"Ms. Ruth, what's going on?"

"Deputy Murphy got a call," she replies like it's no big deal.

She's no help. I can tell that much. I don't know why people around here make me dig for information. It's like pulling teeth.

"Does he need backup?"

"He didn't say, but even if he did, you can't with your arm." Ms. Ruth gestures to my broken arm.

"Where's he headed?" Maybe knowing this will give me an idea of what's going on.

Ms. Ruth drops her head and pretends to shift some papers around on her desk. Now, I'm even more concerned. Why doesn't she want to tell me where Spencer's going? A thought strikes me, causing my head to snap toward the front doors of the station. Spencer patrols the north side of town.

"Ms. Ruth?" I press her for an answer.

"The inn," she finally replies.

"E." Oh, no. Please let her be okay. I rush toward the door. I have to get to her.

"Aiden! Wait! You shouldn't!" Ms. Ruth calls out, but I ignore her.

I jump in my truck and head the few blocks to the inn. I haven't been assigned a deputy cruiser since I'm still on light duty. I could probably run to the inn on foot from here.

Pulling into the parking lot at The Magnolia Inn, I don't see anything that looks out of place. There's no ambulance here, so it's not a medical emergency. Not that a medical emergency would be any better.

I park next to Spencer's cruiser and run to the front door. Inside, I see no one. There's not even anyone at the front desk. I take a few more steps inside as a young girl comes through a door down the hall. She's younger than E. I know her, but it takes me a few seconds to place who she is. I haven't seen Avery Wilson in years. She's grown up.

"Hey, Aiden." Avery waves at me.

"Hey." I look around again but still don't see anyone else.

"Can I help you?"

"Spencer? Emergency?" This has me totally baffled. I can't even make complete sentences.

"Yeah, Mr. Hayes called him." She's really not explaining anything to me.

"What happened?"

"I don't really know." Avery narrows her eyes and shakes her head, but she doesn't look worried.

"Where is Spencer?" I have to ask bluntly.

"In E's office." Avery looks at me like all of this is normal.

"Take me to E's office," I request in my deputy's voice.

Avery turns, and I follow her down the hall. She pauses outside the door with E's name on it.

"I don't think I'm supposed to interrupt them." Avery looks up at me. She's an employee and doesn't want to get in trouble.

"It's fine," I assure her. "You can go back to the front desk."

Sometimes, giving people directions is the better way to go. It's what I should have done from the beginning with her. My panic state has me on edge to the point I can't think straight. I have no idea what's going on. This involves E. I'm not leaving without answers.

They aren't going to keep me on the outside of this situation. With a light knock, I push the door open and step into the room.

The sight before me knocks the air from my lungs. Spencer and Mr. Hayes are talking over at E's desk. That's not what gets to me. My attention goes straight to E. She's sitting on the couch, trembling in her aunt's arms.

"Aiden?" Spencer looks up at me.

"What's going on?" I close the door and lean back against it.

I want to walk over and pull E into my arms, but I'm not sure she'll let me. She won't even look at me. Instead, she buries herself deeper into her aunt's arms.

"You shouldn't be here." Spencer takes a step toward me.

I hold my hand up to stop him. "If it involves her," I pause and point to E. "I'm not going to be anywhere else but here."

Spencer runs his hand through his hair. Mr. Hayes looks between E and me a few times. I'm not sure if he knows how much I care for his niece. Still, no one speaks. Okay. Whatever this is, they don't want me to know. Only, I'm not leaving. There's no way I can walk away after seeing how broken E is.

The sight of my girl trembling does me in. I need answers, and I'll get them. Right now, I want to wrap her in my arms and comfort her. I've made two steps when Spencer steps in front of me. He looks over his shoulder at E. She drops her head and wipes a tear from her eye.

That's it. I've had enough. Seeing her cry, even when she was a little girl, made me want to kill people. I go to push Spencer aside, but he grabs both of my arms, stopping me.

He looks back at E again. "I told you, as long as you were safe, I'd stay quiet." Without waiting for a reply from her, Spencer walks over to the desk and picks up a piece of paper.

When he walks back over, he looks me in the eye. He's in full deputy mode now. Friendship means everything to him, but his oath to protect means more.

"At the moment, I won't tell you everything. I want to give her that chance." Spencer nods once. I return it. I understand. He holds up the paper. “I don’t know how serious this is yet, but I don’t think we should take any chances.”

Again, I nod once, and he hands me the paper. It’s some kind of huge postcard from a casino and hotel in Vegas. From the looks of it, it’s an invitation to a huge party that will last from Christmas Eve until New Year's Day. I don’t understand what this has to do with E. From what I’ve heard, Hotels and Casinos in Vegas throw parties all the time. They’re announcing this one three months early. I don’t know a lot about Vegas, except it’s wild there. Maybe the bigger the party, the more they need to advertise.

The writing in the bottom right corner catches my eye. *‘Attend the wedding of Garrett Preston. The final date and time will be announced on Christmas Eve.’* My stomach turns as I read over the card again. I look at Spencer and back down to the card in my hand.

I don’t know E’s ex-fiancé’s last name, but I have a feeling this is him. Why would his wedding affect her like this? Does she still have feelings for him? Surely, she doesn’t after what he did to her. I don’t have all the details yet, but I will soon. Sensing that I’m not connecting the dots, Spencer flips the card over in my hand. My heart stops for a moment. Not to worry. Anger has it pumping hard when I read the writing on the back.

‘I’ll see you soon, Sweetheart.’

This fool cannot be serious. Is this a sick joke or a warning that he’s coming for her? What kind of idiot announced something like this? A mentally ill one or an overconfident one. Both types are extremely dangerous. During my training, I saw cases where the victim and the stalker didn’t survive. Spencer and I share a knowing look. Yeah, this could be very serious, and we’re not going to take any chances here.

Chapter Twenty-Six

Etrulia

Finding that postcard in this morning's mail freaked me out. After everything that happened in January, I thought I'd never hear from Garrett again. The postcard was addressed to the inn, but the message was clearly written for me. Does he really think we're still getting married? He's insane if he does.

That message had me so distraught I couldn't form a coherent word. Aunt Sara took the card and handed it to my uncle. He immediately called Spencer's cell phone. Calls on this subject have never gone through dispatch or the main number at the sheriff's office.

Before his retirement, Deputy Whitlock handled my case. I hate those words. *My case* makes me feel even more like a victim. He was kind and understanding. He's a sweet elderly gentleman, and I felt comfortable around him. His ability to keep this matter quiet in a town full of gossipers amazed me. I still don't know how he managed to pull it off.

When Deputy Whitlock left for Texas, Uncle Silas asked Sheriff Barnes if he would assign Spencer to our side of town. I don't understand that program, but I admire the sheriff for trying to appease the town council.

Thankfully, Spencer agreed to switch sections. He was there that day and already knew everything about the case. I don't want to have to tell my story to another deputy. I had mixed emotions when I heard Aiden was taking Deputy Whitlock's place. I was really happy he was coming back to Montana, but I didn't want him to know what happened to me. It only confirmed I was the quiet, weak little pushover this town thought I was.

Spencer got here within minutes of receiving the call from my uncle. I wasn't expecting Aiden to follow him. As much as I want to keep this from him, I won't be able to much longer. His job will require him to know all the details.

Only Spencer, Deputy Whitlock, and the sheriff know what happened. They just don't know who's responsible. Until now, there hasn't been any communication with Garrett. Beth is the only one who knows Garrett assaulted me. The others have figured it out. I'm sure of it. Still, whenever anyone asks who hurt me, I clam up and cry for days. My anxiety over the situation is one of the reasons my aunt and uncle insisted I see a therapist. Sheriff Barnes and the victim's advocate in Billings suggested it several times. Finally, I gave in.

"Treat this as a Priority One." Aiden hands the postcard back to Spencer.

"My thoughts exactly." Spencer pauses. His eyes dart to me and back to Aiden. "I'll need your help on this."

"Not a problem." Aiden's eyes stay locked on me.

Beth rushes through the door, startling everyone. She hurries over and sits down on my other side. Immediately, she wraps her arms around me. Being sandwiched between her and my aunt is comforting, but it's not enough to settle my fears.

"What do you need?" Beth's voice is full of panic.

"I don't know," I admit honestly.

"Why don't you give Rachel a call?" Aunt Sara suggests.

Rachel Montgomery is my therapist. Her office is in Missoula. She came highly recommended by the victim's advocate in Billings.

Surprisingly, Rachel is only in her late twenties, which made it easier for me to connect with her. After a few weeks of visiting her, I felt I could trust her. Slowly, I began to open up to her. If she had been the forty-something-year-old strict therapist I was expecting, I would have ended sessions with her after a couple of weeks. Most of our talks are now through phone calls and video chats. They cost the same as an in-person visit, but I don't have to leave the safety of my apartment. There were a few times when I desperately needed that security.

"Come on. I'll take you home and get you settled in. When you're ready, you can call Rachel." Beth's always knows what I need.

It sounds like a good idea, so I nod and wipe my eyes with a tissue. Beth and Aunt Sara help me stand. Spencer steps in front of us before we can get to the door.

"I don't know if he's messing with you here, but due to the past circumstances, I have to treat this as a serious threat." Spencer looks over his shoulder at Aiden and back to me. "I'm sorry, E, but I can't keep my promise to you on this any longer. I'll look into this." He holds up the postcard. "As long as nothing else happens, I'll give you a few days to talk to him."

I know he means well, and I'm grateful he's kept his promise this long. Still, this day came sooner than I thought it would. I nod, but I keep my eyes downcast.

After Spencer moves, Aiden steps forward. He's struggling to be my friend and a deputy. This puts us all in a tough situation. I want to tell him everything, but I'm scared to. What will he think of me? Will he still want to go out with me? When he finds out how broken and battered I am, he will never look at me the same way. I'm not sure I can handle that.

He doesn't speak. He reaches his hand up to touch my face. Any other time, it would have been a sweet endearment. Today, it causes me to automatically take a frightful step back. I lean closer to Beth. As if my actions slapped him in the face, Aiden drops his hand and takes several steps back. He can already see how damaged I am. It's probably for the best.

"I'm sorry." I drop my head and wipe the tears from the corner of my eye.

"Don't apologize." Aiden's voice is calm and even. He's in cop mode. "I'll check on you later."

"Thank you." I keep my eyes on the floor. This hurts us both, but I do appreciate his understanding here.

Sensing that I need to get out of this room, Beth tightens her arm around me.

"Come on. Let's get you home." Beth leads me out of the inn and to my apartment.

Once we're inside the apartment, Beth and I collapse onto the couch, where I break down completely and cry even more. I hate falling apart like this, but I don't know how to overcome my fear. This is no way to live, and I don't want to do it anymore.

I'm still on the couch in Beth's arms when I wake an hour later. Best friend ever. I didn't mean to fall asleep, but I guess that's what my body needed.

"Why don't you get a shower, and I'll get us something to eat," Beth suggests.

"You're going to cook?" I'm surprised.

"I said *get* not *make*." Beth rolls her eyes. Even she knows she's not the best cook. "I can order us a pizza or something from the diner. Which do you prefer?" She already has her phone out.

"Pizza sounds good."

Beth shoos me away with her hands as she places our order with Antonio's Pizza Palace in town. We have no idea who Antonia is. The restaurant is owned by a guy named Ed. Still, our little pizza parlor has the best pizza within a hundred miles.

The moment I step into the shower, I start to feel a little better. The warm water eases the tension in my body. It feels so good. I stand under the spray until the water starts getting cold. After adjusting the temperature, I hurry to finish. I have no plans on going out again, so I slip into my pajamas. When I return to the kitchen, the pizza box is already sitting on the counter.

"That was fast," I say as I sit down at the table.

Beth gives me a look that says I was in the shower longer than necessary. She understands and doesn't call me out on it.

"I called Rachel and told her you needed to talk." Beth hands me a plate. "You can call her after we eat." She grabs a plate for herself and sits down next to me.

"Thank you, Beth." I take her hand in mine and give it a little squeeze. I don't know what I'd do without her.

"Are you going to talk to Aiden?" Beth asked.

With a deep sigh, I lean back in my chair. I can't avoid this forever. Eventually, Aiden will find out whether I tell him or not.

"I guess I have no choice." If I could find a way out of this, I would. "You heard Spencer. He's going to tell him."

"Please don't hate Spencer." Beth grabs my hand. "Aiden is his best friend, and he's kept this quiet for eight months. He hates lying to Aiden. He doesn't want to break his promise to you, but you're in trouble now. It's his job to protect you."

"I could never hate Spencer." I blink back tears. "He shouldn't have to lie to Aiden because of me."

"Why are you afraid to tell Aiden?"

"It will change everything. He'll see how broken I really am and run back to Karlee. I wasn't ready to date, but I did it because it was him." Beth probably already knows all this, but I could never lie to her.

"Look at me." Beth waits until I look up. "You're not giving Aiden enough credit here. He will *never* take Karlee back. He loves *you*. You should have seen how he took care of you that night you were drunk."

"What?" I remember dancing with Aiden, but not much after that.

"He held your hair while you were sick and put you to bed. You asked him never to leave you again, and he promised he wouldn't. Girl, that man cried. Aiden is in this with you for the long haul."

Her words surprise me. Why hasn't she told me this before now? Does it make a difference? My heart wants it to. My mind is so clouded with fear that I can't process all this.

After we ate, I called Rachel and told her what happened. She agrees with Beth and Spencer about almost everything. As always, she encourages me to move forward in my relationships, even the ones with my family and friends. She never pushes me too far out of my comfort zone. She firmly believes that baby steps eventually get you to bigger ones. We set up an in-office appointment for the middle of next week. A day trip to Missoula with Beth would do me some good. Sitting at home in fear makes me feel caged in.

At the end of the day, Beth refuses to leave me. My couch pulls out into a bed, so she makes herself at home. I don't even try to protest. I need her here tonight. Spencer stopped by to let me know he hasn't found anything out yet. Still, he's having the third-shift deputies make extra rounds by the inn for a while.

I lay in bed staring at the ceiling. There are nightlights throughout the apartment, but my bedside lamp will be on all night. I hate feeling scared. I glance at my bedside table when my phone dings with a text. With shaky hands, I reach for it. Garrett doesn't have this number. I'm safe.

Aiden: *Hey, Sunshine.*

I smile. He's still using his nickname for me. That means a lot to me.

Me: *Hey, Cowboy.*

Whether I lose him or not, I'm going to have to be honest with him. One of my biggest fears is that Garrett could show up here and hurt my family. If my aunt and uncle get hurt because of me, I'll never forgive myself. I'd feel better if my cousin, their only child, was here. Tyler's a travel photographer. He's in Australia on a photoshoot. He's abroad more than he's in the US nowadays.

Aiden: *I'm here.*

He's not pushing for answers right now. I'm so grateful for that.

Me: *Thank you. Goodnight, Cowboy.*

Aiden: *Goodnight, Sunshine.*

Chapter Twenty-Seven

Aiden

Patience is definitely *not* a virtue. I don't care who claimed it was. It's a lie. The past few days have surely tested my patience. Since the postcard from Vegas showed up, I've sent E Good Morning and Goodnight texts. That's it. That's all the contact I've had with her.

I've made regular rounds by the inn, like every deputy on the force. The other guys tell me they don't know the details. They've only been told we need to keep a close eye on the inn for a while. Spencer is the only one who knows what's going on, and he won't tell me anything. He wants to tell me, and if E doesn't soon, he will. The only problem is, it's not fast enough for me.

I've stopped by E's apartment at the end of each day. She won't see me. At least she's being taken care of. One of her friends spends the night with her every night. Beth, Katie, Sammie, and Ally take turns staying with her. It's good she has a close and loving friendship with each of them, but I want to be the one to watch over her.

Going against everyone's wishes might be a bad idea, but I can't sit idle when there's a threat against my girl. I have Wednesday and

Thursday off this week. Wednesday is my scheduled day for physical therapy and doctor's appointments. I don't have a doctor's appointment this week. So, after physical therapy was over, I left Missoula, heading for Billings.

Brady and E went to the same college in Billings. I got a hotel room near the college last night. Today, I'm going to pay a surprise visit to my little brother. That's just my cover, so I brought my uniform with me. Technically, I am here on business even if the Sheriff didn't send me. I'm here to investigate what happened to E back in January.

Brady was surprised when I texted him. He happily met me for lunch in the café across the street from the college. He didn't think it was odd I showed up in uniform today. A few students eyed me closely, though. I might need to make a few more unannounced visits here just to make sure my little brother isn't running around with the wrong crowd.

Brady was shocked to hear about E getting the postcard. No one has called or texted him about it yet. Like Spencer, he doesn't want to betray E. He also said if she doesn't tell me soon, he'll tell me what he suspects. He's already told me all he can prove.

After leaving my brother, I make my way to the college security office. I'm not officially assigned to E's case, but it doesn't mean I haven't snooped around. While Ms. Ruth was at lunch on Tuesday, I slipped into the records room and pulled E's file. Surprisingly, it had little information that would help me. That's why I'm here today.

The lady at the front desk sends me back to see the guard on duty today. I lightly tap on the door before entering the office.

"Deputy Maxwell, how can I help you?" Cole Willis stands to shake my hand.

"I'm here to discuss a case that happened back in January. If you have the time?" I shake his hand before taking the seat he gestured to.

"I'll help if I can. Which case are you referring to?" Cole folds his hands on the desk.

"It involved Etrulia Hayes."

Cole's face loses all expression. He sighs and nods.

"That was a bad one." He takes a deep breath.

"I know, and I would really like to get to the bottom of it."

"I don't know how I can help you. I've already told the police here and your office in Hayden Falls what I know."

"You were on duty that day?" This might be my lucky day. He nods again. "Have you remembered anything new? Has another student come forward with more information?"

"No, and I've watched the security footage for weeks afterward, trying to find something. The assault didn't happen on campus. So, there's not much in the videos." Cole blows out a breath.

"Do you mind sending me those? Maybe a fresh set of eyes can catch something." I hand him my card.

"Has something new happened?"

"Miss Hayes got a postcard from Mr. Preston on Monday."

"So, she finally named the jerk." Cole sounds relieved.

"Not officially, but everything points to him." I watch him closely. It's clear to me he's had no formal training in law enforcement.

"I agree, and I hope he pays for hurting that sweet girl. It's bad enough what he did, but dropping her off on the side of the road like that." Cole pauses and shakes his head. His eyes are full of hate. "He's evil. He shouldn't have been allowed to stay and graduate."

"Where exactly did he drop her off?" This is new information for me.

"A few miles outside of town. The poor girl had to walk at least a mile to a gas station, Hank's Gas and Go. They called 911, and she was taken to the clinic not far from here." Cole has no problem giving me the information. He wants Preston arrested as much as I do.

The clinic is next on the list of the places I plan on visiting today. I'll stop at the gas station on my way out of town.

"Thank you for your help, Mr. Willis." I stand and shake his hand again. "I'll watch for your email."

"You'll let me know if you finally get this guy, right?"

"I'll make a point to do just that," I promise and leave the office.

At the clinic, I'm sent to speak to a nurse named Glenda. She's an elderly lady who seems to genuinely love her job. She gasped loudly when I told her I was here about E's case.

"We gave your office a copy of her medical records at her family's request. Due to privacy laws, I can't give you another copy without written permission." Nurse Glenda gives me a tight smile.

"I understand, Ma'am." I smile and give her my country charm. "I stopped by today to see if someone might remember something more from that day. Even a small detail could help the case."

Sometimes, lying and sweet-talking helped to get information out of people. I hate doing it, but I'll do anything for E.

"Sadly, there's not much else we can tell you other than what's in the medical records. She didn't talk much while she was here. She gave us her name and asked us to call her family. We moved her to a private room we have for assault victims and contacted the police department. Several hours later, your Sheriff showed up with her family. An aunt and uncle, I believe." Nurse Glenda's face drops. She closes her eyes for a moment. She's as emotional as the security guard at the college was.

"Yes, Miss Hayes lives with her aunt and uncle."

"I wish I could help you more. Whoever hurt that sweet girl needs to be in prison." Nurse Glenda pauses and looks me in the eye. "I will say this. She knows who assaulted her."

"She does," I agree.

"Did she finally name him?"

"She got a postcard a few days ago. Her reaction was enough to confirm the matter. Sadly, before charges can be pressed, Miss Hayes will have to officially give us his name." I stand and shake her hand. "Thanks for your time."

"Deputy Maxwell, promise me you will protect her." Nurse Glenda doesn't let go of my hand.

"I promise. I will protect her with my life," I vow.

She releases my hand, and I walk out to my truck. I have one more stop, and I have a feeling I'm not going to like what I find there. I get in the truck and drive to Hank's Gas and Go. Hopefully, they'll talk to me.

Luck's on my side today. Once again, I found someone who was on duty the day E was hurt. Professionally, I should say assaulted, but personally, the word is hard for me to say.

"There were only a couple of cars in the parking lot when she walked up. I didn't find out until the police came that she walked about a mile in the snow to get here." Monica points to the counter in the center of the store. "I was making coffee when I saw her collapse outside the door. A couple of guys at the pumps helped to get her inside."

I look from the coffee pots toward the doors. There's a clear view from there. The image the clerk describes makes my stomach turn, and my blood boil. I want to scream and punch something. Preferably, one Garrett Preston, but I have to hold it together.

"She was badly beaten. She had a black eye, busted lip, and was freezing. I'm pretty sure her arm was broken, too. The ambulance took her. The cops came later and asked questions, but that's all I know. I never heard anymore."

"Cameras?" My voice cracks with that one word.

"The manager gave the video to the police."

"Thank you." I turn to leave. I have to get out of here.

"Officer, is that girl okay?" Monica's question halts me at the door.

Usually, I wouldn't give information like this out, but Monica helped E that day, and she seemed genuinely worried.

"She physically healed. Emotionally? She's getting there."

"Good." Monica sighs with relief. She lifts her hand to say goodbye. I return the gesture.

The five-hour ride back to Hayden Falls was one of the longest of my life. There was too much going through my mind. At one point, I had to pull over and get myself together.

I assumed what happened to E was heartbreaking. With all of my training, I thought I could handle it. I was wrong. When I think of E, all I can see is pure happiness. That jerk hurt her and took her happiness from her. Eventually, I'll have to see those videos the Sheriff has. There's no point in trying to prepare myself for what I'll see. After everything I've heard today, those videos are going to break me wide open.

While sitting on the side of the road, I vow to myself, and silently to E, that no matter what it takes or how long, I'll do everything in my power to help her heal. One day, her happiness will be real again. There'll be no more fake smiles and pretending for her. I know she's faking it most of the time. She never liked attention being on her.

I make another vow before pulling back onto the road. I'll see to it that Garrett Preston pays for what he did to her.

Chapter Twenty-Eight

Aiden

Calm, cool, and casual are part of my character. My father and grandfather helped to instill those traits into me when they raised me to be a gentleman. My law enforcement training took it to another level. Since Thursday, I've been struggling to hang onto it. Only one thing gets under my skin and sends me over the edge. Well, it's someone, Etrulia Hayes. I haven't seen her since Monday, and it's seriously starting to drive me crazy.

My little day trip to Billings has cracked my control. I don't have all the details, but for the most part, I can piece it together. If it would do any good, I'd storm into the Sheriff's office and demand to see the security footage he has on E's case. It won't work. Sheriff Barnes can be hardcore when he wants to be. That's probably why everybody, including myself, wonders why the man went easy on me. Waiting around for answers is getting harder by the day.

First thing Saturday morning, Spencer walks into my little office and closes the door behind him. I avoided him yesterday. I haven't told him about my trip. I'm still trying to process everything I found out.

"How's Brady?" Spencer drops into the chair in front of my desk and stares at me for a moment.

I sigh and lean back in my chair. He knows. There's no point in trying to deny it now.

"He's good."

"You couldn't wait, could you?" Spencer never takes his eyes off mine.

"Could you have?"

Spencer's shoulders slump, and he breaks eye contact with me. I hate I hid this from him, but no one would tell me anything.

"No," he finally replies. "How much did you find out?"

"I wasn't shown any evidence. All of that is supposed to be here somewhere. I'm guessing the Sheriff has a hidden file on the case tucked away," I tell him. Spencer nods. "I can still put most of it together."

"I contacted a friend in Vegas. Garrett Preston's wedding is the highlight of that party. However, the bride's name hasn't been released yet." At least he's sharing information now.

"Why hasn't he been arrested? We all know he hurt her."

"She won't name him, and there's nothing of him on camera except in the college parking lot. Brady witnessed that. Preston admits they argued. He said they stopped at a park near her dorm, and she walked away. He thought she was going back to her dorm room. He claims he has no idea how she got to that gas station." Spencer knows it's a lie.

"Who's Rachel?" I remember Beth and Mrs. Hayes mentioning this woman on Monday.

"Her therapist."

She's in therapy. Good. She sure needs it after what she's gone through.

"I just want you to know I never liked keeping this from you. I begged her not to ask this of me." Spencer looks me in the eye again. This has bothered him for a long time. "If you had seen her, you would understand why I gave in to her pleas."

"Don't worry about it. We're good here," I assure him. Our friendship will never be in danger. "Why doesn't she want me to know?"

Spencer lightly laughs and shakes his head. "For two of the smartest people I know, you're both dumb."

I gape at him. He only laughs harder.

"Aiden, she's loved you just as long as you have loved her, if not longer. I don't know why you didn't pursue something with her when we were younger."

"Because of the legal aspect of it. Eighteen and fifteen is a problem. We all saw what happened to that boy in Willows Bend," I remind him.

"Yeah. That was bad."

When we were sixteen, an eighteen-year-old boy in the neighboring town was caught in a girl's bedroom. The girl was fifteen. Her father went into a rage, causing the boy to jump out the window without any clothes on. It didn't matter that the two had been dating for nearly a year. In the end, all that mattered was that he was an adult, and she was a minor. The girl's father pressed charges, and the boy went to prison for statutory rape. Even though they got married later, had two kids, and are still together to this day, that man will forever have a record.

The case in Willows Bend was exactly why I didn't try to date E during high school. When she turned eighteen, I was coming back for her. Only, I destroyed my plan less than two months before I graduated. I stayed in Hayden Falls through July of that year, working off the debt. Once most of the financial debt was paid, Sheriff Barnes shipped me off to Tennessee.

"If she doesn't tell you soon, I'll tell you the case details. The personal details, I'll leave those to her." Spencer slides a picture across the desk to me. "That's him. Just in case he shows up in town, you'll know what he looks like."

Picking up the photo, I get my first look at Garrett Preston, the lowest form of life on the planet. I'd say he wasn't bad-looking if I didn't know how evil this guy was. He's clean-cut, with dark blonde hair, and wearing a business suit. His expression says he's cocky. No doubt he has a problem with authority. The way he holds himself, he comes from a lot of money. He's nothing like someone I'd expect E to be with.

"Do the other guys know?" Surely, I'm not the only one out of the loop.

Spencer shakes his head. "The Sheriff is going to talk to them and have everyone look out for Preston. All they'll know for now is that he could be causing problems at the inn."

It's only a matter of time before the rest of the deputies figure it out, but I appreciate how the Sheriff is trying to respect E's privacy. I stand and hand the picture back to Spencer. If I look at this jerk's face any longer, I'll punch something.

"Thanks for taking care of her," I walk over and put my hand on his shoulder.

"She's family. It's what we do." Spencer puts an arm around my shoulders. "I knew how much you cared about her. You couldn't be here, so I gladly took your watch."

Wow. He's going to make me cry. Instead, we give each other a bro hug and walk out to the front lobby.

"I'm going to walk around town for a while." I wave to Ms. Ruth and head out the door.

It's Saturday. E usually walks around town. If she's feeling better, I just might run into her today. A coffee from Beth's Morning Brew sounds good right about now.

Before going to the coffee shop, I walk around the town square first. As I pass one of the side streets, movement catches my eye. Usually, I wouldn't have noticed it, but I have this weird ability to sense whenever she's near.

E's standing in front of the post office, dropping envelopes into the blue outdoor mailbox. When she sees me, she doesn't smile. That sure hurt. I love her smile. She gives me a shy little wave, though. I wave back and gesture toward the square. Surprisingly, she doesn't run away. Instead, she nods and walks up to me.

"Hey, Cowboy."

"Hey, Sunshine." I want to touch her, but after the way she flinched on Monday, I don't risk it. "How are you feeling?"

"Better." She quickly looks away. "I'm sorry you had to see me like that."

"Don't be." As much as I want to talk more about what happened, I don't think she's ready yet. "I'm heading to Beth's. How about a cup of coffee?" It's better to change the subject for now.

"That's where I'm heading." She looks up at me and smiles.

That's what I want to see. She's so beautiful.

"Well, let's go together," I suggest, and we start walking towards the coffee shop.

When her tiny hand goes around my right arm, I try not to sigh too deeply. Her simple touch feels so good. Being a gentleman, I bend my elbow and place my left hand over hers on my arm. People are already looking at us, but I don't care. If E does, she doesn't show it.

"We need to talk."

"We do." The ball's in her court here, so I don't push. We'll take this at her pace.

"How about dinner on Wednesday?"

"Why, E Hayes, are you asking me on a date?" I pretend to be shocked.

She giggles at my silly antics, and just like that, the world feels right again.

"I guess I am." She giggles again. She's not the type of girl to ask guys on dates.

"Where would you like to go on this date?" I'll take her anywhere.

"My place?" she suggests nervously.

To keep the humor going, I put my left hand to my chest and gasped loudly. For a moment, I gape at her.

"E Hayes? Your place? I might not be that kind of guy," I tease.

She drops her head back and wholeheartedly laughs. It's the best sound in the world.

"What would you like for dinner? I'll pick it up."

"Oh, no need for that. This was my idea."

"I don't care whose idea it is. I will never let you pay for anything on a date." As much as I want to keep the humor going, I'm dead serious about this.

"I was going to cook dinner." She bites her bottom lip.

We pause on the sidewalk and stare at each other. A home-cooked meal? No woman has ever done that for me. I happen to know she's already one of the best cooks in town. Mom told me about some of the dishes E brought to the town cookouts and dinners when our families got together.

"You're going to make me dinner? At your place?"

"No." She shakes her head. "In the gazebo."

Is she serious? I quickly look over to the gazebo in the center of the town square and back to her. For a moment, she has a straight face, but she can't contain her laughter. Okay. I admit it. She got me there.

"Okay, Sunshine. You cook dinner, and I'll pick up dessert from Sweet Treats. What would you like?"

"Cake."

Yeah, I knew that.

"What kind?" I ask, even though I doubt her favorite has changed.

"White cake with buttercream icing."

Yep. It's still her favorite. I'll place a special order today and surprise her with blue roses on it.

"I think I can handle that." I nod.

"Oh, I'm sure you can," she says softly.

E lifts her chin and looks me in the eye. The humor is gone. We're not talking about cake anymore. Every primal instinct I have wants to grab her around the waist and haul her against me. *Can't do that here.* I'm fighting hard to hold it together.

"What am I going to do with you?"

"I can think of a few things," she whispers.

Oh, my heart just stopped. I'm going to lose it right here on the sidewalk. This little temptress will be my undoing. We gotta change the subject.

"What were we doing?" I swallow hard and force myself to look away from those big blue eyes.

"Getting coffee."

Yeah. No. That's not what we were just doing, and she knows it.

"Right. Coffee." Getting coffee has never affected every part of my body before. "Let's do that."

Surprisingly, somehow, we're standing in front of the coffee shop. I blow out a breath and open the door for her. I'm shocked. I can't fully process what just happened between us. This is a side of her I didn't know existed. Oh, I've dreamed about it but never did I expect to see it. For now, she needs to get past some things. Once she does, I'm going to unlock every ounce of passion Etrulia Hayes has in her. Today, we're getting coffee. Yeah, even though I can smell it, coffee is the furthest thing on my mind right now.

Chapter Twenty-Nine

Etrulia

This morning, I had an in-office appointment with Rachel in Missoula. Beth took the day off to go with me. At my request, she even sat in on the session with me.

Over the past few months, I've told my therapist almost everything that's happened to me. From the abuse I experienced as a child, which brought me to live with my aunt and uncle when I was eight, to the attack in January. The only thing I haven't done, once again, is to name my attacker. I've talked with Rachel about my relationship with Garrett and the attack, but I've never linked the two together.

Rachel is a professional. She's probably put the pieces together already. After today's visit, I'm sure she has. She told me I have what's known as Battered Women's Syndrome. I shuddered when she said those words. It's wrong to have a medical name for this. My little online search on my phone while Beth drove us home revealed that this condition is linked to an intimate partner. Rachel knows.

I'm not sure if my situation is one of the cases where Rachel is required by law to report it to the authorities. It's why I haven't admitted that Garrett was my attacker. I don't know why I'm so scared to say it. Garrett deserves to go to jail for what he did. Whenever someone asks me who hurt me, other than Beth, I clam up.

Aiden had physical therapy in Missoula today, but we didn't run into him. Usually, after a visit with my therapist, I get quiet and spend a few days processing everything. I don't want to do that today. It's why I asked Aiden to have dinner with me at my apartment tonight. We need to talk. I'm going to rip the band-aid off and get it over with.

Around six, Aiden shows up with a box from Sweet Treats Bakery. I reach for it, but he holds it away from me. He's such a tease. I mean, come on, that's cake.

"If I give this to you now, you'll eat dessert before dinner." He winks at me and puts the box in the fridge.

"You're no fun," I pout.

"Oh, I'm lots of fun." He walks over to me and tucks a lock of my hair behind my ear. "I promise you can have cake after dinner."

"Fine." I have no choice but to give in.

"You, my dear, have made fried chicken. There's no way we're ruining our dinner with cake first."

Yes, I made fried chicken. It's one of Aiden's weaknesses. Aunt Sara shared her family recipe with me. Her fried chicken is famous around here. It's one of the first dishes to disappear at cookouts and events. Rumor has it that Uncle Silas married her for her fried chicken. The joke is cute, but I know it's because he loves her.

Aiden and I make small talk all through dinner. It's weird, but it helps to ease my nerves a little bit. It's been two months since the bus accident he was in. The cast might come off his arm next week. He's beyond ready for that. He's also started remodeling his house. Well, the plumbing and electrical contractors have been sent in to get everything up to code.

"You should talk to Sawyer Gibson if you need help with the carpentry work. He started his own business a couple of years ago. Everyone says he does excellent work."

"I didn't know that." Aiden leans back in his chair. "Next weekend, Spencer and some of the guys from the station and the Fire Department are coming over to help get things started."

"Oh, that's great." I stand up and take our plates to the sink. "Four and Pit are really good helpers, too."

"E, I kinda want to live in that house." Aiden shakes his head. "There's no way those two are touching it."

"They're not *that* bad."

Aiden stares at me. He doesn't agree.

"Look. I know you are friends with Four. I don't understand that relationship at all, but I respect it. Still, he's not touching my house." Aiden gets up to help me put the leftover food away.

"Okay, but he really is a good painter." I refill our tea glasses.

"E, we aren't using spray cans to paint the house." He looks absolutely horrified.

I laugh at the thought. Four does tag. Aiden's house would be an original if Four got ahold of it. Still, I let the matter drop. Aiden's not going to let Pit and Four help.

"Are you ready for cake?"

"Sure." This is cozy, but we both know it's not the only reason we're here tonight. "We can take it and our tea to the couch. If you'd like?"

Aiden nods and picks up both glasses of sweet tea while I cut two cake slices. It was so sweet of him to get blue roses on top.

I'm not sure if I'm ready for this conversation, but the small talk is starting to drive me insane. He follows me to the living room and sets our tea on the coffee table. We sit on the couch quietly eating cake for a few minutes while I figure out where to start. Once our empty dessert plates are on the coffee table, it's time to talk. Stalling isn't helping my nerves.

"As a cop, I'm sure you're already figured most of it out." I sigh and look straight ahead. The tv isn't on, but it's my focus point right now. "I don't know where to start, but there's something I need to know first. Am I talking to the cop or my friend?"

Aiden takes my hand in his and gives it a little squeeze. We're sitting shoulder to shoulder. I look up and find his soft brown eyes tenderly watching me. His eyes are full of compassion and maybe something more.

"I'm not a cop tonight," he whispers. "But I am definitely more than just your friend."

I nod and look back at the tv. I want to read a lot into his words, but I can't right now. I need to do this.

"Garrett and I were engaged for a year." I hate telling Aiden this story. "He was angry because I wouldn't set a wedding date."

"Why wouldn't you set a date?"

"Because I didn't love him," I reply honestly.

"You accepted his proposal." His voice is filled with pain.

"Yes and no. I mean, I did. But not because I wanted to marry him. He floored me with it one night while we were out with some friends from college. I hate having all those eyes on me. I froze. All the girls were nodding their heads, so I nodded mine, too. I shouldn't have." I take a deep breath and sit up straight. Telling this story doesn't get any easier.

"What ended the engagement?"

Even though he said he's not a cop tonight, he's asking a lot of questions. Maybe I need it this way.

"He wanted a wedding date, or he was taking me to Vegas to elope. I still put it off. A couple of weeks into the new semester, he found me and Brady building snowmen. Garrett hated Brady. No matter how much I insisted that Brady and I were just friends, he didn't believe me." I take another deep breath. Aiden patiently waits.

"Garrett was furious that day. He accused me of having an affair with Brady. I've never thought of Brady like that. Still, he insisted I was cheating on him. His driving was wild, and it really scared me. I finally convinced him to pull over. We stopped at a park near my dorm room." I pause and run my fingers through my hair.

"Why would he think you were cheating on him?"

"Because nothing remotely romantic happened between us in over ten months."

Aiden shifts next to me. I'm not sure why. Does he think I was having an affair?

"I wasn't cheating on Garrett," I assure him. I don't want Aiden to think I would do something like that. "I knew I didn't love him. He had a temper. I didn't see it the first few months we dated, but he got worse each time it happened. I just didn't like him touching me."

"You felt trapped and were afraid to end the relationship."

For someone who's *not* a cop right now, he sure sounds like one. He probably can't help it, though. It's part of his training.

"I was. I was afraid he would hurt me. A lot of good putting it off did. I got hurt anyway."

Aiden squeezes my hand again. I take a few deep breaths, just like Rachel taught me.

"Garrett was going to go back and hurt Brady that day. He said he was going to break Brady's arm so he couldn't play baseball. Garrett knew I didn't love him. We fought in the car. He said he knew I was in love with somebody. He was shaking me really hard, my nose was bleeding, and like an idiot, I admitted that I was, but it wasn't Brady." I wipe a tear from my eye. I've always loved Aiden.

After a few minutes, I continued, "He started driving again. I couldn't see where we were going. He was screaming at me the whole time. He pulled over and started hitting me again. I raised my arm to block the blows. He grabbed it and bent it until it snapped. My head hit the passenger window. The next thing I knew, I was shoved out into the snow. I managed to walk to a store. I have no idea where it was. I woke up at the clinic near the college." I blow out a breath and lean further back against the couch.

"E," Aiden whispers my name.

I turn my head towards him, but I don't look him in the eye. I can't.

"Can I hold you?" he asks softly.

Slowly, I lift my eyes to meet his. He looks as broken as I feel.

"Please." I can barely get the word out.

Aiden turns sideways into the corner of the couch. I don't have a chance to move. With his right arm, he pulls me against him. His muscular arms feel safe. I haven't felt this safe in a long time. Closing my eyes, I lean into him. He doesn't have to tell me he loves me. I can feel it.

Aiden knows everything now. Telling him didn't make the pain go away. It's a step toward healing, though. If Aiden doesn't walk away from me, it's worth reliving what happened. Hopefully, love will be strong enough to hold us together.

Chapter Thirty

Aiden

Sometimes, you want to know things until you do, and then you wish you didn't. Hearing E's story broke me in ways I didn't know were possible. She admitted to her ex that she was in love with someone. She meant me. That douchebag hurt her because she loves me. It was all I could do to hold myself together in front of her that night. When I was alone, I lost it on several occasions.

It didn't help when Spencer took me to his office, locked the door, and showed me the security videos of the day E was attacked. Those videos sent me further over the edge than I already was. I'm going to kill Garrett Preston on sight. Okay, I know I can't actually do that, but man, do I want to.

Some of the videos were at odd angles, but they were clear enough to understand what was happening. That scumbag grabbed her wrist and practically dragged E out to the parking lot. In one frame, there was no mistaking how frightened E was of this guy. He shoved her into the car, and my brother even chased the car through the parking lot. I now understand why Brady felt responsible for what happened that day. He failed to reach her in time, but he sure tried. According to the college security files, Brady contacted them immediately. Still, it wasn't enough.

The video from the gas station and the medical file from the clinic will probably haunt me for a long time. Seeing her collapse outside the gas station and the photos taken at the clinic ripped my heart out. Spencer stood behind me with his hands on my shoulders. It took all of his strength to hold me down.

Some days, I was so out of control I had to go to the lower pasture where my brothers and I set up a target range when we were kids. I lost count of how many targets I destroyed, but it was the only way I could release what I was feeling.

Naturally, at dinner one night, Colton complained. I was scaring the cattle. He told me I needed to chill out. Too bad for him he caught me on a bad day. I told him *exactly* where he could shove his opinions. It was too bad for me that our parents were present.

I'm now in hot water with my mom. Dad pulled me outside for a long walk. He politely lectured me on my character and reminded me what my grandfather taught us about cussing. *A man that cusses isn't smart enough to think of a better word.* Dad insisted he and Mom had not raised a bunch of idiots. Naturally, I apologized to my mom. I haven't found it in me yet to apologize to my older brother.

Today's the major remodel party at my house. To my surprise, several of the guys showed up at 8 am. Mom was there with coffee and her homemade biscuits and sausage. Dad showed up thirty minutes later with three boxes of donuts from Sweet Treats. None of my friends would let me pay them for their labor today. I got the same reply from all of them. *This is how we do things in Hayden Falls.* Montana has some of the greatest people in the world.

For lunch, Dad helped me grill out hotdogs and burgers. There were chips, sodas, and water. We didn't pull the beer out until around five. That's when Dad came back with steaks to grill. It's been a long but productive day. These guys deserve more than steak and beer. Apparently, I'm not the only one who thought so. Mom and the Hayden Sisters showed up with more dishes and desserts. Someone turned on some music, and this became a real party.

My biggest surprise of the day came when E and her family showed up. She had a party to oversee at the inn earlier this afternoon. Seeing her brought a smile to my face. Since our talk last week, she shut herself off for a few days. Beth stayed with her at night and gave me updates when I stopped by the coffee shop during my rounds. Since E told me what happened, Beth's more apt to share info with me.

The guys cheered when Mrs. Hayes revealed her famous fried chicken. Mom brought baked potatoes and everything for a salad. Several ladies pulled out folding tables, and within minutes, every side dish known to man was spread out. The support of our community when someone needs help is one of the reasons I'm proud to be from Hayden Falls.

"How's your arm?" E finally makes over to me and hands me a beer.

I watched her while she helped set up the tables of food. She even carried a beer to each of the guys before coming over to me at the grill. She's a natural hostess. This didn't start out as a party, but she quickly took over and led it.

"Sore but good." I flex my hand a few times.

"Do you need something for pain?" She lightly touches the brace.

I've worn the brace off and on, so I wouldn't overdo it today. The guys wouldn't let me do any heavy lifting, so I was probably safe without it. I voiced my opinion, but my protesting didn't do any good. My friends weren't letting me reinjure my arm. As much as I want this house ready so I can move in, I don't need a setback.

"I took some ibuprofen earlier. I'm good."

"How did it go today?" She looks over her shoulder towards the house.

"Come on. I'll show you." I hold up the spatula, and Levi Barnes takes over grilling for me.

Levi is Luke's twin brother. Sheriff Barnes has two sets of twin boys. Levi and Luke are firemen. They aren't identical, but they look so much alike that people have to look twice sometimes. Lucas and Leo are identical, and they're deputies. It gets confusing really fast when all four of them are together. Thankfully, Levi isn't as obnoxious as Luke.

Seeing the delight on E's face when we walked into the house made every minute of this day worthwhile. We discovered original hardwood flooring under the carpet in the living room. I'll have it properly cleaned later. The bedrooms, however, will have carpet in them. I hate stepping out of bed onto cold floors in the winter.

There's a twinkle in E's eyes as she walks through the kitchen. The cabinets were replaced. I took her advice and went with wood cabinets. She runs her hand over the countertop and smiles. We disagreed on those, but in the end, I gave up the idea of a butcher's block, and her gray quartz top was installed. The design has a little brown and beige mixed in, and it went really well with the cabinets.

I wanted stainless steel appliances. Again, those sticky little fingers were mentioned. The associate at the hardware store showed me a finish that looks like stainless steel, but it's much easier to clean. I call it a compromise. Still, everything else in this kitchen is what E suggested. This is her kitchen. She just doesn't know it yet.

"It's beautiful." She smiles up at me.

She's beautiful. She seems stronger today, so I take a step closer to her.

"Well, I did have some great advice." I grin as I look her over from head to toe.

Standing with her in the middle of the kitchen, I can see us living here with a family. The need to touch her is so strong I can't stop myself. I gently run my fingertips across her cheek. She lifts her chin, and her smile widens. I haven't seen her much since we talked. Something changed between us that night. My fingers move down to her neck as my thumb moves back and forth across her chin. I want to kiss her.

"Hey, man! We're out of ice!" Miles calls out as he comes through the back door. "Oops."

With that, the spell is broken. I drop my hand and take a step back. Looking over my shoulder, I glare at my friend.

"I'll just send Luke for that." Miles motions over his shoulder with his thumb as he walks backward toward the door. "He's already gotten on my nerves anyway."

"Good idea." Why didn't he think of that before coming in here?

E giggles, drawing my attention back to her.

"Sorry about that."

"It's not a problem." She shakes her head.

My grin widens when she takes the final few steps between us. Having her this close to my body automatically puts me back under her spell. She raises her finger and motions for me to come closer. I tilt my head and narrow my eyes. Closer? She wants closer? Now, who am I not to comply?

She motions me closer with her finger again, so I slightly lower my head. E pushes up on her toes and presses her lips to mine. It's a chaste kiss, and it's over far too quickly for my liking. Still, it was her idea, and that has an even bigger grin on my face.

"You have guests." E takes my hand and starts pulling me towards the back door.

"Yes, we do." I happily follow her outside.

After everyone finishes eating, Miles and Levi build a makeshift firepit with some rocks and start a fire. I have no idea who brought the bags of marshmallows, but roasted marshmallows it is.

"You'll probably be able to move in next weekend." Spencer sits down in the chair next to me.

"I think so. Thanks for your help today." I take the beer he's offering to me.

We accomplished a lot today. This house is huge, but we mainly concentrated on the rooms I needed the most to move in. Upstairs, the master bedroom and bathroom are ready. The kitchen and half bath downstairs need another cleaning, but they're ready. The living room just needs the hardwood flooring redone. I called Sawyer Gibson earlier. He and his work crews are coming on Monday to start working on what we didn't finish today.

Next Saturday, I'll move in. I really need to get out of my parent's house. Colton and I are at odds. We usually are. He lost all respect for me six years ago. For the most part, and only because of our mom, we tolerate each other. It's kind of sad when one of the people who won't forgive you is your brother.

E sits on my other side. She leans closer to me to where our shoulders and arms touch. Her tiny hand reaches over to take mine. She has me instantly turning my head toward her. Oh, her smile does me in every time I see it.

"You okay?' I keep my voice low so no one else can hear me.

She nods. The flames from the fire reflected in her eyes.

"Can I get you anything?"

She nods again.

"What can I get you, Sunshine?" I'm concerned. She's quiet, but she looks happy.

"You," she whispers.

I freeze. Blood, nor oxygen, manage to make it to my brain. This woman is going to shock me to death right here in front of everyone. I lean my head closer to her. My voice is already deep, but I swear it drops a couple more octaves.

"Sweetheart, I can take that a whole lot of ways. You're going to have to be a bit more specific."

"Kiss me," she says softly.

Yep. I just died.

"Here?" I ask. She nods. "In front of everyone?" She nods again.

Well, that's enough for me. I lean down and press my lips to hers. I was going to make it a quick kiss, but the way her lips move against mine has me lingering. I still have to keep this kiss chaste. Her aunt and uncle are here, and so are my parents. I could care less what anyone else thinks.

Slowly, I pull my lips from hers. My heart explodes a little when she wraps her arm around mine and lays her head on my shoulder. This is heaven. I kiss the top of her head before sitting up straight.

Everyone's looking at us. Most of them are smiling. A few are nodding their heads in approval. Luke Barnes, however, is glaring at me and shaking his head. He doesn't matter, so I ignore him. Spencer pats my knee as if to say, *job well done*. I glance back down at E. I don't exactly know what caused this change in her, but I like it. It feeds into my hopes and dreams. She's really mine.

Chapter Thirty-One

Etrulia

Thanks to the flyers we gave out during the fall festival, the party planning at the inn has picked up. I enjoy doing parties. It's a nice change from weddings, and there are no angry brides to deal with. These parties even help out a few other businesses in town. The flowers and balloons come from our local florist. Sweet Treats makes the cakes unless the mothers or grandmothers prefer to bake them. The inn's kitchen staff usually prepares the food unless they want pizza. Naturally, we call Antonio's for pizza. Plus, a few small groups of women are now booking regular luncheons. Needless to say, I've been busy this month.

Aiden moved into his house a few weeks ago. I haven't been back there since the night of the remodel party. To be honest, I'm scared to go to his house. Well, scared might be too strong of a word. It's not that I don't trust him because I do. The problem is I don't trust myself.

After I opened up to him, not that I told him everything, I felt lighter. I didn't tell him about the panic attacks or just how hard it's been for me to move forward. But still, something shifted within me. While I rested in Aiden's arms that night on my couch, the bond with him went to a deeper level. Well, at least for me, it did. He didn't ask any more questions that night. He just held me until I fell asleep. When I woke up hours later, he made sure I was okay before going home. He has no idea how much his patience with me means. He's tearing down my walls faster than I thought possible.

We held a Halloween party at the inn for the kids last week. It was a huge success. Most of the parents preferred the party rather than taking their children out trick or treating, and they requested we have the party again next year. Thanksgiving is a few weeks away, which means the town tree-lighting ceremony is the following weekend. I'm already preparing gift bags filled with candy for all the kids.

"Knock, knock." Aunt Sara walks into my office. "How are you this morning?"

"I'm good. I got a call from a bride earlier this morning. She wants a Christmas theme wedding the Saturday before Christmas." I lean back in my chair. I'm grateful for this little break.

"Wow. That's a little short notice, but I'm sure you can pull it off." Aunt Sara pauses, and her face scrunches up. "Will that be outdoors in the snow?"

I laugh. "That does sound pretty, but no. There are only twenty guests total, plus the bride and groom. She wants to hold the ceremony in the Grand Room, and there will be a small reception in the dining room. We can handle that easily."

Aunt Sara nods her approval. She sets the mail and a small box on my desk before sitting in the chair across from me.

"You got a package." Aunt Sara points at the small box on top of the mail.

I reach for the little box. It's wrapped in white paper and addressed to me at the inn. There's no return address. The postage stamp is from Missoula. Maybe this is from Rachel. She's given me little gifts with encouraging sayings on several occasions. It's a little early for Christmas gifts, but this is really sweet of her.

"Tyler will be home for Christmas." Aunt Sara's entire face lights up.

“Really?” I jump from my chair and rush to hug her. “Oh, my gosh.”

My cousin hasn’t been home for Christmas in years. Even though Tyler calls his parents every year, I can tell how much it hurts Aunt Sara when her only child doesn’t come home for the holidays.

“Your uncle and I are over the moon right now.”

“I bet. I am, too.” I go back to opening the little box.

One look inside, and my entire world goes still. With one hand at the base of my throat, I sit perfectly still, staring into the box in my other hand. This is definitely *not* from Rachel.

“What is it?” Aunt Sara springs to her feet. She takes the box from me. “Oh my.”

She steps away and pulls out her phone. I can’t hear her conversation. Her voice sounds muffled in my ears even though it’s not. I can’t think straight. Breathe. I need to breathe. I need, I need something more. For a moment, I can’t focus. Aiden. I need Aiden.

I pull out my phone but can’t focus enough to text. Scrolling to his contact information, I hit the call button.

“Hey, Sunshine.” His happy voice comes through the speaker. I don’t speak. “E, are you okay?’

“Aiden.” I barely get his name out.

“Hang on, Sunshine.” I hear him running. “I’m on my way.”

Closing my eyes, I lean back against my chair. I didn’t hear Uncle Silas come in. But he’s standing in front of my desk. Aunt Sara is off the phone now and rubbing my shoulders. Aiden doesn’t hang up. He keeps talking until he bursts through the door with Spencer behind him.

Uncle Silas talks with Spencer and shows him the box. Aiden hurries around my desk. He turns my chair to face him and kneels in front of me. He gently places his hands on my neck as his thumbs caress my cheeks. His touch is calm and soothing.

“Sweetheart, I need you to take some deep breaths with me. Okay?” He slowly nods. I can’t move. “Focus on my voice, Sunshine.” My eyes lock with his. “Take a deep breath in. Now, slowly blow it out.”

He and I do this several times while I focus on the sound of his voice. Wow. Was he taught this as part of his police training? I don't think so. Spencer and the other deputies haven't done this with me. Closing my eyes, I shut my mind off. I continue to concentrate on Aiden's voice and our breathing. Rachel taught me this breathing exercise during my first session with her. Sadly, I usually forget to do this when I freak out. After a few minutes, I open my eyes and nod.

Spencer lays the black rose and the 4 x 4 napkin on my desk. Aiden picks up the rose. His eyes meet with Spencer's briefly.

With the napkin in his hand, he turns back to me. "E, does The Maple Room mean something to you?"

I hate that college bar. It's a couple of blocks from the college I attended in Billings. The elite crowd hung out there. The regular students, like myself, preferred meeting up at The Punch Bowl across the street from the college.

"Garrett proposed there." I drop my eyes. I hate admitting this to Aiden.

"He's crazy!" Uncle Silas shouts. "Can't you arrest him?"

"Unfortunately, no." Spencer shakes his head. "We can't prove he's the one harassing her. We know it's him, but until we can legally prove it, there's nothing we can do except guard E."

Spencer's been pleading with me for months to name my attacker. I don't know why I'm so afraid to do it. Maybe I've seen too many crime shows where it didn't work out so well for the woman. I haven't watched one of those shows since last year, but they're etched into my mind.

"Why don't I take you home," Aunt Sara offers.

"No." I abruptly stand and hold up my hands. "I'm tired of hiding. I'm tired of being afraid. I'm tired of feeling like a victim. I'm just tired."

Aiden steps closer and takes my hands in his. He waits until I look up at him.

"You don't have to feel any of those things, but it's okay if you need a few minutes to clear your head. Anyone would need to do that. Spencer and I will go with your uncle and work out a tighter security plan. You and Aunt Sara can stay here and call Rachel if you need to talk this out. We can call Beth if you want us to."

"I'm already here." Beth walks through the door.

Aiden lets my hands go so I can hug my best friend. I will always need her, no matter what happens.

"Do you have an E radar?" I lightly laugh.

"Of course I do." Beth smiles. "Best friends are supposed to."

Beth is awesome, but I don't think she really has a radar on me. I look over at Spencer.

"I didn't call her." Spencer shakes his head.

Beth laughs and keeps her arm around me.

"I was putting some Thanksgiving decorations in the front window of the shop when I saw these two heading this way. I decided to follow them," Beth explains.

"We'll go to another room and let you ladies talk." Aiden kisses my forehead.

"Are we going to your apartment?" Beth asked.

"No. I don't want him controlling me anymore."

"That's my girl." Beth hugs me again.

Aiden growls and narrows his eyes at Beth.

"Oh, come on, big guy. She'll always be mine. You're just going to have to learn to share." Beth tilts her head and grins at Aiden.

"I don't share." Aiden shakes his head at her. He sounds serious.

His expression softens when he looks at me. I could stare into his brown eyes forever. I'm so glad he came back to Hayden Falls. He winks at me before following my uncle and Spencer across the hall.

Once the men are out of the room, we call Rachel. My newfound strength is shaky, but this is progress. Everyone, including me, is proud of how I'm handling things today. This is new territory for me, and I'll do whatever it takes to conquer this fear once and for all.

Chapter Thirty-Two

Aiden

E's ex is one sick man who definitely needs to be in prison or a mental institution. Until she officially names him as her attacker, there's nothing we can do. Finding out the package she received was postmarked in Missoula had me on high alert. That douchebag already graduated college. He should be in Vegas, not an hour away from Hayden Falls. He's too close to my girl. That thought caused me a few restless nights.

We tightened our security around the inn. It wasn't enough for me. A little talk with Beth had her and their other friends having regular sleepovers with E. Sometimes at their places and a few at E's apartment. I asked a few business owners who are friends with my family to watch out for E whenever she's in town. Telling them I was worried someone would give her a hard time because we were getting close was enough to persuade them to help me out. If they noticed anything suspicious, they agreed to call Spencer or me. If E figured out what I was doing, she never said anything.

Lucas Barnes needed to trade shifts with someone tonight. I didn't ask why, but I took his shift since I was off tomorrow. Hayden Falls sure is quiet at night. Even the bar and tavern are closed at 3 am on a Tuesday morning. I ride by the inn and the backstreet to E's apartment at least once an hour. All quiet. I don't think any animals are roaming about tonight. It's the middle of November, so it's too cold to be out anyway. If I weren't working, I'd be all warm and cozy at home like everyone else.

Movement near Cowboys catches my eye. Something ducked behind the bar. It was crouched low to the ground, so I didn't get a good look. It could have been a dog. Still, I'd better check it out. Turning my headlights off, I pull into the parking lot. Before getting out of my SUV, I radioed Leo and let him know what I was doing.

Easing around the back of the building, I see nothing. Maybe it was just a dog. Except dogs don't break windows. One of the back windows is broken, and I can hear movement inside. The camera on the corner looks broken, too. Whoever is in the bar must have thrown a rock at it. It's hard to tell from here. I step back around the corner and radio Leo for backup. A quick call to Noah got me the security code for the back door. Noah's on the way. He'll let Leo in the front door.

Silently, I work my way to the bar area. I wasn't expecting to find a teenage kid trying to clean up broken bottles on the floor. I holster my gun and flip on the light. The boy freezes. Fear flashes in his eyes, and he starts to bolt for the front door. I block his path with my hands held up.

"Easy. It's okay," I assure him.

"I'm sorry." The boy drops his gaze to the floor. "I didn't mean to break the bottles."

"We can worry about that later." Lowering my hands, I step closer to him. "What are you doing, Chase?"

His head snaps up. "You know my name?"

I nod once. "Why did you break in here?"

"I smelled the food earlier. I couldn't find anywhere to stay, so I came back." Chase's voice drops. "I was hungry."

Chase is standing behind the bar, so I walk over and sit down on the stool in front of him. He backs up against the back counter where the glasses and several bottles of alcohol are stored. His fear heightens when Leo and Noah come through the front door.

"Have a seat, guys." I motion to the barstools next to me.

They eye Chase and me closely but take a seat. Chase is trembling by this point.

"This is Leo and Noah. Noah owns the bar," I introduce my friends, hoping it will calm this kid down a bit.

"Chase Ashford, we've been looking for you." Leo rests his forearms on the bar. He's a big guy and would look intimidating even out of uniform. "You know, it's illegal to run away."

"I didn't run away," Chase says quickly.

"Your parents filed a missing person's report three months ago." I continue to watch Chase closely. There's a lot more to this story.

Chase laughs, but there's no humor in it. With his eyes cast downward, he shakes his head. "My parents threw me out."

"Why would your parents throw you out?" Noah asked.

"Who knows? They were high on something. They always do crazy stuff when they get like that." Chase swallows hard. His eyes remain on the floor.

That's what I was afraid of. Reading through this kid's files had me believing drugs were involved somehow. I thought maybe one parent but not both. This sixteen-year-old kid has survived three months on his own. It's nothing short of a miracle he's safe.

"Does that happen often?" Leo asked.

Chase looks down again and nods. My heart goes out to the kid. I lean forward and look down the bar at Noah.

"Why don't you get Chase a coke and something to eat," I suggest. "If you have something to board up the window with, we'll get that taken care of for the night."

"It would take a while to fire up the grill and fryers, but I can make him a club sandwich, and there are bags of chips." Noah starts heading toward the kitchen. "You'll find a few extra pieces of plywood in the backroom from where I had to fix a section of flooring in my office."

"I got the window." Leo hops off the barstool and heads to the back.

“Am I being arrested?” Chase looks around nervously.

“Well, that’s going to be up to Noah here. You did break into his bar and caused a bit of damage. He’s a good man, though. Maybe we can persuade him into letting you work off what you owe him around here while the bar’s closed.” It’s a shaky solution, but it might work.

“I would.” Tears well up in Chase’s eyes. “I gladly would.”

Noah sets the sandwich, a couple of bags of chips, and a soda on the bar. He motions for Chase to take the seat between us. He’s still nervous, but Chase comes around and sits down.

“Where’s he going to stay?” Noah asked.

“If Sheriff Barnes agrees, I’ll call my parents and get him a bed in the bunkhouse at the ranch.” It’s only a temporary solution, but it’s the best I can come up with tonight. “Unless you want to press charges. If so, I have to arrest him.”

Chase tenses up. He stops eating and turns to face Noah. This kid has been through a lot lately.

Noah shakes his head. “We’ll try your plan first.”

Noah and I shake hands. If the sheriff doesn’t agree to my plan, I’ll pay him for the damages Chase caused here tonight.

“Thank you.” Chase drops his head and wipes a tear from his eye.

Noah and I pat him on the back. He’s had a tough life so far. Hopefully, we can make it better for him from now on.

After Chase finishes his sandwich, I drive him to the station. Leo called his father on his cell phone to keep Chase’s case off the radio for now. Sheriff Barnes comes in thirty minutes behind us.

The Sheriff sits quietly, pulling on his bottom lip while I update him on Chase’s case. Leo took Chase to the breakroom and got him another soda. The kid smiled when Leo gave him one of the leftover cupcakes Ms. Ruth brought this morning. I’m glad he’s not in the office with us. The lingering silence from Sheriff Barnes has me nervous. Chase would probably bolt out the front door.

“Why do you want to help this kid so badly?”

“He’s young. His school report shows he has great potential. He can’t help that his parents are drug addicts. I knew there was more to this case than just a run-a-way kid.” I shake my head. “He needs help. He doesn't need to be arrested as a runaway. Chase shouldn't have to pay the price because somebody else messed up."

Sheriff Barnes eyes me closely. It's unnerving. I feel like I'm under a microscope here.

"So, you see a lot of yourself in this kid?"

Now it's my turn to eye him. This is about Chase, not me. There's no need for him to drag what I did into this. As much as I want to say something smart back, I don't."

"Yeah, I guess so," I finally admit.

"You know, it's been over six years. I'm pretty sure the statute of limitations ran out on all that." Sheriff Barnes taps his fingers on his desk.

Rehashing that night won't do any good. I want to forget it, not talk about it.

"It's up to you how long you carry it. I'm surprised it's lasted this long. I understand why you did what you did, but I won't force you to admit anything." He's disappointed in me. I see it on his face.

"What about Chase?" I quickly change the subject.

"Okay, son. We'll let it go for now." Sheriff Barnes shakes his head. "As far as the kid goes, I think it's admirable that you want to help him like this. However, I don't know what the Sheriff's Office and Social Services in Missoula will say."

"Sending him back to his parents will be a huge mistake. Putting him in juvie or state custody will be an even bigger one," I snap.

"I agree with you on everything, but I can't make promises here. For tonight, take him to your family's ranch. Tomorrow, I have to call Missoula whether I want to or not. We'll do what we can for him and hope that Social Services agrees with us. Since Noah isn't pressing charges, I will leave that part out of the report." Sheriff Barnes folds his hands and leans back in his chair.

"Okay." I nod and blow out a breath. He's giving the kid a chance. That's all I can ask. "Thank you," I say and get up to leave.

"Aiden," Sheriff Barnes calls out. I pause at the door and turn to face him. "This kid doesn't know how lucky he is that it was you who found him."

"I know," I say before walking out of the office.

Chase seems more at ease when I join them in the breakroom. Leo has him laughing with some of the crazy stories about our little town. Chase thanks Leo before following me out to my cruiser. He opens up more on the drive out to my parent's house. The kid bombards me with endless questions about living on a real ranch. Honestly, Colton needs to answer some of these questions, not me.

When we get to the ranch, I drive down to the bunkhouse. Graham Bradley, our ranch foreman, is waiting at the door for us. Mom sent Chase a plate of leftovers from dinner. This kid is going to be stuffed if he eats all this. Mom also got together some of Brady's old clothes. They look a little big for Chase, but they'll do for now. If Social Services lets him stay, I'll get him everything he needs.

Graham shows Chase his room. It's nothing fancy, but it's a warm bed for the night. The thought of this kid sleeping outside in the cold sends a shiver down my spine. I say goodbye to Chase before Graham shows him where the shower is. The kid hasn't had one in a while.

"It's a good thing you found him." Graham walks me out to the SUV.

"I hope he gets to stay." I look back towards the bunkhouse. I feel bad for leaving the kid like this.

"He seems like a good kid. Don't worry. We'll take good care of him," Graham assures me.

"Thanks, man. I really appreciate it." I shake his hand. "I'll check in on him later."

Getting back into the SUV, I say a silent prayer of thanks that this kid was found safe. A lot of cases like this end badly. Chase has a real chance here. Well, that is if the authorities in Missoula agree with my plan.

When I get back to town, I make another round by The Magnolia Inn. Still quiet. I sit at the end of the driveway for a moment and stare up at E's apartment. She's safe and sound asleep. I'd walk up those steps and see her if it weren't the middle of the night. Beth's car is here. She's not alone. With a deep sigh, I back out of the driveway and head back to the station. I need to finish this shift and get some sleep.

Chapter Thirty-Three

Etrulia

My life is so strange. Even I have a hard time believing everything that's happening. No one should have this much craziness going on in their life. On the surface, and for the most part, everything looks okay. It's what lies underneath the surface that gives me nightmares, and I do mean actual nightmares.

I never told anyone, not even my therapist, about the horrible dreams I've been having lately. My friends know because I sometimes wake up screaming when we have sleepovers. Thankfully, they don't ask me what happens in my dreams. It's a good thing because if I talk about them, I'll have to relive them. The support from my friends is a true blessing. They sit quietly with me until my breathing returns to normal, and I'm ready to go back to sleep.

There's been no more contact from Garrett since the napkin and black rose arrived in the mail. I do my best to hide it, but I'm scared. The closer it gets to the party in Vegas, the jumpier I become. I no longer open any mail or packages without a return address. Spencer opens those when he stops by the inn during his daily rounds. He doesn't think I notice, but he's making more stops at the inn than usual.

Thanksgiving is a couple of days away, and the Tree-Lighting Ceremony is next weekend. I have plenty of things to focus on. The town doesn't do anything big for Thanksgiving. Family gatherings keep us busy enough this weekend.

It was quiet around the inn today, so I spent the day helping Aunt Sara bake pies for Thanksgiving. Cooking with her was always fun. She taught me everything I know about cooking and baking.

Tonight was one of the few nights I was home alone. It's strange, but I have an odd feeling. Maybe it's because there's no one here with me. Hopefully, it doesn't mean I've become dependent on having my friends with me. I'm trying to get stronger and prove my independence again. Whatever the uneasiness is, I shake it away and settle down on the couch to watch a movie after getting a shower.

Shortly after midnight, I jolt awake. Where am I? My eyes dart around the room. Closing my eyes, I blow out a breath and relax. I fell asleep on the couch. The TV is off. That's good. I must have been so tired I forgot I turned it off.

The uneasy feeling washes over me again. It's stronger this time. Did I have a bad dream? I don't remember dreaming. What woke me up like that? I have nightlights throughout the apartment. They automatically come on when it gets dark. The dim lighting allows my eyes to adjust easily. Nothing seems out of place.

A sound at the door catches my attention. Every muscle in my body freezes as I stare at the door. My uncle installed a streetlight back here years ago. He didn't want Aunt Sara and me to get out of our cars in total darkness if we came home late. The top half of my door is glass. Through the curtain, I can see the silhouette of someone on the other side of the door.

Grabbing my phone off the coffee table, I duck down and slowly move over to the corner of the room under the counter that separates the living room and kitchen. On the living room side, the counter is a bar. It only has room for two stools. From here, I have a clear view of the door. I need help. I pull up my contacts and hit the call button.

"Hey, Sunshine." Aiden sounds sleepy.

Covering my mouth and the phone with my hand, I whisper, "Aiden."

"E, what's wrong?" He sounds wide awake now.

"There's a man outside my door," I'm still whispering.

"I'm on my way. Stay on the phone." Aiden's already in his truck.

I can hear him talking on what I assume is his police radio. He notifies the Sheriff's Office and Spencer. I suck in a breath when the doorknob jiggles. I force myself to take a few deep breaths and pray someone gets here soon.

Sirens in the distance send the man at the door bolting down the steps. I breathe a sigh of relief. Aiden tells me to stay where I am until he or one of the other officers arrives.

Within minutes, everyone descended upon my little apartment. Leo, Lucas, and Sheriff Barnes are outside. My uncle showed up carrying his shotgun. Spencer must have called him. Uncle Silas gave them the spare key. Before I could get to the door, it flung open. Spencer rushes in with Aiden on his heels.

Without giving Aiden time to speak, I crash into him and wrap my arms around his waist. His arms come around me, pulling me tighter against his chest. Safe. I'm safe here.

People talk all around us, but none of it registers. Closing my eyes, I let the sounds around me drift away and cling to Aiden. At some point, the real world comes back into focus. Aiden pulls away, but he doesn't let me go. He leads me to the couch and only releases me when my aunt rushes through the door. Naturally, Beth isn't far behind. I take it back. Beth does have an E radar.

"E, what happened?" Spencer kneels in front of me.

I tell him how I fell asleep on the couch, and something woke me up. That's when I saw the man on the other side of the door. Aiden's pacing behind Spencer. He's fighting to stay in control.

"Was it him?" I asked.

"I think so. This was taped to the glass." Spencer hands me a paper.

One look at the paper confirms my worst fears. It's another napkin from The Maple Room with the word *Soon* written on it in red. There's no doubt in my mind. Garrett was outside my door tonight.

He's never been to Hayden Falls. He refused every invitation to come and meet my aunt and uncle. How did he find me?

"Why won't he leave me alone?" My voice shakes with fear.

"I don't know," Spencer replies.

"Arrest him!" Uncle Silas demands. "This is trespassing."

Spencer stands and faces my uncle. "If your cameras clearly show that it was him, I'll gladly arrest this scumbag."

Sheriff Barnes sends Spencer with Uncle Silas to check the security footage. Garrett's crazy, but he's also smart. Even with the streetlight, unless he looked up at the camera, I doubt there will be enough proof to arrest him.

"E." Sheriff Barnes kneels in front of me. "I don't think this guy is going to stop. We don't have enough evidence to link any of this to your ex-boyfriend. I really hate saying this, but with that party in Vegas a month away and him showing up here tonight, I look for him to try and kidnap you."

His words hit everyone in the room hard. I suck in a breath. Aunt Sara starts to cry, and Beth's arms tighten around me. Aiden growls, causing Sheriff Barnes to look at him over his shoulder. Aiden's chest rapidly rises and falls. His hands are clenched into fists at his sides. The sheriff shakes his head, but it doesn't settle Aiden down.

"What do we do?" Aunt Sara wipes tears from her cheek.

Aiden speaks before Sheriff Barnes can. "Beth, go and help E pack a bag."

"Good idea." Beth pulls me off the couch. "You can stay with me for a while."

"No," Aiden says sharply.

We pause outside my bedroom door. No? What's he saying?

"Just where is she going then?" Beth pops her hands on her hips.

"With me," Aiden replied.

Everyone in the room pauses and looks around at each other. Did we hear him correctly?

"Is that a good idea?" Lucas narrows his eyes and crosses his arms.

"She can stay with us. We just moved her out here to give her some independence," Aunt Sara said.

"She'll be fine at my place," Beth insists.

"No." Aiden's voice hardens. He's struggling to hold it together. "He knows she lives here. With Beth being her best friend, he more than likely already knows where she lives, too. She'll be safer at my place."

Yes, we heard him correctly. Me at Aiden's place?

"Being that far out of town might be risky. It would cause us another ten to fifteen minutes in response time," Lucas points out.

"We have ten year-round ranch hands. Plus, there's me, Colton, and our dad. Brady will even come home on weekends to help. She'll be safe there," Aiden insists.

"That might not be a bad idea." Spencer stands in the doorway.

"Anything useful?" Sheriff Barnes asked.

Spencer shakes his head. "He knew exactly where the cameras were and avoided showing his face."

"He's watching me. He knows where I am." I lean back against the doorframe. "Until six months ago, I lived in the house with Aunt Sara and Uncle Silas."

"Don't you have family in another state?" Sheriff Barnes asked Uncle Silas.

"None that I'll allow her to go to," Uncle Silas snapped. "Biologically, she may be my niece, but E's my daughter. The people who hurt her when she was little will *not* get their hands on her again."

Uncle Silas has a horrible temper, but he rarely lets it show. He's my father's brother. He and Aunt Sara met the social worker and me at the airport in Missoula when I was eight years old. Uncle Silas declared that day he'd never forgive my parents for hurting me. He's right. Biologically, he's my uncle, but legally and in every other way that matters, he's my dad.

"I'm sorry, Silas," Sheriff Barnes apologizes. "I was just trying to think of a way to keep her safe."

Uncle Silas nods to the sheriff before looking at Beth, who is still standing in my doorway with me. "Beth, go help E pack. She's going with Aiden."

Wait. What did he just say? Everyone in the room is shocked to hear that.

"Are you sure?" Aunt Sara places her hand on my uncle's arm.

"It's one of the safest places I can think of here. Preston doesn't know anything about Aiden's house. If he knows she's in this apartment, he knows a lot more about where she goes." Spencer looks around the room and nods his approval.

"Do I get a say in this?" I ask.

It's unsettling how they all talk about me like I'm not standing in the room. I appreciate their concern for my safety. The situation is serious, but I'm not eight anymore. Aiden walks towards me but not close enough to touch me.

"Of course, you get a say in this." His eyes narrow. His expression is serious, and his tone is protective. He cares for me. I know it. "Just know, wherever you stay at night, I'll be there too until he's stopped."

From the look in Aiden's eyes, I've no doubt he means it. My uncle wouldn't have agreed to this if he didn't trust Aiden to keep me safe. I look at each person in the room.

"It's your choice," Sheriff Barnes said. "We'll do everything we can to protect you no matter what you decide."

"Nobody will protect you like Aiden will." Leo shares a knowing look with Aiden. He nods once.

"What about work?" I ask Aiden.

"I will bring you to the inn every morning," he assures me.

"Okay. Let me pack a bag."

Beth and I hurry into my room. We pull out a middle-sized suitcase and quickly fill it with clothes. A smaller bag is filled with the personal things I need from the bathroom. Since I'll still be here during the day, I can get anything I forget tonight.

I can't believe this is happening. It's too crazy to make up. Never in a million years would I believe I'd be stalked by a crazy ex-boyfriend. Then there's Aiden. Staying with him is a long-forgotten fantasy. Somehow, in all this madness, it's now my reality.

Chapter Thirty-Four

Aiden

Once E packed her bag and said goodbye to her aunt, uncle, and Beth, I quickly ushered her out the door. Spencer and Sheriff Barnes will oversee the rest of the investigation at her apartment tonight. One of them will call me later with an update.

Thanksgiving is two days away. Mr. and Mrs. Hayes can handle everything at the inn for a few days. Well, since it's after midnight, Thanksgiving is technically tomorrow. After what happened tonight, E can rest today and get herself together.

Due to the holiday, I don't have physical therapy today. We can spend the day getting E settled in at my house. The fact this is even happening is unbelievable, well, happening this soon anyway. From the moment I bought this house, I dreamed of sharing it with her. The reason she's staying with me is far from ideal. It shouldn't be happening, but here we are.

It's still dark outside when we pull into the driveway. E sits quietly in the passenger seat. We don't speak or move for a few minutes. We're at some weird standstill. It's probably my fault. I didn't mean to blurt out my plan the way I did. I couldn't help it. My need to protect her is so strong. Nothing matters more to me than her safety.

"We should probably go in." E breaks the awkward silence.

"Oh, yeah. I'll get your bags."

I unlock the back door and motion for her to go in first. I flip the light on so she can see the fully decorated kitchen. All the decorations and small appliances are either blue, black, or silver. Every bit of it was her suggestion.

"This is amazing." She walks around the island counter I added to the center of the kitchen. It's something she's always wanted.

"Thank you." I beam with pride. She loves to cook. I want her to fall in love with this room and with me. "If you'd like something to drink, I can make us a cup of coffee. There's also tea and water in the fridge, and of course, there's hot chocolate.

"Definitely, hot chocolate, but I can make it." She goes right to the cabinet where the mugs are.

"Milk is in the fridge." I pick up her suitcases. "I'll put these upstairs."

When I get back to the kitchen, E's at the stove warming up the milk. I stand in the doorway and watch her for a few minutes. She looks like she belongs here. Sadly, she hasn't smiled yet. I can understand why, though. Her world is a jumbled mess right now. Still, I miss her smile.

"I see you found everything okay." I grab the jar of extra mini marshmallows on the counter. "Even these."

"Everything was easy to find." E pours the warm milk into two mugs.

"Some people just heat up water in the microwave," I point out.

E gasps as her hand flies to her chest. "That's illegal."

Teasing her has always been fun. When she first came to Montana, Mom made us hot chocolate with milk instead of water on a snowy day. E refused to use water after that.

"Should I start arresting people?" I tease.

"Yes. Definitely." She dumps an extra spoonful of mini marshmallows into our cups.

The corner of her mouth twitches. She's trying to be serious, but I think I'm wearing her down.

"I should probably warn Sheriff Barnes that the cells will be full all winter." I take a small sip of my hot chocolate to test how hot it is. "We might have to ship a few to the state prison."

E giggles as she sits down on the stool next to me. I knew that smile was in there. Too bad it fades quickly.

"I know we need to talk, but you've been through enough tonight. We should get some rest and talk later."

"I'm scared." She looks down into her cup. "But I'm not as fragile as everyone thinks I am." Her eyes lift to mine. "If you want to talk, I can handle it."

"I don't doubt your strength." I tuck a lock of her hair behind her ear.

She is absolutely beautiful. She's one of the strongest people I know. Just because she has a sweet and delicate side that has me wanting to protect her with every fiber of my being doesn't mean she isn't strong. She just started to find her strong side again. I don't want to see her lose herself to fear now.

"Tonight sucked some life out of me," I tell her, and it had. Knowing she was in trouble scared me as badly as the tour bus accident had, if not more. "I need a little bit to get myself together."

I will never admit to her just how scared I was tonight. Every guy on the force probably saw it, though. It's one of the reasons we're here now. Having her with me at night will settle me a bit. I won't fully rest easy until Garrett Preston is behind bars where he belongs.

"Okay," she agrees. "Because you need it. We'll get some rest first."

I chuckle. She really is cute.

"Thank you. I really appreciate that."

After we finish our hot chocolate and put the cups in the dishwasher, I take her hand and lead her upstairs. E pauses inside the bedroom doorway and takes in the room. Her expression doesn't give me enough to know if she likes the room or not.

"Your bags are there." I point to the suitcases on the chest at the foot of the bed. "And the bathroom is there." I point to the bathroom door.

"This is your room," E says, still looking around.

It wasn't a question, but I replied anyway, "It is."

E doesn't move. I'm not exactly sure what she needs right now. Maybe some privacy? I pull a blanket from the closet and grab a pillow from the bed.

"What are you doing?"

The terrified look on her face halts me in my tracks.

"I'm going to the couch."

"Why?"

"This is the only bed in the house right now. I'll get another one as soon as I can."

I wasn't expecting to have overnight guests yet. The stores in this area will be closed until after Thanksgiving. Besides, I don't mind sleeping on the couch for a few nights so she can be comfortable up here.

"I can't take your bed." E puts her hand on my arm.

"I'm *giving* you my bed. There's no way I will let you sleep on the couch."

"Don't go," she softly pleads.

Don't go? Surely, she's not suggesting what I think she is.

"E." I glance at the bed and quickly back to her.

"Please. I don't really want to be alone." She looks up at me. Her deep blue eyes do me in.

"I'm not sure I can sleep in the same bed with you and not touch you." I have to be honest with her.

"We'll figure it out." She blinks a couple of times. "I trust you."

Oh, dear. How can I refuse her? Giving in will make me less than a gentleman. I can't do that to her. Only, *this is her*. I'm powerless where she's concerned.

"Aiden, please stay with me," she whispers.

Her big blue eyes continue to plead with me. And just like that, I'm putty in her hands.

"Okay." I give in. "We'll give it a try."

Immediately, she relaxes. I toss the pillow back on the bed and return the blanket to the closet. This will not be easy.

"I'll give you a few minutes to change." I hurry downstairs to lock the house up for the night.

What have I gotten myself into? Having her here was the only thing I could think of to keep her safe and me sane. However, at the same time, having her here will completely unravel me.

When I get back to the master bedroom, I find E sitting on the side of the bed. She quickly stands up. My eyes take in the pajama pants and a t-shirt she's wearing. They should be enough to keep me from losing my mind tonight. No. They probably won't.

"Do you have a side you prefer?" Her eyes drop to the bed.

"It's not a big deal. If you like the side you're on, that's fine with me. I'll take the left." I prefer the left, but I'll give it up for her.

E nods and climbs into the right side of the bed. Well, from where I'm standing at the foot of the bed, it's the right side. Since I don't have nightlights in here yet, as she does in her apartment, I leave the bathroom light on and pull the door almost closed. I take off my boots and unbutton my jeans. I pause and look down at her.

"What's wrong?"

"Uh…" I have no idea what I should do here.

"Do you need me to turn over so you can change?"

Is she teasing me? She tries but fails miserably to hide a little giggle.

"I don't usually *change*."

She narrows her eyes. Oh, for goodness sake. I can't tell her.

"Never mind." I grab a pair of gym shorts from the dresser and hurry into the bathroom.

E's still lying on her side, facing me, when I get into bed. So, I turn on my side to face her. Having her in my bed has way too many emotions running through me right now.

"You don't usually sleep with clothes on, do you?"

"Not really," I admit. "But it's okay."

"So, would I have woken up later to find you naked on the couch?" She grins at me.

"That would have been bad." I laugh at the thought.

"Maybe. Maybe not." E shrugs.

The humor is completely gone now. I close my eyes and groan. This woman is going to kill me.

"Thank you for staying with me." Her voice sounds sleepy.

"There's nowhere else I'd rather be." I gently run a finger down her cheek. It's just too hard not to touch her.

"Aiden," Her voice is softer.

"Mmhmm?"

"Hold me," she whispers.

And once again, I'm putty in her hands.

"Come here, Sunshine." I wrap an arm around her and pull her to my chest. She easily comes to me.

With her wrapped in my arms and her head on my chest, E soon falls asleep. The feel of her body against mine will no doubt keep me awake for a while. That's okay. She's resting, and that's all that matters.

"This is exactly where you belong," I whisper. It's doubtful she heard me, but it's true.

E sighs and settles closer to me. I kiss the top of her head and close my eyes. She's here, and she's safe. After a while, I drift off to sleep, lost in the magic of her.

Chapter Thirty-Five

Etrulia

Thanksgiving was wonderful. It was Aiden's first one in Hayden Falls since he left years ago. I never understood why he didn't come home more than he did. We had lunch with my aunt and uncle. For dinner, we all went to Aiden's parents' house. I love how the Maxwells always include my family in their special occasions.

Chase, the teenager Aiden found, was here. Mrs. Maxwell instantly fell in love with the boy. She convinced the social worker assigned to Chase's case to go along with Aiden's plans.

The social worker can't discuss all the details of Chase's case with Mrs. Maxwell. All we know is the boy can't return to his parents at this time. When Mrs. Maxwell wants something, she usually gets it. It's not because she's spoiled, rude, and demanded things. Her husband and boys love her so much. They do everything possible to see her smile. Maybe it does make her spoiled, but in a loving way.

Aiden's parents are now taking foster parent training so that Chase can stay with them. The only disagreement the social worker had with Aiden's plan was the bunkhouse. The bunkhouse wasn't allowed since Chase is now officially in the state's custody. So, Mrs. Maxwell happily moved Chase into Aiden's old room.

Brady's home for Thanksgiving. He'll leave after lunch on Sunday so he can be ready for classes on Monday. He was furious when Aiden told him everything that had happened. While he's home, Brady gladly helps keep watch over Aiden's house. He never said it out loud, but I know Brady wants a chance to go after Garrett.

I don't fully understand their system, but Aiden's family and the ranch hands watch over the house day and night. Colton's dog, Bo, stays inside the house at night. Bo's a beautiful German Sheppard, and he's extremely protective. Everyone was surprised he left Colton's side.

After Thanksgiving dinner, we decorated Aiden's parents' Christmas tree. On Friday, I helped Aunt Sara decorate theirs and the one in the inn. Avery and Marcie helped with all of the inn's decorations. Without their help, we wouldn't have finished on time. You'd think by now I would be sick of putting up Christmas decorations, but I'm not. I love Christmas. It's my favorite holiday. Tonight, Aiden and I are decorating his tree. It feels special, very domestic, and beyond wonderful.

After decorating the tree, we step back and admire our work. Aiden stands behind me and wraps his arms around me. I lean back against him, enjoying the feel of his muscular arms. The multi-colored lights shimmer off of the ornaments and garlands. I don't like all having white lights on the tree, not that those aren't beautiful. I just love the different colors.

For me, the tree is the best part of Christmas. When I was younger, I would sit by the tree and sing Christmas songs, even if I did it alone. Sadly, on most occasions, it's what I did because my family refused to join me. Most people get caught up in Santa or the presents, but not me. The tree is what makes the season magical for me.

"It's beautiful," I say softly.

"Beautiful," Aiden echoes and places a kiss on my temple.

Somehow, I don't think he's just talking about the tree. I'm more than pleased with our first Christmas tree. Whoa. Our? I'm getting too wrapped up in our new living arrangements. This can't go on forever. I have to get ahold of myself here. I will only be here until Garrett's behind bars.

"Dinner?"

"Yeah, it should be ready." I look up at him over my shoulder and smile. I want to stay here forever. *Get a grip*, I tell myself.

Aiden is as reluctant to move as I am. Finally, he moves. With one arm around my shoulders, he turns us towards the kitchen. Thankfully, with all the ranch hands, the Thanksgiving leftovers were polished off yesterday. I don't think either of us could eat any more turkey. The roast with carrots and potatoes has been baking for hours and smells so good.

Aiden sets the table while I pull the roast from the oven. We've fallen into a sweet domestic routine in the evenings. How it happened in such a short time surprises me, but I love it. We sit at the smaller table next to the kitchen rather than in the formal dining room. It's fine because this feels cozier. We talk through dinner about the Tree Lighting Ceremony.

"There's a snowman building contest if you want to sign up."

Snowman contest? Yeah, I know all about it. Beth, Sammie, Katie, and Ally have been my partners every year. We have so much fun goofing off. We never finish our snowman, which means we never win the contest.

"I know," I say softly.

"If you want to sign up, we can."

"Can I let you know?"

I love building snowmen. Well, I used to. It's snowed many times since January, but I haven't built a snowman since Garrett found me building them with Brady at college. Now, I just watch the snow falling from my window. It's pretty when it falls. Watching the snow falling is another thing that's magical for me during the winter. It's different from waking up and finding the ground covered. I look up to find Aiden watching me. The twinkle in his eyes fades. He knows why I'm reluctant to agree to the contest.

"Well, if you decide to, I'll happily be your partner." His smile is back, but the joy isn't there.

"I'll let you know." I return the smile, and we let the matter drop.

"Would you like to watch a movie tonight?" Thankfully, he changes the subject.

"Yes. That would be great," I reply. It is great, but I feel like something is off between us now. Why can't I move past what happened to me?

"What would you like to watch?" Aiden stands up and takes our empty plates to the dishwasher.

"*Star Wars*." I clap my hands and grin.

"You don't want to watch a Christmas movie?" He sounds shocked.

"I don't start watching Christmas movies until after the Tree Lighting Ceremony." I get up and put the leftover food away.

"You're so weird." Aiden lightly laughs. "But in a good way," he quickly adds.

I will take that as a compliment. At least the awkwardness is now gone. After we clean up the kitchen, we settle on the couch, and Aiden starts the movie.

"Okay. Let's watch some *Darth Vader*." He clicks play.

I gasp and put my hand to my chest. "What? No. No. No. We are watching *Obi-Wan Kenobi*," I correct him.

"Why would we do that?" Aiden pauses the movie, which is still in the opening credits.

"Because he's the best *Jedi* EVER," I say with pride, emphasis on the word ever.

Aiden looks horrified. "*Vader* is the best," he insists.

"My guy beat your guy." I poke him on his thigh.

"My guy *kills* your guy," he reminds me.

"Only because my guy let him," I inform him.

We stare at each other for a moment before bursting out laughing. We used to debate like this when we were kids. It was cute back then, and it still is.

"Sunshine, we're just going to have to agree to disagree on this one." Aiden leans over and kisses my forehead.

"Okay." I sigh deeply for the dramatic effect and fall against his side.

Aiden puts his arm around me and starts the movie again. Maybe I can talk him into a *Star Wars* marathon. It would mean I'd be here for a while. As much as I like being here, Garrett needs to be caught. Once his harassment stops, I'll have to go home. The thought saddens me more than I want to admit.

Aiden and I pick at each other throughout the entire movie. I've missed doing things like this with him. Being friends with him when we were kids was wonderful. Sadly, we drifted apart as Aiden got older. He couldn't hang out with the shy little girl forever. When he went on to do other things, it left a huge hole in my heart. His dating phase was my least favorite. Now, a weird twist of fate has brought him back to Montana, back to me.

Somewhere toward the end of the movie, I must have drifted off to sleep. I wake as Aiden lays me on the bed and pulls the covers over me.

"I need to change." I shove the covers back.

I yawn as I walk across the room to grab my shorty pajama set. I could have slept in my leggings just fine and the t-shirt, but the bra would have been torture. After changing, I walk back over to the bed and start to climb in. Aiden stands on the other side with his mouth wide open and his eyes about to pop out of his head.

"What?" I have no idea what was wrong.

A sly grin crosses his face as he looks down at my pajamas. "I knew they'd be blue."

I look down and pull my top out slightly. "Yeah, most of my pajamas are blue."

I look up. He's shaking his head.

"Sweetheart, I'm not talking about pajamas." His sly grin widens.

His eyes move over to the dresser. My clothes are lying haphazardly on the floor. I sure hope it's not a problem. I'm not usually messy, but I'm sleepy. Looking back at me, his grin grows even wider. Oh, no! I gasp and cover my mouth with both of my hands.

"Oh my gosh," I exclaim.

Aiden laughs and pulls off his t-shirt without any modesty. Why should we worry about it now after what I just did? He toes off his shoes and pulls off his jeans. Nope. No modesty here. With just his boxers on, he climbs onto the bed, reaches across, and pulls me down with him.

"Sunshine, you can do that any time you want."

"You saw me." I'm so shocked at what I did.

"Not *all* of you." He kisses my forehead. "Yet."

Yet? Oh. My. Gosh. I don't know what to do right now.

"Aiden, I…" What do I say? He places a finger over my lips, silencing me.

"Don't say you're sorry." He kisses my cheek. "I'm not." His lips move to the corner of my mouth. "You look *amazing* in blue."

His lips press against mine, and all thoughts of embarrassment and protests are gone. My half-asleep self just took our staying together to a whole new level. The way he makes me feel when I'm in his arms makes me want more of him. It's not happening tonight, though. After several long, passionate kisses, Aiden pulls me against his chest, and I fall asleep in his arms.

Chapter Thirty-Six

Aiden

I've been taking cold showers every day for the past week and a half. Sometimes, more than one a day is necessary. Having E in my house and in my bed is great, but I don't know how much longer I can keep this up. Being a gentleman isn't supposed to be this hard. A man's not expected to be a gentleman when the woman he loves is in his bed. Well, yes, we are, but man, it's hard.

The Tree Lighting Ceremony is going great. E's set up outside of Beth's Morning Brew again. This is probably her spot for all the town celebrations. Who could blame her? She has an endless supply of coffee and hot chocolate just a few feet away, courtesy of her best friend. And yes, every deputy on the force, plus several of our trusted friends around town, are keeping a watchful eye on E in case that jerk shows up today.

People come and go all day long. Even though the Tree Lighting Ceremony isn't until dark, just like every other Hayden Falls festival, this one starts at nine o'clock. The Christmas parade starts at three, and the tree lighting closes things out once the sun goes down.

It's two, and my shift for the day has just ended. After signing out at the station, I hurry back to the town square. I love this ceremony. This is my first one in six years. Closing this one out with E by my side will be amazing.

When I round the corner of Frozen Scoops, I come to an abrupt halt. My blood boils, and I see red. It's a wonder all the snow in town hasn't melted from the heat coming off me. Roman Crawford is at The Magnolia Inn's booth talking to my girl.

Several people glance my way when I growl. Whatever he just said to her causes E to smile. Her smiles are for me, not this jerk. I have to put a stop to this madness. While glaring holes into the back of my long-time enemy's head, I storm down the sidewalk to the inn's booth.

I'm not sorry for how I'm feeling. She's mine, and I don't like how half of the guys in this town look at her. In fact, every man in town greatly irritates me when it comes to E.

When I reach her, ignoring Crawford, I put my arm around E and pull her to my side. She comes to me with ease and puts her arm around my waist. It feels good and natural, like we've done it for years. Her smile widens when she looks up at me. Roman Crawford is not an issue.

"Hey, Sunshine," I say like I haven't seen her all day.

I lean down to kiss her forehead, but E lifts her chin and presses her lips to mine. The kiss is brief, but wow. She just kissed me in the town square in front of everyone. Guess we aren't hiding what's growing between us.

"Hey, Cowboy." E's eyes twinkle. "Is your shift over?"

"Yep. I'm all yours." And I really am.

Roman huffs. I turn to look at him. Well, look may be too kind of a word. I'm actually glaring at him. I seriously do not like this guy.

"Oh, hey, Crawford." Sure, I knew he was there the whole time. He just isn't worth acknowledging.

"Roman was telling me Santa has some new elves this year, and it should be interesting." E hands me a cup of hot chocolate she got from Beth's.

"So, the rumors are true?" Roman asked E.

"What rumors?" She looks scared for a moment but recovers quickly.

"You two are together?" Roman ignores me and only looks at E.

Unsure of how to answer, E looks up at me. We should have already talked about what's happening between us. Her confusion is my fault.

"That's nobody's business," I answer for her. I'm only being snappy because this is Roman Crawford.

Roman rolls his eyes but stays focused on E. He and I usually pretend the other isn't around. It's better than fighting every time we see each other.

"I thought you were smarter than that." Roman's voice and expression harden towards E.

"Hey, man." I move E behind me and step in front of Roman. "You can talk to me like that all day long, but you're not talking to her that way."

"You're nothing but a screw-up. You don't belong here." Roman looks past me to E. "Or with her."

"Your opinion doesn't matter," I tell him.

"It's not just me. Everybody in this town knows it." Roman tips his chin towards E. "And if she'll admit it, she knows it too."

My hands ball into fists as I take a step toward him. I'd love nothing more than to knock him out cold right here on the sidewalk. I stop my advance when E grabs my arm.

"Aiden, don't." Her fearful eyes plead with me to stop.

Looks like it's Crawford's lucky day. With a sigh, I nod and step back.

"It's not right." Roman shakes his head. "You shouldn't get to waltz back into town and get a cushy job. You darn sure shouldn't have the sweetest girl in town."

He's right. I already know all of this. I don't deserve E, but I'm grateful for the chance I'm getting with her.

"You ruin everything you touch." Roman isn't through. He turns to E. "You're setting yourself up for more heartache. When things get tough, he'll bail. In the end, he'll ruin you too."

"That's enough!" I roar.

Closing the small distance between Crawford and me, I get in his face. A large hand clamps down on my shoulder. It's the only thing stopping me from knocking him out.

"Crawford, you got a problem?" Spencer pushes his way between us. He's on duty for the rest of the day.

Roman holds his hands up in surrender and walks away. He had no problem going after me, even while I was still in uniform, but Roman won't risk a confrontation with Spencer. He and I have fought plenty of times over the years. Every one of those fights was broken up by someone. Spencer, on the other hand, has managed to knock Roman out not once but twice in high school.

"Okay, everyone. It's over. Go back to enjoying the ceremony." Leo directs the onlookers away.

"You ok?" Spencer asks.

"Yeah." I take my hat off and run my hand through my hair. "It's Crawford."

I don't have to say anything more. Spencer knows. From the look on Leo's face, he knows, too. Roman Crawford is a class-A jerk.

"Don't let him get to you," Spencer says.

I've tried for years to push things with Roman aside. The man just knows how to push my buttons. My anger settles a little when I feel a small hand slip into mine. Taking a deep breath, I release as much of my anger as possible before looking down at E. She's smiling at me. It's forced, but it still helps.

"The parade is about to start," she says.

"Take your girl and go see Santa." Leo pats me on the shoulder and walks away, laughing.

"Go on," Spencer urges. "Just stay clear of Crawford."

That's not a problem. I have no desire to see Crawford anymore today. It can't be avoided forever, though. As much as I hate to admit it, things will probably come to blows between us sooner or later.

"Come on, Sunshine." Putting my arm around her, I lead her over to the center of the square. "Let's go watch the parade."

We find a spot along the sidewalk around the gazebo. We're on the South Main Street side. We could have stayed at the coffee shop since it's on the corner of North Main Street, but that side is where the little kids and their parents line up. Most of the candy gets thrown out over there for the little ones. Besides, I've drawn enough attention on the north side for the day.

The parade starts down North Main Street and turns by the pizza parlor and florist shop before making its way to South Main Street. This leads them back to the parking lot where they started. We aren't a big town, so it isn't a long route.

Since it's crowded, I put E in front of me and wrap my arms around her. Hey. She kissed me in the town square, so I have every right to hold her like this now. Soon, we're surrounded by E's friends. Ally, Sammie, and Katie are having a blast today. All three have no doubt been by the booth for Cowboys for a drink or two. Ally let it slip that they even stopped at O'Brien's Tavern's booth and got an Irish Hot Whiskey. Hot Whiskey? Who would have thought such a thing existed? Leave it to the Irish to heat up whiskey.

Avery and Marcie join us before the last parade participant rides by, which is Santa's sleigh. They stand on either side of E. Both girls are a little younger than E and work with her at the inn.

"Oh my gosh." E's hands fly up to cover her mouth.

The other five women around me are doing the same thing. The guy next to us has to catch Katie to keep her from falling. Everyone on both sides of the street is laughing. I'm not sure if I want to look up. Something tells me I'm going to regret it. If Santa is causing this kind of reaction, I don't want to see it.

Looking up, I greatly regret my decision. Santa and the horse-drawn sleigh are a normal sight. They belong in a Christmas parade. Santa's elves, however, belong in an insane asylum. What idiot in this town thought it was a good idea to let Pit and Four be elves? I sure hope those two didn't act the way they are now on the other side of the street. I don't know how parents could explain this to their children.

"Oh my gosh. I'm ruined for life." Marcie covers her eyes and quickly turns her back to the street. "I can't believe my brother."

For a moment, I forgot that Marcie is Four and Jesse Calhoun's little sister. I can't see how this sweet girl was a part of that family.

Well, her green eyes are a sure sign, but that's where it ends. It's clear all the brains in the Calhoun family went to Marcie.

Four catches sight of E. He does an awkward dance. We won't even discuss that part. The idiot tosses her an entire bag of candy. She wasn't able to catch it right side up. Naturally, candy flies everywhere.

"I'm going to have to kill this fool," I mumble.

E leans her head back against my chest and laughs. The people around us hurry to pick up the spilled candy. It's one of the craziest things I've ever seen in my life.

"Do I need to give you a dollar to throw at him?" I whisper in E's ear.

That only makes matters worse. E doubles over laughing. I wrap my arms around her waist to keep her from falling. I glare at Katie from the corner of my eye. Surely, they didn't slip my girl an Irish Hot Whiskey.

"That was awesome." E finally has her balance back, but she's still laughing.

"E, I can't unsee that." I have no words to describe what I just saw. It's going to be etched into my mind for a long time.

"I know. That's what makes it so great." She can't stop laughing.

"You're so weird." I take her hand in mine as we walk around the square.

"But in a good way." She repeats what I said to her last week.

"In the best way," I correct her.

She's the best thing in my life, and I'm glad to be spending today with her. However, I'm sure complaints are already pouring in at the station about Santa's elves. This weirdness can only happen in Hayden Falls.

Chapter Thirty-Seven

Aiden

The sun has gone down, and Mayor Martin is giving a little holiday speech on stage. I'm glad he never turns The Tree Lighting Ceremony into a political event. His wife and son, Quinn, are up there with him. Quinn will more than likely be the Mayor of Hayden Falls someday.

After the Mayor flips the switch to light the tree, Jake Campbell and his band will play one or two more Christmas songs. The vendors have already started packing up to go home. The day went well except for the run-in with Crawford and the weird elf dance.

As the tree lights up, E snuggles closer against my side. She's smiled for most of the day. That's progress. She happily greeted everyone we knew as we walked around town. Most of them smiled back. A few people gave us odd looks, but my girl held her head high and kept moving. Maybe she didn't notice. If she did, her nonreaction proves she's the better person.

Of all the fun things we've done today, something's still missing. I want to encourage her to try something before we leave. Hopefully, I'm not about to ruin everything.

"Come on." I pull her to the corner of the square.

"What?" She looks confused.

"I thought we could build a snowman."

Immediately, her face drops as she looks around the square. This might be hard, but I know she can do it.

"The contest is over." She motions around the square. "There are snowmen everywhere."

"I know." I pull her into my arms. "We're not part of the contest. Come on, E. Build a snowman with me."

"I don't know." She continues to look around nervously.

"Just a little one," I coax. "Right here."

She looks down at the snow around our feet. "A little one?"

"A teeny tiny one," I assure her.

She looks up at me and takes a deep breath. "Okay."

Her voice is a little uncertain, but wow. She's really going to do this. I grin as we kneel and start gathering up snow. There's a tiny twinkle in her eyes. Good. Building snowmen used to be one of her favorite parts of winter. I hate her ex stole this from her. It would mean so much to me if I could give it back to her.

I roll up a ball of snow for the base. E playfully glares at me and shakes her head.

"What? It's perfect," I insist.

"You said tiny." She points at the snowball. "That's huge."

She swats my hands away. I laugh and let her do her thing. When she's finished, I stare at the little snowman in awe. When we agreed on teeny tiny, she meant just that. This little guy is less than a foot tall. E pulls a red ribbon from her pocket and ties it around the snowman's neck. Who carries ribbons in their pockets? My girl, apparently. She begins to look around like she's searching for something.

"Do you have a pocket knife?"

"It's snow, not cake." Still, I pull out my pocket knife, open it, and hand it to her.

"I'm not cutting it, silly." She looks at me like I've lost my mind.

She pulls on one of the large buttons on her coat and starts to cut it off.

"What are you doing?" I gently grab her wrist to stop her.

"She needs a hat."

"*She* needs a hat?" I'm stunned. "This little, tiny snowman is a girl?"

"Of course." E smiles at me. She looks as though I should have known this. "And Tiny Tina needs a hat."

"And you named her." I laugh and throw my hands up.

E naming snowmen is nothing new. I watch as she cuts the large button on her coat free. She happily places it on Tiny Tina's head. It's just another normal day in Hayden Falls. We stand up and admire her little snowman.

"I can't believe you cut off your button for a snowman." I lightly brush my lips to hers.

"Snowwoman," she corrects me. "And I have more at home. These aren't the original buttons, anyway. Those were ugly." E scrunches up her nose.

"Well, I think Tiny Tina looks great." I pull out my phone and take a couple of pictures.

Call me crazy for taking pictures, but I want a memory of this moment that wouldn't just be in my mind. She might not realize it yet, but this is a huge step for her.

I bump into someone as we start across the street to help pack up the inn's booth. Quickly, I reach out and catch the man before he falls to the pavement. Inwardly, I groan. I almost knocked over Mr. Wentworth.

"I'm sorry, Sir."

"Nothing new," Mr. Wentworth grumbles and walks away.

If only that were the end of it. With this being my life, things are far from over. Elijah Wentworth is standing in the street glaring at me for almost knocking over his grandfather.

"Man, I swear that was an accident." I hold my hands up. I don't want to argue with this man.

"Accidents seem to happen around you a lot. Don't they?" Eli is not happy.

"I don't know what to say." Talking to this family doesn't do any good.

"You can say a lot, but you won't." Eli folds his arms across his chest. He's not going to let this go tonight.

"What do you want from me?" I bluntly ask.

"It would be nice if you'd man up and tell the truth."

"You have the truth!" I shout. I'm so tired of going around this circle.

"Do we?" Eli's not convinced.

There's nothing I can say, so I stay quiet. Eli isn't finished, though.

"My grandfather's barn burnt to the ground. A Maxwell is responsible. Yes, you helped rebuild it. You bought my grandfather two horses to replace the one we couldn't get out. You even bought him a new tractor. If it had been anyone else, they would have been arrested, but not you. You get a slap on the wrist and whisked out of town." Eli's voice raises with every sentence.

"Sorry the gossip was so bad you had to stay away." Eli steps closer to me. "Now, here you are. A deputy in the town you ran from. All that talk has started up once again. You were raised better than that, Aiden. The sad part is, you're letting them pull her down, too." Eli points at E.

"She has nothing to do with this!" I roar.

"She's not part of what happened," Eli agrees. "She's one of the few people in this town who believes in you. It won't matter to the folks around here. Just being with you puts her in the gossip circles. Is that what you want for E?"

"No!" I shout.

"Then fix it!" Eli yells.

This shouting match has halted the entire square. Thank goodness the families with small children have already left. Glancing over my shoulder, I see Beth holding E back so she won't run out into the middle of this.

"Stop!"

Everyone turns to look at the man screaming in the middle of the street. Oh no. This can't happen. I step forward to stop him, but he holds his hand out.

"Stop," Brady says again. His chest heaves with every breath he takes. He looks Eli in the eye. "Leave him alone. Aiden didn't do it. I did it."

Shocked gasps are heard from the crowd. Sheriff Barnes, Spencer, and Leo watch from the sidewalk in front of Sweet Treats. Our parents are here along with our older brother Colton. Eli folds his arms across his chest and waits.

"Dad said Mr. Wentworth needed one of us to work on his tractor. I rode my bike out there and started on it. It was cold, so I turned on the space heater. I forgot to turn it off and unplug it. While I was eating dinner at the diner, I heard people talking about the fire. Yeah, I heard the fire trucks go out, but I didn't know where they were going. Someone in the diner said the person responsible was going to prison. I panicked and found Aiden." Brady stands defeated in the middle of the street. "The next morning, I was going to turn myself in, but when I got to the station, Aiden already claimed responsibility."

Mom rushes out to the street and wraps her arms around my brother. The crowd remains quiet. No one knows what to say. I walk over and pat Brady on the back. Colton, Dad, and Chase join us. Eli's grandfather is now standing next to him.

"He was fifteen and guilt-ridden. He had too much ahead of him. He's my little brother and my friend. I couldn't watch him go to prison for an accident," I tell the Wentworths. I no longer care what they think.

"We know," Mr. Wentworth said.

"You know?" I'm shocked.

"I saw the boy come and go." Mr. Wentworth tips his chin toward Brady. "I didn't think to check the barn after he left. By the time we realized it was on fire, all we could do was get the animals out. We weren't able to get one."

That one horse was Mrs. Wentworth's favorite. The loss of it caused a lot of gossip and anger around here. People in Hayden Falls think of their animals as family. Mrs. Wentworth considered that horse her pet.

Mr. Wentworth walks over and pats Brady on the arm. “Took you long enough, but you finally grew a pair.” He goes to walk away.

“Are you pressing charges?” My dad asked.

“No.” Mr. Wentworth looks between Brady and me. “These two have paid enough.” With that, he walks away.

Eli is still standing in the street. His expression is unreadable.

“You did that on purpose.”

“I did,” he admits. “We just wanted the truth to be told. There’s no honor in a lie, even if it is for a noble reason.”

“You didn’t have to use her.” I nod towards E.

“You’re right. I was wrong for that.” Eli turns to E. “If I hurt you, I’m sorry. Please forgive me. It was not my intent.”

E shakes her head in reply. She and Beth hurry over to Brady. Together, they wrap their arms around him and my mother.

“Take care of her, Maxwell, and welcome home.” Eli clamps his hand down on my shoulder. He nods to Sheriff Barnes. “This matter is done.” And just like his grandfather, Eli Wentworth quietly walks away.

Chapter Thirty-Eight

Etrulia

Brady Maxwell's admission tonight gave the citizens of Hayden Falls a lot to process. A secret that divided the members of our community was finally out in the open. I don't think I've ever seen a time when our townsfolk were shocked into silence. Usually, someone had something to say. Not tonight. No one said a word. They only stared at Brady and Aiden. Sheriff Barnes and his sons, Leo and Lucas, step forward and begin ushering people away. That's when the whispering started.

The members of the Maxwell family are handling this differently. Mr. Maxwell and Colton are quiet. Both are hiding their thoughts and emotions. Maybe they need time to figure out exactly what they thought and felt. To busy themselves, they help my uncle load the inn's booth onto the trailer and secure it while Aunt Sara and I pack up the decorations and supplies. Aiden stands behind Brady with his hands on his brother's shoulders. Mrs. Maxwell is an emotional mess. It's understandable.

Unsure of how people will react, Colton, his parents, and Chase surround Brady and lead him to their truck. The Wentworths may consider the matter finished, but the gossip circles are just getting started. I'm sure Megan is already typing up her blog posts for tomorrow. Brady and Aiden will be the headline for sure.

After hugging my aunt and uncle, I help Aunt Sara into the truck and close the door. Aiden's there when I turn around. He takes both of my hands in his and lightly squeezes them. I squeeze back. He looks so broken. I want to wipe the sad look from his face forever.

"If you want to go home with them." Aiden nods toward my aunt and uncle. "I understand."

Surely, he doesn't think I would bail on him at a time like this. He's only saying this to keep me out of the gossip that's already started. We haven't officially given a name to what's happening between us. Maybe tonight, we should.

"I'd rather go with you." I reach up and place my palm against his cheek. He leans into my touch. "Always the protector."

"It's kind of my job." He takes my hand that's touching his cheek and kisses it.

"You were eleven when I met you," I remind him. "You weren't a cop then."

He's been protecting others for as long as I've known him, probably even before that. Hopefully, now, this town will see him for the man he really is. It doesn't matter if they do or don't. I know his character and his heart. Aiden Maxwell is an honorable man, and I will never let him forget it. His grandfather would be proud of the man he helped raise.

"Are you sure?"

He looks around at the people still lingering nearby. Some only stare. Others are on their phones, no doubt already spreading gossip. This town is unbelievable at times.

"I'm sure." And yes, I glare at the people staring at us.

Aiden puts his arm around me, and we walk to his truck parked at the Sheriff's Office. The ride home is unnaturally quiet. I know the dark places a mind can go at times like this, so I don't push him to talk.

When we get to the house, I hurry upstairs for a shower. Aiden needs a little more time to himself anyway. He calls Brady, which is good. They need to talk. We do, too, but I'll wait until after Aiden gets his shower.

It's a little weird that the shy, quiet girl wants to talk. Does it make me a hypocrite? After all, I've kept things locked away for a long time. I don't know. Maybe it makes me an expert. That thought is kind of depressing. Who wants to be an expert at being sad and alone? I did it without even realizing it. I've gotten really good at staying quiet and hiding things. I sort of have first-hand experience with what Aiden is going through now.

While he showers, I make us a cup of hot chocolate, turn the Christmas lights on, and sit down on the couch. I want to call Brady, but I'm sure he's ready to talk to anyone other than his family. I understood that. So, I decided to send him a quick text like he used to send me.

Me: *I'm here, my friend.*

When Garrett hurt me, Brady sent me the same message two or three times a week. Sometimes, it turned into a few texts between us, but when I didn't want to talk, he didn't force me.

Brady: *Thanks, E. You're the best.*

And that was basically the same text I sent him in reply when I wasn't ready to talk. He and I will talk soon. I think Brady should know some of the things I want to say to Aiden tonight.

"What are you doing down here with all the lights off?" Aiden joins me on the couch.

"All the lights aren't off." I hand him his cup of hot chocolate.

We settle close together and silently watch the tree while we drink our hot chocolate. This is great, but it's not talking. I'm starting to realize how other people felt when I was quiet. I don't think I like this too much. Still, sometimes, it can't be helped. At times, you have to heal a little before you can talk.

"How's Brady?"

"He's not sure how to handle things now. None of us was prepared for that to come out. I'll give them tonight and go over there tomorrow. I told Brady if Colton or Dad starts in on him, he can come here tonight." Aiden lays his head back against the couch cushion.

"Do you want to talk about it?"

"I don't know." Aiden leans forward to set his empty cup on the coffee table. "No matter what any of us say, this town will still give my family a hard time. Eli's right. They'll drag you down with us."

"It doesn't matter what this town thinks." I rub my hand across his back.

"It doesn't matter what they do to my family and me." He leans back and looks at me. "But it matters to me what they do to you."

"You can't lock me away in a cocoon."

"No, but I don't have to cause you more pain. You hate gossip and being the center of attention. I lied to you and this town. That's going to have some serious repercussions. We've added extra security to the inn. If you want to go to your aunt and uncle's house, I understand."

Yes, it's true. I hate gossip and people staring at me, but that was the old me. I've become a different person this year. I'm not fully sure who I am yet, but scared and quiet aren't what I want anymore.

Is he serious about me going home? Wow. This is not where I wanted this conversation to go. Maybe I read too much into our relationship. Now, I feel stupid. I may not be sure of a lot of things, but I know I don't want to stay where I'm not wanted. I knew I'd have to go home sooner or later, but this hurt more than I thought it would.

"Okay." I guess there's only one thing left for me to do. "If that's what you want, I'll go get my things."

I stand to go upstairs to pack my things. Aiden jumps to his feet. He grabs my upper arms to stop me. The hurt in his eyes matches my own. Seeing him like this makes me wish I hadn't asked to talk tonight.

"No, E." He shakes his head. "That's not what I want at all."

"Then what do you want?" We've been sidestepping this since he came home in August.

"I want you safe."

"My uncle and Leo think I'm safe with you." Neither of them would have let me come here if it wasn't true.

"You're safe from your ex here but not from this town. I'm sure rumors are already flying around. I lied. Even though I did what I thought was best at the time, I lied to the Sheriff, to this town, to my family, and to you. That's going to matter, and not in a good way." Aiden sighs deeply and lets me go.

"You didn't lie to me."

"I lied to everyone."

"Not to me." Releasing a deep breath, I gather my strength. It's time for me to be honest, too. "We didn't talk after that night. You shut me out. I only saw you in passing, and that was from a distance. It was the first year I didn't see you on my birthday."

"I'm sorry." He tosses his hand in the air. "I was building a barn."

Yeah, I knew where he was. I wouldn't let my aunt and uncle take me out to dinner that year. Instead, the three of us stayed home and grilled out steaks. It wasn't as great as the cookouts at the Maxwells were, but it was fine. I didn't feel like celebrating that year anyway.

"I knew you didn't do it," I admit.

"I know you have always believed in me. You're the only one in this town who did." He takes my hands in his. "Thank you for that."

"No, Aiden." I shake my head. "That's not what I mean. I mean, I did believe in you. I always will, but I *knew* the truth."

He narrows his eyes. "Brady told you."

"No." I take another deep breath. "Well, yes, but not directly. I heard him, but he wasn't talking to me. He found you on the town bridge that night and told you what happened."

Aiden steps back and runs a hand through his hair. "How do you know that? Nobody knows that." He closes his eyes, and his head falls back for a moment. "You were under the bridge that night."

I drop my eyes to the floor and nod. "I didn't mean to eavesdrop."

In middle and high school, I used to walk out to the town bridge sometimes when I wanted to be alone. There's a perfect spot under the bridge to sit and do absolutely nothing. Aiden and Beth found me there a few times when we were kids. I was even quieter back then than I am now. Hayden Falls is a safe place, so I wasn't scared to go out to the bridge at night. That night, the sun had just set, but it wasn't dark yet. Still, I always took a flashlight with me when I wasn't sure what time I'd get home.

"You tried to tell Sheriff Barnes I didn't do it, but you left that part out." Aiden tilts his head. Again, I nod mine. "Thank you for keeping my brother's secret." He walks over and lifts my chin until our eyes meet. "And I don't want you to leave."

"I don't want to leave. I've never felt as safe in my life as I do when I'm with you." Wrapping my arms around his waist, I lay my head against his chest.

This town can talk all they want to, but nothing they say or do will make me love this man any less. His arms come around me, holding me tight. This is the safest place on Earth. If I could stay here forever, I'd be the happiest woman in the world. He should know that.

"Aiden?"

"Yeah, Sunshine?"

"I love you."

Chapter Thirty-Nine

Aiden

My heart just stopped. No, that can't be right. I'm still breathing, so my heart is still working. Even though it just exploded inside my chest. My mind is taking a bit longer to catch up, though.

Words I've dreamed of hearing for years were just spoken. They're the most important words in my life. Only, I didn't say them. *She* did. This is beyond great, but it's wrong. A gentleman should say those words first. I just rolled my grandfather over again. My dad will lecture me for years to come because of this.

Maybe I didn't hear what I thought I heard. No, I'm pretty sure I did. I should probably make sure, though.

Releasing her, I cup her adorable little face in my hands and search her eyes. Her big blue eyes are holding back unshed tears. Strange, I've never noticed someone's eyes filled with tears before.

"E, you just…" A tear escapes her eye, and I wipe it away with my thumb. "You said." She nods. "Say it again." I need to hear it.

"I love you, Aiden," she says again. "I always have. I always will."

My heart exploded again. Thankfully, the rest of me is starting to catch up. In one swift movement, I wrap my arms around her and claim her lips with mine. She tastes sweet and chocolatey. Hot chocolate is definitely one of my favorite things now.

My mind finally starts to catch up with my heart, emotions, and body. I let her say those words twice. She's 2 and 0 here. That's not good. The gentleman in me needs to stand up and make himself known. Only my lips are seriously enjoying hers.

Slowly, and I mean very slowly, I pull my lips from hers. Her deep blue eyes flutter a few times. The flush on her cheeks is cute. Her breathing is as ragged as mine. She looks drunk from our kisses. It's fine. I feel drunk. She's the only woman to affect me this way.

"I love you, too." My breathing still isn't normal. "Always have. Always will."

She starts to say something, but I cut her off with another kiss. Words can come later. Right now, I need more of her. She doesn't seem to mind. E wraps her arms around my neck, pulling me to her. My arms tighten around her waist as I lift her off the floor. Her being a lot shorter than me has some cute advantages. When the kiss ends, I set her back down on the floor.

"So, does this mean I'm staying?" she asks with a grin on her face.

"Oh, Sunshine, you're definitely staying. I just hope this town doesn't destroy you because of me."

"I don't care what this town says or does." E wraps her arms around my waist again. "Losing you would destroy me."

"You could never lose me." I kiss her forehead before letting mine rest there.

"I hope not. After all, you did promise not to leave me again."

I lift my head just enough to look at her. "You remember that?"

She was really drunk that night. I'm surprised she remembers anything.

"Not all of it. Most of it is fuzzy, but Beth told me."

With my hand on her neck, I run my thumb along her jaw. "You don't drink often. I don't ever want to see you like that again."

"I wasn't planning on getting drunk, but I couldn't help it. I was nervous and mad." E drops her eyes and tries to look away, but I tilt her chin up with my thumb.

"Why were you nervous and mad?"

"I didn't really want to go. And you were there. And Karlee was there. I didn't like her touching you." She tries to look away again, but I don't let her.

"You were jealous." It's all I can do not to grin. Doing so will probably get me punched.

"No more than you were." Her chin lifts slightly, and her eyebrows raise.

She's got me there. I did *not* like seeing her dancing with Jesse Calhoun. His brother Four has me threatening to kill him on a weekly basis.

"You're right." I press my lips to hers for a quick kiss. "I can't stand the thought of another man touching you." I kiss her again. "And you have nothing to worry about from Karlee or any other woman."

I softly kiss her again. Slowly, I pepper little kisses across her cheek to her ear. There's not a woman in the world who holds a candle to her.

"You have nothing to worry about either." Her voice is breathy.

She tilts her head slightly to allow my lips better access to her neck. She smells like coconut and flowers. She's intoxicating. Slowly, my lips work their way back up to her mouth. I never want to stop kissing her.

"Promise you'll never leave again," she whispers.

"Only if you go with me." I kiss my way across her other cheek.

E's small hand slips into mine. She takes a step back, breaking our kiss. Her cheeks and neck are flushed. I like this shade on her. Those beautiful pink lips of hers are a shade darker and swollen from our kisses. Her eyes are so full of love that they draw me to her. Oh, how I love this look on her.

She leads me up the stairs and into the bedroom. Still holding my hand, she pulls the covers back with the other. When our eyes meet, I see the love I have for her mirrored back at me. Dropping my hand, she reaches for the hem of her pajama top. I grab both of her hands in mine.

"What are you doing?" I'm no fool. I know what she's doing.

"Playing *Scrabble*."

"*Scrabble*?" My eyes widen as I practically choke the word out.

Yeah, she loves that game, but this is ridiculous. She giggles, causing me to laugh too. She's cute, but I need to be serious here. I cup her face in my hands again. She needs to look me in the eye for this.

"E, if we cross this line, it changes everything. Even without a ring or a license yet, this means you're forever mine." I lean close, and my voice drops lower. "I can't have you one night and lose you. If it's not forever with you, it will kill me."

She places the palm of her hand against my cheek. "I'm already yours, but this makes you forever mine, too."

"I'm already yours." And I am. She completely owns me.

With every ounce of passion we have, our lips come together. Our other kisses have nothing on this one. Her arms slide around my neck, pulling me closer to her. I scoop her up. Without breaking the kiss, I settle us under the covers.

My life is a mess. I don't know what will happen tomorrow with this town or my family. None of it matters tonight. Tonight, after years of longing, waiting, and heartache, the woman I love is in my arms in a way I've only dreamed of. She's the only part of my life that's perfect. Tonight, I'm making Etrulia Hayes forever mine.

Chapter Forty

Aiden

Mondays have a way of being the absolute worst or totally creepy. Today, it's totally creepy. I've avoided the town square since Saturday night's fiasco. My job won't allow me to do it forever. This little officer program with the business owners in town is grating on my nerves. How in the world am I going to keep it up now? I don't know. Maybe I can convince the Sheriff to let me patrol the rural areas of Hayden Falls, and he can give my section of the town square to someone else. Nah. There's no way he'll go for that. The only choice I have here is to suck it up and do my job.

It's getting close to lunchtime, so I might as well walk to the square. I can stop by Beth's and get E her favorite coffee before walking to the inn. I've been having lunch with her every day since she started staying at my place. Oh, how I love having her in my house.

E thinks I only have lunch with her every day because I want to keep an eye on her. Well, her safety is extremely important to me, but it's not the only reason. The closer we get, the more I need to be around her. She's like a drug to me. I might need to be careful here. The last thing I need is for her to think I'm clingy. Guys don't get clingy. Do they? Surely not. That has to be a girl thing.

As I walk past Sweet Treats, Ms. Taylor heads into the bakery. I open the door for her with a smile and a tip of my hat. My job is to protect and serve. This is me serving. Besides, the bakery is part of my wonderful little section of the square.

Ms. Taylor can be a problem, though. She's one of the biggest gossipers in town. More than half of the rumors around here are either started or added to by her. She's also unforgiving. No one can hold a grudge like this woman can. I swear she has journals where she keeps a record of every offense that happens in this town. I try never to speak to this woman. She's been known to swing her oversized handbag at people. To my surprise, Ms. Taylor pats my arm before walking into the bakery. See? Creepy.

I'm not sure if the moment with Ms. Taylor caused it or not, but every nerve in my body is on edge now. It feels like somebody's watching me. A glance around the square proves me right. It's not just *somebody*. Practically every person in town is looking at me. A few glare openly while others duck their heads and go about their business. The people in this town can be so annoying at times. With a sigh, I reach for the door of the coffee shop.

Stepping inside Beth's Morning Brew did not provide me with a peaceful oasis. The room goes silent as everyone turns to stare at me. Well, except for a few employees working behind the counter. I now understand why E hates being the center of attention. When I was younger, being stared at didn't bother me. Now, it's beyond creepy. I would turn around and leave if this coffee wasn't for E.

"Aiden," Karlee squeals.

She grabs my arm and pulls me further inside the coffee shop. The way she turns us has my back toward the other customers. It doesn't matter. I can feel their eyes on me. Yep, I should have left the moment I opened the door. There's bound to be a recipe online for E's favorite coffee. I can just make it for her when we get home.

"I knew from the beginning you didn't do it." Karlee is bouncing and practically gushing. She's creeping me out even more. "You should come over to my grandparent's house for dinner on Friday. We so love having you over."

Okay. I'm seriously creeped out now. I may have entered the *Twilight Zone* here. I haven't been to her grandparent's house since my junior year of high school. I've only spoken to Karlee once in the past seven years. It's probably been longer than that. When I saw her back in August at Cowboys, thankfully, Miles was there to send her on her way. I have no idea why she's acting this way.

"Karlee, I'm going to have to decline the offer." I turn her down as politely as I can. Since I'm on duty, I don't want to be too rude to her.

"Oh, come on, Aiden. You used to love it." Karlee's voice is whiny and sugary sweet. It grates heavily on my nerves like sandpaper. She can whine all she wants. I don't want anything to do with her.

Before I can turn her down again, a to-go cup of coffee is shoved in front of my face. The hand wrapped around the cup I know *very* well. I've kissed this wrist several times over the past couple of days. I can still feel both of these hands moving across my chest and those fingers digging into my back. My eyes follow the trail my lips took up this arm last night. Long, soft, light brown curls fall loosely over her shoulders. When my eyes reach E's face, she's not looking at me.

"Your coffee, Cowboy," E says without taking her eyes off Karlee.

My eyes dart between the two women as they glare at each other. I groan inwardly. This is why Karlee was acting so strange. I need to do something before my beautiful, sweet, quiet little girlfriend claws my ex's eyes out. I can call E my girlfriend now, right? After the past couple of nights with her and the fact we agreed on forever first, I think so. Yeah, she is, without a doubt, my girlfriend.

I wrap one hand around hers and the coffee cup, lowering it from where E's still holding it in front of my face. My other hand gently fists the hair behind her head. I tug just enough to tilt her face up.

"Thank you, Sweetheart." I softly press my lips to hers.

Am I being dramatic? Oh, definitely. I don't break the kiss until I hear Karlee huff and storm out the door. E looks a little dazed when I pull my lips from hers. I love the effect my kisses have on her.

"I told you. You don't have anything to worry about."

"Oh, I know." E nods. "*She* needed to know it."

Whoa! My girl has a possessive streak. That's kind of a turn-on, and the last thing I'll do right now is tease her about it. What's that saying about poking the bear? Or maybe the one about kittens having claws? At this moment, I believe E might be a bit of both. It's really cute. Of course, I love everything about her.

When I first walked into the coffee shop, I didn't realize E was here. After a quick look around, every alarm in me goes off.

"You're alone?"

"Yeah. I picked up lunch at the diner."

Two to-go bags from Davis's Diner sit on the counter. I slip my coffee cup into one of the two to-go trays with handles Beth gives me. Beth adds several more to-go cups. Looks like she's grabbing lunch and coffee for everybody at the inn. I grab the bags from the diner and let her get the drinks. I'm not about to risk dropping a woman's cup of coffee. I do value my life.

"I'm not sorry I did that," E says when we're about halfway to the inn. "I *am* sorry we'll probably be in Hayden's Happenings tomorrow."

For a minute, I thought we would walk all the way to the inn in silence. It's a good thing my hands are full, or I'd reach over and pull her against my side. Her ex could be watching, so I don't risk it. The last thing we need is for him to figure out she's staying at my place. She hasn't said so, but I see the little flash of fear in her eyes when I drop her off at the inn in the mornings. She's staying strong, though, and I admire that.

"We won't," I assure her.

"Megan used to leave me out of her blog posts, but I don't trust her to do that anymore."

"Don't worry. She won't link us together." She looks at me questionably. I might as well come clean. "The Sheriff and Spencer talked to her. She only knows that it's a serious matter and an active case. She won't post anything about us. If she does, her blog will be shut down."

Thankfully, E lets the matter drop. If she's upset, she shows no sign of it. This isn't to keep the town from knowing about us. We're trying to keep her location concealed from her ex.

The inn is only a few blocks from the square. Still, I take notice of every possible corner or shadow her ex could hide in along the route. There are a few places where someone could hide. Even one is too many for my liking. After we eat, I'll talk to her about leaving the inn alone. She was just starting to discover her inner strength again. I hate to tap that down, but her safety is more important.

"Maybe you shouldn't make this walk alone," I suggest cautiously. She glances up at me and frowns. I can tell she wants to debate this. Yeah, I should have waited. "At least, not for a little while."

E sighs deeply, but she doesn't agree or disagree with me. Hopefully, she'll see the danger of being alone without me reminding her of what that jerk did to her. If she has to remember what happened, it will force her to relive it in her mind. I want to keep her safe and moving forward. It's hard to find a happy medium here.

We don't talk the rest of the way to the inn. Seeing her go into quiet mode concerns me. Another thing that worries me is seeing Spencer's cruiser here. Nothing came over my radio. Maybe this is his regular daily visit to the inn. It's wishful thinking on my part. The moment we step inside, the look on Spencer's face tells me something happened.

"What's wrong?" E asks before I can.

"Why don't you set that up in the breakroom and meet us in your office?" Spencer points to the food and coffee we're carrying.

"Okay," E's voice trembles a little.

Her aunt and uncle give us a weary smile before heading down the hall to E's office with Spencer behind them. I have no doubts this is about her ex.

"Come on, Sunshine." I motion toward the employee breakroom at the back of the inn. "Let's get Marcie and Avery set up with lunch."

After getting the girls settled in the breakroom, we head to E's office. She doesn't bother going to her desk. She has a good idea of what this is about. E straightens her shoulders and lifts her head to face this bravely. She's come a long way. I want to hold her, but I don't want to crowd her. When she's ready for me, she'll give me a sign. However, I can offer her some encouragement. I was going to put my hand on her shoulder, but she takes a step back. With her standing against my chest, I wrap an arm around her waist. If she needs my strength, I'll gladly give it to her.

Spencer walks over and hands E an envelope. "This came in today's mail."

The envelope doesn't have a return address, which is why her uncle called Spencer's cell phone instead of the Sheriff's Office. The postage is stamped in Billings. No matter what the postage says, I have a feeling Garrett Preston is nearby. With shaky hands, E pulls out a single picture and stares at it.

"Is this a church?" E stares at the photo.

"You've never been here?" Spencer asks.

"No." E shakes her head.

"I called a friend to confirm it. This is the chapel inside the Preston Hotel and Casino in Vegas." Spencer's eyes meet mine. Yeah. We need to catch this creep.

His words hit E hard. She presses further back into me. Wrapping my arms tighter around her, I hold her against my chest. Her ex is not going to stop. Sadly, this still isn't enough to arrest him. My chest tightens. Christmas is getting closer, and my girl isn't safe.

Chapter Forty-One

Etrulia

The wonderful lunch I planned with everyone isn't happening today. My appetite is gone, but my aunt insists I eat something. So, I grab a plate of fries and my coffee. I return to my office, not wishing for idle conversations with the staff. Of course, the food from the diner didn't go to waste. Everyone polished that off in less than half an hour.

"Mr. Hayes got in a few more security cameras. You wanna help me install those right quick?" Spencer asked Aiden.

"They're really just upgrades for what we have now. These give a better view with more angles. They even have motion sensors," Uncle Silas adds.

"Sure," Aiden agrees before turning to me. "If you need anything from your apartment, you should get that ready."

"I will after I call Miss Donaldson back." I smile and wave as they head out the door.

Miss Donaldson is the bride for the Christmas-themed wedding this Saturday. She's sweet and nothing like my bridezilla back in

August. I really enjoy working with her. We have a few last-minute details to confirm for her reception.

"Oh, Aiden," Aunt Sara calls out as she hurries to the door.

"Yes, Ma'am?" Aiden meets her in the doorway.

"Will you and Spencer check the windows in E's apartment while you're out there?" Aunt Sara asked. "I don't think anyone has made sure they're secure."

"No problem," Aiden assured her. He winks at me and disappears from the doorway.

He's a wall of strength I need in my life. I'm struggling to hold it together. So far, I haven't had a panic attack since seeing the picture. This is a huge accomplishment for me. Still, none of it makes any sense. Why would Garrett think I would marry him after what he did to me? Could he just be messing with me for the fun of it? His mind is twisted, so I don't know. One thing's for sure—Aiden's right. I shouldn't walk to the town square alone anymore until this is over.

After finishing the phone call with Miss Donaldson, I clean up my desk and head to my apartment. Aiden and Spencer have already finished installing the new cameras. Uncle Silas is pleased with the new setup. Aiden's work with the band in Tennessee came in handy today. He tweaked the system and got my uncle a better resolution on the recordings.

While they check the windows, I go to my room and quickly pack another suitcase with more clothes and a box of personal items I need to take to Aiden's house.

"Looks like you're moving in with me," Aiden teases as he walks by me. He's teasing. Right?

"Looks like." I grin at him. I'm pretty sure I'm blushing too. The thought of moving in with him has my mind drifting to places I shouldn't go right now.

Aiden checks the window in my bedroom while I grab a few more things from the bathroom. When I get back to my room, he's standing in the middle of the room with a devilish grin on his face.

"What?" He's so cute. I want to throw myself at him.

"Thank you." His grin widens.

I don't understand. Why is he thanking me? Aiden raises his hand. I suck in a sharp breath when I realize what he's holding between two fingers.

"Aiden, I…" There's not really anything I can say. He's caught me.

"Will I still get one every week?"

How could I have been so careless? With everything going on, I forgot about the craft table in my room. Aiden had to move it to get to the window.

"You don't have to mail them anymore." He walks over and wraps his arms around me. "You can just hand them to me or leave them around the house as little surprises."

"You're not mad?"

He kisses my forehead. "Not at all, Sunshine. And I thank you for always believing in me. These little cards lifted me up many times."

"You weren't talking to me. The cards were the only way I could talk to you." It broke my heart when I lost him as my friend.

"I'm sorry about that. I didn't want what my family was going through to affect you. I always planned on coming back for you when you turned eighteen. This town isn't forgiving, and after what I did, I was afraid I lost my chance with you."

Oh, my gosh. He planned on coming back for me. My heart just melted. Well, it melted again. He's been breaking through to my truest emotions for a while now.

"I knew all along that you were protecting your brother." I push up on my toes and kiss him.

From the sound of it, there was some serious miscommunication between us during the past six years. He did what he thought he needed to do at the time, and I talked to him the only way I knew how. The cards let me feel close to him when he was thousands of miles away.

"I figured it out a few months ago." He reaches for my suitcase.

"How?" I grab his arm. "I was careful."

"You were," he admits. "The cards stopped mid-January and didn't start again until the end of February."

He doesn't have to explain the time frame to me. It was after Garrett hurt me. It took about a month and a half before I felt like doing anything other than crying and feeling sorry for myself.

"Then there was the day I saw you coming from the post office, and we walked to Beth's shop together. I got a card the next day. So, I figured it was you."

I should have known better than to try and fool a cop. Well, in my defense, when I first started sending him the cards, Aiden wasn't a cop. I knew he was in Tennessee training in law enforcement. It's why I went to different towns to mail some of them. Because he wouldn't talk to me, I thought if he knew they were from me, he would throw them away without reading them.

"What you did for Brady was brave and heroic."

"I'm no hero." Aiden shakes his head.

I tap his chest with my finger. "This uniform says otherwise. Even without it, you gave up your future to save your brother. That matters."

Aiden takes off his hat and runs his hand through his hair. He doesn't believe he did anything grand, but he did. The entire town sees it now. Megan's blog has praised him for it. Of course, Brady is now taking a Hayden Falls bashing with the gossip circles.

Aiden gave up his future of being a pitcher in Major League Baseball to save his little brother. He was willing to go to jail for arson rather than letting it happen to Brady. That was a lot for an eighteen-year-old boy to do. There are grown men around here who wouldn't take another person's place like that. He will always be a hero in my eyes. At the time, he wasn't aware Sheriff Barnes would go easy on him when he confessed to burning down Mr. Wentworth's barn. It had to have been a scary situation for him. Still, he gave up everything to save his little brother. Did the Sheriff know the truth back then? It's possible.

"Yeah, but I lost you." Aiden huffs out a breath.

Placing my palm against his cheek, I draw his attention back to me. "You didn't lose me. We just took the long way to get here."

The road here has been an extremely long one. I've loved this man for most of my life. Sadly, the road ahead still isn't clear for us to have a happy life together.

"Does that mean you are officially my girlfriend?" Aiden leans his head closer to mine. The way his eyes dance and his voice deepens, he has every part of me wanting to melt into his arms.

"I thought we cleared that up when we played *Scrabble*." My eyes dance, too, as I slightly lift my chin.

"*Scrabble*." Aiden leans even closer. His lips hover above mine. "I *love* playing *Scrabble* with you."

"Can we play later?" I whisper.

"Oh, Sunshine. We'll play *Scrabble* any time and for as long as you want," Aiden promises. His lips press against mine.

"Oh, please," Spencer groans from the doorway. "I'll never be able to look at *Scrabble* the same again."

Aiden chuckles and grabs my suitcase off the bed. Dipping my head to hide the blush on my cheeks, I pick up the small box of items from the bathroom.

"Man." Aiden narrows his eyes at Spencer as he walks out the door. "You don't play *Scrabble*. You can't put words together."

"Jerk." Spencer punches Aiden on the arm.

Aiden laughs harder. It's good these two never lost the friendship they had growing up. When I reach the door, Spencer puts his hand on my shoulder.

"I don't want to scare you." Spencer's expression is full of concern. "It's getting close to Christmas. I don't want anything to happen to you. Maybe you could take some time off until after New Year."

I want to flat-out refuse his suggestion, but Spencer means well. Even though I'm trying to hide it, I'm scared. Garrett can't be trusted. A two-week vacation does sound nice, but I can't take it. There's a wedding at the inn on Saturday. I can't bail on Miss Donaldson.

"I have a wedding this weekend and a few ladies' luncheons the first of next week. I'll limit my time to just those for now." It's a compromise.

“Good.” Spencer sounds relieved. “You can handle everything else over the phone with your aunt and the staff.”

That’s a good idea, and I agree with it. I’m not happy about it, but Spencer wouldn’t ask me to do this if it wasn’t necessary. If Garrett tries anything else, I fear Aiden and Spencer will insist on hiding me out somewhere. How did my life become such a mess? Will I ever be free of Garrett Preston?

Chapter Forty-Two

Aiden

Christmas is my favorite holiday. For the past six years, no one would have believed it. I was grumpy and rude to almost everybody. Christmas was a big reminder of what I lost. It hurt to come home to Montana and only stay for a couple of days. Staying any longer only caused the gossip to start up again. If the gossip and hateful actions of this town only affected me, I wouldn't have cared about any of it. What it did to my mom broke my heart.

My mom is a kind woman. She has a heart for helping others. She has a lot of friends in Hayden Falls and the surrounding towns. If she saw someone in need, my mom was there to help in any way she could. Dad said Mom had what my grandmother called a servant's heart. Growing up, I never understood what that meant. I do now. Mom loves openly and big. She latched onto Chase the first day he was at the ranch. She and Dad are now legally his foster parents. It's proof of how she goes out of her way for others.

My entire family was ridiculed when I took the blame for Mr. Wentworth's barn burning down and the loss of his wife's favorite horse. Some of the women in town would cross the street so they wouldn't have to walk past my mom. Hearing her cry at night because a few of her so-called friends had joined in on the shaming of our family broke my heart. My mom didn't deserve that. Nobody does.

As much as it hurt to stay away during the holidays, it kept my mom from being mistreated again. Thankfully, E's aunt helped my mom. Mom shut herself off for about a month. Mrs. Hayes, being a true friend, pushed her way in and got my mom out and about again. I will forever be grateful for her kindness.

Christmas is E's favorite holiday, too. She loves everything about it. The tree, decorations, and even the food are all special to her. Growing up, we spent a lot of time together during the Christmas holidays. It hurt coming home and not being able to share the time with her.

My heart shattered two years ago when I came home and found out she was engaged. I couldn't have her, so I should have been happy for her. I wasn't. Joy and happiness were gone from my world. So, what did I do? I exploded. I caught an early flight back to Tennessee and took my anger at the world out on one of my friends in the band. Yeah, I did apologize to Evan later, but I hated myself for yelling at him. Bryan and Harrison talked me through that time in my life. Of course, it took me months to tell them why I was so angry.

This year is different. It's Christmas Eve, and I'm spending it with the people I love the most. From lunchtime until after dinner, E and I will be at my parent's house. Mom feels that Christmas Day belongs to families, so she always plans a huge party for Christmas Eve. Many of our friends will drop by throughout the afternoon.

I groan when the bed moves. E giggles, and I wrap my arms tighter around her. I don't have to open my eyes to know what's happening. The same thing happens every morning.

"What a good boy," she coos. "Yes, you are. Are you ready to go outside?"

How she can sound so cheery right now is beyond me. My groan becomes a growl when my brother's dog barks at her. It's a happy sound. I swear he's telling her yes.

"Come on." E pushes the cover back and sits up.

Before she slides out of bed, I grab her wrist and pull her down against me. Waking up with her makes mornings a happier time for me. Usually, I need coffee to get me going. Now, I need her.

"Morning, Sunshine." I softly kiss her cheek.

"Morning, Cowboy." She lightly presses her lips to mine. "I'll take him out."

I don't want to, but I let her go. I told Colton if his dog does his business in my house, I'm taking it out on him. Bo is well-trained, and we've had no accidents so far. He's also latched onto my girl with a serious protective streak. Bo has always liked E. She's been around since Colton got him as a pup. Still, I swear that dog can sense there's a problem. The way he protects E makes me think about getting a German Shepherd someday.

"You're too kind to that mutt," I grumble. I don't mean it. I actually like my brother's dog. Bo is the best thing about Colton.

"Awe, there's no such thing," she says in a sweet voice as she pets Bo behind the ear.

E slips on her fluffy blue bedroom shoes and grabs a robe off the chest at the foot of the bed. My body protests as I climb out of bed and head for the kitchen. While she takes Bo out, I'll fix us a cup of coffee. The smell of freshly baked cookies still lingers in the air. E spent the past few days baking every Christmas cookie she could find a recipe for. *Pinterest* is awesome, or so I hear. I have no idea what it is.

Since we're heading to my parent's house this morning, Colton doesn't show up to get Bo like he has every morning. It's really shocking he lets Bo stay here at night. Colton has one friend and a dog. That's it. He's just weird. Colton and I don't get along, so I don't even try to figure him out.

As much as I want to stay here and cuddle up with E on the couch, we need to get to the ranch. After a quick breakfast, we load up a hundred boxes of cookies. Okay. It's probably not a hundred, but it's close. I think so, anyway. I open the back passenger-side door for Bo to jump in the truck. The huge dog cocks his head and looks at me with those big puppy dog eyes like I'm crazy. I pay him no mind and open E's door for her. Before I can close the door after she's settled inside, Bo jumps in the front at her feet and lays his head on her lap. This dog is fighting me for my girl's attention. It's the strangest thing I've ever seen him do. E laughs as I close the door. Colton and I are going to have to talk about his dog.

Walking into my parent's house, the happy sounds of family surround us. Well, most of them are happy anyway. Brady is sitting in the corner of the couch with his head ducked down. He slipped in sometime late last night. It rips my heart out to see my happy brother so broken. Our situations have reversed now. If I could flip things back the way they were, I would. He's a good man and doesn't deserve the pain he's feeling now. I'm the one who took his choice away from him when I confessed. Brady was going to turn himself in. This is the only thing he and I argue about.

Chase seems happy. At times, I see a bit of sadness in his eyes. He should be spending this time with his family. I don't want to tell him, but from the looks of his parent's case, he's probably never going back there. I'm really glad I found him that night and brought him here. I recruited him to help me carry in all of the cookies E baked. Several platters are for all of us to enjoy, while the small boxes are gifts for anyone who stops by today.

After helping Mom and Mrs. Hayes set all the cookies on the counter, I find E in the living room. I'm not sure how to react to the scene before me. My girl is sitting next to my little brother on the couch. Their shoulders and heads touch. One of the boxes of cookies sits on E's thigh. She and Brady pull out a cookie. The random words they're saying make no sense to me. It sounds like a grocery list.

Colton nudges my shoulder and points to the backyard. His narrow eyes and hard expression make me want to punch him in the face. It's been this way for years. I hate his judgmental glares. Reluctantly, I follow him outside.

"They're just friends," Colton says when we're far enough from the house that nobody can hear us.

"I know that." Now, I seriously want to punch him. "Do you have a point you want to make here?"

"Yeah. Leave them be," Colton snaps.

"Whatever, man." Throwing my hands up, I turn to go back inside. Conversations with Colton are one of my least favorite things. My brother has no people skills.

"He was there for her." Colton's words stop me. "When nobody else could get through to her, Brady did somehow. They would have a bowl of popcorn or some kind of snack between them. One of them would say a random word, and the other would say the first thing that word made them think of. Sometimes, it was about food, movies, sports, or songs. Other times, it made no sense at all."

Colton blows out a breath. He's fidgeting. I've never seen him like this. My *'I have it all together'* brother doesn't have it all together today. Hopefully, he's not having a stroke here.

"I can't even begin to explain how it worked, but on a few days, it helped E heal. Brady needs that now." Colton finally looks me in the eye. This is the most he's said to me in a long time. "She loves you. She's just returning the favor to him." Colton points at me. "So don't you dare get mad at either of them." Ah, there's my bossy no-it-all brother.

Still, his words floored me. My grumpy brother has a protective streak. Even though he gives me a hard time, I'm glad to see him standing up for our little brother and E like this.

"I'm not mad at either of them," I tell him, and I'm not. "They're two of the people I love the most."

"I saw the look you had when you walked in there." Colton's eyes are hard again.

"I won't lie. I'm extremely jealous where she's concerned," I admit. "But I'm not a jerk, regardless of what you think of me. I won't do anything to hurt E or Brady."

My brother is really pissing me off here. If it wasn't Christmas, I believe I would actually punch him. You'd think he and I would be close with only two years between us, but we're not. Colton is not as fun and outgoing as Brady and me. All he does is sulk around here in his own little world. He's got no right to tell anybody what to do. Well, other than the ranch hands, that is. Colton will one day inherit this place.

Colton takes off his cowboy hat and runs a hand through his hair. He takes several deep breaths before he can look at me again.

"I don't think you're a jerk." My eyes widen. Colton walks up to me. His face twists like he's struggling to say what he wants to say. "What you did for Brady was honorable. Sorry, I thought you were a punk kid who didn't give a crap about anybody but yourself."

"Thanks." I'm not sure how to respond to him. I might be the one to have a stroke today. "That means a lot."

"You not being here hurt our family. I don't want to see Brady shut himself off the way you did. Mom can't handle that," Colton said.

He's right, and his concern sounds genuine. Mom and Brady are close. Mom loves all three of us deeply, but Brady clung to her as a baby. We used to tell him because we didn't have a sister, Mom petted him the most because he was the baby. It didn't faze Brady at all. He enjoyed it.

"We will find a way to keep that from happening," I assure him.

"Welcome home." Colton holds his hand out to me.

Took him long enough. I've been home for four months. Instead of telling him that, I take Colton's hand. I'd hug him, but we aren't close like that. This is a start for us, but hugs are a long way down the road.

"She really does love you," Colton says as we walk back to the house.

"I know." It's the one thing I am sure of.

Colton put his hand on my shoulder. "No, man." He shakes his head. "I don't think you realize how much. One of their little word games was about you. I heard a lot that day. It told me how big of a fool you really were."

"They said random words about me?" I let the rest of his statement go. That last part was the beginning of a fight between us.

"Yeah." Colton nods his head and pokes me in the chest. "So, don't hurt her."

"Not happening," I say firmly.

There's no way in the world I'll hurt E or my little brother. It's good to know Colton is as protective as he is. I always thought he didn't pay attention to anything if it didn't involve the ranch. Things will be different now, with the two of us having an odd sort of truce. Mom will be thrilled. I guess the Christmas season really does have a way of changing things.

Chapter Forty-Three

Aiden

The week from Christmas to New Year's Day, I became a complete and total overprotective jerk. E's practically pulling her hair out. I can't help it, and I won't apologize for it.

Since I'm only a few months in with my job at the Hayden Falls Sheriff's Office, I don't have any vacation time saved up where I could take the week off. Thankfully, I was able to convince the Sheriff that E didn't need to be in town this week. He granted Spencer and me permission to put E in a sort of protective custody. It isn't official, but still, we're hiding her out at my place and my family's ranch.

"When will this be over?" E glares at me with her hands on her hips.

"Soon," I reply.

"Ugh!" She throws her hands in the air. "I hate that word!"

She probably does. It's the same answer I've given her all week. Spencer has his contact in Vegas watching the Preston Hotel and Casino. No wedding took place. Part of me hoped Garrett Preston would get married, and all the little messages he sent E were just a joke. It would have been a messed-up, cruel joke, but it was better than the alternative. However, my gut tells me her ex's messages are serious. He's stalking her.

Keeping my girl caged in is wrong, but it's necessary to keep her safe. She knows it as well as I do. She wouldn't be so upset right now if I hadn't taken protecting her up a few notches. I hired a private investigator to tail Preston this week. If he's planning on kidnapping E, I want a heads-up on his movements. Sadly, the PI lost Preston, and we have no idea where he is right now.

E's not upset because she can't go to work this week. Well, I don't think so, anyway. My nagging and demands are the real problems. Well, she calls it nagging and demanding. I call it being safe. I only let her out of the house when we drive to my parent's house for dinner. I won't even let her take Bo outside for a walk. Too much? Probably. But she's safe. Mission accomplished.

"You have to stop this, Aiden." E jabs her finger at me.

"You're safe. That's what matters," I snap.

Her eyes go wide, and her mouth falls open. Oh crap. I just messed up big time. She's the last person I should raise my voice to.

"That right there proves it." She starts pacing in front of the Christmas tree, tossing her arms in the air.

"I'm sorry I snapped at you." I toss my hat on the couch and run my fingers through my hair. "It's just…"

Nobody seems to understand how I feel here. I need to keep her safe. Even my mom has tried to get me to loosen up this week. E's my heart and my future. I can't lose her.

She walks over and puts her arms around my waist. "I know why you're doing it, and I thank you for keeping me safe."

"Then why are we arguing?"

"Because you're not sleeping. You sneak out of bed at night. Even though Bo and Colton or one of the other ranch hands are down here on the couch, you still make regular rounds through the house at night. You're on edge, and it's making you ill to the point none of us can take it anymore. If you don't rest, sooner or later, your body is going to put you down."

She's right about all of it. With a loud sigh, I wrap my arms around her. I'm seriously on edge. Fear grips me to the point I insist someone sleeps on my couch every night. I don't trust just having Bo inside at night this week. Every little noise has me checking it out, even with the extra help inside the house.

If this were any other case, I'd be calm and sure. Only this is her, and all sense of normalcy is out the window for me. That douchebag already hurt her once. He isn't getting another chance if I can help it.

When my phone rings, I release her to pull it from my back pocket. Spencer's name flashes on the screen. He's been updating me and checking in several times each day. So far, everything's quiet.

"I'll make us a cup of coffee and start breakfast," E whispers and heads for the kitchen.

I swipe to answer the call. "Hey, man."

"Hey." Spencer sighs. That's a sure sign this isn't good news. "My friend in Vegas called. There's a note on the doors of the Preston Hotel and Casino stating Mr. Preston's wedding was postponed due to a family emergency."

"I don't like the sound of that." I sit down on the couch and drop my head into my hand.

Canceled would be better. No. Married to someone else would be better. Postponed means this fool isn't giving up.

"Neither do I. But you can let up on E a little today."

"Look…" I start.

"No, man. You can relax today," Spencer interrupts me. "My friend sent me a picture of Garrett Preston walking into the hotel less than an hour ago."

Okay. Hearing that does relax me a little. With him in Vegas, he can't get to E. Vegas is about thirteen hours away by car but only around two by plane. I'll get the PI back on him. I won't give up my watch over my girl, but I could use a few hours of sleep.

After ending the call with Spencer, I call the PI to get him back on the job. Now, to tell E what Spencer found out. We update her with the information we can so she understands just how serious this is. I find her at the stove cooking pancakes and bacon. There are two cups of coffee sitting on the counter.

Standing at the edge of the counter, I watch her for a few minutes. My oversized t-shirt is practically a dress on her. She looks great in her shorty pajama sets, but there's something special about seeing her in my shirt. She has an invisible pull on me. When I can't stand it any longer, I quickly cross the room and wrap my arms around her from behind.

"I love you," I whisper next to her ear before placing a kiss on her temple.

"I love you too." She leans back against me.

Looking over her shoulder and lifting her chin, she offers me her lips. I gladly accept the invitation and press my lips to hers. Just as the kiss starts to turn passionate, E pulls her lips from mine to flip the pancakes.

I grab my coffee and go to the table. She doesn't say anything when I tell her about the note on the doors of the hotel and casino. Hearing that her ex is actually in Vegas at the moment relaxes her a bit, too. When she sits down next to me, I give her hand a little squeeze and bring it to my lips.

"I want you to go to Tennessee with me," I say about halfway through our meal.

E sets her fork down. She drops her head and quietly considers my request for a few minutes.

"Do you really think that's necessary?"

"Yeah, I do." I yawn and rub my hands over my face. Coffee isn't keeping me awake this morning.

"I hate that it's come to this." E leans back in her chair.

"What?" I cover another yawn with my hand.

"That we have to leave to escape Garrett."

I snap my head toward her. She's breathing hard with her arms folded across her chest.

"That's not what I meant." I turn in my chair to face her and lift her chin with my finger. "But if it keeps you safe, we can do that."

"Then what did you mean?" She gets up to fix us another cup of coffee.

"Before you came downstairs, Bryan and Harrison called. They're both getting married in June. We're invited. Well, they asked me to be a groomsman for both weddings," I explain.

"A double wedding?" E sets my cup in front of me. Rather than sitting back down, she leans into me.

"With their fiancées being best friends, you would think so, but no." Wrapping an arm around her waist, I pull her closer. "I don't understand the reasons their fiancées gave for not having a double wedding, but one is getting married the first weekend in June, and the other is the last weekend."

"That's sweet." E kisses the top of my head.

"We could stay the whole month," I suggest. I still have a house in Dade's Creek.

"That's a lovely thought, but I can't stay an entire month." Her answer has me looking up at her. Before I can ask, she continues, "June is the busiest month for weddings. I already have several booked at the inn."

I hadn't thought of that. The wedding and party planning services at the inn were her idea. She's a natural at organizing events. From what I hear around town, the ladies here love E's parties.

"We can still go for the weddings, though. If you need to stay the entire month, that's fine." She leans down and kisses me.

"Sunshine." I pull her onto my lap. "I'm not sending you back to Montana on a plane by yourself."

"Cowboy." E's fingers curl into my hair. "I think I can handle a plane ride by myself."

"Still not happening."

"Are you always going to be like this?" Her lips feather soft kisses across my forehead.

"I will *always* protect you," I vow.

The feel of her fingers playing with my hair has me closing my eyes. My head falls against her chest as my arms tighten around her waist. She's here, and she's finally mine.

"What would you like to do today?" I ask without lifting my head. "We could go to town or play *Scrabble*."

"We played *Scrabble* last night," she reminds me as her fingers massage my scalp. "And again this morning."

I chuckle and look up at her. The look in her eyes has my hand behind her head, pulling her to me for another kiss.

"I'll never turn down playing *that* kind of *Scrabble* with you." I kiss her again to prove it. "But I meant the board game."

She was being funny when she gave me the board game for Christmas. Opening that gift at my parent's house on Christmas Eve messed me up. Spencer's the only one who knows our private meaning for the board game. My friend isn't letting me live it down, either.

"You need a nap."

She's right. We do. Having her in my lap like this isn't allowing for a nap, though. In one swift movement, I'm on my feet with her still in my arms. E shrieks as her legs wrap around my waist.

"Oh, Sunshine." I press my lips to her neck. "*Scrabble* first, then we can take a nap."

Chapter Forty-Four

Etrulia

This was the worst week of my life. If I could go back in time, I would have never accepted Garrett's proposal. The whole hindsight is 20/20 is a horrible concept. It doesn't help fix anything. In most cases, it makes people feel worse. It did for me, anyway.

In two days, it will be a year since that horrible day happened. Thinking about it has already caused a couple of panic attacks this week. Spencer asked me again to name my attacker. After a year, he's not sure if charges can be pressed or not. After being hurt and shoved out into the show, I'm scared of Garrett. Even if I give his name, Defense Attorneys have a way of twisting things in court, and a guilty client could be set free.

I should do it. I don't understand why it's so hard for me to do so. Rachel thinks it's psychological. Leave it to my brain to not work normally. Whatever it is, it was probably ingrained in me when I was younger because of my parents. I've blocked most of those years from memory. I don't want to relive the first eight years of my life, nor do I want to remember what happened a year ago. Trauma has a way of messing up a person's mind.

"It's so cold out there," Avery says as she and Marcie come through the front door.

"Morning, E." Marcie takes off her gloves and blows into her hands.

"Good Morning, ladies." I close out the screen where I was updating our records. "There's hot chocolate and muffins in the breakroom."

The girls hurry off to the breakroom. Two families had to extend their stay because their flights were canceled. Avery and Marcie are here today to help prepare meals for them for a few days. I don't really expect any more guests this week. When I called to give them the day off, both girls insisted on coming in to help. Marcie's brothers dropped them off this morning. Jesse and Four are first responders. They often help the local mechanic shop search the roads for stranded travelers in the snow.

I'm surprised Aiden and my family let me work at all this week. My panic attacks freaked everyone out, but they saw my need to stay busy. Plus, Rachel encouraged me to work as long as there wasn't a dangerous threat. Aiden's Private Investigator, which I didn't know he had until this week, saw Garrett in Vegas two days ago. That and my agreement not to go anywhere are the only reasons I'm here now.

I'm not stupid. Going out alone would be a bad move on my part. I've seen enough movies and read plenty of books where the female lead, or heroine, made stupid decisions that always landed her in trouble. That's not going to be me. I already know what Garrett is capable of, and I don't want a repeat performance.

Breakfast is a simple meal to prepare. Aunt Sara and I handled things easily this morning without any help. Uncle Silas is sitting in the lobby with his newspaper. He'll watch the front desk and answer the phone if necessary while I help the girls in the kitchen. We're preparing a few meals my aunt can warm up for our guests if they need to stay longer. Soups, stews, and casseroles will be their main choices.

Shortly before lunchtime, a loud bang comes from the lobby, interrupting the funny stories the girls are telling me. We freeze and stare at each other. The shouts and screams send a chill down my spine. I recognize Uncle Silas' voice. He doesn't shout like that. Another loud bang comes from the lobby, causing us to jump. I swear it sounds like furniture turning over.

As I slowly open the kitchen door, my uncle falls to the floor near the front desk. From here, I can't tell what happened to him. Two steps out into the hallway, I freeze. A man steps from the sitting area of the lobby into the hallway. His dark eyes lock on me. With an angry growl, he rushes toward me. I need to run. Spinning on my heel, I hurry back to the kitchen. He grabs my ponytail as I open the kitchen door and roughly pulls me back into the hall. Avery and Marcie scream. They need to get out of here.

"Run." I barely get the word out before the door closes, separating us.

"You have caused me enough trouble!" Garrett slams my back against the wall.

"Let me go!" I demand.

"Oh, no, no, no." He shakes his head. With his mouth next to my ear, his voice is like a knife cutting into my flesh. "You are going with me, little wife."

"I'm not marrying you." I push against him, but he doesn't budge.

"You agreed to, and you will." His voice is deep and hateful.

He doesn't love me anymore than I love him. It makes no sense for him to want to marry me. Plenty of girls at college would happily agree to be his wife.

"I don't love you," I say each word slowly and with emphasis. My head hits the wall again.

"I don't care," Garrett snarls in my ear.

"We need to go!" A man shouts from behind Garrett.

Garrett jerks me off the wall and drags me toward the front doors. I gasp when I see my uncle's body lying on the floor. He's too still.

"What did you do?" I cry.

I fight against the powerful arms holding me, but it's useless. I can't get to Uncle Silas. He has to be alive. The more I struggle, the tighter Garrett's grip on me becomes.

"The old man should have stayed out of the way." Garrett pauses long enough beside my uncle to let me look at his face. "That's your fault."

"If we don't go now, I'm leaving you," the man at the door threatens.

The faint sound of sirens can be heard in the distance. Help is on the way. I can't let Garrett take me, but he's stronger than me. Fighting won't do any good, but I have to try. I'll never go with him willingly.

"No!" I scream.

With everything I have in me, I kick and push against Garrett. He slaps me, but I don't really feel it right away. With his hand in my hair again, he slams my head into the front desk.

"You are mine," he growls as he twists my arm.

"Leave her! She's not worth it!" the other guy shouts before running out the door.

The sirens are louder now. The sound is piercing yet welcomed. My head hurts, and I can't focus anymore. My arms and legs do not respond to my mind's commands. Men shout around me, but they sound far away. The last thing I hear before my world goes dark is the unmistakable sound of gunshots echoing through the room.

Chapter Forty-Five

Aiden

Never, *ever* get relaxed when a possible threat exists. It won't happen to me again. That one mistake has me sitting here in this hospital room. The small hospital in Walsburg, a town about twenty minutes from Hayden Falls, is more like a huge clinic. It's the closest hospital without having to go to Missoula.

This week has been draining E emotionally and mentally. The memory of what happened to her a year ago plagues her mind and haunts her dreams. The closer we get to the day her ex attacked her, the more she drifts into her own quiet world. I hate it. At times, she can hide it. When she can't, all I can do is hold her. A couple of nights, she bolted upright in bed. Each time, I pulled her trembling body into my arms and whispered to her until she fell back asleep. We don't talk about it later. That's probably another mistake on my part.

Her aunt talked with Rachel. She encouraged us to keep an eye on E and to give her the time she needs to work through it in her mind. Rachel taught E coping tools to walk her through tough situations. Usually, those help her. Now, I can see the signs I missed where those tools failed her. I guess that's mistake number three on my part. Rachel said if there wasn't an obvious threat, to give E a little space this week. That was therapist mistake number one, my mistake number four. I shouldn't have listened to her.

When the 911 call came from E's aunt and uncle's house, it was where Marcie and Avery ran to, every officer on the force was dispatched to the inn. Sheriff Barnes didn't stop there. Until today, I didn't realize how much he watched over E. The Hayden Falls Fire Department and every first responder in the area descended upon The Magnolia Inn.

I ended a call with the PI in Vegas minutes before the emergency call came in. Preston entered his family's hotel less than two days ago and hasn't been seen since. His family lives in the penthouse suite on the top floor. They also have a house in Los Angeles. Yesterday morning, a helicopter left the hotel's roof, heading southwest. The PI assumed the family was going to California. That was PI mistake number two. He had lost sight of Preston before.

The fingers of the small hand inside mine slightly twitch. I sit up straight and wait. My heart drops because there's no other movement. The waiting is killing me. I squeeze my eyes tightly shut and lay my head back down on the edge of the bed. The hand on my back is there for comfort, but I feel none. I've already exploded on half the hospital staff. Spencer is here as support and control. I greatly need both.

Spencer is my best friend, and I owe him a debt I'll never be able to repay. He and Leo Barnes were the first to arrive on the scene. Leo apprehended Preston's accomplice while Spencer rushed into the inn. As first responders, Jesse and Four showed up before Lucas and I did. The Calhoun brothers helped Leo with the accomplice. Eli Wentworth and Pit were right behind us. Behind them was every deputy, on duty and off, plus the fire department. There were more, but I can't remember who they all were.

Before Lucas and I made it to the door, shots rang out. My heart stopped when I entered the lobby. E and her uncle were lying on the floor with Preston a few feet away, screaming at Spencer. How the world moved after that was a blur to me. I still haven't processed it all. My mind is focused on one thing right now. My Sunshine needs to wake up.

Her left arm is in a brace like my broken arm was months ago. That has me sitting on the right side of her hospital bed. We've only been here a couple of hours, but it feels like forever.

My world is a dark place. The unknown can gut a man's soul. In the back of my mind, I know she'll be okay. Still, I won't fully believe it until E wakes up. At times, her blue eyes are deep, like the sky just before the dawn takes over or after sunset. Other times, they're bright and dancing. Her smile is warmer than the sun to me. Right now, my life has no sky or sunshine.

With my head still face down on the bed, I press my lips to her still fingers. They're warm. She's alive, but I need more. I need to see her eyes and hear her voice. I don't even try to stop my tears. I need my Sunshine.

"Hang in there, man." Spencer pats my back.

"I'll check on her uncle." Sheriff Barnes stands and quietly leaves the room. I didn't realize he was still here.

Her uncle has a broken leg and a nasty head wound. He's fine, but they're keeping him overnight for observation.

Silas Hayes is a brave man. He was serious when he said E was his daughter. When he came to, he crawled with a broken to where he could reach the shotgun hidden behind the front desk. From his position on the floor, he managed to shoot Preston in the leg. Spencer shot him in the right shoulder. The douchebag is alive and under guard. Spencer and the Sheriff have tried to update me, but I've waved them off. It's handled. That's all I need to know right now.

Spencer taps me on the back when E's doctor enters the room. I wasn't expecting it to be Matt Larson. He's young, but Matt's a good doctor. E's aunt must have requested him. It makes sense. Matt's everybody in Hayden Falls' primary physician. He looks around at all the people in the room and pauses. His eyes go from me to E's aunt.

"We can clear the room so we can talk about E's condition," Matt suggests.

Mrs. Hayes looks at each of us. Spencer and Beth are here, along with E's friends Katie, Sammie, and Ally. My parents stand behind me. Leo and Lucas Barnes wait by the door. I don't care what anyone says. I'm not leaving this room.

"No. It's fine. Everyone here is family to E." Mrs. Hayes turns down the offer.

"Okay." Matt looks at the clipboard with E's file. "Her arm isn't broken, but there's some bruising. It is the same one that was broken a year ago, so I put it in the brace just as a precaution."

"Why won't she wake up?" I ask.

"She came to while we were x-raying her arm. She was hysterical to the point I feared she would hurt herself before I could run the tests to confirm her injuries." Matt takes a deep breath before looking me in the eye. "I'm sorry, but I had to sedate her. She should be waking up any time now."

Sedate her? I jump to my feet. A growl rumbles deep in my chest. A hysterical image of the sweetest girl I know rips through me. I want to scream and punch something. Spencer grabs my upper arms from behind. My mom is quickly at my side. Mom has a special way of grounding me.

"Is she going to be okay?" Mrs. Hayes asked.

That's enough to settle me down. E's condition is more important than what I want. I look down at her beautiful face, bruised and bandaged from where her head hit the front desk.

"She has some bruising and a few stitches on the side of her head." Matt shakes his head. "She'll be sore for a while, but there are no broken bones, and the MRI looks fine."

Mrs. Hayes closes her eyes and puts her hand on her chest. The entire room sighs with relief. It's good news, but my Sunshine still isn't awake.

"Thank you, Matt." Mrs. Hayes hugs him.

"Don't worry. She's going to be fine," Matt assures Mrs. Hayes. "I'll be here as long as your husband and niece are. I've given her something mild for the pain, but don't worry. I promise she will wake up soon."

Something mild for pain? That doesn't sit right with me. I remember the pain I had when I woke up after my surgery. Yeah, I toughed a lot of it out so my mom wouldn't worry too much, but I don't want that for E. She didn't have surgery, but she's in pain.

"Mild?" I asked. "She was knocked unconscious. Just looking at her, you know she's in a lot of pain."

"Aiden, I can't give her anything else right now." Matt shakes his head again and looks at me like I'm crazy. "It's too dangerous."

"Dangerous?" I snap. "You just said the MRI was fine."

"Easy, son." Dad puts his hand on my shoulder. "Matt knows what he's doing."

"Does he?" I glare at Doctor Larson for a moment and turn to Dad. "She's in pain. I don't want her to hurt. How can giving her something to stop the pain hurt her?"

Everybody turns to look at Doctor Larson. I don't want to be mad at him. He was great with my broken arm, but I see no logic in this.

"It won't hurt *her*," Matt replied.

"See?" I throw my hand in the air, motioning toward the good doctor.

"Why can't she have something stronger?" Spencer, like me, prefers to get straight to the point.

"Are you waiting for E to wake up to see if she needs a stronger medication?" Mrs. Hayes asked before Matt could answer Spencer.

"No, Ma'am," he replies to Mrs. Hayes. His eyes move to me again. "It's too dangerous," he says each word with emphasis.

I blow out a ragged breath and run my hand through my hair. I don't get it. Is this fool really a doctor?

"Why?" I demand.

"It will hurt the baby," Matt replied.

Baby?

Chapter Forty-Six

Aiden

Baby?

He said, baby. The stunned silence in the room doesn't register. All my attention falls on the unconscious woman lying in the hospital bed. My eyes take in E's face before moving to her flat stomach, where my hand now rests.

"Baby," I whisper in awe.

"Aiden?" Mom wraps her arm around mine. Her voice shakes.

"Did you not know?" Matt asked.

I shake my head in reply, not taking my eyes off the beautiful woman lying on the bed. I couldn't speak right now if I wanted to. She's carrying our baby. More questions are going around the room, but I don't hear them. Spencer has to shake me to bring me back to the present.

"How far?' I ask Matt.

"About four weeks."

"Does she even know?" Mrs. Hayes blinks back tears.

Beth sighs and bites her bottom lip. I look between E and Beth. Did they know and not tell me?

"Beth?" Spencer grabs his sister's arm. I'm not the only one who caught her reaction.

"I don't think she knows for sure. She hasn't been feeling well the past few days. She was tired, and food made her nauseous. She thought it was her nerves because of what this week was. She promised if she didn't feel better in a couple of days, she would go to the doctor. I joked with her and told her she was pregnant, but we laughed it off."

I softly place my hand back on E's stomach. Baby. My heart explodes with a love I didn't know existed until this moment. My entire world lies quietly in this hospital bed. I swallow hard and lose my balance when a thought hits me. That douchebag was trying to take them from me. Spencer guides me back down into the chair I've been sitting in for over two hours.

"Is our baby okay?"

I'm a little choked up. Preston hurt E today. Is there more damage we can't see? E will survive this, but will our baby?

"I don't see any signs of distress right now. We'll watch her close tonight and start prenatal care soon."

I sigh with relief and nod. My eyes never leave E's face. Good. They both will be fine.

"If you want to come with me, I'll check in on your husband now," Matt said to Mrs. Hayes.

Mrs. Hayes wipes tears from her eyes as she hurries around the bed and cups my face in her hands. "You watch over them. I'll be back in a few minutes."

"Yes, Ma'am." It's a vow I'll honor until the day I die. E's aunt kisses my forehead before leaving the room.

"Oh, Aiden." Mom wraps her arms around me.

"Congratulations, son." Dad pats my shoulder. There's pride in his voice and tears in his eyes. I guess the first grandchild can break a strong man.

Everyone else hugged me and said their congratulations before leaving. Mrs. Hayes returned but decided to go back to her husband's room. E started to stir, and her aunt wanted to give us a little time alone. I didn't know of any situations where the father knew before the mother about their baby. I can't wait to tell E. Maybe she suspected it. Even Beth wasn't sure. If E knew, she would have told her best friend.

Holding her hand, I place soft kisses on her palm while watching her eyes flutter. My Sunshine is finally waking up. Her breathing grows stronger. When reality came back to her, E's eyes popped open, and she tried to sit up.

I'm quickly on my feet, leaning over her and holding her down by her shoulders. "Easy, Sunshine."

Finally, her eyes focus on me. "Aiden?" she whispers. I smile and nod. "Where am I?"

"Hospital." I lean down and kiss her forehead.

"Uncle Silas," she cries, trying to sit up again.

"Shh." I gently hold her to the bed. "Your uncle is fine. Well, he has a broken leg and a head wound, but he'll be okay. He's in the room next door."

She relaxes and settles her head back against the pillow. Seeing fear flash in her eyes, I cup her face in my hands.

"You're okay," I assure her.

"Garrett?" The fear is still in her eyes.

I don't want to talk about this guy right now, but she needs to know she's safe so she can relax.

"He's in a hospital in Missoula. He can't hurt you anymore. He's under arrest and heavily guarded." That's all she needs to know for now.

"I heard gunshots." She's still trying to piece it all together.

I didn't want to go into details yet, but it looks like I have no choice.

"Spencer and your uncle shot him, but it's not life-threatening." I blow out a breath and look away. It would have ended differently if I had been the first officer on the scene.

She groans when she shifts in the bed. My protective instincts kick in again. It's probably going to get worse now that she's pregnant.

"What do you need?" I ask, trying to hold her still.

"Water, and can you raise the head of the bed?" When she's sitting up, she lifts her left arm. "Oh, no," she cries.

"It's not broken." I take her hand and lightly squeeze it. "Your arm is bruised, and it was broken last year. The brace is just a precaution."

A growl rumbles in my chest from the memory of seeing her arm before it was bandaged. Preston's finger marks were visible on her skin. The Sheriff had Spencer and Leo take pictures of the bruises and marks her ex left behind while I watched. There was no way I was leaving her side. The nurses nor my friends were able to remove me from the room.

A light knock comes on the door, and Sheriff Barnes walks in. If he's here on official business, it can wait.

"Oh, good. You're awake." Sheriff Barnes walks over to the other side of the bed. "That was quite the scare there."

E nods. It was the worst scare of my life. E closes her eyes, and my heart breaks when silent tears run down her cheeks. With my thumb, I gently wipe them away.

"I'm glad you're okay." Sheriff Barnes takes E's right hand and squeezes it before gently laying it back on the bed. The love and concern this town has for my girl warms my heart. "You rest tonight. We have Garrett Preston under arrest with a long list of charges."

"Do we have to do this right now?" I ask.

"Not officially." Sheriff Barnes sighs deeply. "Unless she has something she wants to tell me."

E wipes the tears from her cheeks and drops her head. It's too soon for questioning.

"Maybe tomorrow," I tell the Sheriff. "She needs to rest."

"That's fine." Sheriff Barnes gives E a tight smile and starts for the door.

"Sheriff?" E calls out. Sheriff Barnes pauses and looks over his shoulder at her. She takes a deep breath before speaking, "Garrett was the one that hurt me last year."

"Are you officially saying that?" Sheriff Barnes won't do anything if she's not. E nods. "Good. That'll ensure a longer stay with the state for him. We'll start the paperwork tonight and talk about it tomorrow."

"Thank you." E drops her head and tries to smile, but she can't manage to do so.

"You rest tonight, little lady." Sheriff Barnes looks between me and E. "And congratulations, you two."

"Congratulations?" E's head comes up. She blinks a few times.

"I haven't gotten that far yet, Sheriff."

"Oh, sorry." Sheriff Barnes holds up his hand. "I'll leave you to it then." He waves and hurries out the door.

"What was that about?" E sniffles.

Cupping her face in my hands, I wipe the last of her tears away with my thumbs.

"I love you," I whisper and press my lips to hers.

"I love you too." She sighs and waits for me to explain.

"You're supposed to be telling me this." I run my thumb back and forth across her cheek. "While they were running tests, Matt found something."

"You said I would be fine." Her breathing quickens as she tries to sit forward. I ease her fears with a kiss.

"Oh, Sunshine, you are fine." I give her another quick kiss.

"Then, what's wrong?" Tears well up in her eyes again. Not how I wanted this to go.

"Nothing is wrong." I can't help but smile as my hand moves to her stomach. "Sunshine, we have a little sunbeam."

With eyes wide and her mouth open, E looks down at my hand on her belly. She covers my hand with hers and looks up. Her expression proves she didn't know.

"I'm pregnant?" she whispers her question.

"You are. *We* are." She playfully narrows her eyes at me. "Well, you'll do all the work, but I'll be right there with you."

"Did Matt know how far along I am?" She bites her bottom lip.

"About four weeks or so. Just before Christmas." I've already been doing the math in my head. "Looks like *Scrabble* got us," I tease.

She presses her head back against the pillow and giggles. Oh, how I love that sound. E slides over and pats the bed next to her. I don't want to crowd her, but I need to hold her. As carefully as I can, I join her on the bed and wrap her in my arms.

"You're happy?"

"Oh, I would say I'm on cloud nine, but that's a lie. I think I passed Pluto an hour ago." I'm not teasing. I mean it.

Still, she giggles again. I'm the happiest man on this planet. If there are any off-planet, I have them beat, too. E puts her hand over her belly. Reaching down, I entwine my fingers with hers, and that's how we stay until we both fall asleep.

Chapter Forty-Seven

Etrulia

My life changed drastically over the next week. My deranged attacker ex-boyfriend is behind bars where he belongs. I no longer have to worry about him coming after me. Naming Garrett as my attacker last year added to his charges. He will enjoy a longer prison sentence in the end. Well, that is, if his lawyers don't find a way to get him a shorter sentence.

During the interrogation, Garrett's accomplice gave up most of their plan. Garrett would inherit his family's hotel and casino, along with a hefty trust fund from his grandfather when he turned thirty. He could only inherit it before then if he went to college and got married. Garrett was pushed to anger during his interrogation and admitted he didn't love me. He thought I was gullible. He was using me to get the money faster. The end of our relationship fueled his anger, so he came after me.

I have some mental issues I'll have to work through from all this. Being used as a pawn in a game of greed and being attacked twice left some lasting marks on me. Rachel is helping me. I'm glad I found a therapist I can easily talk to and be friends with at the same time. She thinks I should take self-defense classes. Jasper Ramsey started a gym in Hayden Falls a few years ago and offered the classes. Spencer is all for it. Aiden, on the other hand, needs to check it out first and make sure it's safe for a pregnant woman to take the classes.

"I can't believe you finally got your cowboy." Katie laughs as she seals up a cardboard box with tape.

Today, my friends are helping me pack up my apartment. When I mentioned going home, Aiden lost his mind. He's just as protective now as he was before my ex got arrested, if not more so. Granted, it's for a different reason now. He goes out of his way to make sure the baby and I have everything we want or need. It's sweet but nerve-racking at the same time.

"I can't believe she's pregnant." Beth hugs me with one arm and puts her hand on my belly. There's no baby bump yet. "I'm going to be such an awesome auntie."

Beth will be an amazing aunt. We aren't related, but the position is hers anyway. She's already bought my baby a beautiful pink dress to wear home from the hospital. It looks like someone is hoping for a girl.

"I can't believe it either." I cover Beth's hand with mine. "I can't wait to meet this little guy."

"Um. Don't you mean, little girl?" Beth scrunches her face up and playfully points at me.

"Oh, please." Katie rolls her eyes.

"If Aiden Maxwell has a daughter, he will wrap her up in bubble wrap, and E will never get to take her out of the house." Sammie holds up her hands to make her point. We all laugh, but she's right.

"I'm glad she's moving in with him. They belong together." Ally brings in more empty boxes.

I was practically living with Aiden anyway, so the move makes sense. The love and support from my friends are more than I imagined. We're close, and I don't doubt these four ladies. Feeling it and seeing it in action shows me how loved I truly am.

My parents never wanted me. No one had to tell me that because I knew it. My aunt and uncle took me in and gave me a home and a huge family. My family isn't all blood-related, but they're mine. The people in Montana are as different as night and day from the people I knew in Georgia. This weird little town loves to gossip and spread rumors, but they know how to pull together when one of us needs help. The outpouring of help I got last week still makes me cry happy tears. Nearly every male member of our community showed up when my ex tried to take me.

At first, I feared how everyone would treat me because I was expecting a baby and not married. That fear got squashed rather quickly. My friends don't look down on me because I'm pregnant, and neither have my aunt and uncle.

The entire town already knows I'm going to have a baby. The gossip circles are in full force. Megan and her blog are leading the way. A few of the older ladies in town eyed me up and down while shaking their heads. Guess you can't please everyone. I never expected to be pregnant without being married first, but I love Aiden. I don't care what the gossip groups say about it anymore.

"How's it going, ladies?" Uncle Silas shouts from outside.

Hearing his voice, I hurry down the steps to greet him. My uncle's leg is in a cast, and Aunt Sara and I have forbidden him to climb the stairs on his crutches.

"We're doing great." I wrap my arms around him for a hug.

"Your aunt is in town and wants to know if the little one wants anything." Uncle Silas holds up his phone. It's still funny seeing him use a cell phone.

"Hey, Aunt Sara," I speak loud enough for her to hear me. "Donuts?"

Uncle Silas laughs and finishes his call with my aunt. He's more than just an uncle to me. He's the greatest man I know. He risked his life to protect me and carries some battle scars to prove it. Since I was eight years old, he has stepped up and done his brother's job.

"Here." I motion toward his house next to the apartment. "Let me get you home."

"Ah, girl." Uncle Silas pats my hand. "I'm fine. I hate sitting around waiting on this leg to heal."

My uncle is an active man. Sitting around is driving him and my aunt crazy. Still, Aunt Sara won't let him out of the house when she's home. Being out now is his little rebellion. I give in and allow him the little break he has while she's running errands. I did manage to coax him to one of the rocking chairs on the front porch.

"I wanted to talk to you." I bite my bottom lip. I've wanted to have this conversation with him for a long time. After last week, I don't want to wait any longer.

"What's on your mind?" Uncle Silas relaxes and gently tips the rocking chair.

"Well." I twiddle my fingers on my lap. I'm not sure how to start this conversation. Taking a deep breath, I decide to just say what's on my mind like he asked. "You always said it didn't matter, and you'd never force me to do it. You and Aunt Sara took me in. You loved me when I didn't feel loved. You're legally my parents, and I thank you for everything you've done for me."

I pause to wipe the tears from my cheeks. "You told Sheriff Barnes that night that I was your daughter."

"You are," Uncle Silas states firmly with pride.

"I feel the same way." I look him in the eye. "You're my dad." He and I nod, but this isn't enough for me. "I was wondering, would it be okay if I called you and Aunt Sara Mom and Dad from now on?"

"I'd like that." Uncle Silas wipes a tear from his eye and wraps his arms around me.

It's an awkward position while sitting in the two rocking chairs. Still, we sit this way until Aiden pulls into the driveway. I wasn't expecting him this early. My friends and I haven't finished packing up my apartment yet.

"Hey, Sunshine." Aiden walks up onto the porch. He gives me a quick kiss and shakes my uncle's hand.

"You're early."

"No such thing," he replies and looks at my uncle. "Do you mind if I steal her for a while?"

"Not at all." Uncle Silas shakes his head.

"Bye, Dad." I kiss his forehead. I don't miss the tear he tried to hide.

It's going to be weird for a while until we all get used to me calling them Mom and Dad. It's something I should have started doing when they officially adopted me. It took two years for the state to fully take away the parental rights of both my biological parents. They're not legally married anymore. The woman who gave birth to me fought the process for about a year. Finally, she caved and gave up. I can never again call those two people my parents. My child will never go through what I did.

"Where are we going?"

"You'll see." He smiles and offers me his hand as he opens the passenger door of his truck.

My friends are all standing on the steps of my apartment, waving at us. Guess they don't mind me deserting them in the middle of packing. If they have no problem with me being stolen away like this, then who am I to complain? I take Aiden's hand and climb into his truck.

The smell of something sweet and wonderful fills the truck. There's a box in the backseat from Sweet Treats Bakery. I reach for it as Aiden pulls out into the street. He grabs my hand before I can get the box oozing with a sweet aroma.

"No. No." He winks at me. "Patience, Sunshine."

"But that's donuts," I whine. I'm sure of it.

He wholeheartedly laughs. "I know, and you'll get them in a few minutes."

"But our baby wants them now," I say sweetly and bat my eyes at him.

"I promise, our little sunbeam can have the entire box." Aiden doesn't give in.

Obviously, I'm not getting those donuts now. With a huff, I cross my arms over my chest and pout. I can't believe he's keeping food hostage from me. My actions only make him laugh harder. He better not be like this through this entire pregnancy.

"I promise, Sunshine, it's worth the wait. I even got your favorite." Aiden winks at me as he drives through town.

I gasp loudly. "Chocolate-covered with vanilla icing filling?"

"Mmhmm," he replies.

Oh, how I love this man.

"You could have gotten me two. One for now and one for later." I smile sweetly. Food has seriously become my happy place.

"Sunshine, you're going to be so much fun the next eight months." He still doesn't give in. And yes, it looks like he's going to keep doing this.

Thankfully, the drive is short. I'm a little confused when Aiden pulls off the road at the edge of the park. I already have the box of donuts in my lap when he opens my door. Seeing the box, Aiden laughs and shakes his head. I'm pregnant. I have a right to this.

"Come on." He holds out his hand to help me down.

"Why are we at the bridge?"

"Because it's one of our favorite places."

This bridge is one of my favorite places, but I didn't realize it was his, too. Most people around here prefer the lake or the waterfall. Both of those are great, but they're make-out spots. You never know what you'll come across when you go there. The waterfall has a small bridge near it, but this one is within walking distance of the inn.

Clutching the box of donuts to me, we walk out to the middle of the bridge. Aiden reaches inside his coat pocket and pulls out a rose.

"You used to stand here and drop petals into the water," he says, handing me the rose.

Wow. I didn't think anyone knew that. When I was sad or unsure of things, I'd come here and drop petals into the water. It wasn't always roses. Still, I made a wish with each petal as it fell. Setting the box of donuts on the railing, I take the rose.

"I don't need to make wishes anymore." I look from the rose to his soft brown eyes. "I have more than I could ever wish for."

"Then perhaps you should open that box." Aiden nods toward the Sweet Treats box.

Finally! This little sunbeam really wants a donut. Maybe it's just sugar the little one is craving. Don't know. Don't care. We're about to be two happy people. I mean, who wouldn't be happy with a chocolate-covered donut with vanilla icing filling? I open the box and gasp.

"Aiden?"

The box has four donuts inside. All of them are the kind with filling. Three are regular glazed with writing on them, spelling out *I love you.* The fourth one, the one that holds my attention, is indeed chocolate-covered, and I'm sure it has vanilla icing filling. What it holds has me speechless. Standing in the chocolate icing is a diamond ring.

When I turn to face him, Aiden is already down on one knee. He reaches into the box and plucks the ring out. The band has chocolate icing on it. To my surprise, he has an alcohol wipe and cleans it. I should have known he would come prepared.

"You and I have come to this bridge many times to think. At times, we came alone. Other times, we sat together under this bridge and tossed pebbles into the water. This bridge is one of my favorite places because we shared our first kiss here." He takes the box of donuts from my shaky hands and sets it on the wooden boards next to him.

"I was going to get cupcakes." He lightly laughs. "But since you and Sunbeam changed things up today, I got donuts."

"Cupcakes would have been fine."

It didn't matter how he did this. I would have loved it if it was just the two of us at home. It is so sweet he went out of his way to make this moment extra special.

"To some people, this might be too soon. We've technically only been dating for about five months, but I have loved you for most of my life." His words already have tears in my eyes.

"For a long time, I thought I'd lost this chance with you. I'm sorry for the wasted years, but I'm thankful God gave us this chance. I don't want to waste another day. I want you to be forever mine." Aiden swallows hard and squeezes my hand. "So, Debra Etrulia Hayes, will you marry me? Will you be my wife and build a home, family, and future with me?"

I have waited more than half my life to hear those words from him. Still, there's something I need to know.

"Are you asking because of the baby?"

"No." He shakes his head. "I won't lie. Our little sunbeam speeded the process up. My original plan was to ask you in May on your birthday. We don't have to get married right away if that's not what you want. We can wait until after the baby is born if you want to. I just want you to know how serious I am about us. I love you. That's not going to change no matter how long I have to wait for you to say you're ready for that step."

"Thank you for that." I place my palm against his cheek. He's still holding my left hand. "But I don't need any more time. I love you, too. And yes, I want to be your wife."

Aiden slides the ring onto my finger and stands up to kiss me. I no longer have to dream of this. My dream has come true. I'm going to marry Aiden Maxwell.

"When would you like to get married?"

"Valentine's Day." It's only three weeks away, but I'm so ready to marry this man.

Chapter Forty-Eight

Aiden

How time can move fast and slow at the same time is a mystery. Three weeks is a short time. However, when a man is waiting to marry his other half, it feels like years. I was thrilled when E said she didn't want to wait to get married. We've waited long enough. Still, I would have waited if she wasn't ready.

She's fully moved into our house now, and she's carrying our little sunbeam. Both of those things make me happy. Today, she's becoming my wife, and that fact has my heart about to burst from my chest.

How E and her friends put this wedding together in such a short time is beyond me. From the looks of things, I think the entire community pulled together to make this day happen. Even though we tried to keep this low-key, The Magnolia Inn is overflowing with guests today. By the time we realized how many people were coming, it was too late to rent a tent and space heaters.

The ceremony will take place in the Grand Room, where E holds the larger parties. Still, the room wasn't large enough to hold everyone. Nearly every room on the first floor and the hallway are lined with people today.

Thankfully, Cooper Jackson, our local computer nerd, saw the problem before everyone else. He showed up this week to set up TV screens throughout the inn so we could run a live feed of the ceremony. Most people will probably watch the feed from their phones anyway. Cooper didn't ask for a fee, but I slipped him a nice size bonus for doing it.

The reception will be buffet-style in the restaurant dining room. This part of the inn was added a few years ago to accommodate more guests and to meet updated building codes. The Hayden Sisters rallied together and completely handled the food for the reception. There's no chance we'll run out with those ladies in charge. People will still have to eat while standing up throughout the inn. Thankfully, no one complained.

It's not an ideal situation, but E refuses to change the date so we can rent a tent. I'll marry her any day, but my Sunshine wants Valentine's Day, so we're making it work. We can laugh about it later on in life. I suggested moving the ceremony to the church, but that didn't go over well at all. So, here we are.

The decorations aren't what I expected. When I think of Valentine's Day, I think of pinks and reds. E's favorite color is blue. Yes, there are hearts, flowers, and candles everywhere, but my bride put her own little twist on them. Everything is in several shades of blue, with white and silver to accent them. It's beautiful. I can see why the women around here love E's party ideas.

Rather than going to Missoula to find a gown, E had Mrs. Wallace, the local seamstress who owns the clothing store in town, make her gown. It's long, white, with lace sleeves. She's absolutely gorgeous in it. The first sight of her almost brought me to my knees.

Of course, Beth is her maid of honor. Katie, Ally, and Sammie are her bridesmaids. Spencer is my best man. Brady and Miles stood up with me, too. The last groomsman was the only member of Dawson who could make it on such short notice. Bryan Dawson was here, but he was pushed for time. After a few pictures were taken at the end of the ceremony, Bryan rushed to the airport to get home to his fiancée, Dana.

"How are you feeling, Mrs. Maxwell?" I whisper in my wife's ear as we dance.

"Never better." She looks up at me with that warm smile of hers.

"Our little Sunbeam behaving?"

Morning sickness, which we discovered could be all-day sickness, has been brutal for her this past week. I promised to be right there with her, so once again, and for a much better reason, I was sitting behind her on the bathroom floor to hold her hair while she was sick.

"He wants cake." Her grin widens.

"He? What if our sunbeam is a girl?" I slowly move us around the dance floor. Sudden movements made her queasy.

"If we have a daughter, you won't let her out of the house until she's thirty."

"Try fifty." I wink at her. I'm not teasing, though. I mean it. She giggles. So cute.

"I'm sorry I didn't get to really meet your friend." She briefly met Bryan while the photos were being taken.

Her face is a little flushed, so I lead her to one of the tables. Someone already prepared plates for us. That's a blessing. I'm not sure if she'll be able to keep anything down, though.

"I'm glad one of them could make it." I lift her hand and kiss her wedding ring.

Inside the band of both of our rings are the words *Steady On*. Harrison Shaw, the drummer of Dawson, wrote one song, *Hold Her*. It was for his girlfriend, Tru, when they were separated. It's a prayer for God to watch over her because he couldn't be there with her. I never told anyone, but I prayed those words for E from the first time I heard the song. To Harrison and Tru, *steady on* means, I love you, I believe in you, I'm here for you, and many other things when those words can't be said. They're perfect for E and me.

"I'm sorry I rushed the ceremony. They all should have had a chance to be here for you." She places her palm against my cheek. "I didn't mean to take that from you. We should have waited."

"No, Ma'am. We shouldn't have. Dawson just started a tour. It would be months before the entire band could come." She feels bad about this. I can see it in her beautiful eyes. "They already had plans for today. I'm honored that Bryan made it. Don't worry. We'll see them soon. We're going to Tennessee in June for their weddings."

She nods, and I give her a quick kiss. I know she wasn't trying to keep my friends from being here when she asked for this day. I'll never let her feel bad about it. Every member of the band understood.

"Now, sunbeam gets cake." Taking her hand, I pull her over to the cake table.

She puts her hand on her tummy and giggles when I pick up the knife to cut the cake. If we have a daughter, I hope she has that little giggle just like her mother.

People linger around the inn for hours. It's great having the town support us today. The hard glares I used to get have softened, for the most part, anyway. Still, some of the old-timers are having a hard time believing the truth. They've believed a lie for so long. No doubt it wounded their pride to have to admit they were wrong. When I walk around the square now, I'm greeted with smiles and handshakes. It's eerie at times. Occasionally, I still get a glare and a shake of the head. I think it's more at themselves than at me. Nobody likes being proven wrong.

The only sad person at our wedding is Brady. Whispers go around the room whenever he walks by. Brady found a corner to hide in when he could no longer handle it. My brother isn't the same carefree guy he used to be. He hasn't even teased Beth today like he normally does. The only time I saw him smile today was when he danced with E. I have to get my fun-loving brother back somehow.

E enjoyed dancing today. Thankfully, the morning sickness didn't hit during the reception. She danced with her uncle. Well, they swayed. He still has a boot on his broken leg, and he did walk her down the aisle. She was being cautious not to hurt him while they danced.

A few others danced with her as well. It was evident very quickly that I was not a fan of men dancing with my wife. Jesse grinned at me and tipped his chin when he gently twirled E around the dance floor. Of course, Four made a show of his dance with her. I swear, I'm going to have to kill the Calhoun brothers before it's over. Surprisingly, when he's sober, Pit can actually dance.

Brady hung around until the end and walked us out to my truck. I know the sad, faraway look in my brother's eyes all too well. It's brutal when this town is against you.

"Welcome to the family, officially, that is." Brady gives E a hug. "You've always been one of us anyway."

"Thank you." E leans back enough to look Brady in the eye. "I love you, dude. You're one of my best friends."

"I love you too, shortcake." Brady genuinely smiles. I haven't heard him call her that since we were kids. "You're one of my best friends, too, and now you're my little sister."

Brady is only a couple of months older than E. Normally, it would make me mad to hear a man tell my wife he loves her. My little brother has a special friendship with E. They know how to make each other smile. I'm glad they can help each other heal, and Brady sure needs help healing right now.

When we got home, I carried E inside in true bridal fashion. She protested, but naturally, I won. She shrieked with excitement when we walked in. I couldn't put a Christmas tree up for her on Valentine's Day, so I improvised. I found strands of all-clear and all-blue lights online. Mom strung them up in the living room and our bedroom. Some of the decorations from the reception were brought to the house. Colton had a fire going. Two mugs of hot chocolate are sitting on the coffee table. Mom must have just left.

I settle us on the couch and pull my lovely wife into my arms. Wife? That's so amazing. There's also a slice of wedding cake on the table with the hot chocolate. E happily polishes the cake off. Our little sunbeam likes sweets.

"We did it." E settles back against me.

"We sure did." I tighten my arms around her and kiss her temple.

"Today was perfect." She looks at me over her shoulder.

"You're perfect." I press my lips to hers.

Our hands automatically go to her stomach. She's not showing yet, but I'm looking forward to the day she does.

"Do you think we'll have more?"

"If you want more. I have no objections." I kiss my way down to her neck.

"Well, the sun does have lots of beams." Her breathing turns heavy as I kiss my way back to her ear.

A sensual growl rumbles in my throat. The thought of more children with her is intoxicating.

"I guess we'll be playing a lot of *Scrabble*," I tease.

"Yes." E turns in my arms so fast it takes me a moment to recover from the shock.

"We should practice," I say, totally agreeing with her.

Scooping her up in my arms again, I carry her upstairs to our room. *Scrabble* is definitely our favorite game. We fall side by side onto the bed.

"You, Mrs. Maxwell, are forever mine." My lips hover above hers.

"Forever yours," she whispers.

Unable to wait any longer, my lips claim hers. Mine. Now. Tomorrow. Always. She's forever mine.

Letter from the Author

Welcome to Hayden Falls!!

I hope you enjoyed Aiden and E's story. I really loved writing this one. As you can see, we have a quirky little town with lots of characters. I hope you found several that you love and can connect with. This is just the beginning for our dear little town. You can find Miles Hamilton's story next in *Only With You ~ Hayden Falls ~ Book Two.*

If you'd like to know more about the country band, Dawson, that Aiden used to work with, you can find that story in The Dawson Boys series. You can fall in love with Harrison, Bryan, Calen, Grayson, and Evan as they try to handle music and relationships. Start the series with Harrison Shaw in *Holding Her* ~ Book One.

Please consider leaving a review for Forever Mine on Amazon and Goodreads or other book sites you have. I would really appreciate it. Continue the Hayden Falls journey in Only With You ~ Book Two.

Check the Follow Me page out for ways to connect with me. I'd love to see you on my social media sites. Be sure to sign up for my Newsletter. Stay tuned. There's lots more to come from Hayden Falls, Montana!

Blessings to you,

Debbie Hyde

Follow Me

Here are places to follow me:

Sign up for my Newsletter:
www.debbiehyde-author.com

Facebook:
Debbie Hyde & Nevaeh Roberson - Authors

Facebook Groups:
Debbie Hyde Books – This is my reader's group. You'll find all of my books here. I hold giveaways in the group often.
Get Lost in Books with Debbie Hyde – In this reader group, we have other authors to pop in from time to time.
For the Love of a Shaw – This group is dedicated to the series. I hold giveaways here, too.
Debbie Hyde's Book Launch Team – I would love to have you on my book launch team! The team gets all my book news first. They sometimes help with cover designs. The Team can get FREE ebooks for an honest review. Join me today!
The Fireside Book Café – This is a book community I created to help readers, authors, narrators, bloggers, and cover designers connect. If you love books, check us out. We have lots of giveaways!

Instagram:
www.instagram.com/debbie_hyde_author

TikTok:
debbie_hyde

Hayden Falls

Forever Mine ~ Book One (This book)
Aiden and E
Today I'm going home to a town that wrote me off years ago. Home to watch the woman I love marry someone else. I'm not going to survive this.

Only With You ~ Book Two
Miles and Katie
My career was strong and sure. My personal life was a mess. My only regret was keeping her a secret. Winning her back won't be easy, but I have to try.

Giving Her My Heart ~ Book Three
Jasper and Hannah
The dance teacher annoys me at every turn until she twirls her way into my heart and my daughter's. Now, I need to find a way to get her to stay.

Finding Home ~ Book Four
Luke and Riley
I was the fun brother until my twin almost died in a fire. Now, I'm a mess. Then she came along. I'm charming, but am I enough for her to stay?

Listening to My Heart ~ Book Five
Phillip and Tara
My family took the biggest part of my heart from me. A piece I didn't know existed. After nine years, the woman who holds every piece of my heart returns, bringing a huge secret with her. This time, no one will keep me from her.

A Hayden Falls Christmas

Spend Christmas in Hayden Falls. Enjoy a short story about the five couples we've met, plus two of the town's beloved families.

Falling for You ~ Book Six

Lucas and Hadley

I'm a career-minded deputy. I wasn't looking for love. Until my little brother butted into my love life, I never even noticed the woman right in front of me.

Finally Home ~ Book Seven

Aaron and Kennedy

If I had known joining the Army would have cost me her, I never would have enlisted.

Protecting You ~ Book Eight

Leo and Kyleigh

I'm the quiet brother. Nothing gets under my skin. Well, not until a little blonde stranger with a bat swings her way into my life and changes everything.

A Hayden Falls Christmas – Two is Coming Soon!

The Dawson Boys

Holding Her ~ Book One
Harrison & Tru
Losing her destroyed me. One letter gave me hope. Like a man on a mission, I went after her.

I Do It For You ~ Book Two
Bryan & Dana
Sometimes slow, steady, and sweet are not the best way to go. Did I wait too long? Did my plan fail? I don't know, but I'd do anything for her.

Everything I Ever Wanted ~ Book Three
Calen & Daisy
"Get out!" I've shouted those words every day. Does she listen? Not a chance. She challenges me. She tests me. How did she become everything I ever wanted?

Book Four is COMING SOON!

For the Love of a Shaw

When A Knight Falls ~ Book One

Gavin & Abby

A battle at sea with a notorious pirate leaves Gavin Shaw wounded and far from home. He will battle his long-time enemy more than once when he falls for his nursemaid. Will Abby marry the wrong man to save an innocent girl?

Falling for the Enemy ~ Book Two

Nate & Olivia

Nathaniel Shaw takes a job to prove his worth to his father. He loses his heart to the mysterious woman in his crew only to discover she isn't who she claims to be.

A Knight's Destiny ~ Book Three

Nick & Elizabeth

Nicholas Shaw is a knight without a title, but he's loved the Duke's sister for years. When Elizabeth needs protection and runs away, rather than sending her to her brother, Nick goes with her.

Capturing A Knight's Heart ~ Book Four

Jax & Nancie

Jackson Shaw isn't bound by the rules of society. He's free to roam as he pleases until he stumbles across a well-kept secret of Miss Nancie's. Will Nancie guard her heart and push him away? Or has she truly captured this knight's heart?

A Duke's Treasure ~ Book Five

Sam & Dani

Samuel Dawson, the Duke of Greyham, has loved Lady Danielle Shaw for years. Dani stumbles into his darkest secret, leaving Sam no choice but to steal her away.

A Knight's Passion ~ Book Six

Caleb & Briley

Caleb Shaw feels lost, alone, and misunderstood. His mind is haunted by his past. While running for his life, he devises a plan to save Briley. The bluff is called, trapping them together forever.

A Mysterious Knight ~ Book Seven

Alex & Emily

Alexander Shaw had no light, peace, or love if he didn't have her. The day she sent him away almost destroyed him. Emily's trapped in her father's secrets and can't break free no matter how much she wants to. Alex will risk his life to free hers.

Other Books by the Author

Forest Rovania series: Middle-Grade Fantasy

Written with: Nevaeh Roberson
Jasper's Journey ~ Book One
Forest Rovania's only hope begins with an epic journey.

Women's Christian:

Stamped *subtitle:* Breaking Out of the Box
Her *subtitle:* Beautiful, Loved, Wanted, Matters, Priceless!
Her: Beautiful, Loved, Wanted, Matters, Priceless! Guided Study Journal.

Blank Recipe Cookbooks:

My Thanksgiving Recipes
Store all your holiday recipes in one place. Choose from 4 cover designs.
Burgundy, Orange, Peach, and Cream & Burgundy.

My Halloween Recipes
A great place to store fun children's recipes.

My Christmas Christmas Cookies and Candy Recipes
You'll find Two books—one with black and white graphics and one with colored graphics.

Cover Background Art

Cover Background Photos are provided by Carrie Pichler Photography ~ located in Montana!

Acknowledgments:

Thank you to my awesome *Toon Blast* gaming friends, Four!, Pit, and Mags! You guys gave me some great character names for this series. Stay tuned! I'm sure those guys will be doing a lot more throughout the series!

A very special thank you to the members of the *Facebook* group *For All Who Love Montana.* Your stories are so great! If you liked or commented on the post for stories, I have included your names here. It meant a lot to me that you took the time to share with me. Christine Migneault, Tammie Duran, Jim and Coleen Larson Done, Andrea Phillips, Joy Rasmussen, Kelli Vilchis, Sandra Stuckey, Sarah Jobe, Gracene Long, Dennis Fabel, Deb McGann Langshaw, Janice Berget, Ruth Collins Johnson, Roxanna Malone McGinnis, Shawn Wakefield, Alan Johnson, Judy Shockley, Danielle Mccrory, Larry Campbell, Maureen Mannion Kemp, Nancy Ray, Jerry Urfer, Kris Biffle Rudin, Holly Good, Vic Direito, Mozelle Brewer, Joseph Hartel, Cheri Wicks, Stephanie Schuck-Quinn, Travis Frank, Kamae Luscombe, Dianne Eshuk Ketcharm, Patty Ward, Tina Griffin Williams, Steve Kline, Jim Lidquist, Christina Mansfield, Glen Hodges, Teri St Pierre, Lalena Chacon-Carter, Eric Wolf, Jennifer Ahern Lammers, Marilyn Handyside, Lynnette Graf, Arianna Dawn Fake, Cody Birdwell, Doug Jeanne Hall, Mary Thomas.

About the Author

Debbie Hyde is the author of the Historical Romance series For the Love of a Shaw. The seven-book family sage begins with Gavin in When A Knight Falls. She is currently working on The Dawson Boys series and the Hayden Falls series.

Debbie has a love for writing! She enjoys reading books from many different genres, such as Christian, Romance, Young Adults, and many more. You will always find wonderful clean stories in her fictional writings.

When not reading or writing, she enjoys using her talents in cooking, baking, and cake decorating. She loves using her skill as a seamstress to make gowns, costumes, teddy bears, baby blankets, and much more.

Debbie started Letters To You on Facebook after God put it on her heart to "Love the lost and lead them to Jesus." This wonderful community of amazing people allows her to continue her mission to Just #LoveThemAll.

Debbie started The Fireside Book Café group on Facebook to connect Authors, Readers, Narrators, PAs, Bloggers, Cover Designers, and as many people in the world as possible.

Debbie would love to hear from you and see your reviews!

About the Author

Made in United States
Troutdale, OR
10/20/2024